DUKE I'D LIKE TO F...

SIERRA SIMONE **JOANNA SHUPE** **EVA LEIGH**
NICOLA DAVIDSON **ADRIANA HERRERA**

The Chasing of Eleanor Vane, Copyright © 2020 by Sierra Simone

My Dirty Duke, Copyright © 2020 by Joanna Shupe

An Education in Pleasure, Copyright © 2020 by Ami Silber

Duke for Hire, Copyright © 2020 by Nicola Davidson

The Duke Makes Me Feel..., Copyright © 2020 by Adriana Herrera

Cover Design: Natasha Snow Designs

Cover Image: Magdalena Żyźniewska / Trevillion Images

Editing: Sabrina Darby

Proofing: Dee Hudson and Michelle Li at Tessera Editorial

First Edition of All Titles: November 2020

Print Edition ISBN: 978-1-949364-09-5

Digital Edition ISBN: 978-1-949364-08-8

THE CHASING OF ELEANOR VANE

SIERRA SIMONE

PROLOGUE

1794

SHE'D ONLY BEEN at Far Hope a week, and she'd already broken two of the three rules her mother had given her. She was about to break the third.

The kitchens were busy supplying treats for the party above, and Eleanor was able to move through the chaos largely unmarked, thanks to the forgettable gown of coarse gray wool she'd borrowed from her maid. She'd brushed her blond hair free of powder and curls and tucked it under a simple linen cap, and she'd washed all the carefully applied cosmetics from her face, scrubbing her fair skin into a state of red splotchiness to make it look like she'd been running back and forth in the hot kitchens all evening.

And, finally, under her skirts, Eleanor had traded her pointed silk heels for leather half-boots. Much better for walking over the rutted Dartmoor roads.

She didn't take much once she was downstairs—even dressed like a servant, there was only so much suspicion she could evade, and swiping a week's worth of food would have definitely been suspicious. After her visit to the kitchens, she stuffed her ill-gotten gains into a haversack along with a leather costrel full of water. She left Far Hope under the cover of night, hopeful that her maid would be able to spin out the lie of her illness long enough for her to escape, and hopeful that no one would discover the real reason Eleanor wasn't at her own betrothal ball until it was much, much too late.

CHAPTER ONE

THE LADY ELEANOR VANE had been resigned to her fate—more or less. She had been a dutiful daughter, had spent the last four years helping her father, the new Marquess of Pennard, restore the old pile he'd inherited in Somerset, all while also tending to her mother's vague malaise of the gut. She was an accomplished young woman in every metric: she was a faithful churchgoer; she dedicated herself to various philanthropic pursuits; she could play the pianoforte, sing, dance, embroider, and converse in three different Continental languages; and other than her vocal support for William Wilberforce and his abolition bills, she was otherwise as placidly unobjectionable as her father wanted her to be.

At least, that was how she appeared on the outside.

Inside, she roiled.

The renovation she didn't mind; the languages and charities she didn't mind. She didn't even mind caring for her mother, who was an objectively terrible patient in every way.

But the *restraint*, the relentless serenity and calm that was demanded of her . . . the constant entitlement of everyone else to her time . . .

That she did mind.

The worst part of it all was that—at some point along the way—she'd begun to lie to herself. She began to feel like this was just a phase of her life, merely a stage on her journey, and that at some undefined point in her future, things would get easier. One day, she would spend her days however she wanted. She would go anywhere she liked, whenever she wanted, and she would reach for the things that excited her. She would live her life for *herself*, no one else, and that would be the reward for being so perfectly competent, efficient, and respectable.

She never could exactly picture what living for herself looked like, however, and whenever she tried, the images and imaginings darted and flashed their way out of reach, like fish scattering away from a thrown pebble in a garden pond. She didn't know any women who lived for themselves, except spinsters, but even they were often dependent on their family for their means . . . and anyway, she didn't necessarily want to be a spinster. Outside of spinsters, there was Mary Wollstonecraft—but Eleanor wasn't a writer. There was the Duchess of Devonshire, Eleanor supposed—but the duchess had also been forced into an unhappy marriage. There was the Countess of Kellow, but Eleanor didn't know enough about her to know if she was happy or fulfilled.

All Eleanor knew was what this ideal life *wasn't*. It wasn't tepid; it wasn't tedious. It wasn't a trap. Perhaps there would be marriage, perhaps there would be a great move across oceans, perhaps there would be danger —the point was that *anything* could happen, in the same way nothing ever happened in the present. She would be free to leave, free to roam, free to think. And if she did anything like marry or move or manage another estate, it would be because she wanted to. Because she'd chosen it for herself, claimed it for herself.

It was a fiction, she knew that from the beginning. Except, unlike other kinds of fictions, this story she told herself began to feel truer and truer over time, instead of less. Until it felt like the truth after all. Until it felt like it had been the truth all along.

She'd believed her own lie, and that single act of foolishness had begun her unraveling. Two months ago, Lord Pennard had pronounced that Eleanor was to be betrothed—sight unseen—to Gilbert Gifford, Earl Sloreley.

She was to marry a stranger.

Without delay.

Gilbert was the Duke of Jarrell's nephew and heir, and he was a squirming embarrassment to his entire family. A man just past his majority, there had been the usual slate of gambling, womanizing, and intemperance that was generally tolerated in heirs—but then came the scandal in Italy during his grand tour, something involving an elderly contessa's racehorse and a baptismal font full of madeira, and Sloreley had been summoned home in shame. The duke had paid, bribed, and donated in order to assuage the wounded sensibilities of the contessa and the Church—and possibly of the horse—and now the duke had clearly had enough of his nephew's dissolution. Sloreley would be married, and married to the most respectable girl the duke could find, and that girl was Eleanor.

All of this Eleanor's father disclosed to her in his study as if he were explaining the weather, as if it would be as impersonal and bloodless to her as it was to him.

"So I am to marry this earl," she'd said, trying to keep her pulse steady. "Even though we have never met, and he is rumored to be an unrepentant lecher."

Not that Eleanor minded lechery *per se*, but she did mind ridiculousness. She did mind inheriting another project.

"And he *baptized a horse*," she added, to clarify her point.

"The priest baptized the horse. Sloreley only watched," her father had corrected cheerfully. There had been florid blooms of early morning drink on his otherwise chalky cheeks. "He's young still, Eleanor, you can control him. You can help him corral his vices and grow into a proper man." He'd given her a fond look. "You are a born manager, you know. Just look how easily you've managed Pennard Hall while your mother's been ill. Everyone sings your praises! And besides, Sloreley is Jarrell's heir, which means you'll be a duchess someday. Your first son will be a duke."

"But why is *he* the heir? I know the current duke is unmarried, but surely he's not too old to find a wife?"

Her father had waved his hand. "Jarrell's first wife died some years ago, and he's never made a secret of his wish not to remarry. And what does it matter? The important thing is that Gifford is the heir and you'll marry Gifford. I have no doubt you'll be able to take him in hand. None at all."

So this was to be her reward, then. She'd succeeded at every task she'd set her mind to, and now she'd been given her prize: another unending task of impossible proportions.

Like Sisyphus with his stone, but her boulder was a living man. With loose morals and even looser habits.

The loose morals she could live with. She often thought she'd like to try some loose morals herself, actually. She'd long ago found a hoard of rather salacious books and pamphlets stashed in a trunk in the attic, and her imagination and her right hand had made good use of the stories and accompanying illustrations. And of course, there had been that house party, where Eleanor had wandered into the Foscourts' temple folly at the wrong moment and saw things that hadn't left her mind since.

However, loose morals rarely ran both directions in married couples. Men were allowed these things; women were not. And while it was tacitly accepted by society at large that husbands would stray, Eleanor wasn't interested in playing the expected counterpart: the meek wifey, embroidering cushions at home while her husband caroused and dallied however he pleased.

But perhaps Sloreley would consider her argument if she made it to him. Perhaps they could come to an agreement, and if that were the case, then the morals would not bother her very much at all.

No, it was the loose habits that bothered her. It was his reputation for missing important functions, for making public scenes, for inveterate rudeness, and for constant sloppiness. While she'd never been able to picture her ideal future with any real clarity, she knew that Gilbert Gifford was its exact opposite. She predicted that marriage to him would be a trap of thanklessly spent time, of smoothing over his gaffes and crudities. Of trying to improve someone who gave no indication he wanted to be improved.

She appealed to her father to no avail. She appealed to her mother with even less success. No one could understand why she didn't want to become a duchess someday; everybody seemed to think Sloreley would eventually be brought in line by her quiet, efficient personality.

Indeed, that's why she'd been chosen.

A graceful bride for a disgraceful man.

And what were her choices? Truly? If her parents would not change her mind and the duke was intent on having her as a bride for his nephew, what else could be done, other than run away?

If she ran away, where would she go? And to whom? And with what money?

So, as the invitations were penned and the trousseau was packed, she'd resigned herself.

She would marry Sloreley at the duke's seat of Far Hope, where she and

Sloreley would rusticate afterward until he could possibly be seen as respectable by society again.

She would begin the project of making him a fit heir and preparing him for a dukedom.

She would marry him and she would find a way to bear it, just as she'd always found a way to bear everything.

WHEN THEY'D FIRST GLIMPSED the ancient manor tucked away in the moors, her mother had taken one look at the frowning stone edifice and told Eleanor, "This will all be yours someday. You must remember to be grateful."

For a very brief moment, Eleanor agreed. Far Hope looked like an etching in a book—moody and wonderful—and there was something about this wild, lonely land that made her feel like she'd stepped into a story. Her very own story, where there would be adventures and romance and—

Abruptly, she remembered that wasn't the case.

Her story was already written, the book already closed and put back on the shelf. The beauty of Far Hope might indeed be hers, but there was no mystery or adventure here.

As per usual, her mother was never ill when she didn't want to be, and so had accompanied the Lord Pennard and Eleanor down to Dartmoor for the nuptial celebrations. Eleanor had never really begrudged her the malingering—if anything, she was jealous of her mother's ability to dodge work—but right now, in the face of this terrible marriage, it chafed. Especially since her mother was using her convenient good health to exhort Eleanor to her famous serenity when all Eleanor actually wanted to do was leap from the carriage and run as far as her legs would carry her.

"Anything else?" Eleanor had asked, trying and failing to sound composed. "Anything else I must do while I'm marrying a reprobate?"

"You must not do anything to jeopardize the marriage," her mother said seriously. Gray shadows had moved over her face, turning her porcelain features into an ominous, inhuman silver. "You mustn't, Eleanor. Nothing outrageous, nothing scandalous. The dukedom of Jarrell is the chance of a lifetime."

Eleanor had nearly snorted at her mother's warning, but her mother didn't notice.

If Eleanor hadn't done anything outrageous during her first twenty years of life, she hardly saw how it would happen out here in this gorse-ridden wasteland. "Of course, Mama."

"And," her mother pronounced, "you must not leave."

"Leave?" Eleanor asked, not bothering to hide her incredulity this time. "Where would I go?"

She gestured out the carriage window to prove her point. They were surrounded by miles and miles of gorgeous but desolate hills. Heather, growing brown and rusty under the fading autumn light, covered everything. Fog laid heavy in the dips and valleys and the road was a single muddy track, occasionally diverted around cheerless granite crags. There was not another inn, house, or hovel for miles.

They might as well have been at the edge of the world.

Her mother had nodded then, satisfied. There was no escape.

SHE BROKE the first rule that very night. After they were received at Far Hope and allowed to rest, they took dinner with a sallow-faced Sloreley, who was already drunk and sulky beyond belief at Eleanor's presence. He alternated between glaring at her and avoiding her gaze altogether; he practically flung her hand off his arm when they reached the table. When he scratched his neck under his lacy neckcloth, she caught a glimpse of a fresh love bite on the pallid skin below his ear.

Why was it that Sloreley could cavort with whomever he pleased and could show up to the dinner table with bites on his neck, but she was made to promise all sorts of good behavior when she'd been nothing but well behaved her entire life?

It wasn't fair.

Maybe you're the one not being fair, she countered to herself. She'd already told herself she would make the best of this, and all successful projects started with determined optimism.

"So, my lord," she started, trying to cast about for any topic that would give them common ground, "have you been at Far Hope long?"

Sloreley didn't bother looking at her when he answered. "No."

"When did you get in?"

"Yesterday. And I'm ready to leave," he said shortly.

This surprised her. Far Hope was lonely, yes, and even the interior had an austerity to it that bordered on bleakness, but it was still beautiful for all that. There were stained glass windows in the great hall and the attached family chapel, and there was a library three times the size of Pennard Hall's. There were sheltered gardens outside that went right to the very edge of the hills, and there were parapeted towers she was told gave expansive views all the way to the far end of the valley. Far Hope had the feel of a place caught out of time, and it had never occurred to Eleanor that someone wouldn't like that.

"I suppose you miss London," she said, trying to keep the conversation going. "Far Hope is quite isolated."

"It's a prison," he said. He still didn't look at her. "Like marriage."

"What did you say?" she asked.

He didn't answer her, scratching again at his neck and then taking a drink of his wine. She couldn't tell if his silence was due to his own inner turmoil or because he simply did not think she deserved a response.

"It doesn't have to be a prison for either of us," she said quietly, deciding to lend him the benefit of the doubt, and also grateful her parents were too occupied with Sloreley's mother and sister to pay her unusual conversation with her fiancé any mind.

"But it is. I'm too young to be married," he complained. "Many dukes don't marry until they're twice my age or older." He glared at his wine glass. "It's not fair."

Almost nothing in their Empire was fair—nothing at all—which anyone with any sense at all would see if they paid any attention. But that was perhaps a conversation for a different time . . . or at least for when Sloreley was sober. "Surely you cannot begrudge your uncle his wishes when you stand to gain so much by remaining in his good graces?"

"I'm owed the title by my birth as his nephew," Sloreley said, still glaring at the glass. "I don't have to earn it by wedding the daughter of some country lord."

It was only years of being Serene, Equanimous Eleanor that kept her voice steady and her hands in her lap. "Then why are you marrying me, Lord Sloreley, if I may ask?"

"Jarrell's got his fist around my allowance," Sloreley admitted in a mumble. "If I don't marry, he'll cut me off."

So it was money. She might have guessed as much.

She considered for a moment, then decided she had very little to lose by being frank. "Is there any agreement we can come to, together, to make this arrangement more palatable?"

Sloreley turned to blink at her. "What do you mean?"

"Only that I imagine some of your objections to marriage come from the restrictions that typically come along with it. I don't consider myself prudish, and I want to assure you that I will not ask you to tailor your appetites or your pleasure-seeking, so long as you can promise discretion in your private affairs. So long as you allow me the same freedoms."

Her heart thudded as she spoke the last part—she had very little practice declaring things she wanted for herself—and though she'd spoken in a low voice, she was still aware of their parents just across the table.

Sloreley's face twisted. "What?"

She was used to putting other people's comfort ahead of her own, and there was a real urge to undo what she'd just done, to assure him she'd misspoken and hadn't meant it. Except she *had* meant it, and unfortunately, this was too important to leave unsaid. "I've no argument with liaisons on your part. But I must insist I be granted the same latitude, my lord, that's all. I know it's rather unusual, but I have seen people with arrangements like this before."

Well, she'd only personally seen it the one time at the Countess of Kellow's party, but *still*, there were others. Lady Melbourne, Lady Jersey. The Duchess of Devonshire herself. It wasn't unheard of, even if one only heard about it through gossip. Not that Eleanor had any plans to be the subject of gossip.

She would be like the Countess of Kellow instead and evade all whispers.

"I think if we can both agree to—"

"Absolutely not," he sniffed. "I'll not have any wife of mine embarrassing me—"

"I have no wish to embarrass you," Eleanor assured him. "I'd be extremely discreet, as I myself have no wish to be embarrassed."

"—and it's not natural," he continued. "How else will I ensure my heirs are my own?"

"That can be negotiated around," Eleanor pointed out. "I can wait until I've born an heir. We can try periods of exclusivity, or I'm told that there are prophylactic measures . . ."

"*No*," Sloreley said, this time loud enough that he startled her parents and his family into looking at them. He didn't bother to apologize or explain. Instead, he turned to glare at Eleanor and said in a voice only she could hear, "You're a means to an end, Lady Eleanor. If I must marry in order to inherit, then I'll do it, but let me make it clear how things will be: you *will* do as I say and you *will* behave as I want you to. By Christ, my mother said you were supposed to be easy and biddable."

She wanted nothing more than to slosh her cup of wine all over Sloreley's elaborate wig and snowy-white neckcloth and see how biddable he thought her then. She managed not to, but only just barely, and only by locking her fingers into fists in the folds of her skirt and forcing herself to drag in several long, ragged breaths.

Sloreley gave her a final glare and then drained his cup of wine, wiping at his mouth with his sleeve when he was finished. A maroon smear was left on his silk jacket after.

Grateful. Her mother wanted her to be grateful? Because in exchange for her body and her *biddability*, she would have a title and a fine house?

No. No, she couldn't be grateful. Far Hope was compelling in an Ann Radcliffe novel sort of way, with its medieval bones and with the moors all around, but it wasn't worth this. It wasn't worth *Sloreley*.

The door to the dining room had flung open then, sudden and sharp, and everybody at the table jumped—except for Sloreley, who simply froze with his fingers digging under his neckcloth like a schoolboy caught fidgeting.

A tall, muscular man stalked into the dining room, his sun-bronzed face spattered with rain. He wasn't in dinner clothes, but riding clothes, his mud-flecked boots as far away from fashionable or appropriate as possible.

His features matched the house and the rain outside; they were like something from another time. A time of heathens and heroes. He had roughly hewn cheekbones and a powerful jaw, a high forehead and a rugged nose. His hair wasn't powdered or curled decoratively—it was black as sin and pulled into a loose queue at his neck, and several strands had blown free on his ride to hang around his face.

In the glinting light of the candelabras, Eleanor could only make out the silver near his temples and sprinkled throughout the dark stubble covering his warrior's jaw. A man well into his prime, then. A man old enough to be hardened.

Eleanor couldn't stop staring at him. He was so unlike her father, and so unlike every preening youth she'd met in London. His very existence was forceful, his very being an energy that couldn't be controlled or directed. His eyes were a blue so dark they were nearly black, and his mouth—

His mouth.

Firm and sculpted and a little cruel.

Eleanor shivered just to look at it.

"Apologies for my late arrival," the man said. "Please forgive me."

He said *please forgive me* like any other man would say *fuck off.*

The man strode over to the empty seat at the foot of the table and sat. His eyes met Eleanor's from across the table—a flash of glittering indigo—and then he gestured for a footman to bring him something to drink.

"Your Grace," Eleanor's father greeted him. "How wonderful to see you. May I present my daughter, the Lady Eleanor Vane?"

The Duke of Jarrell looked over at her again, and this time, his eyes lingered over her face and neck, and then over the low neckline of her amethyst gown. When his eyes met hers again, his stare was unreadable.

"My apologies for your impending marriage, Lady Eleanor," he said. "You are far too good for my nephew, but alas—he is too hopeless for me to release you. You are sadly needed."

Her mother gasped softly. Her father sighed and took a long drink of sherry.

"No one seems to care that I don't wish to be married either," Sloreley pouted.

"Then it's a good thing I don't give a fuck about your wishes," Jarrell replied. "Shall I carve the roast now?"

And then Eleanor broke the second rule and did something outrageous.

She fell in love with the duke.

CHAPTER TWO

THE WEEK LEADING up to the betrothal ball was miserable.

Not because the guests for the celebration and wedding had begun to arrive.

Not even because Sloreley's mother and sister were just as dismissive and selfish as he was and seemed to feel that Eleanor owed them a great debt for being allowed to marry their precious Gilbert.

No, it was because falling in love with the duke was the worst—the absolute *worst*—thing she had ever felt.

She had prided herself on being efficient? On being serene? Ha! She could barely dress herself now without rushing and fumbling through it to get downstairs on the slight chance the duke would be down there also. She couldn't make it through teas or tours of the grounds without getting flushed and flustered and restless in a way she'd never been and couldn't bear—except it was also a restlessness she couldn't get enough of. It was a restlessness she sought out in the same way she might've worried a loose tooth when she was younger. It was a delirium that left her speechless and flushed.

She watched out her window in case the duke rode past; she listened for his low, rough voice as she walked through the house. When he sat next to her in the drawing room as they conversed with the first of the houseguests, she couldn't breathe.

Even in stillness he was arresting; even in the constraints of polite small talk, his cold but raw physicality seemed barely leashed. More than once, she caught his eyes on the wild hills outside when he was supposed to be entertaining a guest, as if he wished himself far away from these tiresome niceties and out onto the lonely, howling lands that made up his estate.

In every way, he was Sloreley's opposite.

In every way also, he was Eleanor's opposite.

He was not serene; he was not respectable. His idea of efficiency was brute force, and his idea of patience was not openly growling at his guests.

And the sheer, bodily *presence* of him—his long stride, his large, ungloved hands. His silvering hair and his stern, carnal mouth.

Just the thought of how all of that would feel against her softness—his rough hands on her smooth ones, his hard body against her curves.

His stubble against her neck . . .

It was that particular fantasy that consumed her thoughts as she climbed the stairs to the tower one morning, having seen to her mother's comfort and having made her excuses to Sloreley's mother and sister for not joining them in the morning room. She'd claimed a slight fever, but truly the only fever she felt was in her blood, which pulsed madly at the idea of the duke's mouth on her skin. On her neck, yes, but also on her breasts. Her belly.

Her thighs.

That night at the Foscourts', there had been a woman kissing another woman between her thighs—slow, languorous kisses that had made her lover arch and pant. How would that feel to have kisses there? How would it feel to have a woman's soft lips giving those kisses—how different then, would a man's unshaven mouth feel?

Eleanor wouldn't mind sampling both . . . and then perhaps a few more times each, in the name of the scientific method and all.

But now her only chance to feel such a thing would be with Sloreley, wouldn't it?

An instinctual wave of unhappiness met the realization. For all the desire simmering in her veins at the thought of the duke and his mouth, she had no answering appetite for her actual fiancé. She wasn't sure how she felt about that or if she even *had* to feel a certain way about it, but there it was. She felt nothing for Sloreley, not even curiosity, not even academic interest. She could only muster up mild apprehension. A resigned distaste.

Eleanor emerged from a slender doorway to find the top of the tower and went immediately to the parapet, looking over the crenellated wall out to the narrow valley below. The Hope River, thin and shallow, glinted like a shining ribbon that unspooled all the way out as far as the eye could see. The floor of the valley remained as green as a garden in springtime, while a sharp autumn wind fussed at the moors above it, sending clumps of mist drifting this way and that.

It was beautiful here.

Not like Pennard Hall. Not in an obvious way and not in a safe way, because there was nothing safe about it at all. This place was rugged, old, chilly, stern—a spot that seemed to resist the very idea of modernity. She could never make a project out of Far Hope.

If anything, it felt like Far Hope would make a project out of her.

The thought was rather thrilling once she voiced it to herself.

"I used to imagine," a voice said unexpectedly, "that everything I ever wanted was just beyond that mist."

She turned to see the duke coming toward the wall where she was standing. He stopped a few feet away from her and braced his hands on the two stone merlons in front of him, staring out onto his lands, and onto the moors above them that belonged to no one save for God and the King.

Jarrell didn't wear an overcoat—only a tailcoat made of gray silk, subtly embroidered but otherwise free of ornamentation—and he was in long boots again, which were glistening as if he'd just come from a walk through the hills. His shoulders strained the seams of his coat, and his breeches hid nothing of his legs, and Eleanor suddenly couldn't look at him straight-on, because if she did, she'd do something *outrageous*. Like ask him if he'd like to walk through the hills with her.

Or if she could nuzzle against one of those muscular thighs. Just for a few hours.

Serene Eleanor, at least, regained control of her senses and managed to speak. "Was it?" she asked politely, relieved to hear that she sounded normal and not breathless at all. "Just beyond the mist?"

He turned to look at her, all midnight eyes and that beautiful mouth. "No," he said after a minute. "It wasn't."

"That's the trouble with imagining," she said, tearing her gaze away from his face. "It so rarely leads one to the truth."

He made a low noise of agreement. It almost sounded . . . well, *sad*, if she could believe such a forbidding man capable of sadness.

"What would be just beyond the mist for you?" he asked her. "If you could reach through it and part it like a curtain, what would you find?"

He sounded genuinely curious, and so Eleanor genuinely considered his question. Serene Eleanor would have an easy answer, a simple one—the health of her mother, perhaps, or a good deal on lead guttering—but it had been so long since someone had really cared about her answers that she wanted to savor it as much as possible. She wanted to honor it by being honest.

"A dock with many ships," she finally decided. "Or a hallway with many doors. Or maybe a crossroads, one with many byways meeting and signs pointing every which way."

"Not," the duke said slowly, "a room with many books? Or a room filled with many people?"

She thought for a moment. "No. Those aren't the same thing."

"No," he agreed with her. "They are not."

Wordlessness reigned after that, broken only by the wind crashing against the ancient walls of the house and whipping through the hills around it.

"It is the possibility itself that is the most potent," she said after a while. "The potential of anything. When you are standing in one place, it's almost as if the future is already written, like a branch that's been pruned of anything deemed not productive. But the ability to go anywhere, to do whatever you please..."

She trailed off. She shouldn't say things like this. Not because she thought it better to lie, but because she was supposed to be harmonious. It was why this marriage had been arranged in the first place. Harmonious Eleanor to save everyone's day.

But to her surprise, the duke nodded, seemingly not bothered by her open admission that she wished for possibilities beyond what she already had.

"It took me many years to learn what you already know, Lady Eleanor. And it took me many more to learn the lesson that follows."

"Which is?"

He stared out into the world of silver and rust, his eyes fixed on something she couldn't see. "That we make our own futures, wherever we are. Wherever we're starting from, whatever we feel has been...pruned...the future is still unwritten. It may be beyond the mist just yet."

His words sank into her, warm and sparking and alive, vital in a way that nothing had seemed vital since she learned she was to be married. *Still unwritten.*

"What if I don't know the rest?" she asked in a low voice. She shouldn't ask. She shouldn't betray anything that wasn't gratitude that she was to marry this man's nephew. But she couldn't help it. Up here on the tower, surrounded by mist, and with only the wind and the house and *him*, she wanted to be herself. "What if all I can imagine are the ships—the doors—the roads—and not where they take me in the end?"

When he looked at her, she felt young, and also just the right age, and she was shivery and hot, and also steady as the house underneath her feet.

"Perhaps," he said, "you cannot imagine where they go because you are not on them yet. Perhaps deciding when to go is more important than deciding where."

He said the last sentence like it was something he'd realized long ago and repeated to himself often. He said it like it was a cherished verse or maxim to live by. He looked away from her then, lost in his own thoughts, and below them in the gardens, Eleanor heard the murmurs of guests taking a walk. And out of the mist came the faint jingle and creak of an approaching carriage, more guests for the wedding.

Her wedding.

Abruptly and terribly, she was ashamed of herself. She'd told herself that she would marry Sloreley, that she'd endure. And the first chance she had, she was expressing a sense of ingratitude and talking about running away.

"Far Hope, though," she started. She planned on saying something conciliatory and vaguely dishonest to smooth over her earlier confession, but found the words leaving her mouth to be entirely true. "Far Hope seems a place like that. That whatever I imagine waiting for me just beyond the mist, I could also imagine here too. It's a place of possibility."

A line appeared between his brows and he turned away. "For some," he said gruffly.

Then he bowed to her and stalked away. He disappeared through the doorway, taking the spiral stairs down in a storm of bootsteps, and left Eleanor alone on the roof.

~

IT WAS nonsense to love him—she was too sensible not to know it was nonsense. It had only been a week of knowing him. A meager handful of hours.

Three hours in the drawing room feigning interest in the journeys of their guests.

Six dinners. A moment alone on the tower, in the wind and the mist.

If he were a book, she wouldn't have had enough time to read him—not even half of him.

And yet.

And yet she felt something awful, a slow clamping in her chest like someone had clipped an artery. Like something inside her would starve and die if she had to be this close to the duke for the rest of their lives and yet be nothing more than a relation to him. Nothing more than a solution to a thorny problem.

She had planned to live without her pride, without her dignity even. She had planned to live without joy or ease.

But to live *with* this? This restlessness, this hunger that would forever go unfed? This branch of a life as Sloreley's wife, pruned of all other possibilities? It was unthinkable. It couldn't be borne. No, she wouldn't endure it.

The future is still yet unwritten, he'd told her.

The moment she agreed with his words—the moment she thought *what if I could still write my future?*—she couldn't *un*agree with them.

She thought *what if I just... left?* And then the idea of leaving became its own presence, its own being. Like a shadow, or a pet, it followed her from moment to moment and from room to room. It paced behind her while she ate and crouched at her feet while she made polite conversation in the drawing room.

It curled up next to her while she slept.

It whispered her own words back to her, quietly, urgently, desperately.

What if I just...left?

A week before, she'd dismissed the idea as ridiculous, as dangerous. As foolish as climbing into a hot air balloon. And what had really changed since then? Sloreley was childishly self-centered, but she hadn't expected any better. His mother and sister were unpleasant, but again, she hadn't expected much better there either. All that had really changed was that she had fallen in love with the duke.

She tried and tried, but try as she might, she could not untether the two things from one another. The duke and leaving. Leaving and the duke. Maybe it was what he said on the tower; maybe it was because it was he who finally gave her the words to choose something different, something *other*, but when she thought of leaving, she thought of him, and when she thought of him, she thought of leaving.

It would hurt, leaving someone that made her feel like she'd felt on the tower—young and old and floating and anchored all at once—but it would hurt even more to spend the rest of her life stealing glimpses of him while the rest of her was slowly eaten alive by the Sloreley Project. No, she wouldn't do it.

Her future would be just beyond the mist after all.

～

THE DUKE HAD BEEN RIGHT. Once she decided to go, once she decided *when* to go, the possibilities came like the first flowers of spring—a couple shooting through the earth here and there, and then all of a sudden, there were possibilities everywhere, carpeting her mind and blooming faster than she could pluck them all up.

Jewelry.

A literal dock with many ships.

A godsister in Edinburgh who would help her and keep her visit a secret for as long as she needed to make her final plans.

Truly, it was not so hard to run away as she might have once believed. The answers to her earlier questions about fleeing this wedding —how and where and when—came easily enough once she let go of safety, security, and reason. Once she accepted that whatever waited for her beyond the mist would only be hers if she plunged right in to chase after it.

Pick a time when everyone is drunk and preening.

Pay off everyone who helps you.

Take enough jewelry and petty money to get to Plymouth, where there will be plenty of ways to get to Edinburgh.

She could not even say the choice was hard, looking back at the past few days. She would rather stare into the inky black of a Dartmoor night than into the duke's magnetic blue eyes. She'd rather face down snakes and bandits and lightning than have to watch the duke's thighs pull against his tight breeches as he walked and rode and danced.

She would rather bolt into danger than sit in stillness near the object of her desire for the rest of her life.

No, there was no choice, not in the end. The world had had enough of her time, enough of her patience and energy. It would not get an ounce more. Let them all find some new victim to feed the minotaur that was Sloreley.

And her future and her time and her energy would finally, finally be her own. Whatever she did after Edinburgh would be for her and her alone.

Just beyond the mist.

The night was chilly and damp as she walked briskly down the lane leading away from Far Hope. The fog clung to her skirts and her shawl, and her breath puffed out in front of her. She had decided against lighting a lantern until she was much farther away lest she be spotted, and the darkness soon swallowed her whole. The moon was covered by clouds, the lights of Far Hope quickly did nothing, and even after she lit the lantern, she still tripped with nearly every single step. Over puddles, over ruts, over rocks.

Before long, she fell. And fell again.

Her palms were scraped. Her skirts became heavy with wet and mud. She could hear her own breaths like she was trapped in a small room.

She thought of the duke and refused to turn back.

She thought of the duke, and she kept going.

She thought of his words and reminded herself of how it felt to know they were true.

Still unwritten.

And some hours later, when her teeth were chattering and her lantern wouldn't stay lit in the wind, Eleanor had to admit to herself that she was lost.

Which was when the rain came.

CHAPTER THREE

AJAX DARTHAM, the Duke of Jarrell and uncle to the world's worst nephew, had honestly not given Eleanor Vane much thought until she'd arrived at Far Hope. Until then, she'd been the convenient solution to a most inconvenient problem. He needed someone to straighten Gilbert out —someone who could keep Far Hope running and the dukedom respectable until Gilbert finally settled down and saw to his responsibilities—and she was undeniably that someone, according to every source Jarrell had interrogated on the matter.

God knew he'd waited for this moment long enough. He'd only survived the bleak, miserable years after Helena's death because he knew he'd be free of the dukedom and this wretched estate when Gilbert reached his majority.

The paperwork was all drawn up; the lawyers ready; the dispensation from the King and the Committee for Privileges all prepared. As soon as Gilbert married, Jarrell would give him a wedding present that Gilbert in no way deserved and hand him the dukedom. *Gilbert* would be Jarrell. *Gilbert* would own Far Hope. And Ajax could finally be free.

Free of the memories. Free of the ghosts.

He would retire to the Orkneys maybe, or to the west of Ireland. Or perhaps even Canada, where his isolation could be frozen and utter and complete. He would be alone in body just as he already was in spirit, and perhaps he would eventually find some kind of peace that way. Some kind of relief.

But he could only leave once he'd surrendered the title, and the night-mare of papers, wills, and deeds had all been drawn up with the stipulation of Gilbert's marriage—something Jarrell had thought would be a foregone conclusion when he'd begun the laborious process of begging the Powers That Be for the right to abdicate the title years ago.

It was very much *not* a foregone conclusion.

Having been a recluse for the last sixteen years, Jarrell hadn't seen his nephew for an extremely long time. However, he'd still assumed the occa-sional tales of Gilbert's wild behavior that had drifted all the way out to Devonshire had been partially exaggerated. Indeed, Gilbert's mother had assured Jarrell of it whenever she wrote. Gilbert was a good man, she'd insisted, and had only been caught up in a bad group of friends, or perhaps he'd been mistaken for someone else, or perhaps he'd had a fever and that's why the malicious gossips had assumed he'd been drunk at Lady So-and-So's party.

Jarrell knew the wildness of youth all too well, and so he factored in some degree of willful maternal ignorance in her impression of her son, but he also truly hadn't counted Gilbert's misbehavior stretching this long. He hadn't counted on the Italian incident, and he hadn't counted on Gilbert being so *immature*. Yet when Jarrell welcomed his nephew to Far Hope that first day, he saw it was exactly what Gilbert was.

Not wild, not spontaneous, nor playful. Not the things that could be coaxed and polished into respectability. No, it was pure and true selfish-ness, the kind a spoiled child might exhibit.

Yes, Jarrell had definitely not counted on that when he'd made years and years' worth of painstakingly difficult plans.

More worryingly, he hadn't counted on the Lady Eleanor Vane.

The Lady Eleanor Vane who was selected because of her competence, her managerial acumen, the patience she displayed with her ailing mother and the never-ending work at Pennard Hall. When Jarrell had first heard of her, he'd pictured some kind of Viking maiden—tall and capable, icy and controlled. A jarl's daughter fiercely ruling his land until he returned from his raids. A girl like that would be just fine managing Far Hope, even with its burdens, even with its hidden debts to God.

But when she arrived at Far Hope, Jarrell was confronted not with a shield maiden, but with a petite, rosy-cheeked *damsel*. Though twenty, she barely came up to his chest, and while she was no waif, there was something eminently delicate about her. Her mouth was set not in the determined line of a seasoned administrator, but in the slightly curved frown of someone who'd forgotten how to smile. Her eyes were not iron-dark with rigid authority, but a green that made him think of tender, growing things.

And her manner—soft, gentle, sad—but steady for all that. She reminded him of certain spring blossoms that unfurled with so much bravery and trembling beauty only to be blown away by the wind a week later.

And, somehow, she was the near-heroic daughter that the *ton* loved to praise? This apple blossom of a young woman? He could hardly credit it—and what's more, a deep fear began to slither through his belly at the thought of leaving her with Gilbert. At the thought of saddling her with Far Hope and its wicked, if abandoned, legacy. After all, Helena had seemed to him a proper shield maiden once—buxom and ferocious—and then, in the blink of an eye, she'd been gone.

What chance then could this tiny little Eleanor stand?

FINALLY, on the night of the betrothal ball, Jarrell had to admit some things to himself.

One: Eleanor Vane was made of far sterner stuff than he'd first supposed. Under those sooty lashes flashed eyes of jade resolve, and while the lush fullness of her mouth was often pulled into that subtle, if elegant frown, the words she spoke in her surprisingly throaty voice were never self-pitying or timid. Indeed, she was nothing but serene through the entire week—although he often caught her glancing to the side and swallowing, as if refortifying herself in the face of numbing small talk and Gilbert's petulance. But other than these small swallows, she was as relentlessly tranquil as usual. She evaded Gilbert's sulks with ease, she attended patiently to her mother's many physical complaints in the damp chill of the old stone manor, and she steered her father's thoughtless remarks into neutral waters. She wasn't the blossom at all, Jarrell realized, but the tree. One anchored so deeply that nothing seemed to move her. Fixed fast to a landscape with invisible, subterranean strength.

Two: after six restless, fitful nights, after that moment on the tower when he saw something inside of her that so mirrored his own wishes, his own yearnings, Jarrell had to concede that Eleanor awakened something inside him he thought long dead.

It had begun the first night, after he'd banged into the dining room like the brute he was, and she'd raised her eyes to his. That first look she gave him—it wasn't shy, it wasn't composed, it wasn't even curious. It was not the kind of look that a young woman with sweetly upturned features and a chaste demeanor should give.

No, for a brief moment, she had looked at Jarrell like she wanted to know what his skin would feel like against her teeth.

Then she'd glanced away and the moment had evaporated, leaving him to wonder if he'd imagined it entirely.

It was her voice that infected him after that, low and husky, like the voice of a woman still abed, like the voice of a woman who'd just moaned herself hoarse. It fired his blood when he heard it, and for the first time in sixteen years, Jarrell felt a hot glimmer of the man he used to be. Of the man who would have pressed her over the table, pushed up her skirts, and taken his ease right there in front of his guests.

Of course, his guests were not the same kind of guests that used to haunt the halls of Far Hope, and he was no longer that kind of man.

Not to mention that Eleanor was betrothed to his heir.

But it was still strange. To feel, however briefly, as he once had years ago, when he was young and ravenous, and the hidden kingdom he'd inherited seemed like a gift, and not a reminder of what he'd lost.

The next day had brought more small revelations about Eleanor—and these revelations aroused long-dormant hungers inside him.

He noticed her eyes were hued with a darker ring of green encircling the leafy jade of the iris, a color palette he wanted to study in moonlight, noonlight, and candlelight. Eyes he wanted to see dilated in raw, animal longing.

Her eyebrows were a darker shade of gold than her hair, and often raised and lowered in the tiniest amounts, barely noticeable reactions to Gilbert's pouts or her mother's complaints about the damp. Once or twice they raised at *him*, as if she was amused by something he'd said—or that he'd growled, more probably, he had trouble remembering how to behave in polite society after all this time—and it made him want to toss her over his lap for her insouciance and pinken her bottom until she glistened between her legs.

And when she returned to dinner without her fichu that night, he could see a freckle on the top curve of a breast, like a sweet waypoint on the topography of her décolletage. A stopping point for traveling lips, a guide for wandering hands.

Was her entire body such a map? Would he find more freckles on her softly curved stomach? A birthmark on the inside of her thigh?

Was her body meant for pilgrims looking to find their way?

If he were a younger man, if she were not betrothed to Gilbert, he would have demanded she undress right there in the dining room. He would demand she wear only her stockings when she was in his presence, so he could look at her whenever he liked. He'd have her sit with her legs spread and her back straight, far enough back from the table that he could see every freckle and mark, so he could see where she was soft and—

Fuck.

No.

No, that wasn't allowed to him. For a thousand reasons, this young woman and her freckles weren't allowed to him.

Unfortunately, the following days were no easier—in fact, they were worse.

Much worse.

He wanted to kiss that barely-there frown. He wanted to tousle those artfully pinned curls, and feel her small, curvy body underneath his. He wanted to hear that low voice crackling at the edges with unrestrained lust.

He wanted—oh, this was the most dangerous thing of all—he wanted to tell her about Far Hope, to share the secrets he'd held silently inside himself for sixteen years. He wanted to tell her about the magnificent parties this house had seen, attended by queens and kings and princes of the realm. He wanted to show her the crooked standing stone guarding the entrance to the deep combe which sheltered Far Hope, and he wanted to show her the star-chambered ballroom not as he'd presented it to her earlier, as the single quirk in an otherwise austere home, but as he would have shown an initiate into his family's mysteries.

Here, he'd tell her. *Here is where kings have laid their crowns since the Plantagenets.*

Let me show you, he'd tell her then, his fingers sliding down the center seam of her bodice. His nail scraping over the near-invisible heads of the pins keeping it closed. *Let me show you what they did here.*

But it wasn't until the betrothal ball, as he watched Gilbert slouch onto the dance floor with Eleanor, as he watched Gilbert touch her, hold her, brush against her skirts, that he realized his desire was not the vague thirst of a man too long parched. This was not ordinary lust, tempted into existence by very ordinary circumstances.

This was *instinct*; this was indelible need. This was a craving that was scouring him raw.

And it was an absurdity on every level. *He'd* been the one to arrange the marriage. *He'd* been the one to select Eleanor for Gilbert. He was the one who was twice Eleanor's age, and too old, too bitter, too depraved to be allowed near anyone so innocent and pure. He could not have her, and she would never want him.

And why would she? Gilbert was a monster, but at least he had his youth. Jarrell had already spent his.

Still. Whenever Gilbert touched Eleanor, displeasure gouged Jarrell somewhere deep in his chest. Whenever she smiled or laughed or turned her head over her shoulder so that the button of her nose and the point of her chin were silhouetted with light, something much more pleasant spiked his blood. And when she danced, when her neck arched, when she leaned forward and her pert breasts pressed against the low neckline of her gown, his fingers curled into fists and his entire being vibrated with a hunger so fierce that it threatened to tear him and the world around him to shreds.

Had he still been young—had Eleanor been born twenty years earlier and they met when he was still himself, unravaged by time and grief and despair—

But no. He had to meet her now. When he was forty to her twenty, when she was promised to another. When his desperate misery had become such a knotted tangle around his being that pulling a single thread loose would spell disaster.

Disaster.

Because if he snapped even a lone cord of his restraint, he would do what his Saxon ancestors had done when they'd finally breached the wilds of Dumnonia: he would ransack, despoil, and plunder. He would hoist the

Lady Eleanor Vane with her fashionable taffeta round gown over his shoulder and carry her off to be his wife, and there'd be no further angst over the matter. He saw; he wanted; he'd take.

He'd give her the chance to know what his skin felt like against her teeth—

No.

Goddammit, *no*.

He wouldn't.

CHAPTER FOUR

THE LAST THING Jarrell had to admit to himself was he'd made a mistake.

Not because he'd changed his mind about leaving the dukedom behind —and not because he found Eleanor intelligent, capable, compelling.

But because he saw now how presumptuous, how careless the whole business of arranging marriages was.

Before last week, both Gilbert and Eleanor had been nothing more than sketches to him. How could they have been more? His days were spent with ghosts, or in trying to outrun those ghosts through whatever lonely pursuit he'd found that day: stalking through the hills, or drinking too much whiskey, or galloping down the narrow, winding roads fast as his horse would go. Until there was nothing of Dartham lands around him, nothing at all, and everything was a silver-brown blur of gorse and fog.

His parents would have been ashamed of his decision to marry Gilbert off to a girl he didn't know. Even before Jarrell came of age and was inducted into the Second Kingdom, his parents had impressed upon him the exigency of choice, of assent and acquiescence. Those weren't only the virtues that guided the Kingdom. They also guided their family, and his parents made sure he and his brother had grown up surrounded by all the Enlightenment ideals that they held so dear.

Then, when it came time for him and Alexander to step into the world the Darthams had guarded for centuries, his parents made sure he and his brother both understood there could be no pleasure without philosophy—no indulgence without rules.

But then they died a year after Ajax joined the kingdom. And then his brother died, and Jarrell's new bride two years after that, and it seemed like there was nothing left to indulge in, nothing left to guard. He'd retreated from the Kingdom and Far Hope itself and dreamed of an exile that would take him out of the reach of his memories forever.

A place where he could forget without also betraying the memory of the woman he'd loved before her death.

Jarrell pushed away from the crowd, scraping a hand over his face while he searched for a servant with a drink. Or better yet, an entire bottle. He was choked by his need, choked equally by the reasonable and civilized barriers to that need. Strangled by the tailored silk he'd donned for the ball and stifled by the ball itself—the largest crush of people he'd been in since Helena's funeral.

And stifled also by memories. For when he saw all these people thronged and dancing in the star-ceilinged chamber, he could so vividly remember the time *before*. Before his wedding, before everyone died, when Far Hope was a convergence of primal urges and wicked wanderings. And *he missed it*, he realized with shock. He thirsted for it. For so long, the man he'd been had been buried under a cairn of grief, and now it was as if all the rocks had tumbled free, as if he'd somehow been alive all this time.

He wasn't sure if he liked it.

Yes, a drink of something was called for in these circumstances. He needed to consider what to do next, and he always considered best with a drink in his hand. Plus it would smother the urge to sling his future niece-in-law over his shoulder and carry her off to be *his* wife instead of his nephew's, which he couldn't do for a thousand reasons, starting with his lack of knowledge about her wishes, and ending with this disastrous marriage he'd arranged.

Ending with the fact that you don't want to betray Helena's memory by marrying again.

He found a servant circulating with champagne and requested a glass of something stiff and amber-colored, and within a few minutes, his throat was burning but his head was clearer.

And with that clear head, he thought of Eleanor on the roof of the tower two days ago, of her low voice and her springtime eyes. The longing stamped on her face as she stared into the mist and the subtle way her hands curled into her skirts, as if she had to hold onto herself to keep herself in place.

A dock with many ships.

A hallway with many doors.

It wasn't too late. Yes, the guests were here; yes, there was to be a wedding in two days' time, but it wasn't too late to undo what he'd so carelessly and negligently done. He'd been appalled to discover his nephew was selfish—but really, how much more selfish had Jarrell himself been? For years, he'd been consumed with leaving by any means possible, and he hadn't considered that those means could be the engine of unhappiness for someone else.

But never mind. He would fix it. What good was being a duke if he couldn't fix things?

Unfortunately, since he was technically the host, he found himself much in demand as he began looking anew for Eleanor. Which meant he had to force his way through tedious pleasantries, barely veiled inquiries into his absence from society, and several pointed remarks about Gilbert's infamous Grand Tour, all while trying to decide the best way to approach Eleanor and ask if she wanted to stop this farce and leave Far Hope with her future intact.

He endured a dance with Eleanor's mother—who was feeling perfectly hale and hearty tonight, although she'd been abed all day with nerves—and then with the Countess of Kellow, Arabella Foscourt, whom he'd once known intimately as a younger man.

"Can we expect Far Hope to host more fêtes such as this?" the matron asked him as they touched hands and turned. Though she neared her sixth decade, she was still lovely, with a full mouth and sparkling eyes. Her alabaster skin was mostly unlined, save for a few fine creases around her eyes, a testament to how often she smiled. "More gatherings?"

"As I've only the one nephew and my brother is deceased, I doubt there will be another betrothal ball soon," Jarrell responded. It was a question he was used to dodging, especially from Arabella, who wrote him once or twice a year on the subject.

She shot him a look as they circled each other. "You know very well what I mean. And I'm not getting any younger, Ajax. I'd like to be here again before I die."

"Far Hope is not the only meeting place for people like us."

"No, but it is the oldest. And the safest because of its location." She peered up at him as they came together and touched hands again. "What happened to you, Ajax?"

A young wife had happened to him. Helena had happened. A duke's daughter, so tall and strapping that she seemed like a force of nature on her own. She rode, hunted, drank, swore, and laughed at every joke she'd ever heard—she'd been the most vital, *alive* person he'd ever met.

And then she'd died. Here in this very place.

"If you'll excuse me," he evaded with some relief, hearing the end of the music. "I should make sure Gilbert hasn't caused a scene yet."

It was mostly a lie—he actually wanted to stop thinking about Helena and he also needed to find Eleanor—but it was a plausible enough excuse.

His nephew would be a perpetual hazard to him all night, and potentially for much longer.

And he'd planned on making Gilbert Eleanor's hazard instead.

Guilt flickered through his blood. What had he been thinking?

He needed to see her. Talk to her, ask her what she wanted, he needed to make sure—

But where was she?

She wasn't in the center of the ballroom dancing, and she wasn't along the edges. Jarrell circulated twice, feeling increasingly stormy as he couldn't locate her, a storminess that had no real target except himself. For placing all of them into this mess to begin with. For desiring her.

But his anger at himself didn't slow his steps. He finally asked Eleanor's mother if she'd seen her, but Lady Vane was too tipsy at that point to be much help. No one in the ballroom was any help. Even though she was ostensibly the reason for the ball itself, no one had noted her departure, nor had anyone noticed her absence.

Jarrell didn't bother asking Gilbert.

He left the ballroom in search of her rooms, turmoil muddying his thoughts. Perhaps she wasn't feeling well. But to leave without telling anyone? To slip away from the ballroom as if she didn't want her absence to be noticed at all?

It all became clear once he got to her rooms and the anxious maid immediately—and tearfully—confessed everything without him having to ask a single question.

Eleanor had left.

Not only had she run away from her family and her betrothed, but she'd done it in the most stupidly reckless way possible. To run into the moors at night? In the rain? Alone? It would be dangerous for someone who knew the moors and combes. It would be dangerous even for a sturdy man who'd grown up here. . .

The unease had slid away, and in its place was something he didn't even recognize at first—because it was fear.

Fear cold and viscous; fear chilled and oily in his veins.

He was suddenly *terrified*. And *furious*.

He managed to bark orders at someone, he didn't notice whom, and within minutes the tailored silk jacket and gleaming dress pumps of his ball outfit were exchanged for a greatcoat and Hessian boots. A few minutes later and he was in the stables, mounting his horse.

And with directions for Eleanor's parents to be informed and for a formal search party to be organized, he tore off into the night, hoping to Christ and all the forgotten gods of the West Country that he'd find her.

And that he wouldn't be too late.

CHAPTER FIVE

SHE COULDN'T REMEMBER when she'd sat down, or why it had seemed like a good idea at the time.

She could only remember the rain, the harrying wind, the chilled ache in her feet and hands. She'd worn her wool cardinal—she wasn't so brainless that she'd escape into the Devonshire wilderness without *some* kind of outer covering—but what had been sufficiently warm for the short walk to the Pennard parish church was not nearly warm enough for a wet October night. The wide split in the front of the cloak allowed the wind to ruffle under her petticoats and nip at her ankles and feet, and the hood—sewn deliberately large so it could easily fit over curls and caps without crushing them—only served to allow the cold in around her neck and ears. When she'd sat, she'd tried to draw the garment more securely around her, but it was a losing fight against the wind, even sheltering as she was against a huddle of lonely rocks by the road.

At least, she thought she was still by the road. She'd been following it mostly by instinct and by feel in the pitch-dark night, and she wasn't sure if she'd managed to stay on its path or not.

If only she'd run away sooner. A day ago. A week ago. If only she'd run before she left Pennard Hall; if only she'd left Pennard Hall the day her father told her she would marry Sloreley.

But how could she have known that she would fall in love with the duke? How could she have known that there would have been a way to rewrite her future after all?

And how could she have known that it would storm like this tonight? And how could she have known how lightless this night would be? How desolate? How utterly indifferent to her and her existence?

She thought of the dock with many ships, of the hallway with many doors. Her future, which—when she had been warm and dry—had seemed so close she could reach out and touch it. She would go to Plymouth, then to her godsister in Edinburgh to plan her new future. Everyone knew half a dozen spinsters, it seemed. It could not be that hard to figure out how to become one. Or where to live as one.

But you don't really want spinsterhood. Not like that.

No, she didn't. She wanted room to make her own choices, that was all. She wanted away from her family and the never-ending demands on her time. But she didn't want to live an untouched life either, not at all. She wanted to be touched—often, and preferably by the Duke of Jarrell—but there wasn't a future in which she could see that happening. The afternoon with him on the roof made her realize she only had two choices.

Stay and hunger for the duke...or leave and hunger for the duke.

At least this was the option that didn't require marriage to Sloreley.

But she hadn't expected *this* part to be so difficult. Walking? Down a road? It should have been the easiest part of the whole business, yet here she was, sitting on the hard ground, trying in vain to keep herself warm. It wasn't long before even the brushed wool of her cloak was soaked through, along with her dress and her hair and her stockings and—

Everything was wet. *Everything* was cold.

She knew, in a vague sort of way, that it was probably better to keep moving. That staying still would make her colder yet, that moving might warm her. But the thought of standing, of taking a step after, of placing her feet on the slick, uneven road . . .

Perhaps she could wait a bit longer. Surely the storm must abate any minute now, surely no storm could last all night. And surely dawn wasn't so far off . . .

If she waited for the light or even for the rain to ease, it would be better. She knew it would be better. She rested against the rock and closed her eyes. She thought about Far Hope, and about the ball. She wished she'd taken another look before she left, a final look at the grim and glorious place where anything had seemed possible.

Well, anything except for her own happiness.

She also wished she'd been brave enough to approach the Countess of Kellow at the ball for something more than the usual polite greetings. She wished she could have told Arabella Foscourt how what she'd seen two years ago had fired her imagination like nothing else. Asked how one found other people who liked those kinds of things, how one could be a sort-of spinster, but also get occasional kisses between the thighs...

The memory of the Foscourt party sent sparks of warmth everywhere, and she nestled into herself, as if she could coax those sparks into a little fire, into a cheery conflagration to keep her warm until dawn.

How had it all started again?

Oh, right. Her cousin had laid down for a nap after their meal, but Eleanor hadn't been tired. She'd decided to enjoy her rare chance at solitude instead and take a walk around the lake on the far end of the Foscourt estate. There'd been a footman guarding the path, so she'd decided to detour through the stand of trees instead, coming to the folly from the other direction.

There'd been no footman there, no boundary or warning to alert her. She'd simply been walking, pleasantly lost in thought, and then the next moment she'd been greeted with a scene like something out of ancient Rome. Twenty or thirty people in various states of undress, music drifting through the air, liberal amounts of wine and food piled all over.

Instinct had forced Eleanor's eyes shut; instinct then forced them open again. It was shocking—wrong—almost certainly immoral —and yet—

Well, no one had ever been hurt by simply *looking*, surely? Bacon and Descartes both agreed that observation was key to knowledge, after all, and who was she to disagree with them?

And there was so much to, ah, *observe*. Her cousins had talked to her of kissing, and a childhood in the country meant she was familiar with the mechanics of copulation, but she had never imagined anything like this. Anything so sultry, so languorous. When animals tupped, it was quick and cursory—often with the female of the species still chewing whatever they'd been eating before being mounted, then wandering off to eat some more afterward, as if nothing interesting had happened.

But the guests in the folly weren't doing anything quickly, as if the end goal of procreation weren't the point at all. It was all slow kisses, slow touches. Where there was mating, even the mating seemed leisurely, as if the lovers could do it all day. And there were more than just pairs of people—there were trios and quartets. A group of seven, all tangled silk and entwined limbs. And something else she hadn't considered—but once she had, it seemed rather obvious—the pleasure wasn't restricted only to men and women together. There were men with men, and women with women. The Countess herself was being idly stroked by a woman near her age, while she kissed a man next to her. And that man was being cradled by her husband from behind, who was—oh.

Oh. Yes. Eleanor had needed to observe it all for a very long time indeed.

The trouble was, she'd had no idea how to insert herself into the moment, and later on, she had no idea how to approach anyone about it. Whenever she rehearsed a conversation in her head with the countess or any of the other guests, she sounded fumbling and awkward even to herself, and of course, she'd have to admit to her sneaking around the folly. Her willful voyeurism. She'd been too terrified of being scolded, ostracized...or worse, laughed at.

So she'd kept that afternoon inside herself, imagining that one day she'd be brave enough to ask one of the people she'd seen in the folly about it. Brave enough to ask for some kind of invitation or initiation. The kinds of slow touches and lingering kisses that led to long, shivering releases.

The Duke of Jarrell would be good at those, she wagered. He seemed the kind of man who would scoff at short, cursory pleasure. Her body sparked anew just to think of it.

And it felt quite nice to rest now. Her hands didn't hurt so much, and neither did her feet. The shivers too had eased and melted off, and she nearly felt warm.

Maybe she *was* warm, now that she thought of it. Warm enough not to worry about the gusts that spattered her face with rain, warm enough to stay here like she planned. She could rest and think of Jarrell touching her, of her and Jarrell in that folly, his hand between her legs and his mouth everywhere, everywhere...

"ELEANOR. *ELEANOR*, PLEASE. PLEASE WAKE UP . . ."

She'd rather not. She'd only just fallen asleep, and the dream of her and Jarrell in the folly was too exquisite.

"*Eleanor.*" The voice was rough and deep, and it would not be gainsaid. It was a voice used to getting its way. She frowned and tried to roll away, which the voice did not like. "No, little blossom, come here."

It said more things then, its words low and impatient and threaded with fear, but she couldn't make them out. She was too tired, and the rain was too loud, and she wanted back to her dream now, please.

Then suddenly she was being held. Cradled. Carried.

She tried to turn into the touch, snuggling into it, but this wasn't allowed her. She was hefted, settled, and tugged back into his arms, and then the swaying and jolting began.

A horse, she realized dazedly. *I'm on a horse.*

But further thoughts were beyond what she could do.

She nestled into the shelter of a broad chest, shut her eyes, and fell back into darkness, back to the folly where her dream-duke waited impatiently.

A FIRE CRACKLED. Light moved on the other side of her eyelids—reddish and flickering, and underneath her was something more firm than soft, but not uncomfortable. A blanket spread over a floor, maybe.

Warmth—like melting butter—was everywhere. In her chest and in her stomach, along her thighs and the arch of her neck. Low in her belly and between her legs.

In fact, she was aware of the melted-butter feeling before anything else, before the fire and the blanket, and was aware she'd been feeling it for some time now. It was strange, this warmth, because it made her dozing fitful and full of more dreams of Jarrell and the folly, but the sensation resisted action, it resisted fully waking. She didn't want to wake up and move from here; she didn't want to leave this feeling with its beautiful aches behind.

And the aches were *so* beautiful, but so cruel too. The tips of her breasts throbbed. The soft place between her legs cried out for contact so strongly that she squirmed for it, seeking pressure, friction, relief.

She found it.

There, all along one side, was a wall of firm, wonderful heat. She arched against it, feeling damp linen and silk, smelling something like fresh heather and cold rain, and something else she couldn't identify but that stoked the torment roiling in her body. She continued arching, seeking, until her body was pressed entirely against it.

And then—to her immense frustration—the wall tried to move away, making her hiss softly in displeasure.

She followed it. *Him.* Jarell.

Just like in her dreams.

But better, because he felt—oh, he felt like she thought he might. Long and muscular and superb.

I shouldn't touch him.

I should open my eyes.

But this dream feeling, this sleepy, shivery wonderfulness of him and her—and *finally*—

He was lying on his back now and she could drape herself over him. Just partly. Just enough to make a large arm band around her back in instinctive support, and enough that she could press her neediest spot against a hard, silk-covered thigh.

"Eleanor—" a deep voice said in warning, but she rocked against him anyway, a little noise escaping her as she did. It felt so *good*; it felt necessary. Each time she ground against him sparks flew everywhere in her body, like a blade on a grinding wheel. She was catching fire; she couldn't stop. Inside of her, there was a twisting, a hot and urgent twisting, and all around her was a strong body and the sharp scent of the moors at night, and—

Right as the voice muttered a low curse, the twisting inside of her snapped.

Her mouth opened against his chest and her teeth scraped over the fine linen of his shirt as sweet and agonizing release shuddered through her . . . waves of greedy pleasure wringing everything below her navel into absolute disarray. *Delicious* disarray. She wanted more of it, and more, and more—until the shudders gradually faded away and she slumped back against the muscled arm cradling her close.

The satisfaction of it all was almost enough to lure her back to sleep, but then Jarrell spoke her name again, and with an abrupt mental lurch, she came all the way awake.

CHAPTER SIX

HE DIDN'T KNOW what his face looked like then, only that it must have reflected all the fear he'd felt earlier, all the barely leashed lust, all the needs of a man too long denied.

She blinked up at him, her smile fading but her eyes staying curious and bright.

It was the brightness that undid him. Goddammit, didn't she know what it could do to a person, having her looking at them like that? Right after she'd used their body to give herself pleasure?

What slid through his veins then was something that wasn't rage or terror or lust. It was something far, far more dangerous.

Possession.

"We are going to talk now," Jarrell told her very quietly, doing his best to ignore the possessive burn in his blood, but *fuck*, it burned so hot. "You have choices to make about what happens next."

She pulled her lip between her teeth and then released it, nodding. The sweet sleepiness in her face was melting away, receding, and in its place was a look that brought him back to his senses.

Mostly.

He carefully separated their bodies and reached for the blanket behind him, draping it over her chemise-clad body, studying her as he did. He'd been terrified earlier, terrified in a way that made him realize he barely knew the meaning of terror at all. How could he have when he'd never before felt the chilled, limp weight of Eleanor Vane in his arms?

Only a single day ago, he would not have thought himself capable of so much fear. Even Helena's death—and the excruciating worry which preceded it—hadn't been marked so much by fear as by *dread*. He'd known he was going to lose Helena; he'd already lost everyone else by then too.

But this was not the slow creep of illness; this was not a crawling slog into oblivion.

This was being plunged into the icy waters of hell without warning. This was having a hole blown right through his heart.

He'd ridden as fast as he could given the downpour—the rain meant mud and moonlessness, two things anyone traveling at night tried to avoid —and it had only been pure luck that lightning had lit the miserable night as he was about to pass her huddled, red-cloaked form. For a moment, as he dismounted and knelt beside her, he'd thought she was already dead. That she'd already succumbed to the cold and that it was too late—he'd killed her.

He'd driven her to this. Driven her out into the storm and the desolate wild because he hadn't been quick enough to realize his own mistakes, and now there would be another ghost to haunt his steps—

She'd stirred then. Which should have helped dissipate the terror, but only made it worse, because she could still die at any moment, because in the intermittent flashes of lightning, she looked yet half-dead and safety was miles away. Unless—yes, his refuge at the far end of his property was maybe only a mile and a half away, much closer.

He'd gathered her into his arms and muttered prayers into the darkness the entire way there.

He'd never brought anyone to Far House before.

It was a small but elegant dwelling he'd had built at the edge of Dartham lands, tucked into a forest and girdled on three sides by a loop in the River Teign, and where he'd hidden for the last several years. It was his sanctuary—a place free from the ghosts of Far Hope, or *freer* at least—and no one, save for a few trusted people and his lawyers, knew it existed.

Until tonight.

He'd burst through the door with Eleanor in his arms, barked orders for a fire in his room, and then swept her upstairs. He kept a very small staff at Far House, but just like the staff at Far Hope, they were familiar

with the ways of the Second Kingdom. Which meant that the sight of a
Dartham man whisking someone unceremoniously up to his room wasn't
unheard of, although it hadn't happened in this house or at any house in
the realm since Helena had died, as Jarrell had withdrawn from the Kingdom. From the rest of life in general.

Once the situation was made clear, everyone moved quickly to help.
Blankets, water and wine were sent for, the fire was laid in, and he
dispatched the groundskeeper to Far Hope, to inform her parents that
Eleanor been found and to gather in the search party. As soon as the storm
cleared, he'd return Eleanor to Far Hope or bring her parents to Far
House, since the roads were too treacherous to attempt a journey by
carriage in these conditions. He'd also instructed the groundskeeper to
send a rider from Far Hope to Chagford for a doctor, although he didn't
dare to wait to act until the doctor came. The man could be hours yet, or
more, depending the weather and the roads.

As a young man, Jarrell had once heard a gamekeeper tell a story of a
man caught outside in winter, who'd managed to make it to safety only to
die when an overeager neighbor had plunged him into a near-boiling bath.

Too sudden a shock, the gamekeeper had said sagely. *Slow heat is better for
those who've taken the cold into their blood.*

Slow heat. Slow heat.

He'd repeated those two words to himself like a prayer as the servants
bustled out of the room and he stripped Eleanor out of her wet cloak and
clothes and down to her chemise. He'd peeled off his coat and jacket as
well, since they were both soaked through, wearing only his shirt and a
fresh pair of dry breeches.

He'd spread a blanket some distance away from the fire, wrapped a soft
blanket around them both, and then gathered her into his arms, the way
the old gamekeeper had said was the best way to cure someone sick from
the cold. And he'd held her that way for an hour. Then two.

Keeping his fingers webbed over her ribs to make sure she was still
breathing. Burying his face in her damp, sweet-smelling hair. Swallowing
over and over again in relief as the color returned to her cheeks and lips,
as her skin warmed under the kiss of the fire and his embrace.

Gradually becoming aware—as the fear ebbed away—of her body
against his.

Of the thin chemise that barely hid her skin.

Of the firm curves of her small breasts and the rise of her hip from her waist.

Of her thighs against his own... and of the hollow between her thighs.

He could feel that small cove, that slight dip where her thighs pressed together right beneath her mound, and that lack, that tiny, barely there absence, was just as palpable as any luscious contour or flare. It would take nothing to push his cock into that space, to fill it with himself, and through his breeches and her chemise, he would finally be able to feel her, he would be able to notch himself against her heat and mimic the act he would commit murder to do right now.

An eager erection throbbed insistently against his stomach, and his blood simmered, and his hands shook with the need to haul her even closer, to rub her entire body against his.

How long has it been?

He knew the answer as well as a sinner knew the day of their conversion: he hadn't lain with anyone since Helena. Since his wedding night, if he wanted to be entirely precise.

Sixteen years of chastity. Every day of it hard-fucking-won, but none harder than the days he spent with Eleanor. It wasn't temptation—it was torment, and nothing was more tormenting than holding her like this, knowing so little separated their flesh. All he'd have to do was move a hand, and he'd be cupping her bottom. All he'd have to do is reach down and he could make her come on his fingers.

His muscles began to ache, and not from holding her, but from restraining himself from doing more.

He wouldn't do more. He couldn't.

The kingdom he used to rule over at Far Hope had very few rules, but the eager acquiescence of a partner was an edict they'd all lived by. It had been etched deeply onto his psyche as young man by his parents, and he'd never violated it. So even if Eleanor were awake, even if she were well, he would do no more than hold her until he was certain she was better. And then he would let her go, no matter how much he burned to keep her in his arms.

Half an hour later, he no longer had an excuse to cradle her curvy body against his own. Her cheeks were pink, her lips were rosy, and she sighed and snuggled into him like someone happily asleep rather than someone on the verge of death. It was time to tuck her into the nearby bed and start planning for the morning.

He'd violated the bounds of propriety tonight—they'd spent the night alone, he'd undressed her and held her in only her chemise—even given the extreme circumstances, he wasn't sure that would be enough to deflect her father's ire when he heard. Or Gilbert's ire.

Would Gilbert be ireful though? Would Pennard?

Did it matter?

What truly mattered was how Eleanor felt. Because if she'd been willing to fling herself onto the thorn-choked mercy of the moors, then clearly a marriage with Gilbert had become impossible. Not that he could blame her, although it begged the question: *What next?*

He had hoped to talk to her tonight, yes, but then there would've been time to make a plan, to weigh every consequence and proceed with calculation and care.

Eleanor's flight meant time was no longer a luxury they could afford. There were the guests to think about, and her reputation—because there would be rumors. And selfishly, he wondered how would he bear it after she left and there were no more green eyes, no more husky laughs? No more eyebrows arched in private amusement? The plan had always been to leave after Gilbert married, so he would have been sundered from her anyway, but . . .

Stop being selfish.

He would. He would stop. But the selfishness stirred nonetheless, along with a possessive hunger.

You could have her.

Ask her to be yours.

He dismissed the thought as soon as it came. She wouldn't want him. And he'd already planned the rest of his life—it was meant to be a life alone, a life free from memories and free from violating those memories by wedding another.

I can't.

And that was when Eleanor started moving.

It took Jarrell a long minute to realize what was happening, to understand that her contented little snuggles had turned into a restless seeking, and by then it had become all too clear what was driving her restlessness. Her eyelids fluttered as with fervid dreams, and the tips of her breasts were drawn up tight against his chest under her chemise. Splotches of color bloomed on her cheeks as she began arching against him.

He tried to roll away, onto his back, but even he could recognize it wasn't a very valiant attempt at escape. And she followed him anyway like a needy kitten, rubbing herself against him, pressing her cunt against his thigh and riding it in slow, sleepy waves.

He should stop her. She didn't know what she was doing, and she'd be mortified when she woke up, and his body was strung so tight he feared it would snap. He feared he'd shove up her chemise and kiss her awake—but not on the mouth.

Somehow, he managed not to move, not to touch her other than to support her with his arm as she found her release against his body. As she awakened with a small smile on her lips and sweet, sated eyes fluttering open.

And now here they were, both sitting upright and studying each other, embarrassment, guilt, desire, relief—all of it staining the moment between them.

CHAPTER SEVEN

CHOICES TO MAKE, he'd said.

She adjusted the blanket over her shoulders and tried to meet the duke's inscrutable gaze with a steady one of her own. Steady gaze, steady heart, steady Eleanor.

It was a lie. She didn't feel steady at all. Her body still thrummed from release, her mind brimmed and bristled with scores of contradictory thoughts, and her heart couldn't decide if it belonged in her throat or in her stomach. It wasn't *un*pleasant—the heart feeling—but it did mean that any time the duke did *any*thing—lift a hand, furrow his brow, breathe—her insides melted again and all she wanted to do was giggle. Or purr.

Not steady at all. And why should she be? She'd just—

And in her *chemise*—

And he'd let her—

He'd let her.

Heat bloomed in her stomach all over again, thinking about how he'd held her as she moved against him. She'd found those releases before, but always by herself and always with some effort. But experiencing it with someone else, and so easily—

Should she be embarrassed? Was she embarrassed?

Yes. A little. Maybe a lot. It wasn't done to find release in the arms of a fiancé's relatives, probably not even in the Foscourts' circle. Even though she'd just thrown her family's respect and goodwill into the fire by running away like this, she was too used to the good opinion of others not to crave it now. She'd long ago come to the conclusion that respect and indulgence were not necessarily mutually exclusive. But her entire personality had heretofore been built on restraint and cool placidity. In the span of just a few hours, the duke had seen her behave both recklessly and unthinkingly.

I am both things, she wanted to say—not only to Jarrell, but to everyone. Restrained *and* deeply feeling. Placid *and* agitated.

Cool-blooded and also so feverish sometimes that she felt flames burning along the inside of her skin.

Like this moment right now—she wasn't only embarrassed. She was nervous and excited and scared of what would happen when she left this room, and hungry for more of what they'd just done in this room. She glanced down at the large hand currently resting on his knee as he sat with one leg drawn up, and she wondered how those long fingers and blunt fingertips would feel under her chemise. She looked back to his face and saw the shadow of his beard darkening his jaw, and she wanted to know how it would feel against her breasts.

She almost dared to ask but stopped herself at the last moment. She'd already used up an entire lifetime's worth of boldness, and anyway, more serious things should be discussed now. She'd run away, and he'd caught her. There were only a few different things that could happen next, and Jarrell would be well within his rights to escort her firmly and grimly back to Far Hope if she wouldn't go willingly.

Surely that was what he meant by *choices*.

She didn't like the thought much, and she shivered, pulling the blanket tighter around her, as if she were already back out in the dark.

His brow furrowed even more; he shifted towards her and then shifted back right away, as if fighting some instinct. "Move closer to the fire," he said, a bit gruffly. "You'll be warmer."

She obeyed, crawling forward enough that the warmth of the fire kissed her skin, and then she looked back at the duke, still sitting with his leg drawn up, still pinning her with a stare that seemed as hot as it was troubled. The hand draped over his knee flexed and fisted and flexed again. A muscle jumped in his jaw. She followed his gaze back to herself.

Oh.

The blanket had slipped. And the low-cut bodice of her chemise hid little—she imagined the light of the fire hid even less.

Goose bumps erupted everywhere, as if he was touching her with that restless, flexing hand and not only with his stare.

"Still cold?" Jarrell asked, voice rough, jaw tight. "Do you need another blanket?"

No, she wanted to say. *Warm me up yourself. Push those big hands up my chemise. Cover me with your body.*

The way he looked at her then—like he could read her thoughts. As if he could sense every depraved wish that flitted through her mind.

Could moments be many things all at once, as feelings were? Because this moment felt like that, like it was spilling over with possibilities and futures and promises, as if she was standing at one of those crossroads she'd craved so badly, with many lanes and byways branching off in every direction. And it was her choice where to step next.

She looked at his flexing hand, his dark eyes, his cruel mouth.

And she chose her next step.

"No. Don't get another blanket. I want you to warm me."

His lips, which had been pressed together so tightly she could see lines bracketing the corners of his mouth, parted. His hand flexed once on his knee, out and then back into a fist again. His fist was massive. *He* was massive.

"I beg your pardon," he said. Slowly.

She'd run away, hadn't she? She'd disguised herself and plunged into the wilderness. And wasn't he here looking at her like he craved her as much as she craved him? Didn't he look like it was taking every bit of his restraint to keep from grabbing her and kissing her?

She'd already seized one unwritten future for herself tonight, so why not another? Why not reach for what she wanted, for another hope beyond the mist?

She let the blanket slide all the way off her shoulders. "I want you to warm me, Your Grace."

That jumping muscle in his jaw again.

A sharp swallow sliding down his throat.

"We should talk," he said, sounding like he was trying to convince himself. "There's much to discuss. And I...should not."

Having a mind built for projects was very convenient in this moment.

The new project was convincing Jarrell. Her materials were her words and her body. And she already had a plan.

She started crawling towards him, knowing it made her bodice gape, knowing he could see straight down it. "We could do both at once," she said reasonably. "We could talk while you warmed me——"

He reached out to touch her shoulder, as if to stop her, but the moment his fingers brushed her exposed skin, something seemed to break inside him. A latch, or a lock. A dam.

She was on her back before she knew what was happening, with the duke on top of her, his hands planted on either side of her head. The heat of his body burned against hers, and she pressed up against him with a gasp.

Then she smiled. "See? We can talk just as easily like this."

He narrowed his eyes. Fallen hair from his queue framed his face, and he looked every inch the ruthless heathen. "I have something else in mind, Lady Eleanor."

It was a warning. His eyes blazed with it.

Shivers of delicious fear chased down her spine. *Could* fear be delicious?

Yes, she decided, yes, it could. This wasn't the primordial fear of the moors or the soulless dread of marrying someone she didn't want to marry. This was something thrilling and wonderfully dangerous, like turning to face a prowling wolf and looking into its bright, hungry eyes.

In an instant, all her contradictions, her embarrassments, all the lingering terror of her foiled escape—they vanished. There was only him, this half-wild duke, and the sparkling responses he elicited in her.

Was she afraid? Oh yes. But did it sear her, thrill her, kindle her to have him like this? Did it destroy every ounce of cool *serenity* she'd ever claimed to possess?

Yes.

"I hope whatever it is will keep me warm," she whispered. The whisper didn't make her words any less bold. "Some parts of me are still so cold they ache."

"Is that so?"

Her body was far ahead of her mind in this. Her nipples had gathered into taut, straining points, and they tented the fabric of the chemise, as if rising for his lips.

She took a deep breath. Eyes wide open, she would choose this.

Then, so there could be no mistake which parts of her twinged for his touch, she slid her hands between them and cupped her breasts. It felt so good to have warmth there, and pressure, that she slid her hands over her curves again, squeezing a little this time and savoring the shivering feeling it gave her.

The noise that tore from Jarrell's chest was an animal noise, a feral growl, and it was all the warning she had before her hands were pushed to the side and pinned to the floor. He moved down, ducked his head between wide, straining shoulders, and put his mouth to the curve of her breast.

For a moment, he only breathed there.

Warm exhales tickled her through the near-translucent linen, taunting her, making her restless underneath him. Then he let his eyes rove up from her heaving chest to her undoubtedly flushed face. She had the thought that—despite what she'd sleepily used his body for earlier—this was the actual Rubicon; if he touched her now, if he tasted her, if he made her squirm and pant in the same way she'd made herself do earlier, then there was no going back.

What that meant, she had no idea. A wedding would be the proper outcome from a moment such as this, and yet there was nothing *proper* about the Duke of Jarrell. And there were other impediments to marriage —that he was the uncle of the betrothed she'd just fled from being the largest. But he also had no desire to wed another. Famously so.

What was she *doing*? What road was she stepping on exactly?

What was her desire?

She didn't know. She didn't even know what she hoped for. She only knew this: since the moment he'd stalked into Far Hope's dining room like a villain in a Radcliffe novel, she'd wanted him to touch her. She wanted those rough hands, those flashing eyes, that cruel mouth—and she craved something else that she couldn't put words to. Something beyond sex itself. Something like consumption.

She wanted to consume him.

She wanted him to consume *her*.

Perhaps the road was one she'd been searching for since she'd decided to become a sort-of spinster—maybe even since that afternoon in the temple folly. The liberty to choose her indulgences and pleasures with someone she craved. To join herself to someone who excited her. She'd already run away. She was already ruined. Why not claim this for herself?

And when his eyes met hers, she saw an appetite that more than matched her own.

He would choose consumption, as she had.

He lowered his lips to her nipple and sucked hard, his mouth a shock of heat and wet. Eleanor had no idea—*none*—that anything could feel like that. The difference between her own fingers when she'd touched herself privately and someone else's indecent mouth was so vast it was almost laughable.

His wicked kisses sizzled over her skin and drew need between her thighs. They sent fresh goose bumps everywhere and made her pant in sheer sensation.

How did anyone get anything done when this was a possibility? How were there women who spent hours on embroidery and polite conversation when *this* was an available option? She didn't understand it at all! If she had her way, she'd spend all day just like this, with Jarrell's large hands pinning her wrists to the floor and his hot mouth drawing her need to the surface.

Although, after he impatiently tugged the chemise off her body and she felt his mouth on her naked flesh, she had to amend her previous assertion a little.

This was how she'd spend every day if she could: tongue to bare flesh, teeth to sensitive skin, her eyes on the working of the duke's jaw and the subtle hollowing of his cheeks as he feasted on her.

Jarrell moved to her other breast, kissing the underside and gently biting his way to its peak. She rocked underneath him all the while, shuddering at the feeling of her naked body against the linen and silk of his clothes. It was forbidden, every bit of this was, and she should be horrified with herself. But she wasn't. She wanted *more* actually, his mouth on her breasts stoking tension low in her belly, and she told him so.

"I'm cold elsewhere too," she whispered.

He lifted his head to look up at her with glittering eyes. "Show me," he said.

Eleanor could feel the humiliated flush scald her chest as she took his hand. Her entire body trembled with nervous, reckless yearning, with the awareness of her own daring.

She pushed his hand between her legs and curled it over her sex.

"Here," she murmured, watching the hunger settle over his face. "Right here."

He shot a look up to her face that could have been furious or could have been furiously thankful—she had no time to tell because, in an instant, he was between her legs, pushing her thighs apart with his hands and looking not up at her face, but at her wet opening.

It was *indecent* how he looked at her. It was sinful, shocking. He didn't merely glance at her intimate flesh—he studied it. He inspected her like a connoisseur of fine things, his midnight eyes missing nothing, allowing her no secrets from him.

"I've thought about this," he said in a low voice, a finger trailing up her damp seam, "since the moment I met you. I've thought about what I would do to see this. Touch this."

He moved down to his elbows, and all the distant thoughts and worries in Eleanor's mind burned themselves to ash. The sight of him there, his sculpted mouth hovering over her gold curls, his massive shoulders and arms backlit by the firelight—it was a sight that immolated all reason. If someone had laid out all the logical explanations for why this was a terrible idea, she would only have to gesture to the muscle-hewn silhouette of him to make her argument.

There was no denying herself this. She wouldn't even know how to try.

"I would have given up my entire world to taste you," Jarrell said, right before kissing her in her wettest, hottest place.

The first brush of his lips made her sigh, and the second made her moan. But then he parted his mouth and began exploring her with his tongue, giving her slick kisses that curled her toes. He stroked into her entrance with no shame, nothing even approaching shame, as if she were indeed a feast fit for a king, and when she looked down, his hips were flexing against the plush rug, as if to give himself pressure and friction. As if to—

Oh.

Oh.

It was his erection he was grinding against the floor. It was that hard part of himself he was seeking relief for as he pleasured her with his mouth. Because he was enjoying this as much as she was? It hardly seemed possible, but there was the slow churn of his hips, those were his hungry moans from between her legs. Those were his eyelashes fluttering like those of a mortal drinking the gods' nectar.

Doing this made him as wild as it made her—and ah, the knowledge of that. The feeling of it. She wanted more and more and more of it; she wanted to be dragged under and drowned in it.

"Please," she murmured, not entirely sure what she was asking for, but knowing that it was *more*. "It feels so good. Please, Your Grace."

"Ajax," he said. When he lifted his head, his pupils were blown laudanum-wide and his mouth was wet with her. "My name is Ajax."

"Ajax," she said softly, and the answering grunt of satisfaction was enough to make her thighs and belly tighten dangerously. She was close to the mindless urgency that had overtaken her earlier in her sleep, but it felt different now. Perhaps because she was awake. Perhaps because the wickedness of his mouth was a world apart from pleasuring herself against his thigh. Or perhaps it was because she could actually see him—the large hands wrapped around her hips, the dark fans of his lashes over his cheeks as he kissed her. The restive toil of his hips as he pressed himself against the floor. All of it was so much *more*.

There was only his tongue stroking into her, his mouth at her swollen bud, his flickering kiss in the firelight. There was only the sweet frustration of her release building just out of reach, and she didn't know whether to squirm away from it or seize it with both hands—

When the cataclysm came, it came like the storm outside...in furious, seething lashes that had her crying out to the ceiling. Her whole body shuddered, her belly and thighs quivered with it, and she could no more stop herself from twisting in Jarrell's hold than she could stop herself from trying to rock harder against his mouth at the same time.

Jarrell didn't stop, but he did ease his insistent kisses somewhat. They were more reverent than hungry now. When he finally stopped completely and raised up to his knees, hunger was still present in his glittering gaze. And the thick rod straining against his breeches . . .

Her heart skipped.

With fear or with lust? Terror or delight?

Once again, did it matter?

But her heart still cautioned her. She'd already made the mistake of falling in love with him, surely it would be an even larger mistake to assume he could ever feel the same. But when he looked at her like he was doing now, when he moved over her to trail darkly worshipful kisses over her breasts and throat . . .

Was it so impossible to think he might return her feelings? That he might not regret later what they were doing right now? That he might want to do it again?

She wasn't a fool. She wouldn't expect love. But perhaps a proposal wasn't as farfetched as she'd thought earlier? She hadn't wanted marriage with Sloreley, but with Jarrell . . .

Yes. Yes, she wanted it. She wanted everything. And surely that's what he meant when he mentioned choices. After the night they'd just spent together, there could be only one choice left.

The choice she'd spent the last week trying to keep herself from dreaming about.

But if he doesn't propose?

Well, then, she would take her blows like the soldier of serenity she was. She was capable of that, right? She was capable of surviving a broken heart?

Enough now. Enough of the circular thoughts—she'd already leapt, and there was little sense in regretting the fall. She gave into her deepest urges, slid her hands into his silky hair, and pulled him close.

CHAPTER EIGHT

"I THOUGHT we were going to talk," she murmured against his mouth.

He couldn't answer at first. She was simply too sweet to stop kissing. Her mouth was too soft, her tongue too eager to slide against his. Her hands in his hair were too perfect—tentative and seeking at turns, as if her need to hold him and use him warred with the polite reserve she'd deployed all these years to survive.

Use me however you like, he wanted to tell her. *Use me until we both hurt with it.*

He felt tempted as he hadn't been in years to let the beast free, to tell this quiet blossom currently panting beneath him everything. Everything.

No. He couldn't do that.

What did he think would happen then? If he explained to this well-mannered English rose—who was *still legally betrothed to his nephew*—that he'd like to tie her to his bed, pretty please? That he wanted her naked at his dining room table every night until the end of time, wearing nothing but Dartham heirloom jewelry and white silk stockings?

That he wanted to taste her cunt, not because it was the gentlemanly thing to do, but because it got him hard?

That he wanted to fuck her, and fuck her, and fuck her, until there was nothing left to do but sleep and then wake up to fuck again?

No. She'd asked for his touch, she'd asked for pleasure, but Jarrell was the former master of the Second Kingdom, and he knew better than anyone that there was a gap between gentle lovemaking and the carnal acts of the inherently wicked. Many people enjoyed the former and despised the latter. Also it was absurd to think a woman who'd rather die than marry his young nephew had any wish to further entangle herself with that nephew's far-from-young uncle.

And what does it mean that I haven't thought of Helena this entire time?

Jarrell wanted Eleanor like he hadn't wanted anyone since Helena, and it made him doubt himself, doubt his capacity for loyalty and his commitment to Helena's memory.

With great agony, he tore himself away from Eleanor's mouth.

A pretty frown pulled at her lips as he raised himself to his knees. "Ajax?" she asked.

His name in her husky voice—even huskier post-climax—was enough to make his already-throbbing erection surge against his falls. But what nearly undid him was the sight that greeted his eyes as he got to his knees and was able to see between her spread thighs once more. Her cunt—slick and rosy—was still exposed and waiting for him. Her petals still open and softly swollen. Her tight opening beckoning . . .

His hand went automatically to his aching prick, squeezing to alleviate some of the pressure there. He absolutely would not go any further, but fuck, he thirsted for it, and that troubled him. After sixteen years, anyone would be in physical need, and so he didn't blame himself for that. The problem was that he wanted more than just her body: he wanted *her*. He wanted this little blossom, lush and brave, and so secretly reckless, so privately turbulent, like a churning river hidden underneath a layer of solid ice. Not that there was anything cold about her.

No, when she was being spoiled as she should be, she was hotter than the fires of hell.

He forced his eyes up to her face, his hand still wrapped tight around himself, and then he let go of his erection, wincing at the throb it gave.

Eleanor, perceptive thing she was, noticed. "Does it hurt?" she asked him.

She as curious as she was coy, and it unraveled his control, his guilt, everything. Was it possible to want someone so much that it could change what he thought he knew about himself? Because right now he could taste her on his lips, recall how the turgid point of her nipple felt on his tongue. The need that frothed and simmered in his blood frightened him—he wanted her so much. He wanted all of this *so damn much.*

He closed his eyes, knowing he shouldn't answer. He should cover her nakedness and ask her forgiveness.

That's what a good man would do.

"Yes," he answered, opening his eyes.

He wasn't a good man, unfortunately for them both. "It needs release."

She reached for him, and he didn't stop that first tentative brush of her fingertips over his clothed erection.

"Can I help it feel better?" she whispered. "I felt so much better after —" She searched for the words. "After you kissed me there."

He shuddered as she stroked him again. Even over the silk breeches, her touch scalded him.

"Eleanor," he said, and he meant to say next: *we should not. We should stop right now.* But those weren't the words that left his mouth. "Hold it tighter. Yes, that's it. Like that."

She pulled her lower lip between her teeth as she watched her hand mold over his shape. She squeezed and released, caressed and explored. He wanted so badly to unfasten the falls of his breeches. To show her how deeply she riled him. To teach her how to attend to his coarsest needs.

After a minute of this torture, he covered her hand with his own and halted her attentions. "Enough," he said.

She lifted her spring-green eyes to his. "Why?"

It took him a full minute to understand that she was asking why he stopped her. To understand that she didn't *want* to stop.

"We shouldn't, little blossom," he said, the endearment clearly surprising her—and then, if her renewed flush was any indication, pleasing her. He pushed her hand away.

"But why?" She looked back down to the tumid length between his hips. "I don't want to stop."

"It's been an eventful night for both of us. I don't want to take advantage of that. Of you." He closed his eyes, tried to gather his thoughts. When he opened his eyes and spoke, it was more to convince himself than her. "I won't pretend that your leaving will be unnoticed, and I can't promise it won't cause some damage to your reputation. But right or wrong, you know as well as I do that some boundaries mean more than others. Some acts might mean more to a future husband."

Something moved in her eyes that he couldn't catch: the moment he noticed it, it was gone. "I see," she said evenly. Her expression was neutral. "And you don't wish for that to be the case."

He didn't like it when she was serene with him, when she used her equanimity as a shield to keep him at bay. He didn't like it at all. He wanted her curious and unfettered. He wanted her reckless—although the mere thought of her running away again and putting her life in danger elicited a storm of fury and fear in his blood. "Why would I?" He'd only known her a week, but he felt violently protective of Eleanor and her future. And that extended to protecting her from himself, and also protecting himself from his ravening urge to claim her, to plunder her when he'd already decided his future. It was better for everyone if he stayed away from her and abdicated his title as he'd planned. Right?

Right?

"What choices do I have now, then?" she asked. "At this moment?"

He sensed something else under her questions, but he wasn't sure what it was. Unhappiness, probably, and she had every right to be unhappy. To her, he must represent the marital captivity that awaited her if she was bought back to Far Hope—and he still hadn't reassured her that he wasn't going to bring her back.

He corrected that now. "Firstly, I want you to know that I won't ask you to change your mind about marrying my nephew."

Relief filtered through her face before she schooled her expression again. "Thank you. I'm grateful for that."

He cut her a look. "That doesn't mean I'm happy about *how* you decided to break off the betrothal, Eleanor. You could have died tonight."

Her chin lifted ever so slightly. "But I didn't."

"Because I found you. If I hadn't . . . "

Her mouth tightened, the only betrayal of her placidity. "I'm grateful that you found me as well and brought me someplace safe. Thank you."

Very aware of her nakedness—of her tightly beaded nipples and gold-dusted cunt—Jarrell finally handed her the blanket and then sat back. He was still so hard that half the blood in his body had to be filling his cock right now, but he did his best to ignore it.

"Are you truly? Grateful, I mean?" he asked. "Your unhappiness was not a secret to me, and I let myself pretend that your forbearance was consent when I should know better. If I had handled this matter well, you wouldn't have needed to run away at all."

Eleanor seemed to consider his words, tilting her head. "I appreciate the admission. I suppose whether or not I'm truly grateful depends on what happens next."

Yes. That would inform things, wouldn't it, whether or not he was about to drag her back into the pits of Gilbert-infused hell. He took a deep breath. "The way I see it, you have two paths available to you now. Either I escort you back to Far Hope, and I help you formally break off the betrothal. Or I help you get *safely* to your final destination and then I return and formally break off the betrothal on your behalf. In either instance, you have my full and free assistance in ending the engagement."

Or there's option three, where I drag you to the church myself.

He scraped a hand over his face, as if he could rub away the thought itself. Rub away the keen bolt of longing that struck him in the chest—and elsewhere—whenever he thought of making Eleanor his bride.

She looked away, tucking the blanket more securely around her. "I see," she said quietly. "So in both of these futures, I am unencumbered by any husband."

"In both, you will be free to choose whatever you like, because you will not be burdened by Far Hope."

She kept her face angled away from his. He didn't like it.

"Eleanor, look at me."

She did, after a long moment, reluctance stamped all over those pert features.

"Are you unhappy with these options?" he asked. "Do you want more from me? More help? I owe it to you. I arranged this disastrous betrothal and I should be the one to fix it. I was being selfish, thinking only of myself, but I can find another way to—"

He stopped. He hadn't meant to say that last part, hadn't meant to expose that Gilbert's marriage served a purpose for *him*.

But he should have known she would catch his mistake. Her brow arched subtly. "Another way to what, Your Grace? Marry off your unmarriable nephew?"

He debated lying, then decided against it. It was beneath them both.

"Yes, but that wasn't necessarily its own end. Once Gilbert was married, I'd planned to abdicate my title and move away. He would become the Duke of Jarrell, and I would be free."

Her mouth parted; he'd genuinely shocked her. There was no serenity in those features now, no level neutrality. She could not have looked more stunned than if he'd stood up in front of her and started doing backflips.

"Abdicate?" she asked, then blinked. "Move away? You can't *do* that! And who wishes to be free of a dukedom in any event?"

"Me," he replied simply. "And yes, it was very difficult to arrange, but my need to leave outweighed every other consideration, and so I persevered."

She blinked again. "I don't understand."

He got to his feet, leaving her there on the floor in her blanket. He wandered over to the window where a steady rain fell outside. Heavy, but no longer desolate and howling. Lightning still flashed occasionally, illuminating the grasping branches of the trees and the glinting wind of the river.

He desperately wanted a drink before he filled this airy, modern room with the sad tales of his past, but he didn't move to the desk where he kept his whiskey. He could still taste Eleanor on his lips, and it would be the only time he could savor it. He wouldn't wash it away. Not for any price in the world.

"Far Hope is an old place," he started. An instinctive resistance nearly stilled his tongue—secrecy was one of the highest laws at Far Hope, and only the initiated were permitted to know its mysteries—but it was strangely thrilling to speak of it too. To finally confess. To unburden himself of the things that he'd run away from in his grief. Things he currently craved with a deep and animal hunger.

"The manor house was built sometime in the thirteenth century," he continued, "but there was certainly a structure there at the time of the Domesday Book, and there are recordings of a Saxon abbey there even before that. And like all old places, Far Hope has its secrets—very old ones. Some of the oldest in England."

"But what do those secrets have to do with you? If they are so old, surely they cannot hurt you now, in this day and age?"

He rested his head against the glass, not looking at her. "They only hurt as they serve to remind me."

He couldn't see Far Hope from here. It was much too far away, but it didn't matter. It was vivid in his mind's eye as always. He could see Helena's pale gray eyes reflecting the stars in the star-ceilinged chamber back to him; he could hear her laugh as she danced at their wedding. He could feel the cool, dry weight of her fingers in his as she drew in her last, shaky breaths.

Eleanor shifted behind him in a rustle of blankets and skin. "They remind you of your—your wife?"

Thunder hummed against the glass, and he finally turned around to face the girl he'd rescued from the moors. "Yes. My wife."

Eleanor was perched up on her knees, the blanket wrapped securely around her, although it didn't cover those creamy shoulders or disguise the pert curves he'd just been licking and sucking. Her eyes were wide and clear, and her lips parted.

"What happened?" she asked.

"It's coming in the story, I promise. And Eleanor, I must ask that you do not repeat anything you learn tonight. While my friends haven't gathered at Far Hope for many years, they still meet, and they still risk exposure. Many of them are powerful, but many are not. Even the powerful ones might not escape punishment, if it came down to that."

"Punishment?" Eleanor repeated.

He nodded once. It was a grave reality. The Second Kingdom—so called because it existed like a shadow realm inside the actual monarchy— conferred some safety and liberty for its people to love and fuck whoever and however they wished, and to live how they needed to. But that safety was sorely limited outside the confines of the Kingdom, and the danger of being discovered was all too real.

"Do I have your word that you will keep the things you learn tonight confidential? At least where the revelation would risk someone other than myself?"

"You have my word, Your Grace," she said solemnly, and it was surprising how much he already missed her calling him by his Christian name.

"Thank you," he said, and then continued. "As far back as anyone knows, Far Hope was a place for, well, *baser* needs, one might say. Some think it began at the Abbey, which was a place of pilgrimage for women wishing to conceive. Some think it started before that, with the Romans, or maybe even the Druids. But what is known for certain is that my valley became a place where people could indulge themselves. Carnally." He studied her then, before he continued. She didn't look frightened or disgusted. She wasn't scrambling away from him, begging to leave.

When will you stop underestimating her?

He continued. "It's an entire world—servants and peers alike—and membership is handed down both by birthright and by sponsorship. I learned of the Kingdom on my eighteenth birthday and was allowed to join on my twenty-first. I was elated."

Every family had different customs around how to handle their adult children joining. But like many other parents, Dartham parents retired from public Kingdom events—at least the more salacious ones—once their children were inducted, although they continued their private affairs as they had before. Which meant that Jarrell's initiation had also been a coronation of sorts, since he'd been assuming his father's former role as the Kingdom's figurehead.

Jarrell had been so thoroughly *coronated* that he'd barely been able to walk the next day.

"The Kingdom has very few rules," he continued, "and it follows no law but pleasure. Other than a partner's acquiescence and a dedication to secrecy, there is very little members do not permit themselves. As the master of Far Hope, there was very, *very* little I did not permit myself."

She tilted her head. "Even after your marriage?"

"Helena...she wanted to. There are many married couples who indulge in our world either in tandem or separately. But she took ill with her cough in the days right after our wedding, and I devoted myself completely to caring for her. There were no more Kingdom events at Far Hope after that."

"You said Helena wanted to. Did you want to as well?"

"Pardon?"

"I mean, would you have acquiesced because you also wanted the Kingdom's offerings or only because you loved her?"

"Both, I suppose. Perhaps I fell in love with Helena because she wanted the same things I did."

"Did? Past tense?" She looked down at the blanket pooled around her knees. "Do you no longer want those indulgences?"

"You don't even know what those indulgences entailed, Eleanor."

She raised her eyes to his. "Then tell me."

He'd already learned not to underestimate her, and so he paid attention to his own lesson.

With a deep, trepidatious breath, he told her

CHAPTER NINE

IN HER WILDEST THOUGHTS, in her most secret dreams, Eleanor might have conjured up the world of silk and sex, of velvet and vice, that Jarrell described to her...but learning it was *real*, that what she'd seen at the Foscourts' was not an outlier at all but part of a glimmering, wonderful whole...it was intoxicating.

There were parties—often at Far Hope, but also in London and in other sumptuous locations across the island—and there were pageants and performances, banquets and balls and masques and carnivals. Feasts of the flesh and glittering gatherings that lasted for days and weeks. There were orgiastic rites as elaborate as they were impure and bewitching.

It was a world in which the body was as holy as the spirit. A world in which everyone, not just men, could be physically satisfied without censure. A world in which anyone a person desired—*anyone*—could be loved and embraced without sanction, scourge, or peril. In which someone could live authentically, not only in who they desired, but in whom they desired themselves to be.

There was no division between proper and improper, no demarcation of what was divine and what was damned. As Jarrell had said, there was no law but pleasure. No limit but acquiescence.

No rule but secrecy.

This—though she hadn't had the words for it, the framework for it—

this is what she'd been craving ever since the Foscourts' party. A life in which serenity could be exchanged for sensation, a world where she could have complete autonomy over her choices.

If she were part of this family, this clan Jarrell referred to as the Second Kingdom, then her only duty would be to herself and her own fulfillment. Her faithfulness would be given to whom *she* chose—not whom her father chose.

She glanced up at Jarrell, who looked more like a villain than ever in his shirtsleeves and breeches, with his silver-threaded hair glinting in the dim glow of the fire. Even in this mint-painted, delicately trimmed room—the exact opposite of the gothic wood and stone of Far Hope—he imbued the air with a raw, ungodly thrill.

He could have her faithfulness, her duty. Her time and her body. To him, she would surrender gladly, not only because he was a growlingly magnificent man, but because he would treat her surrender the way she wanted it to be treated.

He would give her victories in return.

He doesn't want you, a soft voice reminded her. *He has made it more than clear he has no plans to take you for a wife.*

"Two years ago, I was staying with the Countess of Kellow, and I saw people. Together, like you're describing."

The duke's eyebrows raised up in interest. "At Arabella's house?"

"Yes. Is she part of the Kingdom?"

"Indeed, she is. In my absence, she's become something of its queen. And what did you do when you stumbled upon her little party?"

"I watched," Eleanor admitted.

His eyes darkened a little in understanding. "You liked what you saw?"

"Very much." She searched for the right words. "I didn't really know before then all the ways that people could be together. I'd found these books when I was younger—smutty books, you understand—but they only ever showed men and women together. When I saw that it could be otherwise—"

She remembered how it felt, seeing the women together in the temple folly, feeling heat curl in her body as her mind crowded full of questions.

"It was like seeing a ballgown under candlelight for the first time," she tried to explain. "Or a jewel in the sun. Of course, all those extra depths and colors were always there, and the minute you see, you can't remember what it was like not having seen."

The duke was nodding with something soft in his expression. "Many in the Kingdom have a marked preference for who they like to share their bodies with, but many others—myself included when I was there—enjoyed pleasure with everyone. It is one of the reasons people are drawn to the Kingdom—and why secrecy and safety are so paramount."

She thought about this a minute, about the secrecy.

"Does the earl know?" Eleanor asked about Gilbert. "Has he already. . . ?"

Jarrell studied his hands. "No," he said after a moment. "He does not know. Traditionally, the heir is told on his eighteenth birthday, but as I said, I'd left the Second Kingdom behind after Helena's death. Our wedding—one of her last good days—was a Second Kingdom affair, and I couldn't bear to be reminded of it. Of her. And so, when Gilbert came of age to be told, I couldn't bring myself to do it. He didn't grow up in the valley, he wouldn't have heard the rumors, and I thought maybe he'd be better off not knowing."

His jaw tightened, and then he said, "No. No, I'm sorry. That's a lie. The truth is that I couldn't bear the idea of talking about it. Of inviting everyone back, of watching everything be as it was with the music and the laughter and the gaiety—everything but Helena. Everyone but my parents and my brother. The Second Kingdom is full of ghosts to me, and those ghosts are best left undisturbed."

"So...you were never planning to tell your nephew?"

Eleanor wasn't sure how to feel about this. She'd only just learned of the world herself, and she understood that the duke grieved his late wife dearly, but it seemed miserly to let this way of life wither at Far Hope because of that grief.

She leveled her gaze at him. "If the answer is yes, I think that's rather shameful. Especially if you are already planning to abdicate. Doesn't Gilbert deserve the chance to know? To bring the Kingdom back to Far Hope if he wishes?"

She braced herself for his anger or his defensiveness, but he gave her a weary kind of smile instead. "It is shameful, yes. I'd made up my mind to tell him after all. But then, Italy happened."

"Ah. The Kingdom approves of orgies, but not of equine baptism?"

His smile deepened a little and a rough noise left his throat.

A laugh! Eleanor didn't know if she'd ever heard him laugh before, and looking at him now, still smiling, his shirt loose around his neck and his cheeks warm from the fire, she could almost imagine the playful young man he must have been before Helena's death.

"Equine baptism is not so bad, I suppose, if one isn't bothered by the sacrilege or the stickiness," he said. Then he grew solemn.

"The Kingdom is mainly for pleasure, but pleasure is serious business. Above all, it must be a *safe* business, and we've already talked about why. It's rare, but sometimes even families decide not to admit their own into the Kingdom, or they decide to wait until the temperament in question is better matured. Gilbert is frivolous and selfish, but I wanted to give him the chance to improve. I'd hoped that marriage and an even-tempered wife would help."

"An even-tempered wife," Eleanor repeated. "That was to be me."

"I know it's not enough, but I do regret how I went about this engagement, ordering you like a tonic to fix the family's ills. I should have known better and done better. I am sorry, Eleanor."

She inclined her head to accept his apology. She was grateful for it—more grateful still because she didn't know very many men who would have given it.

"You wanted to leave. Desperately."

A short nod.

"And if I don't marry Gilbert? Will you still leave?"

"I've planned on it too long not to," he said. There was something in his voice though, something that was too hesitant and ephemeral to be certainty. Something like doubt.

"And the Kingdom?"

"The Kingdom doesn't need me or a Dartham or Far Hope. It will survive."

"But what about you?" she asked. "Will you survive?" If she were Jarrell —if she had access to a world like the one he described—she didn't know that she'd be able to deny herself a single year, much less sixteen.

He stepped away from the window and sat in a chair by the fire. The orangeish light threw the lines around his eyes and mouth into sharp, delicious contrast. "It's too late for me, Eleanor," he said. "At first, people told me that the sadness would pass. That the cure for loneliness was company. But I felt lonelier *with* people. I felt sadder whenever joy was anywhere near. It was a perverse kind of grief, because time seemed to feed it rather than starve it, and no matter where I went or what I beheld, it was right there next to me, like an extension of myself. It made me into a man I didn't even recognize—rough and grim and hard— and incapable of so many things that I used to be capable of. I don't know that I could inject myself back into the Kingdom even if I wanted to."

He recited this last part as if it were someone else's story, as if he had rehearsed it to himself many times. But his fingers curled around the arms of the chair, like he could anchor himself to the world if he gripped hard enough. Like the memory of Helena threatened to snap him in half.

"I suppose it's a sin to grieve this much," he finished in a murmur. "I had a priest tell me so once. But sometimes I think that if I let it go—let Helena go, let the memory of my parents and brother go—I'll no longer know who I am. I've lived with this too long to live without it now."

"It seems to me that your sin isn't grief, then, but fear," she said. Gently.

His eyes were a near-purple in the firelight, his carved muscles visible under the thin linen of his shirt. Even now, in this modern and sophisticatedly furnished house, he was tense, restless, feral.

Of course, he was.

Ajax Dartham, civilized? Ajax Dartham, *mild?* It was like asking the moors to become farmland. Like asking granite to become loam. It simply wasn't possible.

"Do you know yet, Eleanor, what it is like to adore someone thusly?"

Yes, she thought. *I do.*

"It was more than desire or affection," he said. "I *loved* her. Would have died for her. And to watch her die instead in the very place where she was supposed to live and thrive . . ."

"Would she not," she said softly, "still want you to live and thrive?"

"The priest said that also," he mumbled.

She'd never known a grief like his, and it felt unkind to diminish it. But it seemed to her like such a *waste*, like a shipment of cracked tiles or garden tucked too far into the shade. If she at twenty could cope with having seventeen different feelings inside herself at once, then surely he could too.

She could not talk someone out of grief, but she could talk someone into sense.

She clutched the blanket to her chest and slowly crawled on her knees to him, stopping only once she was at his feet.

"Ajax," she whispered. "Ajax, look at me."

The duke looked. His eyes were still dark—nearly as dark as the sky outside.

"You are not broken. You are allowed to keep living."

She put her hands just above his knees. His silk-clad thighs were so firm, so warm, and she couldn't help but slide her palms over the hard muscles, up to his hips and then back down to his knees again. His erection was imprinted on the other side of his breeches—she could make out its length, its ridges, its male topography—and it surged between his hips every time she caressed his thighs.

His hand caught hers and arrested its motion. His eyes were as dangerous as his voice was broken. "Be careful, Eleanor."

"I'm taking a great deal of care," she whispered, allowing her fingertips to brush against his thigh again.

The duke reached a large hand down and touched her jaw—reverently, delicately—and hope slashed through her, as hot and bright as the lightning outside the window.

"Can't you hold it all inside yourself at the same time? The love for who you've lost and the possibility of more?" She kept her voice soft. "I wouldn't ask you to let go. Only to allow yourself more."

"I don't know, Eleanor," he said. "I don't know if I can ever marry again."

Although the regret in his voice was palpable, it did nothing to soothe the bruising ache of his reply. But she should not have been bruised, she should have known better—she *had* known better, after all. He'd never given her any reason to think otherwise. It was only her reaching for more and more, reaching for someone who didn't want her in return.

He is not the only thing you can have. There is something else.

A life that could be almost completely her own, not as an almost-spinster, but as an almost-queen. She bit her lip, ran through all the different possibilities in her mind, imagined each and every sign at that crossroads, each and every ship waiting at her dock.

Every future beyond the mist.

Then she made her choice.

"I'm not talking about marriage," she said, nuzzling into his touch. "Make love to me, Ajax."

He hauled her into his lap as if she weighed nothing and cradled her face in his hands.

"Eleanor...." he murmured. "Sweet Eleanor."

She met his searching stare, watching the reflected flames sparkling in their indigo depths. He was the answer to a question she hadn't known enough to ask. He was a dream she hadn't known enough to dream before she came to Far Hope.

"Please," she asked. "Please."

CHAPTER TEN

HER REQUEST WAS like a hot knife to the throat. How could he say yes?

But how could he say *no*?

He wanted her like nothing else; with her, he could almost imagine living again, *truly* living, with all that it entailed.

What a mistress of Far Hope she would have made, he thought with a sear of regret. *What a world I could have given her.* If he weren't already pledged to his ghosts...

But it wasn't only his past that lay between them.

"Give me this," Eleanor said. She was perched on his lap like a little queen, and there was something very queenly indeed in the lift of her chin and the flash of her eyes. It married quite well with the hunger in her voice and the flush on her chest—and with the subtle squeeze of her thighs and the greedy points of her nipples making themselves known even through the blanket. "I don't expect marriage afterwards, or a declaration of love," she added. "I only expect you."

He let go of her face to sift her hair through his fingers. "You must see that it's not so easy," he replied. "What if you wish to marry someday?"

Something sad flitted through her eyes, but it didn't linger. She looked at him evenly. "If a future husband is upset that I have no hymen, then he may go to hell."

"He may," Jarrell agreed. "But it is a consequence, and one we should consider first."

She gave him a look that many wouldn't have dared to give a duke, and his chest was about to crack open with all the things he felt for this woman. "I'm not a fool," she informed him. "I've been considering it since the moment I woke up here. Since the moment I ran away in the first place."

He'd underestimated her again. "Of course," he murmured. "I just want to be careful with you, that's all. Careful with your future. It should be your own, and no one else's."

He heard his own words then, could imagine her saying them to *him* instead.

His future could be his own too.

She tilted her head enough to kiss his fingers, which were still tangling gently through her hair. "Trust me. Please. In a few hours, you will escort me away from here—and to the beginning of the rest of my life. I don't know what will happen after that...but I do know we can have this. We can have right now." Her eyes were imploring, her cheeks flushed with need. Her words undeniably true.

He wanted to believe her. He wanted to believe that they *could* have this moment, they *could* have right now—that they deserved it precisely because a real future was impossible between them. She would want to leave, and he'd already made plans to. Neither of them would be at Far Hope for long after tomorrow.

In the end, the choice was made much, much easier: she found his hand and guided it under the blanket, pressing his fingers right to the heart of her.

Right to the place that she'd so shamelessly rubbed against him. Right to the place where he'd kissed her so deeply that she'd reached her peak against his greedy mouth.

The place he'd pay any amount of money or pain to be inside of right now.

She was so wet that his fingertips were immediately slicked with her need, and she was so warm that she could have rivaled the fire behind her. And the softness . . . the silky-soft curls and the plush give of her lips . . . the satin of her inner petals...

He already knew the succulence of her, had already tasted her sweetness and felt her delicate warmth against his lips and tongue. But this—the supple heat, the sheer *squeeze* of her—he had no preparation for this, no defense. For sixteen years, he'd starved himself, and now here was a feast of the highest order, his for the taking. No longer could he deny the marauder within, the raiding pagan.

She would be his.

She would be his.

Without her prompting, he slid his finger as deep as he could, deep enough to seat his palm against her little berry and press against it as he explored her. She gave a long, low sigh and practically melted in his arms, her thighs sprawling open to give him access, her head coming forward to rest on his shoulder. Underneath her plush bottom, his organ was harder and thicker than ever, demanding entrance into the tight heaven he was exploring.

He'd denied himself too long, and may God forgive him for what he'd do next.

With a growl, he withdrew his hand to unfasten his breeches, making quick work of the falls and also of his shirt, needing to feel as much of her soft skin against his as possible. "Up on your knees," he ordered, giving himself a rough pump as she speedily complied, remaining astride him but lifting herself a few inches off his lap. The blanket he shoved out of the way, pooling it around her hips and pulling it free from her shoulders. He tugged it impatiently to the sides too, needing to see her cunt.

If he was to break his promises, if he was to indulge, then he would not do it by halves. He would not deny himself a single sight or sound or taste. This one night would have to last him the rest of his lonely, exiled life, and he planned to have his fill.

Once her sex was on display for him, he cupped her, curling a possessive hand around where she was soft and wet. This was to be his. Those delicious breasts in front of him—firm but full, tipped with sweet berry-pink peaks—those were his too. He leaned forward to take a nipple into his mouth, and he relished her gasp as he sucked on it. He relished the unconscious push of her into his hand, as she instinctively sought pressure. Invasion.

He gave it to her, returning his finger to her entrance and slowly sliding inside. He only gave her a moment to adjust before he added a second one, her answering moan shredding what was left of his control.

He needed to fuck.

He needed to fuck this slick little opening; he needed to get inside it and rut; he needed to fill her until neither of them could remember a time when they weren't joined.

"You're going to put me inside you," he said, releasing her breast as he pulled his fingers free. He licked them clean. She tasted good. Like cream with a dash of something earthy and sweet.

"Reach down—yes, like that, wrap your fingers around me—"

His words were cut short as her slender fingers sheathed his root. Her hair, which was every shade between platinum and bronze in the firelight, slid over her shoulders to brush against her breasts as she looked down. Her long eyelashes left fan-shaped shadows on her cheeks, and he couldn't see her eyes as she took in the sight of him, but he could see the slow, wondering part of her lips. The way her tongue peeped out to taste her lower lip, as if she was thinking about tasting *him*. He nearly lost it then and there, and she hadn't even started.

"Good, now put it in," he said, his voice gone guttural. "Just the tip of me, at first. If you want to stop then, we can."

"Yes, Ajax," she whispered. She aligned him with her sex, lowered those plush hips, and—

"*Fuck,*" he swore viciously, feeling her. The slick, wet kiss of her. It was only the press of his head against her folds, but already he didn't know if he could keep still, keep himself from sweeping her off to the bed and shoving into her like a beast.

She placed one hand on his chest, her other still gripped tightly around him. He felt her knees spread as far as they would go in the chair, and then—*Jesus—God*—more, she was taking more. He looked down and nearly perished; the plump head of his cock was nearly inside, and the *clutch* of her, the unforgiving clasp...like he was being wedged into heaven itself.

He wanted to punch his hips up into her. He wanted to thrust, to take, to have that fist-like silk all over him from base to crown. He wanted to find the end of her sheath; he wanted her so filled with him that she milked him as she came. He wanted her swollen bud rubbing against him as she rode him, taking him deep, so fucking deep . . .

"You're trembling," she observed, looking up at him. She was so beautiful like this, with her cheeks pink and her eyes bright. With her pretty mouth not in a frown of forbearance but a pout of pure, untrammeled need.

"You're trembling too," he said. He could feel her quivering, see her stomach contracting as she adjusted to the stretch of his member. "Does it hurt?"

He did not want to hurt her. Well, not this way at least—he couldn't deny that he wanted to discipline her sweet little bottom and redden the curves of her breasts with his stubble. But this was a different kind of pain. Jarrell well remembered the first time he'd been fucked by another man; he'd ejaculated hard in the end, jetting his spend all over his chest while a decadent Michaelmas ball whirled around him, but it had taken time for him to relax around the intrusion, to feel the discomfort melt into a sharp, raw pleasure.

He would go carefully.

His hands were now fisted on the arms of the chair because he didn't trust himself to touch her, to circle her waist or grip her hips, lest he bruise her in his lust. He was close to the brink, skating along the edge of brutal animality, and the only thing keeping him tethered to stillness was the knowledge that this was Eleanor, his vernal Eleanor. Stronger than anyone else he'd ever known, even though she shouldn't have had to be. He did not want her to hurt for this night. He wanted this to be worth every single ounce of the risk she was taking.

With a low whimper and the flutter of her eyelids, she worked her way down another inch as she murmured, "It doesn't hurt, I don't think. It's close to *hurt*, but it's not—oh—"

Another inch. Her head fell back, and the golden hair around her breasts slid and shifted, revealing the bunched points of her nipples. He surveyed the flushed heave of her plump breasts as she panted, examined the subtle quiver of her stomach. He greedily traced the arch of her throat and the bevel of her collarbone with his eyes, committing every last bit of it to memory. He could never forget this, how she looked, how she felt. How huskily she moaned and whispered, the way she murmured his name over and over again like a prayer as she took another inch, and then another, and another, and then a couple. With a final whimper, she impaled herself fully, and then shuddered, falling against him and tucking herself into his chest.

Her trust gutted him. The sweet clasp of her crucified him. He could no more stop himself from wrapping his arms around her once more than he could stop himself from breathing. He slid his hands up and down her bare back, gentling her, soothing her, reassuring her every time she moved and then gasped.

"It hurts a little now," she whispered against his skin, and then nuzzled into him. "I feel it everywhere, in my chest and in my bones, and I never want to stop feeling it. It's like...a song. Or like a strong wine. Every time I think I'm not sure, it lures me back in again."

He kissed her head, her silky hair so impossibly soft against his lips. She smelled so wonderful, like rain and fire and flowers. "Take your time," he said, his voice coming out both reverent and rough. "Take anything you need."

They stayed like this for a few minutes, her speared with his prick and curled trustingly against him, Jarrell stone-still except for his gentling hands on her back and the shaking of his muscles, which he could not control.

The restraint it took not to move or to come . . .

Sweat began to slick his stomach and his chest, but he would not yield to his need. He would give her this, he would give her anything, he would give her everything, because he loved—

No.

Fear, cold and ugly, roiled inside him at the word. He did not love her, he *could not*. It was impossible, because if he did love her—

I don't, he thought, and with a short thrust of his hips, he tried to prove it to himself. *It's only the fucking. I should know better, because, of course, it's only the fucking.*

But whatever he was trying to prove was beside the point, because as soon as he moved into her, she made a noise that changed everything—a noise of curious delight. Of exquisite surprise.

And then, of course, he made a noise, too, because it was the first full stroke into her, the first real thrust, and it felt better than heaven. It felt like dying terribly only to be brought back to life, and he had to do it again, he *had to*, and so he did.

"Oh God," she breathed, lifting her head. Goose bumps covered her everywhere. "Ajax."

He tried to remember himself, to remember that this was Eleanor's first time. "Yes, little blossom?"

A pretty smile curved her mouth. "Do it again."

He did it again, a smile pulling on his own lips as he watched her eyes flutter in rapture. "Does it still hurt?"

"No," she said dreamily. "And yes. I can't describe it. But I want more of it."

"You can have as much as you want," he said, taking her hips in his hands and showing her how to move over him—not up and down, but back and forth, as if she were riding a horse. "Feel how I'm moving you now. Let me lead you—yes, you like that? You like feeling me? Keep going, just like that. Christ, you feel good."

The first rock forward had her shuddering; the second one had her gasping. After that, she didn't need his hands to guide her, to show her the way, because she found it all on her own, following her pleasure as she circled over him, chasing the friction as she ground against him.

And once she found that perfect angle, that perfect rolling of her hips that allowed her to be serviced both inside and outside?

She was lost to him then, lost beyond all reach. He held her, he stroked her, he grunted low, filthy words of encouragement to her, but the pleasure was taking her for its own, stealing her away bit by deliciously flushed bit. Her hands wandered over his muscled arms and firm chest; her fingers toyed with the dark hair there and skated over his nipples. She scratched her nails gently over his stubble and bent low to lick his lips.

She was fucking *him*, using *him*, pleasuring herself with *him*, and he never wanted her to stop.

"That's right," he said. "That's it."

She dropped her head back as she moved faster and faster over him, her breasts moving with each snap of her hips and each desperate breath she dragged in. He could so easily see the sweet anatomy of her like this— the pink berry rubbing against him, the stretch of her wet glove around his erection. Her arched throat and her pouting nipples.

But it was her face he watched the most, the expressions that chased themselves over her upturned features. Astonishment, ecstasy. Hunger. He could watch her like this for hours. For days.

For the rest of his life.

If she were his little wife...

If she were his, then he could. He could have her always, have her in his lap like this whenever she wanted—which, judging by her eagerness now, would be quite often indeed. He'd have his hands full keeping a young bride sated, but it would be the world's sweetest labor, a duty he'd gladly deliver up anything and everything he owned in order to perform.

What if it's not just the fucking?

What if I love her?

What did that mean about him? That he could love again? Did it mean he'd loved Helena any less? Mourned his losses imperfectly? He used to think so, and yet...

"*Ajax,*" Eleanor moaned, her head falling forward and her hands seizing on his shoulders, as if trying to anchor herself against a buffeting storm. As if trying to hold on.

"How is this pretty cunt?" he whispered. "How does it feel?"

"I—good—but—"

The *but* was written all over her face. It was something like panic, something like fear, like the feeling was too big, too overwhelming. He knew that feeling all too well, though he hadn't felt it for sixteen years. It was the feeling of a looming climax that didn't feel like a climax at all but a ruin, an annihilation, something that would rip you in half and leave you dying after. The kind of orgasm you didn't know whether to reach for or run away from.

He held her tight against his chest as the first wave took her, as she cried out his name. "I've got you," he murmured into her hair, once again fighting his own body as it keened to fuck up into her sweetness. "I've got you."

She trembled into his chest as the cataclysm took her, and he treasured —*treasured*—each and every whimper she made, each and every caught breath that blew over his skin. Each and every seize of her quim around his member. "You are beautiful," he said as she quaked in his arms. "You are the most beautiful thing I've ever seen. The most wonderful thing I've ever felt."

My life will be empty without you.

It took longer than a minute, maybe it took two, but after several long, shivering clenches, her climax abated and left her limp and sated against his chest. He continued to be still, save for his arms around her and his hands playing in her hair, because if he moved even a little, if he shoved up just the tiniest bit . . .

"Your Grace," Eleanor said, tilting her head to look up at him. "You have deceived me."

"Is that so, little blossom?"

She liked when he called her that, he could tell, even when she ducked her head to hide her smile. "Yes, it's very much so, Ajax. All that talk about the wickedness and carnality of the Second Kingdom...and yet I'd hardly call you wicked or carnal at all. You were very polite and gentle, maybe like a vicar would be?"

Her teasing was as obvious as it was effective. Patience spent, *gentleness* spent, they were up and out of the chair in an instant, him sweeping her off to the bed and her laughing the whole way—laughs that melted into moans as he threw her on the bed and climbed between her thighs. He wasted no time in piercing her once again, sliding his organ back into her intimate flesh with a rough shove of his hips. *Ah*, that felt exquisite, delectable, divine. To rut and fuck, to watch her breasts move with each thrust. To see those dilated eyes, those flushed cheeks, and feel her greedy fingers squeezing his arms, his hips, scratching along his back.

That it was Eleanor, this deviant little blossom who'd awakened him... obsessed him...

"Does it hurt still?" he breathed.

"Yes," she said. "But I like it."

Abruptly, he needed all of him and all of her to be one. With a growl, he withdrew and rolled her to her stomach.

"Ajax," she murmured, sending a look over her shoulder. "What are you —*oh*. Oh. *Fuuuck*."

The curse on the lips of his English rose was both crudely arousing and adorable as hell. He would have smiled at it if he weren't already mounting her from behind, if he weren't already watching his thick inches disappear into her rosy cunt. He went slowly, for himself, for all the long, lonely nights of the rest of his life when he'd have only his hand to oblige him. He wanted to remember this sight, with her spread out like this. The delicate camber of her back, the generous curves of her bottom, the tousle of her golden hair.

He never wanted to forget the subtle flex of her upper arms as she braced herself to look over her shoulder at him, nor the swoop of her pert little nose silhouetted against his counterpane. The perfect, sinful feel of her private place gripping his cock, welcoming him in. Tempting him to fill her full of himself.

"I didn't realize," she said faintly, moving underneath him. Seeking friction. "I didn't realize it would feel like this. When I saw it in books—at the Foscourts'—I had no idea..."

She sounded both full of puzzled wonder and already kindled for her next orgasm, and oh, the things he could show her, the things he could teach her, the revelations he could give her.

The sins they could invent together.

The way her eyes had gleamed when he'd described the Kingdom to her, shining with fascination and desire . . .

He couldn't let himself have more than this. But as he moved over her, laying his body over hers and sliding an arm under her chest as he lovingly held her throat with one hand, he decided he could pretend. Just for a few minutes, while they were joined, mating, skin to skin and heat to heat. Just while he felt her swallow and gasp against his palm as another climax took her, and while he released into her with something like a roar, pumping and spilling and filling...

Only then would he pretend he could love her and she could love him.

Only then would he allow it.

And then, no more.

CHAPTER ELEVEN

SHE SLEPT.

Caged happily in his arms and trapped against his hair-dusted shield of a chest, she dozed off and on, waking to his kisses in her hair or his fingers running along her spine. Twice, they woke together, and twice more she reached those glorious peaks. And afterwards, each time, he'd tucked the blankets around her as tenderly as he had been rough moments earlier, pulled her against him, and caressed her until she'd fallen back into a deep, contented sleep.

It wasn't until she opened her eyes and realized she was alone in the bed that the harsh enormity of last night came crashing in. The failed escape, the brush with a cold and lonely death. The revelation of the Second Kingdom, and her decision.

The wonderful brutality of Jarrell last night.

No, not Jarrell. *Ajax*.

Named for the warrior who fell on his own sword rather than live in dishonor, which possibly explained why she was curled up in bed alone, with her arms flung around a cool pillow instead of a grumpy, midnight-eyed duke.

When she sat up, she saw him sitting in a chair by the fire, the cloudy morning light catching the silver threads in his hair. "I've sent for a carriage and a change of clothes, and notified your parents of your improved health," he said without looking away from the fitful, popping embers in his fireplace. "They anticipate your return to Far Hope. However, the carriage's destination is in your hands, Lady Eleanor. I can take you to Far Hope, where I will arrange for the wedding to be called off, or I can escort you to some other destination, where you may do anything else you please."

Her two options, according to him. Both leaving her husbandless.

Ajax-less.

What else did you expect?

Still, the disappointment dug into her heart like tiny, awful splinters. Thousands of them, delving into her ventricles and veins. She knew what he was going to say before he said it, and even though she'd expected it—even though she'd formed plans and decisions around it last night—it didn't make it hurt any less.

She wanted to ask him again, plead with him, to reconsider these certainties he'd made for himself, to reconsider the life of abnegation and suffering he thought he deserved after the people he'd loved had died.

But she would not beg. Not because she was too proud—was anyone too proud to ask for what they wanted when it sat not ten feet away, brooding at a fire?—but because she knew it would be futile.

If last night, with its surging pleasure and bliss, had not been enough to convince him, then nothing would. Especially not her words spoken awkwardly into the weak morning light. No, her mother's vague ailments and the Pennard Hall renovations had taught Eleanor all about futility and lost causes, and she was not the type of woman to ignore a lesson.

Now you know the future can be whatever you want it to be. She knew what she wanted—even if it couldn't be with Ajax, she still wanted it—and she knew what price she'd pay to have it. Even if it meant some tense arguments with a certain Dartham heir.

But if she'd renovated an entire estate on her own, there wasn't any reason she couldn't persuade Gilbert to see things her way if she tried hard enough. Right?

"I'll return to Far Hope, Your Grace," Eleanor said, her voice quiet but also very steady. "As soon as the carriage can take me."

~

It was nearly embarrassing to see what a short way she'd come in the night; the road that had seemed leagues long in the rainy darkness turned out only to have been four short miles, and all of them were passed easily —if jouncingly—enough in the carriage. She made the mistake of saying this to Jarrell, who sat scowling out the carriage window, and his scowl deepened.

"There's no such thing as a short mile in the moors," he said.

"I didn't mean to make you angry."

He wouldn't look at her. "The memory of you nearly dying will always evoke powerful emotion in me. I apologize."

Defensiveness spiked through her. "I ran because I didn't think I had a choice, Your Grace."

He didn't like it when she called him that, she could tell by the dark look he shot her. "You always have choices."

"Says a peer who's never had them taken away."

"You have a choice now," he said, ignoring her dig. "Do you not?"

"I allow that I do." However excruciating that choice might be.

"I wish you *safe*, Eleanor," he said. "That's all. Safe and happy."

She couldn't resist, even though she wanted to. "I've already told you how I could be happy."

His eyes were troubled, his sensual mouth pressed into the very shape of unhappiness.

"I know," he said after a moment. "I know you did."

And that was all. If she'd hoped the carriage ride would change his mind, if she'd hoped that at the eleventh hour he would realize he could set aside his grief and that they belonged together after all...

Well, she'd be a fool to hope. That was more than plain now.

I should tell him.

Before they got to the house, she should tell him what she'd decided. She didn't want him to be hurt, to feel betrayed—but she also didn't know if she could stomach arguing with him just yet. Because he *would* argue, but then he still would not offer her what she really wanted, which was his heart.

She took a deep breath as the carriage rattled over a stone bridge and into the deep valley of Far Hope. She would do as she'd always done when faced with a painful future—find a way to bear it and bear it gracefully. The tricks were many; it was imperative not to linger on the unpleasantness, to remember the necessity of her actions, to hold on to whatever small pleasures she could reasonably count on.

At least in that, she was assured some reward. She would make her future life a palace to pleasure, even if that palace were only a mere shadow of what could have been if Jarrell would have opened his heart to her. But at least she'd been completely honest, completely vulnerable.

Finally, for the first time in twenty years, she'd reached for what she wanted. There would be no wondering what could have been if only she'd been braver, because she *had* been brave, she had tried her hardest to carve out something for herself that she thought was impossible.

Now there was nothing left but to face her future.

Alone.

CHAPTER TWELVE

JARRELL'S entire body hurt as the carriage rolled to the front of Far Hope and stopped.

His bones ached, his blood simmered. His heart felt like it had been threaded with slivers of glass, and he was hot and brittle everywhere. As if he were not a man, but ashes molded in the shape of a man.

As if he would crumble into smoldering dust at the slightest touch.

He hated himself, *loathed* himself, could not even stand being himself as he'd sat next to Eleanor and watched her look serenely at the hills as they drove back to his cursed ancestral seat. He'd done that, he'd made her put up her shield of placid reserve once again. Last night she'd been avid, curious, unleashed, and he'd stolen that away from her. With his refusals.

With your cowardice.

A cowardice he wasn't even sure kept him safe any longer.

No, it was better this way. She was better off this way too. He was sure of it, although it was hard to be sure of anything when he could still smell the rain and flowers scent of her, and when he could still vividly recall the way her blond tresses slid like so much teasing silk over the pink points of her nipples.

There was a moment—a dizzying, disorienting moment—as he handed her out of the carriage and saw her silhouetted against the ancient stone house of his ancestors, when he felt a splinter of what could have been. A future in which everything he'd ever wanted and needed flowered together as one vibrant and sacred bloom.

And he'd given it up.

I had no choice, he thought dully. *What kind of husband could I be to Eleanor if I'm already willing to let go of Helena's memory only a week after meeting someone new?*

But the thought no longer felt as true as it had even a few hours ago.

Your sin is not grief but fear.

Could it be that easy?

Could he be more afraid than he was broken?

The questions dogged him as he escorted Eleanor up the shallow steps and into the main hall where they were greeted by Eleanor's parents, an impassive butler, and a thin cloud of interested guests, openly gawking at the returned bride on Jarrell's arm.

"Eleanor!" Lady Pennard exclaimed, rushing forward to pull her daughter into her arms. "We were so worried, we thought you might have been lost out there, that you might have—"

She didn't finish her thought, but it was clear to everyone around her, clear to Jarrell.

They thought she might have died. And when he thought of how easily she could have, of how cold and limp she was when he first found her last night, the glass splinters in his heart burrowed even deeper.

How could he have survived if she'd died?

But he would have to survive without her, wouldn't he? He'd made sure of that last night when he said he would not marry her; he would have to survive just as he had after Helena had died.

You could do more than survive. You could start living instead.

"I'm fine, I'm fine," Eleanor was insisting, giving her mother's arms a squeeze before pulling back. "I simply went outdoors for fresh air and got lost on the grounds, that's all. I'm so grateful to the duke for finding me in time."

It was the story they'd agreed on—the story that would be officially circulated—that, not feeling well, Eleanor went outside for the air and had gotten lost. It was ludicrous, since Far Hope's grounds were all hemmed in by craggy, louring moors, and it was quite difficult to wander off the grounds without being very, very aware of it, even in the dark. The servants and guests would know enough of her disappearance and the ensuing search that gossip spreading to the rest of the *ton* would be inevitable. But so long as there was an official story, the scandal of her flight would be muffled at least.

The scandal of an ended engagement, however...

"I believe we have some matters to discuss," he told Eleanor's parents and gestured toward the library. Eleanor's father seemed to understand immediately, but to Jarrell's surprise and gratification, he only looked thoughtful, not angry. In fact, her father found Eleanor's hand and tucked it through his arm, as if wanting to reassure himself that his daughter was here and close and alive.

"I'm just glad you're safe," the Marquess murmured to Eleanor as they walked. "I wish that you'd come to me instead."

Perhaps the betrothal would be easier to break than Jarrell had thought, which was a relief. He'd, of course, make sure the Vanes were compensated, but a broken engagement was a difficult thing to recompense for. The social costs would be vast, and no less punishing for how difficult they were to quantify. Jarrell pondered this as they reached the library and he closed the doors behind them.

"Now," he said, as the Vanes took seats near the fireplace, looking at him expectantly. "After last night, Eleanor has decided—"

Eleanor interrupted him. "I'm still marrying Gilbert."

The Marquess and the Countess's mouths dropped in tandem.

Jarrell's glass-filled heart stopped beating.

"Excuse me?" he managed to say.

"I plan on going through with the wedding," she explained calmly. Blandly. As if she hadn't just lit him on fire and kicked him into a pit. "I'll be his wife."

"Like hell you will," he said, ignoring Lady Pennard's gasp at his language.

Something glimmered behind Eleanor's serene eyes then—something that looked a lot like fury. Good! He wanted her fury; he'd take her hatred. He'd rather have her hissing and spitting and *real* than acting as if it cost her nothing to marry a man she didn't love and could never respect.

"You have no say in the matter, Your Grace," she said, her eyes flashing and her voice tight. With a deep breath, she seemed to steady herself, and when she spoke again, she was even-tempered Eleanor once more. "I've given the matter much thought since last night, and I've decided I shall marry Gilbert after all."

Over my goddamn dead body, he wanted to yell. But he didn't.

It was Eleanor who angled toward her parents and said, "Could the duke and I speak alone for a moment?"

"It's hardly proper—" the Countess started, but Eleanor interrupted her.

"What about anything I've done since last night has been proper? A few minutes in a library is hardly going to dent my reputation at this point. Besides, you and Papa owe me the chance to handle my own marriage for once, wouldn't you agree?"

The Countess looked very much like she wanted to argue, but the Marquess nodded and then stood, helping his wife to his feet.

"This once," he said. "You have twenty minutes."

And then her parents left, closing the library door behind them.

The moment they were alone, Eleanor set her expression in that resolute mildness that vexed him so much. "My mind is made up, Ajax."

He stepped closer to her. She merely lifted her chin.

"You're lucky I didn't throw you over my shoulder and carry you to my bedroom," he said, roiling with anger and panic and something else he couldn't name. "You're lucky I'm not tying you to my bed so I can talk some sense into you!"

A subtly raised brow. "I think I've made it very clear that none of those things would be a deterrent for me."

"Eleanor, this is no joking matter."

"I'm not joking, Ajax."

With a curse, he spun away, raking a hand over his face. When he turned back to her and saw her arms wrapped around herself, saw the smudges under her eyes from her sleepless night, he could hardly breathe or think. He never wanted her sad; he never wanted her lonely. He never wanted her marching bravely into a marriage she would hate.

And yourself? What do you want for yourself?

He hadn't honestly asked himself that question in sixteen years. And now that he asked it, the answer felt obvious.

He didn't want to exile himself. He didn't want to spend the rest of his life with ghosts.

He wanted Eleanor and his friends and his life; he wanted to keep loving the people he'd lost while he learned to love new people too. Like this library, where old books were shelved alongside the new—couldn't he keep the old and the new inside himself too? Couldn't he have both?

This was what Eleanor had meant about his sins. He'd known it when she'd said it, but he let himself really know it now.

He'd been afraid to make new memories alongside the old ones. He'd been afraid of loving someone else only to watch them die again. All this time he'd thought the answer to that fear was to retreat, to find some kind of numb safety far, far away, but he'd been wrong.

So wrong.

He scrubbed his hands through his hair and tried to focus on the immediate problem. The problem he'd made.

"You don't want to marry my nephew," Jarrell said, trying to understand. "And this morning, you told me—you said you'd chosen, you said you wanted to come back here so I could help you break the betrothal."

"You are correct in that I don't wish to marry Gilbert," she said as she stood and moved over to a deep window looking out to the valley. "But I only said I wanted to come back here. Not that I wanted to break the betrothal."

I'll return to Far Hope, Your Grace.

Why hadn't he seen it then?

She'd said it with so much forbearance, with so much tired courage, and he'd attributed that to the imminent headache of killing a betrothal close to the ceremony—but it hadn't been that, had it? It hadn't been the understandable apprehension of an aborted wedding, but rather the unhappy nerves of contemplating a consummated one.

Fury surged at the thought of that consummation; a dark, possessive anger had him striding over to Eleanor and setting her on the high sill of the window. He braced his hands on either side of her and leaned in. "You aren't marrying him."

"I. Am."

He was too close to her, too dangerously close. He could see the taut curves of her breasts heaving under the diaphanous drape of her fichu; he could see how wide her pupils had blown at his nearness. He could see how she swallowed and shifted and licked her lower lip.

"You're not, Eleanor. Why don't you raise your skirts for me, hm?"

That telltale flush bloomed on her cheeks and chest, and she slowly lifted her skirts over her knees as she said, "Making love to me won't change my mind."

He didn't know what he was doing. He didn't even know what he felt in that moment, except an urgency that nearly clawed him apart. He had himself unfastened and freed in a moment, had her moved to the edge of the sill and her thighs parted wide for him to step between. The minute he wedged the wide tip of him against her furrow, she started panting.

"Don't make me wait," she said, bracing herself back on her hands, as if to see his crude invasion better.

"You're not wet enough."

"I'll get there," she said impatiently. "But I can't wait another sec —*ohhh*."

In his prime, the Duke of Jarrell had been able to divest a woman of a robe a l'anglaise—with its assorted pins, paddings, petticoats, and stays—within a swift two minutes. But the new, simpler fashions meant that he'd unlaced the top of Eleanor's gown and liberated her breasts from her chemise within *seconds*. He had a nipple captured in his mouth and his thumb on the bundle of nerves at the top of her sex so quickly that she was struck speechless, her hand flying to the back of his head to push his mouth harder against her.

She's mine, Ajax thought as his tongue lashed short, hot stripes across her nipple. *Fucking mine.*

She gasped his name as he sucked and stroked her, arching hard against him. "Please," she begged. "If this is going to be the last time, then—"

"This is not the last time," he vowed. "You won't be his. You can't be his."

Because you're mine.

She found his hip with her free hand, still clutching his head to her breast as she urged him closer. "I'm going to marry your nephew," she said breathlessly. "And I'm going to reassure him of that fact right after you're done fucking me."

The filthy word on her lips robbed him of reason—not that he had much left to rob by now. He finally gave into the need burning in him and began to fit himself inside her opening. She was wet now—so wet that her arousal was anointing even his knuckles where they brushed against her— but she was still tight enough to necessitate two or three strokes to bury himself fully. Tight enough that once he was completely seated, they both had to breathe for several seconds before he could start moving in earnest.

Once he did, he lifted his head to bite her neck and growl against her throat. "You belong to me."

"I do *not*," she said, her eyes fluttering when he pulled back to look at her face. "You made that clear, Ajax. Very clear."

Pain ripped at him from the inside, and he rode her harder, as if the pleasure could drown out his guilt and regret. "Eleanor," he said, holding her close so he could bury his face in her hair. Between her thighs, his hips churned. Nothing could ever feel as good as fucking Eleanor Vane— nothing other than holding her, that was.

Nothing other than making her smile. Making her every dream come true.
Giving her a life of ease and satisfaction to replace a life of tasks and obligation.
Nothing other than loving her.

He loved her. *He loved her.* And he was going to give her everything.

"Tell me why you'll marry him," he said, teeth gritted with determination and the gorgeous sensation of his cock gloved inside her. "Is it for the Kingdom?"

Her gaze when it met his was no longer serene—but neither was it anguished or turbulent. Those spring-green eyes were brimming with determination and pride.

"Maybe I can't have you, Ajax, but I can resurrect the world you left behind, and that would be something. It would be worth it."

She could have him.

She already had him.

All along the answer had been right *here*, in this petite warrior of a girl. *Your sin wasn't grief, but fear.*

It was the truth. Fear of loving again, of losing again. Of losing the memories of the people he'd lost.

What could he have if he weren't afraid now?

He could have a wife, one whom he loved and who loved him, and he could have the world left to him by his ancestors. He could have Eleanor and Far Hope both.

"Marry me," he said abruptly, looking down into those wonderful eyes, into that sweet, strong, hungry face. "Be *my* wife. Not Gilbert's, but mine, and I will give you everything, everything you want."

She stared up at him. "Are you lying to me?"

She had every right to ask, but he knew the answer now. Maybe he'd known it hours ago. Days ago, when he first saw her. He was ready to live again. "No."

"Are you lying to yourself?"

He cradled her face with his hands; the movement had him sliding inside her and she let out a low noise that made him shiver. "No, little blossom."

"I want to believe you," she whispered. "Ever since I saw you, I felt—I knew—" She seemed to struggle for words.

He kissed her gently on the mouth. "I know, Eleanor. I know. I felt it too."

"But you were so adamant last night. All your plans...and..." She pressed her forehead to his. "Ajax, I'm not Helena."

"And I don't want you to be," he said, closing his eyes. "I loved Helena sixteen years ago, and while I'll treasure the time I had with her, I am ready to treasure other things too. Other people."

He opened his eyes, studying her. His little blossom, his firmly rooted tree.

He'd been living like a ghost for years, thinking it would keep him closer to the ones he lost. But it hadn't. In the end, he'd only lost himself too. And then she'd come along and found him, reminded him that he was flesh and blood still, with a heart that hadn't yet quit beating.

"It wasn't until I met you, someone I wanted to live for, that I realized I *could* still live at all," he tried to explain. "You were right about me and you were right about my fear. It felt safer than feeling anything else. Because at least in fear, I already expected the worst. But in love—well, in love, I would have to hope for the best. And I didn't think I could bear it."

"But you will bear it for me?" she whispered, her eyes searching his.

"For the rest of our lives, Eleanor. Beginning now."

He drove his hips forward enough that his idea of *now* would be more than clear. She whimpered and laced her arms around her neck.

"If you marry me, then you must stay."

"Yes, Eleanor."

"Remain the duke."

"Yes."

"And bring the Kingdom here once again."

He kissed her lips again. She tasted so sweet, so much like home—like Far Hope. "Yes."

"Then marry me, Your Grace," she said between kisses, their mouths mating in slick, warm wonder just as they mated below. "Make me your wife."

She abruptly broke around him as he murmured, "I will," and when he flooded into her a moment later, filling his soon-to-be bride, he recognized the truth he'd instinctively known all along: Eleanor Vane wasn't the solution, she was the question. The beginning.

For Far Hope. For him.

Forever.

The End.

~

Want more dangerous widowers, gothic houses, and carnal secrets from Sierra Simone?

Check out The Awakening of Ivy Leavold...

ALSO BY SIERRA SIMONE

Thornchapel:

A Lesson in Thorns

Feast of Sparks

Harvest of Sighs

Door of Bruises

Misadventures:

Misadventures with a Professor

Misadventures of a Curvy Girl

Misadventures in Blue

New Camelot:

American Queen

American Prince

American King

The Moon (Merlin's Novella)

American Squire (A Thornchapel and New Camelot Crossover)

The Priest Collection:

Priest

Midnight Mass: A Priest Novella

Sinner

Co-Written with Laurelin Paige

Porn Star

Hot Cop

The Markham Hall Series:

The Awakening of Ivy Leavold

The Education of Ivy Leavold

ABOUT THE AUTHOR

Sierra Simone is a *USA Today* bestselling former librarian who spent too much time reading romance novels at the information desk. She lives with her husband and family in Kansas City.

Sign up for her newsletter to be notified of releases, books going on sale, events, and other news!

www.thesierrasimone.com

DUKE FOR HIRE

NICOLA DAVIDSON

CHAPTER ONE

THE TIME HAD COME for change. No more would the stern expectations heaped upon a clergyman's spinster daughter rule her life and rob her of pleasure.

Miss Ada Blair glanced around the sunny vicarage parlor. Fortunately, the two people who would support her quest most were here today: her honorary godmothers and fellow members of the St. Mary's Church sewing circle, Miss Ruth Lacey and Miss Martha Kinloch. Even so, she should begin with a logical, reasoned argument.

"I'm turning thirty and don't want to be a virgin anymore," Ada blurted.

Both silver-haired women froze. Then Ruth tossed away her sewing and splashed gin from a silver hip flask into her berry cordial. Martha set down the copy of Mrs. Radcliffe's *The Mysteries of Udolpho, Volume One* —cunningly disguised as a treatise on housekeeping—that she'd been reading aloud.

"Hallelujah," said Ruth, offering a silent toast before taking a healthy swallow. "I've been praying for this day."

Ada blinked. "Er...you have?"

"Oh yes. I even made a notebook titled *Aiding Ada: The Grand Cock Plan*."

Laughter bubbled. "I see."

Martha nodded sagely. "To summarize the notebook, we'll assist in any way you wish. Money, an alluring gown, list of potential bachelors, excuses and alibis—"

"*Alibis?* This is not a smuggling operation."

"There are similarities," said Ruth with a wink. "Except rather than goods disappearing in the cover of darkness, it's your virtue. I must say though, I prefer fucking in the afternoon. Warm sun is lovely on bare skin."

"*Ruth,*" scolded Martha, her cheeks pink. "Concentrate. A Grand Cock Plan is certainly required, for there are two significant barriers to success. First, Reverend Blair, bless his terrifyingly righteous soul. Second, handsome bachelors don't grow on trees, especially in Charlton Kings."

At those two indisputable facts, Ada sighed.

Once she'd dreamed of a handsome prince (a nice man with steady employment) who would storm the castle (knock on the vicarage door) slay the dragon (stand toe to toe with her father) sweep her up in his arms (a negotiable point, she was nearly six foot tall and decidedly plump after all) and teach her all the delights of the marriage bed. But as the years passed, that sweet fantasy had withered and died. Reverend Blair enjoyed the convenience and frugality of a daughter who cooked, cleaned, and ran his errands far too much to welcome suitors, and the few men willing to knock on the door had run screaming at the first hint of fire and brimstone. So, while Ada reluctantly accepted being a wife and mother wasn't in her future, that didn't mean she couldn't learn about bedding. Surely *one* man in the county might say yes.

Ruth finished her cordial. The woman had a stomach of cast iron. "What would your dream lover be like, Ada?"

"Experienced," she began, because bold women gave voice to their dreams. "Someone discreet and mature, not a fumbling lad who will reveal all at the tavern after a few ales."

"Sensible. Also, a grown man will know where your clitoris is, and won't forget to spill on your belly when he comes. Far too many girls are forced to leave home because some young fool *forgot* to withdraw. I'm so glad that pussy is my feast of choice...Martha darling, we've been lovers forever. How can that word still make you blush?"

"It just does," mumbled Martha. "Although not quite as bad as fuck. You have the vernacular of a sailor—"

"It makes you wet as rain."

"Utterly beside the point. We are here to assist our girl."

Ada grinned at their forthright speech. Nowadays it rarely shocked her, although she could still recall at age eighteen having scarlet cheeks for days after Ruth and Martha sat her down and said because her dear mama was in heaven, they would give her *the talk*. Her godmothers didn't believe in waiting until a wedding and provided information with jaw-dropping detail. Ada had also learned their truth: the two women were far more than the good friends her father and the parish insisted they were. Martha said they were life companions. Ruth winked and said they'd made each other sing like nightingales in bed for nigh on forty years. It had been a frank and eye-opening conversation about society and tolerance, but also the very nature of love and pleasure.

"Then by all means assist," said Ruth, gracious as an empress.

"Very well. Let's discuss looks," said Martha. "What do you prefer, Ada? Red, dark, or fair-haired? Beard or clean-shaven? Certain eye color? Height? Because you mentioning discreet, experienced, and mature has me thinking of a certain someone."

Ada twirled a blond curl around her finger as she considered her answer. "I am not so attracted to red or fair-haired gentlemen. I like dark hair. Eye and skin color don't matter, nor does his jaw. But for my own peace of mind I'd like him to be taller and broader than me. I couldn't bear the thought of accidentally hurting someone...*botheration*. That leaves no possibilities at all, does it?"

"Actually, you just described the man I have in mind."

Ruth hooted. "Martha Kinloch. If it is the man I'm now thinking of, this is the grandest of Grand Cock Plans."

"Well, of course," said Martha irritably. "It's for Ada."

At the proof—yet again—that she was so important to these women, Ada's vision grew blurry. They'd taken her under their wing when she'd first arrived at St. Mary's as a bewildered, grieving child with her newly widowed father, and had been both her rock and her amusement ever since. While it sometimes stung that she remained alone and her godmothers had found their forever love—someone to banter and share adventures with, who was splendid in bed, and who thought them equally delightful at sixty as twenty —she wouldn't trade their friendship for the world.

"Well," Ada said lightly, when she had regained control. "Don't leave me in suspense, Martha. Please reveal the Grand Cock Plan prospect who is discreet, experienced, mature, dark-haired, *and* taller than me. Because I do not believe such a paragon truly exists."

"On the contrary. The Duke of Gilroy."

She almost fell off her chair laughing. "I adore you, but have you lost your mind?"

"Not at all," said Martha thoughtfully. "In fact, the more I ponder this, the more I'm convinced His Grace would be the perfect pleasure tutor. According to the London scandal sheets, he recently celebrated his fortieth birthday with a magnificent ball. *Mature*. He never talks about his lovers, even after they've parted ways. *Discreet*. And he requires them to sign a contract outlining each delicious, wicked thing they'll do. *Experienced*."

Ruth sat forward. "No wife, fiancée, or mistress, either. Also, village gossip says he is spending this month at his Cheltenham country estate. What if you trotted over to Gilroy Park and tried to hire him as your temporary lover? I'm sure the duke would be *intrigued*."

"Oh yes," Ada replied with a snort. "Intrigued at how I haven't already been hauled away to Bedlam."

"Ye of little faith. A tall, plump blond might be exactly his preference."

She hesitated. No. Attempting to hire a *duke* to be her secret first lover was preposterous. It wasn't like Gilroy needed the money, and he could have his pick of ladies.

But what if he did agree? What if brazenly approaching him resulted in an entire month of pleasure before they bid each other farewell, never to speak of it again?

Bold women pursue their dreams...

"The Grand Cock Plan is perhaps the worst ever," she muttered. "Fraught with risk and the very high likelihood of my utter humiliation. However..."

"That however sounds like a yes," said Ruth. "Huzzah! Now, no dilly-dallying allowed. Tomorrow after we've delivered the charity baskets,

Martha and I shall escort you to Gilroy Park in the carriage. My word, ˎ is thrilling!"

The two older women stood and danced a jig around the parlor, but Ada remained in her chair, her stomach churning with both excitement and anxiety.

Tomorrow could be the best or worst day of her life.

~

GILROY PARK

"Are you truly happy, Gil? Tabby and I could stay longer."

Only years of practice allowed Jasper Muir, thirteenth Duke of Gilroy, to stifle a curse at his younger brother's diabolical threat.

Tristan, his wife Tabitha, and their five children had stalked the ducal carriage from London to Cheltenham after his recent fortieth birthday ball, convinced he was lonely and requiring comfort and good cheer. But enough was enough. A bachelor could only endure so much spontaneous singing, charades, cake stomped into rugs, and lovestruck married couple before his sanity fractured.

"No, no," he replied hastily as they watched Tabitha herd the children into a traveling carriage from the safety of the manor's front steps. "London has the best physicians, so you, your pregnant wife, and thousand offspring must return at once."

His brother chuckled. "It only seems like a thousand. This next babe will be the last...unless Tabby bats her lashes for another, of course. Can't refuse her anything. Wouldn't want to either, not after she scooped up my miserable self and taught me how to laugh. Love is a wondrous thing. Turns your whole life around."

Jasper grimaced at the excessive sentiment. Their late father had taught them to be reserved and stoic men who disdained emotion, but nowadays his brother was almost obnoxiously chirpy and forever wanting to discuss feelings. Worse, he'd become one of those eccentrics who kissed his wife in public, romped with his children in the nursery, and *hugged*. Everyone knew that proper noblemen demonstrated pride and care with an inclination of the head, handshake, or if hearing particularly good news like a military victory, a brief clap to the shoulder. Anything else was decidedly un-British.

"Indeed," he said with acute unease, because talk of love inevitably led to talk of—

"I'm sure Cheltenham is near-bursting with potential brides," continued Tristan, his voice gaining volume with enthusiasm. "It's time to bid farewell to mistress contracts and welcome a Duchess of Gilroy into your heart and home."

Christ.

"There is already a Duchess of Gilroy," Jasper retorted. "Mother."

Tristan shook his head. "Her duty is done after all those terrible years with our shriveled-soul father. She found love with Mr. Winslow. Tabby is my forever. I'm sure you'll find yours as well. There is no need to feel lonely or empty."

Not again.

Jasper rocked on his shoe heels. They'd had this ridiculous conversation on countless occasions, and he was bloody tired of it. Mistress contracts kept his existence neat, orderly, and free of theatrics. He did *not* feel lonely or empty, he did *not* need long conversations or hugs, and he *certainly* didn't need a wife. Not when he already had legitimate heirs in his brother and three nephews.

"Tristan!" called Tabitha, laughing, "From the expression on his face, Gil is about to shove you into that fountain. Better join us in the carriage."

"A timely warning," muttered Jasper.

"But I'll echo my husband's words, please find a wife and sire an heir so he and our sons are cut from the line of succession—"

"Safe travels!" Jasper barked, holding out his hand to Tristan.

His brother pouted, but accepted the handshake then bounded down the steps and into the carriage. As it moved down the gravel driveway, a thousand fingers burst out a partially open window to wave frantically, and Jasper raised a relieved hand in farewell before returning inside. Some time alone in his library would cure the madness of the past few days.

Soon he was settled in his favorite chair—custom made to accommodate his unusually tall six-foot three-inch frame—with a large pile of ball and soiree invitations to peruse.

Lonely and empty? Ha.

No one this popular could feel such emotions, nor had turning forty instigated any kind of panic. He had no complaints; it would be churlish of a man with an ancient title, vast fortune, and numerous estates to be anything other than content.

A minute later, he drummed his fingertips on the carved oak desk. Christ, it was quiet.

Why haven't you secured a new mistress? It's been several months. Could it be that you do wish for more than bedsport?

Jasper glared at an invitation. He wasn't looking for love; in truth, he might not even be capable of tender sentiment. If he was that way inclined, surely one of the courtesans, widows, or well-bred young ladies he'd met would have prompted a grand declaration.

No, the family visit had just addled his mind. He needed a distraction. Immediately.

"Your Grace?"

He brightened when a footman peered around the library door. For once, a swift answer to prayer. "Yes?"

"You have visitors. Three ladies from St. Mary's—not in Cheltenham, but the smaller church in Charlton Kings. Miss Lacey, Miss Kinloch, and the vicar's daughter, Miss Blair. They wondered if they might have a little of your time."

Jasper sighed and stood. Church ladies on a mission; no wonder a heavenly answer had been swift. But granting a funding request for a roof repair, charity baskets, or the upcoming village fair was certainly preferable to sitting here scowling about *love*. "They may. Escort them in."

Soon, three visitors approached his desk and sank into curtsies. Two neatly dressed, silver-haired women, and...

His breath caught.

The third woman was tall, wonderfully so, and wearing a modest pale blue gown that in no way disguised her lush breasts and hips. She certainly wasn't young, yet her creamy skin was unblemished, her eyes the hue of expensive brandy, and her unruly honey-blond curls battled to escape a severe chignon. As for those dusky pink lips...he'd never seen a mouth more suited for long kisses, sultry smiles, and sucking his cock. Together with those ample curves and long legs, she'd be the perfect mistress; even the thought of sinking deep into her wet heat while she moaned and pleaded for more had him harder than stone.

"Your Grace?"

Shocked at his lapse in decorum, Jasper sat. She was here on behalf of a *church*, not seeking a lover at a pleasure club.

"Ladies," he said, his tone more forbidding than he intended, so he tempered it with a brief smile. "Do take a seat. How may I assist?"

One of the older women beamed as she settled on the overstuffed chaise. "I am Miss Ruth Lacey. This is Miss Martha Kinloch, and our dear friend Miss Ada Blair."

Oh. The luscious beauty was Ada Blair, the vicar's daughter.

He'd just fantasized about fucking a *vicar's daughter* senseless.

Inwardly wincing, Jasper inclined his head. "Enchanted. Do you seek funds for charity? Building improvements, perhaps? If so, I should be happy to contribute."

An odd, tense silence met his words. His guests exchanged meaningful glances, and the Misses Lacey and Kinloch stood.

"We'll let Ada explain," said Miss Lacey. "May we peruse your library shelves?"

"I love books," said Miss Kinloch with a sweet smile.

Puzzled yet intrigued by their behavior, he nodded permission, and the two older women hurried to the far end of the room.

Jasper leaned back in his chair and tapped his chin. "I now find myself exceedingly curious to know your request, Miss Blair."

She took an audible breath. "We don't seek funds, Your Grace. I am here to discuss a delicate matter."

"Indeed? Go on."

Miss Blair's cheeks darkened to rose. "It is...most delicate."

Why was she so hesitant? He understood the natural reticence of a country miss toward a high-ranking stranger, but he wasn't an ogre. Perhaps this angel sensed all the wicked things he wanted to do to her, aged guests, servants, and library location be damned.

"Nothing is too delicate for my ears. Is it a complaint, perchance? One of my staff or tenants behaving badly?"

"No, not at all," she replied, taking another deep breath. "Actually, I wondered...that is, if you agree...Your Grace, I should like to hire you as my first lover."

Jasper froze, temporarily robbed of speech. He must be hallucinating. Surely the daughter of a village vicar hadn't just enquired about hiring him for *bedsport*.

Yet Miss Blair sat here, her cheeks now scarlet, waiting for a response. *Bloody hell.*

THE DUKE OF GILROY was the most handsome man she'd ever seen in her life. Even the hushed magnificence of the library, with its floor to ceiling shelves of leather-bound books, priceless artworks, and thick Aubusson rugs, had faded into insignificance when he'd stood to welcome them. Gracious, that face. Piercing blue eyes, square jaw, and glossy dark brown hair attractively streaked with silver. Better still, the duke must be at least several inches taller than she; with massive shoulders encased in a perfectly tailored black jacket, a simple rather than fussy cravat, and thankfully, no lace at his wrists. Probably her upbringing, but she'd never liked garish patterns or excessive trim.

Alas though, the bold request had broken him.

Ada bit her lip in dismay as Gilroy stared at her with wide eyes and slightly parted lips. Should she speak? Snap her fingers?

At last he blinked. "Er—"

"I apologize," she mumbled as she stood, wishing the floor would open up and swallow her. The Grand Cock Plan was indeed the worst in history; she'd been a complete twit to think even for a moment that the duke might agree to bed her. "I've never asked that of anyone, naturally you wouldn't want to. I'm hardly your usual preference, am I? Oh dear—"

"Sit down, Miss Blair," he said sternly.

Ada sat. If this were a Mrs. Radcliffe novel, no doubt she, Ruth, and Martha would shortly be locked in a dank cellar by a loyal footman, or blindfolded and tossed into a rickety carriage for an endless journey around a haunted moor. Heroines were often punished for being foolish, but if she could plead her case...

"Do forgive my impertinence, Your Grace. Is there any chance we could pretend this never happened? I won't darken your doorstep ever again."

"Impossible," Gilroy replied, tilting his head and fixing that startling blue gaze upon her. "It is etched in my memory now."

Ada hesitated. He didn't sound cross. Nor were his cheeks flooding with color the way her father's did when he was about to unleash his volcanic temper. In fact, the duke looked almost *amused*. "You aren't...offended?"

"Surprised would be the word, Miss Blair. 'Tis not every day that a gently bred virgin enquires if she might hire me as her first lover. Is there a particular reason I am your choice?"

"Forgive me if I am misinformed, Your Grace," she began slowly, grasping for words that wouldn't make her sound like a Bedlamite, "but it is my understanding you enjoy short affairs with strict yet naughty contracts. And, you do not gossip about your former lovers. That is what I'm looking for. A man who is experienced, discreet, and mature, so the bedding is pleasant, and I can learn many things without fear of scandal or banishment."

Rather than shock or dismay at her announcement, Gilroy merely nodded. "You are not misinformed. But I wonder why you seek a brief affair rather than, say, marriage? It is an unusual path for a vicar's daughter."

After twenty-nine years in the Blair household, the duke's questions were so calm and reasonable, so lacking in judgement or censure, it was almost confusing. But he seemed to value honesty. In for a penny, in for a pound.

Ada clasped her hands. "My father does not wish me to wed. He prefers I live with him and act as his housekeeper, so he has frightened away every suitor I've ever had. No man in Charlton Kings or even Cheltenham will come near me now. But I really would like to know how it feels to sing like a nightingale in bed," she finished wistfully.

Muffled giggles sounded from the far end of the room; Ruth and Martha were indeed listening intently. Yet Gilroy didn't laugh.

"I see. And how much are you willing to pay for such a service? Lovers who make you, er, *sing like a nightingale in bed* don't come cheap, you know."

She almost gasped at the twinkle in his eye. Had negotiations commenced? Could the duke actually be considering her request?

"I...ah...I'm not sure," she replied unsteadily, rummaging through her reticule with clumsy fingers to retrieve the small leather coin purse that her godmothers had generously added several shillings to. "I'm sure everything costs more in London, including hired lovers, but we are in Cheltenham. Perhaps...a shilling per bedding?"

Gilroy grinned. Not a small smile like before, but an actual grin that revealed a flash of white teeth and turned handsome into devastating. "I'm relieved you think me worth a shilling. Would have been a terrible blow if you'd offered a farthing, even in Cheltenham money."

Good heavens. The duke was teasing her. Men *never* did so. They either assumed a vicar's daughter lacked humor or feared her father's wrath too much to share jests, let alone any bawdy talk. Fortunately, Ruth and Martha shared everything.

"I must warn you, Your Grace," she said, smiling in return, "I hold high expectations of my employees. Should you choose to accept my offer, you will certainly earn that shilling."

"Oh, I intend to, Miss Blair. Every single penny."

Ada shivered as the words rasped across her skin, tightening her nipples and causing her pussy to throb. This was another first: being regarded with such appreciation, as though he were a parched man in the desert and she a glass of cool lemonade. Quite frankly, it was lovely. "You're saying...you agree to be hired?"

The duke inclined his head. "On the proviso there is nothing further or permanent, of course. For I am certainly not a marrying man, nor will I be manipulated or tricked."

"Understood," she replied, almost breathless with excitement. Ada Blair, soon to be virgin no more! "Allow me to reassure you that I have no expectations beyond pleasure for the duration of your visit to Cheltenham. I am nearly thirty years old, not some foolish green miss."

"Then we shall be well-matched companions, as I recently turned forty. I suggest we meet tomorrow to outline contract terms. Do you have a preference where?"

Ada pondered and discarded several options. It was difficult to be discreet in a small town. "What about the old gamekeeper's cottage at the edge of your estate? The Tudor one? All those trees for privacy, and it's an easy walk from the vicarage. Say two o'clock?"

"An excellent idea. Two o'clock," he agreed. "Your friends will provide excuses should anyone seek you?"

"Oh, certainly, Your Grace," called Ruth cheerfully. "We've already informed Ada we are happy to be her alibi, anytime of the day or night, and shall personally ensure you aren't disturbed at the cottage. She needs this."

"My word, yes," added Martha. "Long past time our girl let her hair down."

"Indeed," said Ada wryly. She stood and held out her hand. "Until tomorrow, Your Grace."

Gilroy rose to his feet and moved in front of the desk, and next to him she was almost delicate rather than ungainly. How glorious. Then he took her hand and brushed a brief kiss across her knuckles. "I look forward to earning my pay, Miss Blair."

She trembled at the jolt of sensation. If his warm, firm lips felt that good on her hand, she could only imagine the impact on her lips or breasts. Between her legs...

"Ada," she choked out, barely suppressing a moan. "My name is Ada."

"Very well. *Ada*."

Somehow, she curtsied before turning and walking toward Ruth and Martha, who both winked and grinned. In truth she wanted to dance their little parlor jig, for not only would she at last discard her virginity, it would be with a skilled and exceedingly handsome man.

Today had been a very, very good day.

CHAPTER TWO

"HERE YOU ARE, Your Grace. The food for the estate jaunt. They're all things that won't spoil, and the bread is freshly baked."

Jasper smiled briefly at the maid as he took the bulging leather satchel. "Thank you."

"Oh, there are napkins and cutlery as well, I tucked some into the side pocket. The wine and lemonade are wrapped so they keep cool."

"You've thought of everything," he said, handing her a sixpence for the trouble. "Much obliged."

The maid beamed at him, then scampered away.

Jasper set down the satchel and glanced yet again at the clock resting on his bedchamber mantelpiece. Never had time moved so slowly; despite the passing of at least a thousand days, the hands insisted it was noon. Still two hours before his tryst with Miss Blair in the old gamekeeper's cottage.

No, not Miss Blair. *Ada*.

He couldn't remember the last time a woman had fascinated him so. Yes, he'd been initially startled at her offer, but the more he'd delved into Ada's reasons for wanting a lover, the more they had made sense. A vicar's daughter living in a small village would indeed require a discreet man, especially if her father was an obnoxious boor who made her work as an unpaid scullery maid. If nothing else, Ada deserved numerous orgasms simply as a reward and respite from that.

But the way she'd reacted to having her hand kissed...even now he could recall the satiny softness of her skin under his lips, the way she'd trembled and sucked in a little breath, the visible imprint of taut nipples against the bodice of her gown. She might be innocent, but this was a woman made for carnal delights, and he couldn't wait to show her how good it felt to have tongue, fingers, or cock inside her.

Indeed, he would take the honor of introducing her to pleasure very seriously indeed.

Jasper continued to pace between the enormous four-poster bed and the window overlooking the flower gardens. What a damned difference a day made. Or should that be what a damned difference the promise of a tryst with a beautiful and interesting woman made. He wasn't entirely sure why Ada had captured his interest so completely, when in recent months not even the most accomplished courtesans in London had tempted him. Hell, not a single lady at his birthday ball had tempted him either, and there had been literally hundreds of well-bred daughters, sisters, and widows assuring him in no uncertain terms that they were willing and available.

Perhaps it was the novelty of being the lover hired rather than the one hiring. For a *shilling*.

That still made him smile. Considering most London courtesans expected houses, carriages, servants, and their bills paid, he could well be England's cheapest lover. But it wasn't about the money. It was about helping Ada taking control of one thing in her life, a luxury he suspected she'd never enjoyed. And the benefit wasn't one-sided; he would at last be fucking the woman of his most private fantasies: a tall, blushing blond with bountiful curves. As long as their affair remained a secret, there were no disadvantages here.

"Your Grace? You sent for me?"

Jasper glanced up to see his longtime housekeeper, Mrs. Eden, hovering in the doorway. She was the wife of his steward, an absolute treasure of efficiency who kept secrets like a vault. He'd not wanted to involve her as he filched a jar of her wonderful herbal potpourri, some dusting cloths, and a set of the finest linen sheets to take to the cottage. Alas, though, he desperately needed her assistance.

"Ah, yes. I'm hoping you can help me with something important."

Mrs. Eden smiled quizzically. "Of course. What is it?"

Gah. He could actually feel his cheeks heating a little. But damn it, Ada would not perform household tasks for him. "I need to learn how to make a bed."

Her eyes bulged. "Are you unhappy with a chambermaid in particular? Do they all need further training? Oh dear, I—"

"It's not that. I will shortly be meeting a companion elsewhere, and, er, wish to be responsible for the task."

"Ohhhhh," Mrs. Eden replied, her expression easing to bemusement as she walked over to his bed and yanked the heavy embroidered quilt and sheets onto the floor. "That is a surprisingly sweet reason. Watch closely, now. We start with the first sheet draped onto the mattress evenly, tuck all the corners and around, smooth the fabric…"

Well. That looked easy enough.

A quarter hour later he'd muttered every curse word he knew, in three languages, and pledged to raise the wages of all chambermaids in the household. Mrs. Eden appeared to be torn between strangling him and howling with laughter as his eleventh effort sailed across the mattress to hang drunkenly over the side of the bed like a young buck after his first night out. "This is bloody ridiculous."

His housekeeper's lips twitched. "I'm sure *sheets* won't be front of mind for the lady."

"I want to make it nice," he said irritably. "Someone else shouldering the burden for a change."

Mrs. Eden stilled, her gaze turning thoughtful. "So, that's the way of it, is it?"

Jasper shook his head. He'd lost his noted composure over Ada, first pacing and watching the clock, then attempting to learn bed-making. Yes, he felt an unusually powerful attraction, but she would still be a temporary mistress, nothing more. "Never mind. I'll muddle through. I'm sure you've far more important tasks to do."

"Just remember to tuck in the corners. Enjoy your afternoon," said Mrs. Eden as she bobbed a curtsy, and departed the room.

Annoyed at his excessive preparation, Jasper quickly packed the sheets, cloth, and potpourri into the satchel before adding the final items: quill, ink, and parchment for the contract he and Ada would write together. When finished, he hauled the satchel over his shoulder and made his way downstairs and outside to the stables to find his pure black stallion, Thunder.

The weather was warm and sunny, perfect for a ride and to preserve the fiction that he would be jaunting about Gilroy Park. Thunder was always eager for a good country gallop, and as he lived mostly in London, he didn't indulge the beast as often as he should.

"C'mon boy," he said as they trotted past the extensive herb gardens that surrounded the manor proper. "Let's see what you're made of."

At the lightest flick on the reins, Thunder surged forward. They practically flew across the rich pasture, and with a gentle breeze caressing his face, Jasper nearly forgot propriety and whooped. What could be better than riding prime horseflesh on a summer's day to meet a beautiful woman for a secret tryst?

Although his lands stretched as far as the eye could see—a full two thousand acres that included woods rich with deer and game, hunting lodge, orangery, a lake for trout fishing, tenant farmers, and cornfields—it took Thunder less than a quarter hour to reach the old gamekeeper's cottage. After removing his horse's tack, completing a quick rub down, feeding him some oats and fresh well water, and setting him loose in the fenced paddock next to the cottage, Jasper walked over to the small Tudor-era building. As a family home, the single-story red brick dwelling with diamond-paned windows and dark brown shutters was wholly inadequate. But for lovers it was ideal—private and quiet, with a kitchen, larder, privy closet, solar, and bedchamber.

He unlocked the door and walked inside.

Ugh. He should have given himself an extra day to clean the place. Thankfully it wasn't moldy, or housing any number of creatures, but a thin layer of dust covered everything.

Well, yesterday he'd been hired as a lover for the first time. Earlier he'd attempted to learn the fine art of bed-making. Now he could be a duke who dusted. Ada did expect the highest of standards from her employees, after all.

Jasper snorted and began to unpack the satchel.

Today he truly would earn that shilling.

～

"BOTHER!"

Ada stared in dismay at the mess of hot tea and broken crockery on the kitchen table in front of her. Naturally, the day she attempted to finish her daily tasks as swiftly as possible, everything went wrong. Like the sturdy silver teapot—her late mother's pride and joy—slipping from her hand as she poured and destroying her father's cup with a nerve-shattering crash. Earlier she'd managed to accidentally decorate the hallway with freshly laundered linen, and nearly set the kitchen ablaze with a too-generous scoop of coal. Their maid of all work, Deborah, had delicately inquired if she was *well*.

That was highly debatable. But how could anyone concentrate on housekeeping when a life-changing afternoon of pleasure beckoned?

"*Ada*," barked a familiar masculine voice behind her, and she almost jumped a foot in the air. "All I can hear is the most undignified banging and crashing, which is not helpful when one is trying to write a sermon."

A guilty flush scorched her cheekbones, and she took a deep breath before turning to face her father, Ernest Blair. They were almost the same height; he was perhaps an inch taller and noticeably thinner, with narrow shoulders, iron-gray hair, slightly florid cheeks, and thick eyebrows like two caterpillars about to duel. But as she and the rest of the parish could attest, a great deal of righteous wrath spilled from such an unassuming package.

"Forgive my clumsiness. I promised Ruth and Martha I would meet them at half-past one to...finish darning those trousers for the charity box. They offered berries and clotted cream if I would assist, and you know how I love berries."

Her father nodded impatiently. "As long as you don't become a glutton, daughter. But you are tardy with my afternoon tea, so attend to the task with proper diligence and do not break anything else. Haste to visit your friends is not sufficient excuse for poor effort. Unless there is something else distracting you? Something to confess, perhaps?"

Reverend Blair asked this of everyone, so it wasn't a pointed question. Usually she could honestly reply *nothing*. Not today, though, when she would soon be finalizing a wicked contract with the Duke of Gilroy, and paying him the token sum of a shilling to bed her. On the carriage ride home Ruth and Martha had explained the true cost of a London lover; she now knew exactly how great a favor the duke had granted her, and the generous act made him even more attractive.

"Only the sin of coveting berries and clotted cream," Ada replied, forcing a laugh. She hated to lie, but would tell a hundred to get to the cottage.

Ernest tilted his head and fixed his dark gaze on her, a tactic alongside the fire and brimstone that was remarkably successful in extracting information from his parishioners. Fortunately, she was immune to it after twenty-nine years, and when she merely continued to smile, he huffed out a breath.

"Clean up this mess and bring me my tea. After that you may visit with Miss Lacey and Miss Kinloch. Don't forget to change your gown and brush your hair. You look a fright," said Ernest over his shoulder as he marched from the kitchen.

Ada sank against the cool stone wall, gulping in air. Then she did as she was bid, her movements deliberately slow and methodical as she mopped up the spilled tea, prepared a fresh tray, and delivered it to her father's small study. Afterward, she dashed to her bedroom, Deborah behind her to assist with the gown change.

What did a woman wear for such a momentous occasion?

Ada perused her meager collection of gowns. Reverend Blair would be extremely suspicious if she wore her rose-pink Sunday best to darn with Ruth and Martha, so she couldn't wear that one. Gilroy had already seen her in pale blue, and the white lace-trimmed gown would be a trite and unwanted reminder of her maiden state. That left a dark brown serge more suited to the colder months, a bronze-striped calico she often wore to clean, or a primrose-yellow cotton a little faded now from frequent laundering.

"Yellow, I think," she said.

"You always look lovely in it. Like a sunbeam," said Deborah with a grin. "I'm sure His Grace will appreciate it."

Ada stared in horror at the younger, red-haired woman. "Beg pardon?" she croaked.

"Oh, come now, Miss Ada. We have an actual *duke* nearby. Just about every unmarried woman within fifty miles is putting on a pretty gown for an outing to Cheltenham, hoping that he'll see her from his carriage and fall madly in love."

Relief nearly sent her to her knees. The Grand Cock Plan hadn't been discovered. "From what I hear, His Grace is not a man to fall to Cupid's arrow. But when he crosses my path, as fate insists he will, I'll be sure to smile sweetly."

Deborah giggled. "Then we must ensure you look tip-top. I shall do my best with your hair, but it does have a mind of its own."

Once gowned in yellow, with her blond curls partially tamed, Ada hurried to Ruth and Martha's cottage. The front door opened immediately, and Martha ushered her into the parlor.

"My dear! We'd started to think you had changed your mind."

"It's been one of those mornings," said Ada ruefully. "I've never been so clumsy in my life. Oh, by the by, today we are darning trousers for the charity box, and you bribed me with berries and clotted cream to assist you."

Martha smirked. "Fortunately, I have a pile I darned last night while Ruth read me the next chapter from *Udolpho*. It's so thrilling. Much like your duke."

"He's not *my* duke."

"Not yet," said Ruth as she entered the room. "But given time, who knows? Now. As the Grand Cock Plan continues into its second day, have you given any thought to what you want included in the contract?"

Ada shook her head. "Er...no. Not beyond bedding, anyway."

"How exactly would you like to be pleasured? Kisses? Tongue? Fingers?" asked Martha, as casually as one might inquire about the weather.

Thankfully she was past being shocked by frank talk. "Am I allowed more than one way?"

The two older ladies burst out laughing.

"Oh, hush up," said Ada, rolling her eyes. That was the whole point of this contract. She would learn the things that no one apart from Ruth and Martha even hinted at because she was the vicar's spinster daughter.

"Forgive us our merriment, but you have some treats ahead," said Ruth. "Martha love, fetch a pencil and some paper so she might write our suggestions down. We don't have much time before they meet at the cottage."

When all three women were settled comfortably in the parlor, Ada looked expectantly at her godmothers. "So. What should I definitely ask him to do if he's willing?"

Ruth smiled approvingly. "I'm glad you are entering negotiations with that thought. Pleasure should be pleasure for all, everyone involved willing and excited. One thing that has been imperative for Martha and me over forty years is talking to each other. Discussing our desires and learning what we each prefer. Never should a lover have to do something they dislike or find painful just to please another."

Ada nodded and squirmed on her chair with anticipation. Soon, she would be the one making choices. Back at the vicarage, her preferences didn't matter. At the gamekeeper's cottage, she would first be able to discuss a variety of sexual acts with Gilroy, then agree to those she wished to try. "I shall always keep that in mind."

"As to what you should ask for...well. Where do I begin?"

"Tell her about our treasure chest," said Martha, with a comical wiggle of her eyebrows.

"Treasure chest?" said Ada, pencil poised.

Ruth sighed happily. "Bedsport with my darling is always splendid, but there is something special about adding accessories to heighten sensation. Over the years we've gathered a nice little collection. Quill feathers and lengths of silk. A blindfold, silver nipple clamps, small leather dildos for pussy or backside..."

"Gracious," said Ada, her eyes wide with astonishment as she wrote busily.

Thank heavens she had experienced friends for guidance.

EVERYTHING in the cottage looked as well as it could.

Or did it?

Aware that Ada would arrive any minute, Jasper's gaze swooped about the dwelling one last time. Thanks to Mrs. Eden's potpourri, the rooms held a pleasant herbal scent; but he was proudest of the daybed—after six attempts, the fine linen sheet had settled properly and he'd been able to tuck it in as instructed, and spread a second sheet over the top. His satchel sat on the unlit hearth with the bread, butter, fruit, and pastries still inside, but he'd moved the wine and lemonade into a bucket filled with well water to keep them cool. Most importantly, the rickety wooden table was clean and set with quill, ink, and parchment so they might write and sign a comprehensive contract.

Unless Ada had changed her mind, of course. As he well knew, many a decision had been reversed after the benefit of a good night's sleep, and an unwed vicar's daughter choosing to discard her virginity with a stranger was a significant one. He would quite understand if she—

A knock sounded at the door, neither timid nor imperious, and Jasper crossed the room to open it, more relieved than he cared to admit.

"Do come in," he said gruffly.

Ada smiled shyly as she entered the cottage. With her blond hair and yellow gown she looked like a ray of sunshine, and despite the darkness caused by small windows and dark paneling, the kitchen immediately felt brighter.

For God's sake, Gilroy. Leave the poetry nonsense to Byron.

"Good afternoon," she said, glancing about. "It smells lovely in here... gracious, have you been *cleaning*?"

"Why do you ask?"

"You have dust on your cheek. That always happens to me, no matter how careful I am."

Jasper sighed and impatiently wiped his face with his fingers. "An argument against cleaning if ever I heard one. Better?"

Ada set her reticule down on the table. "Now I'm annoyed. You do that, voila, the smudge disappears. If I attempted such an action, I'd have a gray smear from chin to ear. Must be a ducal skill."

"Taught in the nursery," he replied. "Perfected at Eton. 'Tis the true measure of an aristocrat, the attention paid to ancient bloodlines, estates, and titles is a cunning ruse."

She nodded solemnly. "I learn something new each day. Oh, parchment for the contract, excellent. Wait a moment, is that...wine over there? And lemonade? You brought food as well? My goodness, I'm a terrible guest, I didn't even think to bring a gift, and you've gone to so much trouble."

Jasper cleared his throat. "No trouble. I...wanted to."

"You did?" she asked, her cheeks turning that delightful shade of pink. "Well. I have been looking forward to this all day. You have no idea how much."

"I think I do," he replied softly as his fingers positively tingled to remove her clothing and taste every sweet, silken inch of her.

Ada's blush deepened. "Are you going to lock the door?"

"I think that prudent. Not to keep you in, but to keep others out. The key will be on the table; of course, you are free to leave whenever you wish."

"Shall we...shall we discuss terms?"

"Capital idea. Do sit down," said Jasper as he attended to the door, then gestured to the chair on the other side of the table. "Mind you don't bump your head though, damned Tudor cottages and their low wooden beams. Not designed for tall people like us. That's the reason I approved the construction of a new cottage for the gamekeeper; well, that and a crumbling chimney, a roof that leaks in the rain, the haunted privy closet..."

Christ.

His voice trailed off and he sank into his seat. What the bloody hell was wrong with him? He sounded like Tristan blathering away to Tabitha. Besides, no woman wanted to hear about haunted privy closets. Especially not a woman about to discuss contract terms for an affair.

Displeased at his lapse, Jasper straightened the stack of parchment and examined the tip of the quill. "Let's begin, shall we?"

Silence greeted his words, and he glanced up to see her staring at him. "Ada? Is something wrong?"

She smiled ruefully. "I'm sure you already think me quite mad, so this won't sound so very strange...but now you have mentioned a ghost, I wonder if I might inspect the privy closet. I am an avid reader of Mrs. Radcliffe's novels and find such matters fascinating. This is something else my father would strongly disapprove of, so I am rebelling in several ways today."

In another woman he might have suspected nerves, perhaps a waning desire to proceed with the contract. But it seemed his blathering had provoked her to confide in him, to share an interesting fact few people knew. That trust, fledgling though it was, boded very well for their affair.

Jasper nodded and stood. "Come with me."

The hallway was too narrow to walk side by side, so he went ahead and cautiously pushed open the privy closet door. When certain there were no rodents or other wildlife, he gestured for Ada to stand in the doorway and peruse the room. Personally, he couldn't stand it; even with bright sunlight outside the room remained shadowed and icy cold. To the right was a short wooden bench with two roughly hewn circles cut out, and the faint trickle of stream water running underneath sounded downright eerie, like chains clinking in a dungeon.

"Oh my," breathed Ada. "I swear every hair on my arms is lifting. No wonder there is room for two, no one would dare come in here alone. It's chilly. Unnaturally so..."

He'd never been a man to offer comfort by touch, yet his hands rose to gently rub her bare arms. What was it about this woman that urged such behavior in him? He could hardly blame the damned privy closet; it had started prior to this moment. "Better?"

Ada surprised him once again when she leaned back against his chest. With her head resting on his shoulder, the light citrusy scent of her hair teasing his nose, and her rounded backside pressed firmly against his groin, his only thought was how perfectly they fit together. Like he'd been fashioned exactly for her convenience.

Jasper stifled a groan as his cock began to harden.

He wanted to fuck this woman. *Needed* to fuck her. Taste her honey in his mouth, feel the tight clasp of her wet cunt, hear her unbridled cries of pleasure as she came. Did she know it? Was that why her hips circled and rubbed against him, tormenting him with layers of fabric while promising her luscious curves unclothed?

"Ada..." Jasper growled. It was almost impossible to be a gentleman when every instinct urged him to brace her against the wall and take her so hard and deep that she would never move again without thinking of his cock buried inside her. "You dare to tease me?"

She shuddered. "No. I wrote a list."

"Of what?"

"Of the things I would like you to do to me."

"Did you indeed?" he murmured in her ear as he caressed her arms again, deliberately allowing his knuckles to brush the side of her breasts but not touch her nipples, which now jutted lewdly against the bodice of her modest yellow gown. He yearned to know their color, before and after he'd pinched and sucked and bit them.

Ada moaned, then clamped a hand over her mouth.

"No," Jasper said sternly, hating that she'd been taught to suppress and deny desire. "You may not stifle yourself. In fact, a clause in this contract shall state that every moan, every whimper, every orgasmic scream belongs to me. I will hear your need, Ada, when you beg for ease because the ache is unbearable. And I will hear your pleasure when you come. Do you understand?"

She quivered, her breathing ragged. "Yes, Your Grace."

"Good. Let us return to the kitchen table and attend to this contract."

CHAPTER THREE

GILROY HAD BARELY TOUCHED HER, and she'd turned into a shameless wanton. Leaning against his broad chest. Rubbing her backside against his cock. Moaning so loudly she could scarcely believe the sound had come from her own mouth. What would happen when he undressed her and took her to bed for the first time? When he made her *beg for ease?*

Ada sat on the wooden chair, her trembling knees grateful for the respite. After waiting so long, the sheer anticipation coursing through her body at the wicked pleasures she would soon be experiencing was a little unnerving. Thank heavens the duke would write the contract—even holding a quill felt like a challenge right now.

He took a seat opposite her, both too close and too far away, before setting a piece of blank parchment in front of him and flipping the lid from the inkpot. But he wasn't as cool and calm as he appeared; the way his voice had rasped in her ear and the thick bulge that strained the fabric of his perfectly tailored trousers put paid to that.

"So," Gilroy said eventually, picking up the quill. "Tell me of your list."

Gulping air in an attempt to soothe her racing heart, Ada reached for her reticule. First, she perched the spectacles she always wore to read small print on her nose, then she unfolded the list of suggestions that Ruth and Martha had helped her to write. Gracious. Even as bold as she'd been thus far, it was difficult to share things so personal and intimate. What if Gilroy didn't want to do them?

"I...ah...I'm not sure where to begin."

"Allow me to prompt you with the preamble. A contract between the Duke of Gilroy and Miss Ada Blair, commenced on August second in the year of our Lord 1814, for the purpose of an affair. The two aforementioned parties shall be lovers for one month; the affair conducted in a discreet and confidential manner, including sexual acts or preferences specified below and any others mutually agreed upon. At the end of said month, the parties shall amiably end this agreement with no further requirement or responsibility from either. Are you satisfied with that?"

"Yes," Ada nodded quickly, and he wrote the words, the sound of quill scratching parchment overloud to her ears.

"Good. As I said, the first clause will be mine. Miss Blair shall not stifle herself in any way during the agreed affair. She will make her needs, desires, and pleasure plain, and is free at all times to decline or halt an act."

She blinked back tears at the words. Even cloaked in formal language, he offered *freedom*. It seemed an unlikely location for something so momentous, this small, abandoned cottage with its exposed beams, narrow hallway and eerie privy closet, but finally she had the opportunity to be her true self. To make choices and decisions.

Yet as Ruth and Martha had counseled her, all involved must be willing and eager.

"As are you," Ada blurted. "Free at all times to decline or halt an act, I mean. Pleasure should be for all, not one."

Gilroy inclined his head, his blue gaze heating. "An accurate and excellent sentiment. Beg pardon, Miss Blair, but I must pause to inform you how fetching you look in those spectacles. Do you wear them often, or just for reading?"

A blush swept across her cheeks at the unexpected compliment. "Just for reading. The print in bibles and hymn books is so small, but I have no trouble seeing things in the distance. 'Tis the oddest thing. One would think farther away would be worse...oh dear, I'm rambling."

"Not at all. But we must add a few more clauses to our contract, so I invite you to share that list. How can I give you what you need if I don't know, in great detail, how you wish to be pleasured?"

At Gilroy's low and rich tone, like a large spoonful of treacle-coated encouragement to explore her most decadent and private fantasies, she shivered. He made it sound so easy: ask and ye shall receive. But nothing had ever been easy in her life. "I should...simply say?"

"Yes," he replied, his voice turning implacable. "At once."

Ada shifted on the chair and squeezed her thighs together against a pulse of fierce arousal. One more step. Just one more, and she would know what it felt like to have a man's hands on her naked body, his cock deep inside her...to sing like a nightingale in bed.

Do it. *Do it.*

Her fingers gripped the paper tighter, causing it to rustle. "I should like kisses," she said slowly. "Not only on my lips, but *everywhere.* My neck and breasts and, ah, between my legs. If you are willing."

Gilroy smiled, perhaps the most sinful smile ever seen in England. "Oh, I am most willing. Please do continue."

Emboldened, Ada read the next line. "I understand the best way to prevent conception is for you to, er, spill on my belly. Is that agreeable?"

"Quite."

"I should also like to try bedding with the assistance of...accessories."

For the first time, the duke hesitated. "What kind of accessories?"

Ada bit her lip. The more Ruth and Martha had talked of their treasure chest the more curious she had become to try some items for herself. A man of great experience like Gilroy would surely know of such things. "A blindfold, a quill feather, and oil that is massaged into the skin. Oh yes, and also...um...a little dildo for my, er...backside."

His eyes widened, and he sat back in the chair, tapping the quill against his chin. "You continue to surprise and delight. I myself enjoy using accessories on a lover, so can easily source those items."

At further confirmation Gilroy was indeed the perfect choice for a pleasure tutor, the last of Ada's inhibitions melted away. "You know, it is quite lovely that I can speak so freely about intimate matters without judgment."

He shrugged. "Our tastes coincide; it is harder if they don't. When you mentioned accessories, I feared you might want to be spanked, whipped, or led by a collar about your neck. While others greatly enjoy elements of pain to enhance their bedsport, it isn't my particular preference."

Ada shook her head. "Nor mine."

"But if I understand correctly, you would like to be teased until you beg?"

Heat scorched to her aching center. She whimpered. "Yes."

Gilroy leaned forward. "How do you feel about explicit talk?"

"Do you mean words like fuck or pussy? I've heard those are used sometimes."

He blinked, then nodded. "That is precisely what I mean. For some, using words like fuck, pussy, cock, or cunt in the privacy of the bedchamber adds to the occasion. Others do not care for it."

Ada squared her shoulders. "I should like that," she replied firmly, unwilling to pretend she needed convincing. She *wanted* wicked play and wicked talk, and with Gilroy, felt confident enough to ask for it. "To be told in explicit terms what will happen, to be made to beg for it, and then for those acts to be done to me."

This time it was the duke shifting in his chair, and he wrote so fast the quill near flew across the parchment. How thrilling to know her words affected him as much as his did to her.

"We have one final aspect to confirm, Mademoiselle Employer. Payment. A shilling for each occasion, yes?"

"I am now aware that is ridiculously low—"

"Fortunately, I possess a few other income sources," he said with a very ducal eyebrow quirk. "But in the boundaries of this contract, we both win. I bed a beautiful woman, you pay so you are in control. Sign here...and I am entirely at your service."

Not hesitating for even a second, Ada took the quill and added her signature.

There. Done. The Duke of Gilroy was now officially her lover for a month.

Let the wicked pleasures begin.

~

He was a pleasure tutor in the employ of a village virgin. For a shilling.

Jasper stared in bemusement at the contract as he blew on the ink to assist in drying. The London scandal rags would dine on such a story for weeks, and his family would stalk him like Bow Street Runners for more details, but that paled in comparison to the delights ahead.

Ada Blair would soon be in his bed. A virgin, yes. Unawakened, certainly. But he suspected a lusty, adventurous soul lurked under the prim exterior.

No, more than suspected. He knew. For Ada had confessed as much.

I should like that. To be told in explicit terms what will happen, to be made to beg for it, and then for those acts to be done to me.

Christ, he'd nearly come in his trousers at the decisive words. He couldn't wait to give her exactly what she needed.

"Shall we retire?" he asked.

"Please," she said huskily.

"First we'll get you undressed. Come over to the daybed and I'll act as lady's maid. Do forgive my lackluster attempt at making the bed, though. A good thing I'm a hired lover, not a chambermaid."

Ada's gaze was soft. "I appreciate the effort. You really are making my first time quite special."

Jasper coughed. "Yes. Well. Ducal standards and all that."

She smiled and turned around so he could unfasten the three buttons at the nape of the yellow gown. But her skin was so warm and smooth that he couldn't help gliding his fingertips along her collarbone, upper arms, and the tops of those full breasts.

"Your Grace," Ada choked out. "You dare to tease me?"

He couldn't help smiling as she turned his own words against him. The village virgin was a pert little minx, and he liked her, damn it. "Jasper."

"Excuse me?"

"My given name is Jasper. You may call me that within this cottage."

"Hmmm. Do many people have such leave?"

Jasper frowned. Did anyone? His family affectionately shortened his title to Gil. Everyone else called him Gilroy, Duke, or Your Grace. He couldn't recall offering the option to a previous lover, either. How odd. "Not many," he replied eventually as he helped her step out of her gown and petticoat.

"Then I am honored to accept...*oh*..."

Ada quivered as he kissed her bare shoulder and neck while releasing the cords of her stays. Pleasingly, she made no move to cover her breasts as the constricting garment fell away from underneath them, leaving her clad only in a knee-length chemise.

"Sit on the daybed, Ada," he said, and when she obeyed, he took his time removing her shoes and stockings, giving each foot and ankle a brief massage.

"Hurry..."

Deliberately, he slowed his movements, tormenting himself as well as her, for the chemise only offered a shadowed outline of swollen nipples, soft belly, and thick tangle of bush between her sturdy thighs. "Do you wish to keep your chemise on or take it off?"

Ada toyed with the ribbon at the neckline. "The way you are looking at me, I think you would like to see it off."

Damned right I do. 'Tis a crime to keep these curves hidden.

"This is about your comfort, not my preference."

"You really wish to see me fully naked? When I possess a figure more suited to the Renaissance?"

He didn't dissemble. "Since the moment you walked into my library, all tall and lush and delectable. It was difficult to think of anything else when all I wanted to do was spread you across my desk and fuck you senseless."

She blushed, but removed her spectacles and placed them on the small side table. Next, her gaze locked with his and she tugged the bodice ribbon undone, awkwardly parting the fabric to uncover large creamy breasts tipped with pale pink nipples. Finally, she grasped the hem of the garment and slid it upward to reveal her knees. Her upper thighs.

Christ, he was nearly panting.

Yes, that's it. Show me your pretty cunt.

She smiled impishly and halted. "Shall I continue?"

"Off," Jasper gritted out, ready to tear the chemise from her body.

Seconds later, the garment lay on the bed. He didn't think he could become any more aroused, but she proved him wrong by leaning back on her hands and spreading her thighs just wide enough to offer a glimpse of delicate pink flesh through blond bush. Ada was already soaking wet. Even now, a heavenly spicy, musky scent teased his nose, and those tender folds glistened with honey. Pure need roared through him, and Jasper nearly tore his expensive clothing in his haste to remove it before moving forward onto the daybed to kneel between her legs.

"Well, *Jasper?*" she said, arranging herself against a pile of pillows.

He licked his lips at the mouthwatering sight. He didn't really like his given name; probably why he'd never offered the informality to anyone. But when Ada said it in that sultry tone...

"You requested kisses," he rasped. "Everywhere. I must warn you, I believe in being thorough."

"By all means begin. Oh, wait...can I touch you in return?"

"Not yet. Not until I've made you come. It is imperative you are properly ready before I take you. I'll do my best to be gentle for your first time, but I find..."

"You find what?"

Jasper paused, weighing the confession in his mind. It wasn't the sort of thing one said to a virgin, let alone a vicar's daughter. On the other hand, Ada was rather atypical of both, and with a fledgling trust established, he didn't want to lie. "That I am struggling against baser instincts. To fuck you rough and deep and hard, which is not at all gentlemanly."

She sniffed. "I do not recall any contract clause requesting a gentleman."

A laugh rumbled in his chest, and he found himself cupping her cheek. The pert little minx had indeed come out to play. But while he enjoyed the banter, he needed to taste that carnal mouth. At once.

Ada's lips were soft and warm and yielding as he coaxed them apart with his own and taught her how to kiss. But the more she gave the more he wanted, and he touched her lips with his tongue, demanding entry. She surrendered with an adorable little whimper, her hands clinging to his shoulders, and he kissed her with everything he had until she tore her mouth away, panting for breath.

Yet Jasper gave her no quarter, instead kissing and nipping her neck, holding her close enough to tease her nipples with the wiry hair on his chest.

"Make it stop, Jasper," she gasped. "The ache, make it stop."

He slid one arm under her, arching her back. Then he swooped, capturing her right nipple in his mouth and sucking hard. Ada groaned, her fingers tangling in his hair, holding him to her breast as he flicked with his tongue and scraped with his teeth until the taut peak darkened to carmine.

"I see my lover likes to be kissed," he rasped as he attended to her other nipple, making her cry out. "Where else would you like my mouth, sweet Ada?"

"There," she said, gesturing wildly between her legs.

It took all his will, especially when his stone-hard cock ached for ease, but Jasper pulled away. Ada's stated desire was to be made to beg and he would ensure she got her shilling's worth. "It appears you wish to have your clitoris kissed and your cunt tongue-fucked until you come. Alas, though, you've forgotten the contract clause."

"Please," she whispered, tilting her hips to offer him better access.

"I cannot hear you."

"*Please.*"

"Be specific, and I'll grant your desire."

Ada moaned, her gaze feverish with excitement. "Please kiss my clitoris. And...and fuck my pussy with your tongue until I come all over it. Please, Jasper."

Who could deny such a pretty plea?

In one sinuous movement Jasper maneuvered down the bed.

"Very well."

PEOPLE HAD LOOKED at her a variety of ways in her life: dismay, pity, bafflement, sometimes gratitude or fondness. But never with raw hunger.

Until now.

Jasper's eyes glittered like sapphires as he curled an arm around each of her thighs, holding them open. "Watch me pleasure you," he growled. "I'll stop if you don't."

Ada could only nod. But when he lashed her clitoris with his tongue, her sharp cry echoed in the small room, the sensation so intense it was almost painful. Thankfully he didn't stop; indeed, Jasper was merciless with his lips and tongue as he feasted on her pussy. It was far too much, and yet at the same time, not nearly enough.

"I need more," she whispered.

Slowly, gently, he pushed a finger inside her while fluttering his tongue against her clitoris, making her writhe. "You taste so good, Ada...I can feel your tight little cunt rippling around my finger...yes, that's it, come for me. Give me all that sweet honey. *Now.*"

As though waiting for such a command, Ada orgasmed. Her back arched, her hands gripped the expensive sheets, and she screamed as waves of ecstasy buffeted her whole body. Good heavens! No wonder lovers ignored the dictates of society and the church and risked all for pleasure. What could possibly compare to that?

"Gracious," she stammered eventually. When Jasper didn't reply, but continued to rest his forehead on her inner thigh, Ada reached down to stroke his hair in gratitude.

Unexpectedly, he tensed at her touch. "Don't."

"Jasper? What is the matter?"

The duke finally looked up, agonized desire on his face. Farther down, his engorged cock bobbed against his flat belly, the swollen head dripping with pearly moisture.

"Forgive me," he muttered. "I—"

"Take me," she said, needing to be one with him, to enjoy that last act long denied her which would also ease his suffering.

"Are you sure? I told you how it would be."

Ada nodded. "I wish you to take...no, I wish you to *fuck* me. Please."

Jasper exhaled audibly. Then he repositioned himself on the daybed so one forearm rested beside her breasts, and his other hand slid down to grip his cock. When he rubbed the head against her slick labia they both moaned, and desperate for more, Ada tilted her hips in an attempt to lure him inside her.

"Teasing me again," he bit out. "Wicked minx."

"Yes," Ada agreed, delighted how he could be both playful and stern. "What are you going to do about it, Your Grace?"

His reply was to penetrate her pussy with his thick cock. Even as a brief stinging pain and overwhelming feeling of fullness made her eyes water, Ada wanted to cheer. At long last, a virgin no more!

When buried to the hilt inside her, Jasper paused. Seconds later, he began to withdraw.

"No!" said Ada clutching his shoulders. The pain had vanished; her body had stretched to accommodate his size; surely he wouldn't stop now.

But he completed the movement before thrusting back in, and she cried out in delight. *Oh.* That was how it proceeded. Delicate retreat followed by ruthless advance.

"See?" Jasper said, smiling faintly. "You are too impatient."

"I have much to learn."

He reached down to curl his fingers around her thigh and nudge it upward. "I'll teach you. Wrap your legs around my waist, Ada."

It took a moment to wrangle her limbs into the new position, but when the duke sank even deeper inside her, they both gasped. This felt as good as his talented tongue, and when he circled his hips and ground against her sensitive clitoris, Ada bucked beneath him.

"More," she pleaded.

"Oh, you like that, sweetheart?" he said, bending his head to suck her nipples. "You like my cock buried in your tight cunt?"

Sweetheart?

"Please," Ada sobbed at the tiny jolts of pleasure, locking her hands around his shoulders to hold him closer, needing this man to make her come more than anything in the world. "Please, please, please."

Jasper thrust harder and faster and abruptly she reached that wondrous pinnacle again. An abandoned scream tore from her throat as her inner walls gripped and released his cock in an orgasm even more powerful than the first. Seconds later, with a low roar, he yanked his cock from her pussy to spurt his seed across her lower belly before rolling onto his back beside her, gasping for breath.

Stunned, all Ada could do was stare at the ceiling. Not even in her wildest dreams had she contemplated bedding being like that. Exhausting. Consuming. Overwhelming.

Oh no.

Tears threatened and she dashed a hand across her eyes, but the wretched moisture kept trickling. Worse, she sniffled.

"Ada?"

"I'm quite well," she mumbled, waving a reassuring hand.

"Tears imply otherwise."

The words were light, but carried an underlying edge of deep concern. And he'd called her sweetheart earlier. Botheration. Why did she have to react like a complete twit? Who cried not because of pain or distress, but a toe-curling starburst of an orgasm?

"Oh, hush up," she replied, thoroughly disgruntled at herself.

"One does not simply tell a duke to hush up, Miss Blair. It may in fact be breaking several laws."

Ada turned her head and poked out her tongue. "I wager no one has informed you that your jests are terrible, either."

Jasper's brow furrowed. "I would say I'm cut to the core, but I'm more interested to know why you are, er, not crying."

"Must I tell you?"

"Yes," he replied firmly. "You agreed not to stifle yourself, remember?"

"Argh. Very well. I'm not sad, or in pain. I just...I've waited so long and it was so good, better than I dreamed. I felt a little overcome. But instead of behaving, my eyes started trickling water and I'm most displeased with them," she finished with an irritable sigh.

"I see," he murmured.

Ada shivered as he wiped her tears with his thumb and tucked a lock of hair behind her ear. The warmth in his gaze, like he wanted to hold her...

I know it's not in the contract, but yes you may.

Abruptly he pulled away, swinging his legs over the side of the daybed. "Perhaps some food and drink might help?"

Confused at the sudden distance between them, she replied, "Er...yes. Always. What did you bring?"

"Bread and butter, fruit, and some almond pastries. Wine or lemonade to drink. I did not know what you preferred."

"Let me fetch—"

"Do not move, Mademoiselle Employer," he replied, strolling past her toward the kitchen.

"Good gracious," she blurted. "That backside. You are equally impressive advancing or retreating."

Jasper snorted with laughter as he returned and placed several wrapped items on the bed. "Why thank you. Same to you, although I'll never look as good in spectacles, alas. What would you care to eat?"

"An almond pastry to start," said Ada, suddenly ravenous.

While he ate the bread and butter, she made a mess devouring two delicious flaky pastries and a glass of wine, but the ripe peach was also irresistible.

When she bit into it and juice sprayed across her bare breasts, she groaned in dismay at her clumsiness. Until she saw Jasper staring at her with undisguised hunger once again.

Ada put down her wine glass and tentatively cupped her breasts. "Hmmm. I need a man experienced in cleaning. Perhaps you might know of someone?"

"I may," he said, collecting a drop of peach juice with a finger. "Do you have time? Don't want anyone sending out a search party for you."

"I have all afternoon," Ada whispered, although now that sounded disappointingly short. She offered the fruit to Jasper, whimpering as he trailed it across her breasts and anointed each nipple with juice.

"Good. I can be thorough," he replied, slowly dragging his tongue across one taut, sticky peak.

But even as she reveled in the sensation, the part of her brain still capable of rational thought sounded a warning. Ruth and Martha had spoken of this, the danger of emotions tangling with lust.

This was a one-month contract. Nothing more.

She absolutely could not fall for her hired duke.

CHAPTER FOUR

HE'D NOT SEEN Ada in three days.

Three bloody days!

Jasper refrained from scowling at the looking glass only because his valet was in the process of shaving him, and he preferred a smooth rather than hen-pecked chin.

God knew he and Ada had tried to meet after that lusty and incredibly satisfying afternoon in the cottage that would remain imprinted in his brain forever. But the following day, her father had decided every rug in the vicarage required cleaning, and the day after that, he'd insisted she accompany him to a parish meeting to discuss road maintenance, charitable efforts, and the election of a new churchwarden. Thankfully the vicar could not prevent them seeing each other today to arrange a second tryst; it was the August fifth fair in Cheltenham, one of four each year, and St. Mary's would have a stall selling lemonade, preserves, and baked goods.

No one would question his presence. In fact, they would applaud the major landowner in the area buying goods from local farmers and merchants. As long as he could avoid any matchmaking mamas and their daughters. Or worse, the fervent members of the Cheltenham Pigeon Appreciation Society, who believed the birds had not been adequately recognized for discovering the famous Royal Well and deserved a ten-foot bronze statue in the town square.

"How is that, Your Grace?"

Jasper rubbed a hand across his jaw and nodded at his valet. "Exemplary, as usual."

"And your clothing choice for the fair?"

For the first time in his life, he hesitated. Usually he muttered something like "blue" or "black", and his valet raced between dressing room to armoire to create an ensemble. But his attire seemed to matter more than usual. "Let me see..."

His valet's eye's widened. "Your Grace? Is something amiss?"

Jasper nearly snorted. Anyone who had known him longer than a week would say yes. Making a bed, dusting, and permitting a vicar's daughter to hire him for fucking were hardly run-of-the-mill activities. "Not at all. Er...brown."

Ada's eyes were brown.

He gritted his teeth. One afternoon in an abandoned cottage, and he'd lost his damned mind. Yes, it had been spectacular bedsport and he needed more without delay, but that was no excuse for his increasingly unhinged behavior. Hell, he'd nearly *hugged* Ada when she had become tearful after coming so hard. Tristan and Tabitha hugged. The Duke of Gilroy did not. That was a degree of softness, of intimacy, that he would never be comfortable with. He was too much his father's son for that.

"I've changed my mind," Jasper said brusquely. "Hunter-green jacket and black trousers."

"Very good, Your Grace."

Once dressed, he called for his carriage and was soon on his way to town. As always when traveling in the area, Jasper leaned forward and admired the rolling landscape as it flew by. No scenery could compare to this; there was just so much space, and only in heaven could the pasture be richer or greener. Everyone knew the finest beef, mutton, wool, and game in England came from Gloucestershire; indeed, today's fair would see a great deal of money change hands as farmers sold fat cattle and lambs, and tinkers hawked their goods.

When his carriage approached Cheltenham High Street an hour later, it slowed to a crawl. Hundreds of people had gathered for the fair, and already there were wooden stalls selling food and wares, animal pens, a pavilion for musicians, and a temporary stage for dancing and puppet shows. Understanding it would be infinitely quicker to walk, and eager to stretch his legs, Jasper tapped on the carriage roof to bring it to a halt. His driver would proceed to a popular spot for gentry vehicles in a wide avenue nearby before settling in to play cards and eat pasties with the other drivers.

Jasper stepped out of the carriage and absorbed the activity around him. The air was alive with excited chatter and applause, loud bargaining, restless cattle and sheep, and musicians tuning their instruments. He walked on, nodding in greeting as men doffed their hats and women curtsied, knowing as soon as he passed by the townspeople would be whispering about him. While he was held in high esteem as a landlord and employer, they tutted rather pointedly over his bachelor status.

Well. Everyone except Ada.

"Good morning, Your Grace!"

Jasper turned at the feminine hails and smiled at the sight of Ada's friends Miss Lacey and Miss Kinloch. They had done him several great services after all, assisting Ada in her quest and acting as note messengers between them.

"Ladies," he said warmly. "How are you this fine day?"

Miss Lacey grinned. "Faring well at the fair. We've been watching a troupe of Londoners perform tricks on horseback. My word, such talent! If I attempted to stand up, or lean down and fetch a sack, I would be on my backside in the dust, wailing for a physician. But we've also contributed to the local economy; I sampled a great deal of wine, and Martha purchased enough red and white ribbon to circle the cottage thrice."

"Glad to hear it," he replied. "I also have purchases to make."

"Have you just arrived?" asked Miss Kinloch, stepping closer to avoid a passel of shrieking children with sticks of toffee in their hands. "We were helping Ada at the St. Mary's stall, but there was a lull in customers, so she told us to take a stroll."

"Yes, I've been here ten minutes or so. Is Miss Blair...well?"

Miss Lacey smirked. "Quite well several times over, apparently. I salute the effort."

He somehow stifled a laugh. While Ada's own household might be rather miserable, it was easy to see who encouraged the hidden streak of pert minx in her. "One can only strive."

"Indeed," said Miss Kinloch merrily. "But you won't have had time to donate to St. Mary's yet. Why don't you accompany us back to the stall, Your Grace?"

"You'll find exactly what you've been seeking," added Miss Lacey. "A nice, tall, refreshing...glass of lemonade."

Jasper raised an eyebrow. "Bold."

"As sin," she replied with a wink. "By the by, if you walk with a sweet old lady on each arm, far less chance of being accosted by young misses with suspiciously weak ankles."

"A clever plan. If only I could find some sweet old ladies..."

Miss Kinloch giggled. "Naughty man. Come along, Your Grace, and loosen those purse strings. There is a cart up ahead with the finest apple tarts in the county; we'll need sustenance to find our stall, as it is way down the other end of High Street."

"It would be my honor," Jasper replied, offering each woman an arm.

In truth while he liked them both, far more importantly, they seemed to like him and had proven steadfast in their assistance. Even today, offering to escort him back to the stall. If he walked straight up to Ada by himself it would cause gossip or catch the eye of her dastardly father, but with Miss Lacey and Miss Kinloch accompanying him, all small-town proprieties were being observed.

He *needed* to arrange a second tryst with Ada. Those stolen hours in the cottage hadn't been nearly enough for his recently neglected cock. Logic also promised that once he'd had her several more times and the novelty of fucking a tall, plump, innocently bold minx wore off, all his bizarre thoughts and behaviors would cease and he would return to his old self. He didn't actually require more than bedding from a woman; he just had months of unspent lust to slake.

Pleased and relieved he had a watertight plan to proceed, Jasper relaxed.

It was time to enjoy the fair.

～

"WHERE ARE those jars of preserves I told you to fetch? Good heavens, girl. Your head is away in the clouds today. A son wouldn't be so much trouble."

As always with her father, Ada kept smiling even when she wanted to hurl something and unleash several choice words. Of course, the moment she'd sent Ruth and Martha away to see the sights of the fair, half of Cheltenham decided they wanted a jar of berry preserves or marmalade, and the other half wanted a cool glass of lemonade to ease the late summer heat. While the money would boost the church coffers, she'd been run quite ragged, and her father reprimanding her every few minutes for even the slightest infraction did not help. Nor did talking to every man in the county except the one she wanted most to see.

"I'll get them now, Father," Ada replied, turning away from the temporary stall they'd constructed of three long wooden trestle tables and retreating into the tiny white canvas tent where they were storing their remaining supplies. But her hands were clumsy, and she halted for a moment to calm her agitation.

Had an estate emergency prevented Jasper attending the fair? Was he injured, or ill? Her mind couldn't help leaping to the worst possible reason, for the brief unsigned note she'd received in his distinctive handwriting stated he would be here. And he'd proven to be a man of his word.

Not knowing was a torment. She *needed* to see Jasper.

Apart from Ruth and Martha, he was the only person she didn't have to pretend with. In his company she could laugh, be bawdy, and eat what she wanted, and now she'd had a taste of pure pleasure to boot, her body craved him as much as her spirit did. How utterly frustrating for her father to have unwittingly wrecked their plans *twice*. She was a woman requiring orgasms, blast it all!

Scowling in annoyance—something she could do only when alone—Ada wiped the perspiration from her brow with a linen handkerchief from her reticule. Next, she began loading the tray with full jars of raspberry jam and orange marmalade, all made and donated by St. Mary's parishioners. They had long since sold all the cakes and pies, and only had two jugs of lemonade remaining, so she had fond hopes of being able to stop soon for a rest or perhaps to even stroll the High Street.

Voices outside the tent made her pause.

"Reverend Blair! We bring a most illustrious guest to sample our church's far superior lemonade. Are you acquainted with His Grace, the Duke of Gilroy?"

"Not personally," said her father coolly. "I understand, Your Grace, that you choose to attend St. Mary's here in Cheltenham rather than Charlton Kings. A great shame, I'm sure you would find my sermons beneficial."

Ada inwardly groaned at the peevish words then quickly added a fresh jug of lemonade to the tray before carrying it out to the stall. "Here you go, Father...oh, Ruth, Martha, you're back."

Jasper's glittering gaze seared into her soul. "Hmmm. Is this the wonderful Miss Blair I've been hearing about?"

She bit her lip as her mind helpfully provided explicit recollections of their last meeting. Their wicked talk as they'd signed an erotic contract. Jasper holding her thighs open and insisting she watch him pleasure her. The way he'd stuffed her pussy full until she screamed in bliss. His naked saunter to fetch afternoon tea.

Setting down the tray so she did not drop it, Ada curtsied with unsteady legs. She didn't even trust herself to speak.

"Indeed it is," said Martha. "Ada is such a treasure—"

"Now, now," said Reverend Blair. "Excessive compliments turn a woman's head away from the virtuous path of modesty. Far better to offer advice on how she might improve herself—"

"I know how I might be improved," said Jasper crisply. "With a glass of that lemonade Miss Lacey swears is the best. How much are you asking, Miss Blair?"

Ruth beamed. "A shilling, perhaps?

Ada coughed to halt a wayward laugh. "A shilling does purchase the best, and our fundraising efforts would certainly welcome such a generous donation, Your Grace."

"As I'm very, very thirsty, I'll take two glasses," said Jasper, digging into his money purse and placing the required coins on the trestle table. "Here you go."

"Ada!" said her father impatiently. "Don't stand there like a henwit, pour the duke a drink."

When she handed Jasper his first glass of cool lemonade, their fingers brushed. At the sensual jolt her hand shook slightly, spilling a few drops. "My apologies."

Jasper shook his head and finished the drink, then another, watching her the entire time. "Delicious."

Reverend Blair frowned. "There must be many stalls you wish to visit, Your Grace. Don't let us keep you."

"Oh, you aren't. I must peruse these preserves. I am partial to marmalade on toasted bread, but have recently developed an insatiable desire for peaches."

Even in the heat of the noon sun Ada shivered, her nipples tingling at the memory of having peach juice smeared across them and licked off. She couldn't take much more of this subtle teasing. "Over here on this tray, Your Grace."

"Run along, Ada," said her father, glaring at her. "I will assist the duke."

Martha shrieked. "Good heavens. Look! Over there! Are those young lads smoking a *cheroot*? Oh, Reverend, we must stop such foolishness. You know the kind of dark criminal path that leads to. Ruth, Ada, you stay here and guard the stall," she finished over her shoulder as she towed him in a manner only a devout grande dame could get away with.

Ruth's lips twitched. "I believe there are some more jars of peach preserves in the tent, but they are dreadfully heavy. Perhaps Your Grace would be kind enough to assist for a few minutes? I will serve any customers."

"Of course," said Jasper.

Near trembling, Ada turned and entered the small but blessedly private tent, and when Jasper stepped inside a few seconds later, she practically hurled herself against his chest. He didn't stagger by so much as an inch. One hand clamped about her waist, the other gripped the back of her neck, and his lips captured hers in a hungry kiss.

Oh. Even better than she remembered.

Clinging to Jasper's shoulders for balance, Ada opened her mouth for his darting tongue. He tasted lemonade-tart, and she kissed him back eagerly, unable to stop rubbing her aching mound against the hardness between his legs. Immediately, the hand at her waist moved lower to cup her backside and press her more firmly against him. She whimpered at the feel of his cock, the sweet torment of grazing her taut nipples against his chest, wanting to claw away the fabric preventing him from thrusting deep inside her.

The sound of a small child's wail outside the tent was like a bucket of cold water to the face, and Ada jerked away from him, struggling to catch her breath. Good gracious. Had she lost her wits entirely? Even with Ruth standing guard outside, to kiss Jasper like that behind a church stall on Cheltenham High Street was exceedingly foolish. What if her godmother had been distracted by a customer and didn't see the vicar return? What if someone else had seen them and reported the salacious gossip to the *Cheltenham Chronicle?*

Society would insist on a wedding, and Jasper had already told her quite plainly that he wasn't a marrying man. A secret affair carried out at a private location might be acceptable, but he would never forgive a forced marriage.

Ada closed her eyes briefly. "Is this too risky?" she whispered. "Do we need to end our affair?"

His gaze flared. "Is that what you want?"

She stared at her hands. Certainly not.

But they couldn't behave so rashly again. Their affair had to remain secret.

Had to.

~

JASPER WILLED his heart to stop racing and his cock to soften after that scorching hot stolen kiss. His entire sexual history had been centered around discretion: detailed contracts, private rooms in pleasure clubs, arriving at a lover's home late in the evening and departing before dawn, and never speaking to anyone about his affairs. Bedding Ada in an abandoned cottage with the door locked, safe in the confines of his country estate, was one thing. But an embrace in an old canvas tent barely six feet wide, on the goddamned Cheltenham High Street?

So much for control. He'd never been so reckless in his life.

This wasn't London. Ada wasn't a courtesan or widow with the freedom to indulge in an affair, but a village clergyman's daughter. And Reverend Blair wasn't a kindly vicar, but a prune-faced purveyor of criticism and judgment who treated her worse than a servant.

Jasper exhaled slowly. "Ada. Is ending the affair what you want? I know we said a month, but the very last thing I want is for you to feel any distress. I can tear the contract up—"

"No."

Much like the day she'd knocked on the cottage door, acute relief flooded him. For he wasn't nearly ready to end their time together, even if he was running mad. "What are you thinking, then?"

"This contract is respite from the many aspects of my life I do not enjoy," she whispered, clasping her hands. "I won't give it up. But I cannot be foolish, either. And kisses in public are exceedingly foolish, even if we are in a tent. We must restrict intimacies to the cottage."

"Agreed," he said, nodding.

Ada smoothed the white apron covering her bronze-striped gown. Then she smiled a little. "I do hope our next tryst will be very, very soon, though. The last few days have seemed endless compared to those hours at the cottage, which flew by."

I feel exactly the same way.

"Your decision," Jasper said instead. "My schedule is a lot more flexible."

"Today?" she replied, those big brown eyes widening hopefully. "I just remembered, Father is meeting a possible new curate this afternoon, so won't want me around for their discussion. He believes spiritual matters are too complex for women to understand."

Jasper snorted. "His loss is my gain. I'll wait for you with great anticipation at the cottage. Oh, and by the by, I have sourced those items you wished to try."

Ada sucked in a breath. "All of them?"

"Each and every one."

"I'll be there as soon as I can," she replied in a hushed tone, as she waved her hand in front of her face like a fan. "I cannot wait. Gracious me, this is exciting."

"Then I'll take my leave," he said, turning to glance out through the tent flap. "Ah, bloody hell."

"What? Is Father returning?"

Jasper scowled. "That might be preferable. Have you heard of the Cheltenham Pigeon Appreciation Society?"

"Yes, but I'm no pigeon admirer. I know many like the bill and coo, but they are not the ones who have to scrub bird business from steps and windows."

"Quite. Well, it is the lifelong quest of these bacon-brains to see pigeons properly recognized for discovering the Royal Well. I'm sure all British heroes wish it were as easy as pecking at salt crystals to receive a large bronze statue in the town square."

"How large?" asked Ada, her eyes glinting. "Three or four feet?"

"*Ten.*"

She burst into giggles, her shoulders shaking with merriment. "Oh...oh my."

He'd always thought Ada a beauty, but never more so than when she laughed. For it wasn't a society titter like he heard in London, but a full body activity. Her curls bounced, her breasts jiggled, her feet tapped, and fine lines appeared at her eyes, reminding him that she wasn't a young miss, but a mature woman.

"Miss Blair," he said mock-sternly, "this is not a laughing matter. Especially when they want me to pay for it."

"Do not fret, Your Grace," she said, moving to stand in the doorway of the tent while waving an invisible sword. "I shall protect you and your money purse from the clutches of the terrible pigeon people."

"Thank you."

"No, you may thank me later. Most thoroughly...hmmm, I think they've gone. Best you go start dusting," Ada finished mischievously.

Jasper stared at her for the longest moment, tempted beyond measure to kiss her again. Or something even more foolish, like take her in his arms and hold her tightly so he might imprint himself upon her, a warning to others that they must keep their distance and not even think of hurting her.

Which meant he absolutely had to leave at once.

"Until later," he said, inclining his head as he ducked through the tent flap and walked out to the stall. Miss Lacey was serving two musicians a glass of lemonade, but wiggled her fingers in farewell, and he sketched a bow in return.

Over to the right he could see Reverend Blair lecturing the unfortunate group of cheroot-smoking lads, but Jasper managed to catch Miss Kinloch's eye and nod. Then he turned left and walked back down the High Street, making purchases as he went: lemon drops for his housekeeper, and a pair of elegant silver thimbles for Miss Lacey and Miss Kinloch as a token of his appreciation.

Should he buy something for Ada? In the past he'd bought gifts for his mistresses, so it was hardly out of character. Besides, this would be more like...a gift between friends. Yes, just a man buying his friend a gift. Of course, it didn't mean anything more than that. Although any gift would have to be small so it could be hidden from her father. Nothing too intimate, easily explained away if discovered.

"Will you buy some flowers, sir? Fresh from the garden."

He paused and looked at the young Black woman sitting on a plaid rug spread with colorful blooms and green herbs in buckets of water, and also a collection of pretty satin drawstring pouches containing dried herbs that could be hung in rooms, or stored in chests.

Inspiration struck.

"Those herb pouches there," Jasper said slowly. "This might sound like the strangest question in the world, but I don't suppose you have one that offers, er, protection? I have a friend who greatly admires Mrs. Radcliffe and enjoys exploring old buildings but, ah..."

The woman nodded. "But doesn't actually want to meet a ghost? I recommend dill for your friend, sir. Long believed to assist in protection, prosperity, and good fortune. The pouches are hand sewn and only a shilling each."

He almost smiled as he opened his money purse and retrieved a coin. "I'll take one."

"Here you go," she said, handing him a blue satin pouch about half the size of his palm, and he sniffed appreciatively at the strong, tangy aroma of the herb. Even the haunted privy closet would be no match for this little weapon.

Dangling the pouch from his fingers, Jasper marched on. While he paused to admire a pen of fat cattle, and agreed with several farmers that this year's herds were perhaps the finest in a generation, he was eager to return to his carriage and depart for the cottage.

Like all good dukes, he had cleaning to do.

CHAPTER FIVE

ADA HATED RUNNING. Her breasts and backside bounced, her knees and ankles hurt, she wheezed and puffed, and her face resembled a pink pincushion. But for an afternoon in bed with Jasper—and accessories—she would sprint the length of the county.

Her father hadn't even blinked when she'd told him she was going to Ruth and Martha's for afternoon tea; he was too intent on counting the funds raised from the stall and preparing for the meeting with this potential new curate. As he was offering a pittance for the position, it was easy to see why there were so few applicants. The man would have to be from a well-to-do family, and there were very few society pleasures to be had in Charlton Kings even if the scenery was beautiful.

But that was her father's problem. She had much nicer things to contemplate.

Glancing both ways to ensure she wouldn't be run down by a carriage or cart, Ada swiftly crossed the London road that bordered Gilroy Park, and climbed over the stile cleverly hidden in the trees surrounding the old gamekeeper's cottage. For no other reason but vanity she paused on the doorstep to catch her breath, smooth her gown, and remove her bonnet.

When she raised a hand to knock, the door swung open.

"Good afternoon, Miss Blair," said Jasper, his hot gaze devouring her.

Ada's pussy clenched and she whimpered, so overcome it was difficult to move. "Jasper..."

As though he understood, one strong arm curled about her waist and hauled her inside the cottage, while the other slammed the door shut and latched it. Soon she was pressed against the heavy wood as he crushed her lips with his.

Oh. She'd had a taste earlier in the tent, but this was so much better. Now she could moan and cry out, now she could beg to be pleasured and discover even more new sensual delights with her experienced lover.

"Tell me what you need," Jasper said, as he nipped her shoulder. "Tell me and I'll give it to you."

Ada wound her arms around his neck and shamelessly ground herself against him. "I can't wait. I can't."

He rucked up her gown and slid one big hand along her inner thigh until it cupped her mound. When he discovered her wetness, his satisfied growl reverberated to her very soul, but he tormented her pussy with butterfly-light caresses before finally sinking two fingers inside her.

"Poor sweetheart," he murmured. "That hot cunt all wet and aching... you need to come very badly, don't you?"

Ada moaned as he lazily swirled his fingers while teasing her throbbing clitoris with his thumb. "Please, Jasper. *Please.*"

He began to pump them, penetrating her deeply, and the orgasm hit with the power of a spring tide: brutal and overwhelming. Her wild cry echoed in the kitchen, and if it weren't for the solid door behind her, she would have ended up a puddle on the floor.

"Better?" he asked softly.

Still trembling, Ada rested her head against the wood, panting for air. But eventually she managed to blink pleasure-dazed eyes at him. "Compared to nearly everything, yes. But what about you?"

"I have high hopes you might take pity on me and return the favor. After payment, naturally."

Return the favor? He would let her touch his cock? Huzzah!

She wriggled until he set her feet back on the ground. "Come along, then. The daybed is more comfortable than the door. Your shilling is in my reticule."

Jasper took his coin and followed her into the bedchamber. Once again, he'd made up the bed with those wonderfully smooth and cool linen sheets. It was such a kind gesture. Perhaps it wouldn't matter to others, but it was so lovely to have a bed she didn't have to make. Ada gestured to her gown, and he swiftly removed it and the rest of her clothing until every garment lay in a neat pile on the small side table.

But Ada didn't get into bed. Instead, she perused him, hands on hips. "You were my lady's maid, now I should like to be your valet."

Jasper nodded. "Very well."

Mimicking what he'd often done to her, she took her time removing each item of clothing while stroking and caressing him. First his jacket, waistcoat, and linen shirt, then she knelt to tug off his boots and stockings. Ada perched on the side of the daybed to attend to his trousers, smiling in satisfaction when dancing her fingertips over the bulge of his cock provoked a colorful curse.

"Hmmm," she said thoughtfully. "One moment please."

"Ada?" he spluttered, as she darted back to the kitchen, but when she returned wearing her spectacles, he relaxed and unbuttoned the fall of his trousers.

"Thank you for the assistance," she said with a smile. "I thought since you found my spectacles so fetching, I might wear them while I kiss your cock. You've tasted me. I think it only fair I get to taste you."

Jasper's fingers clenched on his thighs, that splendid erection now bobbing against his lower belly. "You may do so."

Frowning in concentration, Ada glided her fingertips along his length. She circled the swollen head and cupped his heavy balls, brushing aside the coarse dark hair at his groin. Not that she had any measure of comparison, but he certainly had a beautiful cock. So thick and hard, yet smooth like satin as well. "Do you like this?"

"I do," he said hoarsely. "So much."

"But you need to come very badly."

"Wicked, wicked minx. I'll remember this later."

"Now, Your Grace. No need to unleash the bear," Ada replied, both hands encircling his cock and giving it a gentle squeeze.

When her tongue flicked across the purple head, Jasper's breathing grew more and more ragged. Growing in confidence, she lapped at his length, and as his hips thrust in a tiny, unconstrained movement, she boldly took the head of his cock in her mouth and sucked.

He groaned, dislodging the pins from her coiffure as his fingers tangled roughly in her hair. "That feels...so damned good."

"Mmmm," she replied, sucking harder, eager to taste his seed as he'd tasted her honey when she'd come on his tongue.

Jasper groaned again. His cock was enormous in her mouth, but he abruptly pulled out and came on her breasts, his seed releasing in several harsh spurts before he collapsed on the bed beside her.

Ada blinked in affront.

No!

Why hadn't he spent in her mouth? Had she done something wrong? Was she terribly gauche and untalented compared to his previous lovers?

Or had he made a decision on her behalf?

Confused frustration and no small measure of irritation churned within her. But she couldn't stay quiet and smile like it didn't matter. She was annoyed, blast it. And he had told her she mustn't stifle herself.

Ada turned her head and frowned at her errant lover. "Why did you spill on my breasts and not in my mouth?"

He stilled, obviously taken aback by the question. "It was your first time. I did not think you would like it in your mouth."

"What I like and do not like is for me to decide, don't you think?"

"Well, yes," he said hesitantly. "But while I am certainly no expert, I understand the taste is not particularly pleasant. Perhaps not as bad as taking the waters, but certainly not ripe peach juice, either."

Ada squared her shoulders. "You are very kind to think of my welfare and shield me from unpleasantness. But I must ask...no, I must *insist* that I be allowed to learn and experience without interference so that I may decide my own preferences in the bedchamber."

Jasper looked so startled she almost apologized. But no. Even small lines in the sand needed to be drawn.

Would he accept it?

LOST IN THE WORLD-TILTING, consuming haze of an orgasm, he'd done something unwise. And Ada had scolded him.

Certainly a rare occurrence for a duke, and yet with Ada he actually felt *relieved* that she had done so. For as their contract stated, she hadn't stifled herself or behaved as she did with her father, smiling and pretending all was well when she wanted to hurl him into prickly shrubbery. Even better, she'd been so precise in the manner that he'd blundered that he didn't have to stumble around or coax the truth from her.

"You are correct," he said. "I should have given you the choice. That was badly done."

"Yes, it was," said Ada, glaring at him over her spectacles.

"I hope you can forgive the lapse in judgment. And I'm glad you said something. Truly. I want our time together to be...happy. Er, I mean beneficial to you. As per the contract."

She cleared her throat, her gaze softening. "Well. I am glad you understand my position. One must be stern with wayward employees."

Jasper's lips twitched. "Especially a humble pleasure tutor—"

"What have we decided about your jests?"

"I refuse to believe they are *that* terrible."

"I refuse to believe that a body cannot survive on pastries alone, but apparently I am wrong. Now you have two things to atone for. Making a decision on my behalf, and jesting with reckless abandon."

Jasper grinned. Ada was so...*glorious*. A fascinating mix of bold and innocent, proper and blunt. How rare it was to meet someone who could both arouse him and make him laugh. "Perhaps you will allow me to atone with afternoon tea and accessories?"

She squirmed on the daybed, another quirk that he liked. No coyness or feigned modesty, just open and honest excitement. "What did you bring?"

"Everything you requested. A blindfold, a quill feather, scented oil, and a charming little jade dildo for your backside."

Her cheeks went pink. "I meant what did you bring to eat. I find bedsport gives me quite an appetite."

Now he laughed. As someone with an equally large appetite for lust and sweets, that was a sentiment after his own heart. But she looked so damned lush and beautiful sitting there naked on the daybed, it was actually difficult to think of food even after an astonishing orgasm. "I shall fetch the basket like a good employee, rather than a wayward one."

"Excellent."

"I must warn you though, once fed, I will be thorough in the use of those accessories," Jasper said over his shoulder as he walked to the kitchen.

When he returned, he unpacked a small leather sack containing the sexual accessories and placed it on the other side table. Next, he poured Ada a glass of wine, and arranged a small feast of bread and butter, apple tarts dusted with sugar and cinnamon, and fresh raspberries on a starched linen napkin. They both ate their fill, but her gaze kept returning to the leather sack.

"Are you finished?" she blurted, dabbing at herself with the napkin.

Jasper raised an eyebrow as he popped the last raspberry in his mouth. "One might almost think you were eager to be blindfolded, Miss Blair."

"I am. Among other things."

Desire scorched through him, and he quickly moved the remains of their afternoon tea and the basket to the floor. Then he retrieved the sack and tipped the contents between them. A black satin blindfold; a quill; a small glass bottle filled with pale golden oil; and a dildo carved of jade with a sturdy gold ring at the end, about the size of his thumb.

"Before we start," he said gruffly, wanting to be sure she understood the rules of the game, "I wish to remind you that you may decline or call a halt to any act at any time. This is strictly for pleasure, Ada. Not to cause you anxiety or physical pain."

"Thank you," she replied, her gaze warm. "It is reassuring to know you have a care for my well-being. And I will do so if need be. For now I would like to be blindfolded, please. And have the quill feather used on me."

"Very well. Lie down."

Ada settled her head on the pillow, allowing him to arrange her arms above her head in a rather decadent pose, and also remove her spectacles. Next, he took the satin blindfold and placed it over her eyes, gently lifting her head so he might fasten the ribbon behind it.

She wrinkled her nose. "Suddenly it seems like everything has a stronger scent. Me. You. This cottage."

"Often happens when one sense is suppressed," he replied. "You may hear things more clearly and be more sensitive to touch as well."

"Ooooh," said Ada, stretching like a cat on the soft, smooth sheets. "Please do begin."

The only thing better than watching her move so sensually was pleasuring her. But he made her wait until she frowned in consternation.

When she whimpered, he took the quill feather and brushed the tip across her foot and around her ankle.

Ada sighed and spread her thighs wide, an unspoken invitation to plunder. Ha. She thought he would trail a path up her calf, straight toward her glistening cunt. But today his employer would learn a lesson in patience—the thrill of pleasure repeatedly denied and granted at last.

After flicking the quill tip against her belly button, Jasper teased her with long strokes of the tapered feather on the underside of her right arm. Then he slowly circled the taut pink peak of her left nipple.

"You're playing with me," she mumbled, shivering.

"How does it feel?"

"I can't adequately describe it. Like every hair on my body is raised. And blood is pounding in my veins. I can hear you move on the sheets and the rasp of the quill feather, and I think I know where you are going to touch me next, but it's always somewhere else. You have full control and I'm helpless. It's so...so wicked. So delicious."

As a reward for her frank answer, he glided the feather down to nudge her swollen clitoris.

Ada gasped, her hips lifting from the daybed. "There. Touch me there, Jasper."

Naturally, he refused, instead skating the feather tip around her knee and eventually returning to her inner thigh, delighting in her hiss of frustration. That was what he wanted to hear. The slow crescendo toward pure need.

"Something the matter?" asked Jasper innocently.

"I thought we agreed not to tease."

"We did nothing of the sort. I must admit, I'm rather enjoying having you at my mercy. Your skin is flushed pink, your nipples are hard, and your cunt is dripping wet. I'm at a most delectable banquet and unsure which dish to sample first. Perhaps here?"

When Jasper captured her right nipple with his teeth and gently bit it, Ada arched with a ragged moan. But he continued to play havoc with her senses, alternating the tip of the quill feather with kisses to her lips, collarbone, belly, and inner thighs until she writhed on the daybed.

"Let me come," she begged hoarsely. "*Please.*"

Benevolent now Ada had surrendered, Jasper parted the hair between her legs and rubbed her clitoris. She shrieked, soaking his fingertips in fragrant honey as she came. Greedy to capture every pulse, every spasm of her orgasm, he cupped her mound and shallowly penetrated her cunt. When he leaned down and kissed her clitoris, forcing her to come a second time, his name echoed in the bedchamber as a wild, broken cry.

Good. Ada knew exactly who she belonged to.

The shockingly possessive thought crashed through his mind like an anvil.

What the bloody hell?

He wasn't looking for his forever. Ada was a temporary lover, paying him a token shilling each time to be bedded, and at the end of the month they would part ways for good. His existence would remain neat and orderly, exactly as he liked it.

Is that really what you want?

Jasper rubbed a hand across his jaw.

Christ. He didn't even know anymore.

EACH TIME she thought she knew what pleasure felt like, Jasper proved her wrong.

Still blindfolded and shaking in the aftermath of her orgasms, Ada breathed deeply in a futile attempt to calm her racing heart and order her thoughts. But only two remained in her head: that Jasper was a master in the bedchamber, and that walking away at the end of the month would be nearly impossible.

How would she live without this? Not simply the expertise of a skillful lover, but someone she could be herself with, someone who made her feel beautiful and sensual, witty and clever?

No. She couldn't think like that. She had to enjoy this day and the others to come until her duke returned to London.

"Ada?" Jasper's voice was low and soothing. "I'm going to remove the blindfold now."

After complete darkness the sunlight was harsh, and she raised a hand to shield her eyes. "What next?"

He gestured to the remaining items on the bed. "Do you want to try them? Or rest awhile longer?"

Ada didn't hesitate. "Try them. But...my skin is quite sensitive right now."

"I suspect your clitoris might be also. Is it?"

Remarkably, the question provoked a faint wash of heat across her cheekbones. Once a vicar's daughter, always a vicar's daughter it seemed. "Yes."

Jasper smiled briefly. "I won't touch you there. Actually, it will be easier if you turn onto your hands and knees for this."

"Very well," she replied, as she rolled onto her stomach and rose on all fours. "Explain...in great detail...what you are going to do."

When he didn't reply, Ada knew a moment of dismay. Had Jasper changed his mind? Did he find her backside too big and dimpled, her thighs too thick? But when she peeked over her shoulder, he appeared transfixed by her Renaissance figure, an expression of such lusty appreciation on his face that she couldn't help a mischievous little wiggle of her hips. Nor could she resist spreading her thighs so he might look upon the wet pussy he'd pleasured.

How perfectly wonderful it was to have a man admiring her body rather than offering suggestions on how to improve it. In truth, such suggestions were annoying. God had fashioned her tall and plump, and while she sometimes felt ungainly next to women who were petite or slender, and shopping could be a disappointing experience, she didn't feel any urgency to change. Ruth and Martha loved each other as they were, and that was the kind of love she wanted. Something that built up rather than tore down.

Eventually Jasper sighed. "Forgive the silence, I was just admiring the view. You're so...so lush and soft. It is very appealing."

Ada wiggled her bottom again. "Feel free to add some hardness to the equation."

He laughed as he trailed his fingers across her skin and delved between the full globes to lightly caress her back entrance, causing her to shiver in anticipation. "Minx."

"Indeed," she replied. "Now, please tell me in great detail what you are about to do."

"Hmmm. I'm going to take the oil, coat my finger to help ease the way, and penetrate you here. Next, I'll slide the dildo in and fuck your backside with it. That might be enough to make you come. If not, and you beg me prettily enough, I'll use my fingers in your cunt, or perhaps my cock. Your choice, Ada. Dildo alone, dildo and fingers, or dildo and cock."

Ada's hands clenched on the sheets, and she closed her eyes briefly against a powerful wave of arousal. "I want that. Hurry. Please hurry."

Curious at how he would prepare, she peered over her shoulder and watched Jasper uncork the oil bottle and warm some of the golden liquid in his palms before coating his index finger. He circled her tight hole, once, twice. Last of all, he slowly and carefully pushed the tip of his finger inside. In. Out. In. Out.

Ada gasped at the unusual sensation, her confused body both welcoming and rejecting the invader. The stretch burned a little as he pressed on, but the resulting throb in her pussy had her lifting her backside, trying to encourage him even deeper.

"How is that?" he murmured.

"It is very odd. I never thought being penetrated there would feel so good. Can you put the dildo in? I should like to compare it to your finger."

First dipping the jade dildo in oil, Jasper then hooked his finger through the gold ring and began pushing it into her backside. How different it was! So smooth and cool and unrelenting. Ada groaned at the feeling of fullness as her inner walls seemed to melt around the object, her hips circling as her mind debated whether it was too much or not nearly enough. At the same time, her pussy ached, furious at being neglected.

"Talk to me," he said sternly. "Are you comfortable? Does it hurt?"

Ada panted, her forehead resting on the pillow. After the sweet torment of the feather and two shockingly intense releases, wanting another so desperately was hard to fathom. But her entire body clamored for relief, reduced to one critical need. Not air, not food, not shelter, but to orgasm. "Jasper...I need to come..."

"I'll make you scream with pleasure, sweetheart," he said gruffly, stroking her back. "But you must choose: the dildo inside or out, if you want my fingers or cock."

"Inside. And cock. Hard, I need it hard. So deep that we are one...oh!"

Good gracious.

From behind his cock seemed even longer and thicker than usual. The jade dildo was an unyielding presence in her backside, the two held apart by the thinnest wall of flesh. Each time he moved her pussy gripped him tighter, and the friction, the heady pressure of the double penetration, was utterly overwhelming.

Ada whimpered, balancing on a knife edge of pain and pleasure. A cataclysmic orgasm beckoned, and she bucked against Jasper, encouraging him to fuck her properly. When at last he curled an arm around her waist and cupped her left breast as he thrust and withdrew, she moaned in relief. All she could feel was the heat of his body around her. All she could hear was a lusty symphony of flesh slapping flesh, the rasp of knees on sheets, wet pussy welcoming hard cock, and their mingled gasps of delight.

"Who do you need?" he gritted out, as he took her brutally hard. "Who is the only man who makes you come?"

"You," she sobbed. "Jasper. I love it. I love you..."

OH NO.

Even in her passionate delirium she couldn't believe the words that had escaped, and worse, he'd heard them. The infinitesimal pause in his thrusts confirmed that. But just as quickly he resumed, holding her tighter and nipping her shoulder. In seconds she tumbled over the edge into ecstasy, her guttural cries of pleasure blending with his low roar as he withdrew to come on the small of her back, the harsh spurts of his hot seed lashing her sensitive skin.

They both collapsed onto the daybed. It might have been minutes or hours later, but eventually Jasper fetched a damp cloth to give them both a hasty sponge bath. However, he didn't address her words, and she was torn between pique and pure relief. That particular conversation could possibly end their contract. When he'd said not to stifle herself it certainly wasn't in regard to love, and to blurt it out like a passion-addled twit was quite beyond reason.

Determined he should forget her blunder, Ada smiled and chatted about inconsequential topics. Jasper laughed and jested in return, yet she couldn't help noticing that hint of distance creeping back between them.

Fool!

If intemperate words brought the most wonderful experience of her life to a premature end, she would never forgive herself.

CHAPTER SIX

IN A SERIES of exceedingly odd decisions, attending St. Mary's in Charlton Kings for the sole purpose of talking to Ada was probably the oddest. And the most hazardous to his peace of mind.

An Ernest Blair service could only be described as loud. And rather frightening.

From his secluded position at the very back of the church, Jasper winced as the vicar's booming voice bounced around the cool limestone walls, high carved arches, and stone slat roof, and viciously attacked the few hundred souls tightly packed inside. While Reverend Blair stood behind the raised pulpit, he never remained still. From one moment to the next he tossed his head, thumped his fist, and gesticulated wildly, causing his black cassock to swirl menacingly about. Not once did he speak of love or kindness or grace unto others.

How on earth had Ada survived thirty years of this? The relentless judgment and correction? No wonder she'd sought a lover for respite and pleasure.

While Jasper remained more than happy to provide that, the game-keeper's cottage now housed a second troubled specter: the conversation Ada was steadfastly avoiding. He'd tried broaching the topic of her love declaration on several occasions in the past week; each time she very successfully distracted him with her naked curves. And her spectacles.

He had the fortitude of syllabub when she wielded either.

But they needed to discuss the matter. Ada was stifling herself; and in truth everything he thought he believed, the opinions he'd long held on tender sentiment and finding forever love, were becoming unusually...*disorderly*. Perhaps that was why he hadn't yet given her the satin dill pouch. It never seemed to be quite the right time, and the damned thing spent half its days hidden in his satchel, and the rest sitting forlornly on the side table in his bedchamber.

Jasper grimaced. He should have brought the pouch today. Forget protection from ghosts, protection from tempests of hellfire and brimstone masquerading as a vicar was a far more pressing concern.

Three hours later, after confession, psalms, readings from the Old and New Testament, the reciting of the Apostle's Creed, and a sermon on the sins of vanity and pride, it was finally over. Standing up and discreetly stretching his numb backside, Jasper watched parishioners practically sprint for the double doors. The adults congregated outside on the lawn to talk while their children dashed about the neatly-tended gravestones nearby, all thrilled to have left the cool church and unpleasant smell of tallow candles behind. Ada was the last to leave, as she'd been dutifully sitting in the front row with Miss Lacey and Miss Kinloch.

"Miss Blair," Jasper said softly, as she walked past him.

The two older ladies smiled conspiratorially and continued through the door. Ada halted, her cheeks going pink. "Your Grace! What...what brings you to St. Mary's?"

He glanced to his left, relieved to see the vicar was presently occupied talking to a group of elderly men. "If you recall, I was chastised for attending church in my own parish, rather than the one adjoining. Never let it be said I do not welcome a new experience."

"It is an experience for everyone," she replied wryly. "As you lasted the full three hours, I hereby declare you to be stout of heart."

"I shall have new calling cards made. But I had to see you," he murmured. "Outside the cottage."

Her blush deepened. "Why?"

"You know why."

Ada sighed and her shoulders sagged a little. "Those three words."

I love you.

Jasper nodded, fighting the urge to take both her hands and rub his thumbs across her knuckles to warm them. In this public place, they must be seen as nothing more than distant acquaintances politely conversing about the weather or other trivial topic.

"When can we discuss?" he asked. "I think we both know we need to."

"Not here," Ada said quickly, glancing again at her father, who was now talking to a young farmer and his heavily pregnant wife. "I am going to take the waters with Ruth and Martha tomorrow morning. It is our annual pilgrimage to the Royal Well. Perhaps you could accidentally bump into us there?"

"As long as I'm not expected to participate," he said with a small shudder.

Ada sniffed. "Taking the waters is good for the soul. Cleansing. One small tumbler in exchange for my continued assistance in thwarting the terrible pigeon people."

"Miss Blair. Surely you aren't attempting to blackmail a duke? How positively Radcliffe of you."

She batted her lashes at him. Ha. As if he didn't know how perfectly wicked this vicar's daughter could be. But before he could reply, a barked hail of "Your Grace!" assaulted his ears, and they both turned in dismay to see Reverend Blair approaching the church steps.

"Your Grace," the vicar repeated, inclining his head like an emperor. "How gratifying to see you at St. Mary's. I trust you found my sermon both educational and informative?"

"It was unlike anything I've ever experienced," said Jasper truthfully.

"Ah, yes," said the older man, looking pleased. "I write the sermons myself you know. Others are far too meek and mild; one needs to be a lion when guarding a flock. What were you speaking to my daughter about? I can't think of anything you'd have in common."

"The architecture of the church. Norman, I think?"

"Indeed. If you have any questions about it, please do ask me. Ada's interests lie only in the feminine tasks of housekeeping, which is what she should be attending to right now."

Ada's shoulders stiffened. "Of course, Father."

"Enjoy your excursion to the well, Miss Blair," said Jasper with a bow.

Reverend Blair glared at him suspiciously. "I thought you had been discussing architecture. Do you have something to confess?"

Bloody hell.

Jasper lifted a ducal eyebrow. "I commented on the warm weather, and Miss Blair mentioned she would be taking the waters tomorrow with Miss Lacey and Miss Kinloch. Not an activity I would choose to partake in."

"I take the waters each month. So cleansing."

"Then I have great sympathy for your chambermaid."

The vicar's eyes bulged, and to Jasper's right he heard a muffled coughing sound. Ada, trying her best not to laugh.

"Well," bristled Reverend Blair. "Do not let us keep you, Your Grace. By the by, daughter, I have wonderful news. The curate I met with, Mr. Ambrose, has agreed to terms and will be returning to live here. Such a fine young man and so upright in his beliefs. He will make some fortunate woman an excellent husband. Of course, I have counselled him in the virtues of choosing an appropriate bride from Charlton Kings."

Ada nodded. "There aren't too many young women in the parish, but all are quite lovely. Perhaps one of them will look favorably upon the suit of a curate. Now, if you'll excuse me, I must go and attend to my duties. Your Grace. Father."

After she'd bobbed a curtsy and departed, the vicar looked at him again with a dark frown. "My daughter is not for the likes of you, Gilroy."

"Beg pardon?" he asked icily, unable to feign politeness a moment longer. The way this cretin treated Ada was abominable. Hell, if a pigeon flew past and decorated the older man's head, he'd commission a twenty-foot statue for the town square tomorrow.

"You heard me. I commend an attempt to save your wretched soul by listening to one of my sermons, but do not approach Ada again. She is quite content with her life here and I won't have her head turned by a wastrel sinner from London."

"Is she content?" Jasper asked bluntly. "It does not seem so."

"She will be. Good day, Your Grace."

With those rather ominous words, Reverend Blair turned on his heel and went to talk to other members of his congregation.

Jasper's brow furrowed. In other circumstances the warning might have been comical, but not from this man. It was a good thing he would be seeing Ada soon.

She needed comfort and respite more than ever.

THE FOLLOWING morning dawned cloudy and cool, and Ada was grateful for the light rug draped over her lap as Ruth and Martha's small, bright yellow open carriage sped toward Bayshill Road.

The Royal Well was Cheltenham's oldest mineral spring and had been discovered nearly one hundred years earlier by the pigeons she and Jasper so loathed. A man named Captain Skillicorne had developed the site and enjoyed moderate success, but a visit from King George, Queen Charlotte, and the princesses back in 1788 had transformed the area into a bustling spa town. Nowadays Cheltenham had several spring facilities and was highly regarded as a health destination.

However, when the carriage pulled up in the clearing set aside for vehicles, Ada's heart sank to see only two other conveyances, neither of them Jasper's. As she'd finally readied herself for the delicate and long overdue conversation, she wanted it done with as soon as possible.

"He'll be here soon, I'm sure of it," said Martha, patting her arm as Ruth hitched the reins of both horses to one of the wooden posts provided.

Grateful once again for her godmothers' unwavering support—they had been entirely sympathetic when she'd told them what she had prematurely blurted—Ada climbed down out of the carriage and approached the mineral spring and pump room as one might approach the edge of a steep cliff: with great reluctance and extreme caution.

"I cannot believe I agreed to this," she said, shaking her head as the three of them walked on. "And don't say it is good for me; the expressions on those faces there says otherwise."

Ruth laughed as the group in front of them hurried away; lips puckered, brows furrowed, and hands clutching bellies. "You don't have to drink a full tumbler. Martha takes a single mouthful and tips the rest into a shrub. I wonder how many others do the same thing. Must be hardy plants about, none have died yet."

"Let us give praise for noble vegetation," said Martha. "So stoically British."

Ada laughed as they paid the longtime attendant, Mrs. Hannah Forty. Each received a freshly pumped half-pint tumbler of water from the twelve-foot-deep well. On the advice of physicians and men of science, the pump room was only open to members of the public during the summer months, between the hours of seven and ten in the morning. Allegedly the waters assisted with conditions such as indigestion, rheumatism, ulcers, asthma, and feminine complaints, but the only result she'd ever experienced was a headache and rather urgent need for the chamber pot. "Why do you come here rather than the Montpellier well? Far jollier over there with the band playing."

Ruth snorted. "I prefer to take my medicine without some twit beating a drum or blowing a trumpet in my ear. A few gulps of repulsive mineral water shall wash away any guilt related to our excellent and varied collection of sins, and this holy occasion must be treated with great solemnity and decorum."

Ada meekly raised her tumbler. "Let us drink—"

"Oh look," said Martha. "It's Gilroy."

Thank heavens.

She watched Jasper advance with great appreciation. His muscular legs ate up the distance between them, and he looked almost too handsome in a dark brown jacket, gray waistcoat, and black trousers, with highly polished Hessians. No one else here knew that her duke looked even better without that expensive clothing, advancing or retreating.

"Miss Blair. Miss Lacey. Miss Kinloch. Good morning to you all," he said when he reached them. "About to do your watery penance, I see."

"We are," said Ruth cheerfully as she curtsied, then moved to stand beside Martha. "What a lovely jacket, Your Grace. Almost the same color as Ada's eyes."

Jasper's lips quirked. "Er...thank you."

Ada glared at her godmother. Rather fortunate for Ruth that she'd stepped away, otherwise she would have enjoyed a sharp elbow to the ribcage for that mischief. "We all look lovely today."

"You do indeed," he said, nodding. "But don't let me interrupt your water-taking. I understand it must be consumed soon after pumping to enjoy the full benefit."

"You aren't interrupting," Ada said hastily. "I can't think of anything I'd rather sample less than this mineral water...oh!"

As his arm jostled hers, an arc of water splashed out of her tumbler onto the ground, leaving it three-quarters empty. Jasper's expression was the very portrait of contrition, but a glint of amusement lurked in those striking blue eyes, and it made her feel warm and tingly inside. He'd done that deliberately to spare her...but this time *after* she'd stated her dislike of it, not before.

"Miss Blair!" he exclaimed. "I do beg your pardon. How unforgivably clumsy of me."

I love you.

Rather than three words launched unthinkingly in the heat of passion, they settled around her heart like a warm blanket. It wasn't just that he could make her scream with pleasure, or that he admired her curves. It was everything. His care for her well-being. The terrible jests. Their banter. Good heavens, he'd even left her father temporarily speechless at St. Mary's, and no one had achieved that, ever. Her late mother had always inclined her head and murmured "yes, Mr. Blair," even when he was entirely wrong.

She would never have to do that with Jasper. With him, she had a voice and could be herself. No, more than herself. The woman she'd always dreamed of being: bold and passionate and daring.

"Indeed unforgivable," Ada whispered. Then she added wickedly, "The only way to atone is to take the waters yourself."

His eyebrows near flew into his hairline. "Anything but that."

Ruth cackled. "Allow me to fetch you a tumbler, Your Grace."

Soon they stood in a little circle, staring at their tumblers like one might stare at a viper about to strike.

"Who is going to go first?" asked Martha.

"Ladies before gentlemen," said Jasper promptly.

"Since Ruth dragged us here, she may go first," said Ada.

Her godmother rolled her eyes, raised the tumbler to her lips and swallowed the entire amount without so much as a splutter. Martha went next, taking one gulp of water before squawking like an outraged gull and flinging the remaining contents at a hapless shrub.

"My word," wheezed Martha. "It's an assault to the tongue. Worse than seawater. Your turn, Ada, then His Grace."

Ada lifted the tumbler, drained the remaining liquid, and shuddered violently. *Ugh.* It was possible her mind wiped the experience each time she sampled the waters, because she didn't remember it ever being this dreadful.

Her stomach roiled, and she pressed her knuckles to her mouth.

"So very...cleansing," she muttered eventually.

"That leaves me," said Jasper. "I would ask that you all stop smiling in that sharklike manner; I have taken the waters previously, you know."

"*Drink*," chorused Ruth and Martha.

With a shrug, he drained his tumbler. Seconds later, he coughed. Then coughed again.

"Bloody damned pigeons," Jasper said hoarsely.

Unable to stop herself, Ada began to giggle. "And their terrible people."

Martha peered at them both. "What are you two talking about?"

"Private jest," said Ada.

Ruth tilted her head, her expression thoughtful. "The couple that jests together stays together. Martha and I are living proof of that. Now, Your Grace, you wish to speak to Ada privately. Perhaps you could escort us back to our carriage. It's the yellow one with the two red roses painted on it."

Jasper looked startled at the casual revelation, almost as startled as Ada felt, for Ruth and Martha rarely told anyone their truth. But Ruth had chosen to tell him. Which meant in her opinion, he could be trusted.

It was definitely time for an intimate conversation.

TWO VERY DIFFERENT thoughts were assailing him. The first, that dressed in a simple white gown with her blond curls piled atop her head, Ada looked like an angel walking among mere mortals. The second, it was both a surprise and a delight to be informed so casually that Miss Lacey and Miss Kinloch were lovers rather than just friends.

In truth, he'd been curious since the day they'd walked into his library, but he'd not asked Ada nor commented on the matter, for it was their tale to tell. While he knew several ladies in London who bedded women, with Reverend Blair leading Charlton Kings society, it was hard to believe Miss Lacey and Miss Kinloch's true relationship might be common knowledge. Which meant they had *chosen* to tell him. And this acceptance by Ada's friends, two women who obviously loved her like a daughter, meant a great deal. A new sensation for the Duke of Gilroy, when he'd always sat at the top of the society tree and made his own rules.

Yet another way that two weeks in the country had changed his life forever.

His thoughts might be muddled in terms of what the future held, but one thing he did know: he could never sign a contract with another woman. Not after Ada.

"So, Miss Blair," he began, as they strolled toward the yellow carriage that almost resembled a barouche, Miss Lacey and Miss Kinloch retreating discreetly to walk several feet behind them. "I know some things said in the heat of passion can be regretted later. Or not truly meant—"

"I meant it," Ada said quietly. "I love you."

Jasper almost stumbled at the certainty in her voice. How could she know for sure? "I see. Hmmm. Forgive me if I...that is...I'm not sure I truly understand love. My brother Tristan and his wife Tabitha are in love. So is my mother and her companion Mr. Winslow. But I didn't think it was for me. Emotions and so forth. I'm not an emotional man and don't enjoy talking about feelings. I was happy with mistress contracts. Well, perhaps not entirely happy, but they sufficed. Now they don't. They bloody well don't. And I purchased you an extremely bloody silly gift," he finished with great irritation.

Ada glanced up at him, her gaze warm. "I heard about the thimbles. It was so kind of you to buy them for Ruth and Martha, they were thrilled. Am I allowed to know what the bloody silly gift is?"

At last they reached the carriage parked about twenty feet from his curricle; he'd not wanted his ducal carriage with its instantly recognizable crest here today. A plethora of witnesses were certainly not required for an act of sentimentality that no one in London would believe. Fortunately, apart from Miss Lacey and Miss Kinloch, the only other party currently at the Royal Well were standing a great distance away in front of the long rectangular building adjacent to the pavilion, a room that occasionally hosted balls.

Jasper sighed and delved under his jacket sleeve to remove the little blue satin pouch dangling around his wrist. "Here. It's filled with dried herbs."

She took the pouch and lifted it to her nose. "Mmmm, is that dill? Such a pleasant fragrance."

"Yes, but I didn't get it for the scent. Dill is for...er...protection."

"Protection from what?"

Now he felt even more unsure about the gift. What if it went against her personal religious beliefs?

Jasper looked away, but he could hardly halt the conversation now. "Ghosts," he said abruptly. "Now you need not ever fear the privy closet. Or any haunted room for that matter, should you be on a Radcliffe-esque adventure."

Ada went very still. "How did you know?"

"How did I know what?"

"That this would be the p-perfect gift."

At the wobble in her voice, Jasper shifted uncomfortably and glanced across at Miss Lacey and Miss Kinloch, who were feeding their horses handfuls of oats and pretending not to listen to the conversation. "It's not a diamond bracelet. Only cost a shilling."

Ada sniffled. "What would I do with a diamond bracelet? And we both already know the delights that can be purchased for a shilling."

Indeed. Hours and hours of lusty bedsport with a pert minx who had somehow burrowed through his defenses to stake a claim in his heart.

"You truly like it?" he asked instead.

"It is a gift given with careful thought for my preferences. I shall cherish it always."

Jasper cleared his throat against a boulder that had unaccountably lodged there. After a lifetime of being in the position of power and knowing the words to say, of neatly arranging his world with emotionless contracts, it was very disconcerting to suddenly be floundering. Ada wore her heart on her sleeve. His had been locked in a vault beneath two feet of solid rock.

How, exactly, did one go about taking the first step of a declaration?

Damn it, this might actually be something Tristan could be helpful with.

"Er...well. Good. Ada—"

"You don't have to say it back, you know. I don't expect that. I feel what I feel, but I am also a practical woman who understands how the world works. You are a duke who reigns over society in London. I am a vicar's daughter from Charlton Kings. You made a dream of mine come true and I will forever be grateful for that, but I know what happens at the end of August."

Jasper blinked, utterly nonplussed. While he knew next to nothing about declarations, he was quite certain they didn't include the words "practical woman who understands how the world works." Weren't there supposed to be hearts and flowers? A unicorn prancing along a rainbow? Goddamned bloody fireworks?

"What happens at the end of August, Ada?" he asked. "Perhaps you tell me."

They stared at each other for an endless moment. But before she could reply, a flurry of movement caught his eye, and Jasper turned his head to see a hackney and several gigs approaching. Even with Miss Lacey and Miss Kinloch standing nearby the two of them talking intently would still cause gossip, and with Reverend Blair already having warned him away, he didn't want any unpleasantness for her at home.

"Can we meet at the cottage?" Ada asked eventually, stepping away from him and moving toward the yellow carriage. "Anywhere else there will be tattling tongues."

"Tomorrow," he said brusquely, so annoyed at the ill-timed arrivals that he wanted to kick stones. How dare visitors visit. Did they not understand the importance of the occasion? A ducal declaration, for God's sake!

"Tomorrow," she agreed, and minutes later the three women were on their way.

Jasper unhitched the reins of both horses from the wooden post, and soon his curricle headed in the opposite direction. His mood only grew darker on the journey back to his estate, but as he rounded the stable block an unwanted surprise awaited him: one lavish and very familiar travelling carriage sitting in the driveway.

"Darling!" called his impeccably gowned, silver-haired mother from the front steps as she waved madly in her exuberant style, the dashing but completely bald Winslow at her side.

What on earth were they doing here?

After jumping down from his curricle, he tried to march but instead staggered a little toward them. They both rushed forward.

"Are you ill, Gilroy?" asked Winslow, frowning with concern. "Do you need a physician?"

Lavinia, Duchess of Gilroy laughed merrily. "No, Winny. He's never looked this...this *thwarted*. Which leads me to believe my son, the duke renowned for contracts, composure, and control, has at last succumbed to a matter of the heart. Come along, Gil, you may tell us everything over tea."

Jasper grimaced.

Christ.

CHAPTER SEVEN

YESTERDAY, Jasper had given her the perfect gift. But in true Blurting Ada fashion, she'd interrupted his thoughts and quite ruined the moment. Worse, she'd done the thing she'd scolded him for—deciding she knew the answer without discussion.

Why? Why had she leaped in to assure him he didn't have to say he loved her back, and that she knew what would happen at the end of August? There was only one word to describe such behavior. Henwit. And being overly emotional at receiving the little satin pouch of dill was no excuse whatsoever.

With a muttered curse, Ada gave up trying to re-sew a loose button on her father's best black jacket and stabbed the needle into a tattered velvet pincushion. Then she stroked the pouch that hung reassuringly from her left wrist as she attempted to wrangle her thoughts. She'd not slept a wink last night, and the clock on the parlor mantelpiece mockingly advised the time to be eleven in the morning rather than two in the afternoon when she could escape to see Jasper at the cottage. They needed to settle this once and for all. No assumptions, just honest conversation.

"Ah, there you are."

She looked up to see her father standing in the parlor doorway. Oddly, he appeared almost...cheerful. The back of her neck prickled. "Was there something you needed, Father? Tea perhaps? I can prepare you a tray before I go and visit Ruth and M—"

"You won't be visiting them today; I think you've spent far too much time in the company of Miss Lacey and Miss Kinloch lately. But you'll be delighted with my surprise, which will make you very, very happy."

Ada's stomach curdled, both at the denied request to leave the house, and the way he'd already announced the expected reactions to his news. Ernest Blair did not care—and had never cared—about her true feelings. "Surprise?"

"Indeed. I have arranged a marriage for you!"

Shock hit her like a blow to the solar plexus, and for a moment she struggled to breathe.

Marriage?

The father who'd turned away every genuine offer made in the past decade had abruptly undergone a change of heart and now wished her a happy and love-filled future?

She didn't believe that for a second.

"To whom?" Ada managed.

Ernest tugged on his jacket lapels, resembling a preening rooster. "My new curate, Mr. Micah Ambrose. It makes great sense. To truly be accepted in the community he needs a wife from Charlton Kings, and you are unwed. Even better, there is sufficient room here for us all to live, so you won't be faced with the burden of finding a new home. Ah, what a blessing it shall be. Ambrose and I are in accord in so many ways; he'll make you a most satisfactory husband. I will officiate the ceremony; the only thing you need concern yourself with is the trim on your bonnet and perhaps a posy to hold. Your future husband is in my study; I'll go and fetch him so we can celebrate your betrothal."

Ada pressed her knuckles to her lips so she didn't unleash a bloodcurdling howl. This couldn't be happening. After her discoveries of the past two weeks, the joy and pleasure of being with a man she desired and had fallen in love with—under no circumstances could she wed another. Especially not to live here at the vicarage forever, housekeeper to two men rather than one.

No. She had to flee this house at once. Hurl herself through an open window if need be. If she made it to Ruth and Martha's cottage, they would transport her to Gilroy Park to be reunited with Jasper.

"Ada," said her father jovially. "May I present your new fiancé, Mr. Micah Ambrose. I'll be in my study; you may have a little time to become acquainted."

As he turned and left, a slender, blond-haired young man marched into the room, and she loathed them both for assuming her compliance and delight at such a sudden and heartless arrangement. Perhaps the old Ada who'd not known true love or pleasure might have acquiesced to their wishes. But she was a woman who had at last found her voice. What would a Radcliffe heroine do?

Ada slowly rose to her feet, her gaze darting about to assess her best method of escape. If she could get the curate to move, she would have a clear path to the hallway and the front door. "Mr. Ambrose," she gritted out, bobbing the barest curtsy.

"Miss Blair," said Mr. Ambrose, with a stiff bow. "I consider myself fortunate to be marrying the daughter of Ernest Blair, a man I have long admired. We shall post the banns this Sunday—"

"Oh, please do take a seat, sir. So we might...discuss this further."

He stilled in obvious bewilderment. "What is there to discuss? I am quite a catch; well-dressed, healthy, from a good family, modest of income but with excellent prospects. I'm also willing to overlook your advanced age and unfortunate height. I would, however, chide you to begin a fasting diet prior to the wedding."

Ada's fingers positively itched to stab him with a darning needle, but it seemed her heart wouldn't quite permit crossing the threshold into blood-thirsty heroine. Instead, she forced a smile onto her face that was hopefully sweet and dutiful. "Then let us discuss fasting. Please do sit down and I'll order tea. The chair by the fireplace is particularly comfortable."

"Thank you," he replied, as he settled into the armchair. "I do agree it is important that you are aware of my expectations of a fiancée, and indeed a wife. I am a traditionalist in that sense. For your future reference, I prefer tea without the decadence of milk and sugar."

"Of course," she chirped. "I'll go at once and see to that. Excuse me."

Ada walked along the hallway as though on her way to the kitchens. But rather than turn left, she continued on to gather her reticule and pelisse from the iron hooks by the front door. After one quick, furtive glance over her shoulder, she carefully opened the door and hurried down the front steps.

Only to halt, for about thirty feet away on the road, an elegantly dressed older woman was being assisted out of a grand carriage.

"Wait!" Ada yelped, running as best she could down the uneven gravel path toward the open carriage door. "Turn back and take me with you!"

The stranger stared in openmouthed surprise, yet something about her face was oddly familiar. "Miss Blair?"

"Yes—"

"Ada!" her father roared from the vicarage front steps. "*Stop.*"

The older woman slid gracefully back into the carriage. "Get in, my dear."

With no time for decorum, Ada flung herself into the carriage and sprawled face first onto a cream leather squab, wincing as her knees connected with the hard floor. Soon they were speeding down the road, leaving her father bellowing behind them.

"Er...thank you," said Ada awkwardly as she righted herself. "I would like to clarify that I'm not a thief absconding with the silver. Or someone who has lost their wits."

The woman beamed. "I know. And I must thank you, for I've always longed to bark *drive* like that. It was very exciting to rescue you from the clutches of a dastardly man, like we are two characters in a gothic novel. My late husband was also dastardly, so I consider it my sacred duty to assist."

Utterly bemused, Ada shook her head. Why did she look so familiar? They certainly hadn't met. "I don't know how to say this without sounding horribly gauche, but may I ask who you are?"

"Oh! Forgive me. I am the Duchess of Gilroy. I believe you know my eldest son rather well...no need to blush, dear, I am a thoroughly modern woman. I invited Miss Lacey and Miss Kinloch for tea to hear the gossip, and we decided to step in and assist you and Gil in settling this love matter once and for all. I've been waiting my whole life for this, and it seems my timing was impeccable. Now we have a few miles to get to know each other. Pray tell me more about yourself."

Still reeling, but not about to challenge an actual miracle, Ada leaned back on the squab.

"Well..."

How could it only be bloody noon?

Jasper glared at the clock in his library. Much like the day of his first tryst with Ada, time had slowed to a near standstill; he was ready to begin hurling objects from the window, just for something to do. His mother had informed him earlier that she would be taking tea with a few friends, and even the thought of a chattering horde of ladies gave him hives. So he'd retreated here. But now he was as trapped and bad-tempered as a bird in a cage.

Really, he needed to get her and Winslow back on the road to London before they extracted any more information from him. If his mother found out about Ada...

He shuddered. All meddling hell would break loose.

Surely it wasn't a bad thing that he wished to figure out the love matter for himself. At his own pace. Without interference. Quite frankly, that he thought of love at all was a miracle when he'd always shunned it for being chaotic claptrap, as his late father had insisted. Besides, love matches were so rare in society; most wed for money to save or restore estates, to elevate position, or to unite two ancient families. It wasn't as though he'd been surrounded by happy couples his entire life. Christ, he'd been in his thirties when Mother and Winslow, then Tristan and Tabitha happened.

A brisk knock sounded at the door.

"Enter," he called.

Expecting a footman with a tea tray, he raised an eyebrow at the sight of his mother sashaying through the door instead. But one look at her cheery grin, and he groaned inwardly. He knew that expression. It was her signature "after much prodding I shall eventually confess to the mischief I have been dabbling in, but will remain utterly unrepentant" face.

"Mother," said Jasper, pinning her with the most forbidding of frowns. "What have you done?"

Lavinia hesitated, her smile faltering for an instant before righting itself. "I'm sure I don't know what you mean, darling."

"You know *exactly* what I mean. You've meddled, haven't you?"

She took a seat, her cherry-red skirts swirling about her ankles. "Meddle is such an ugly word. I am merely smoothing the path of true love, as I did for your brother."

Jasper's jaw clenched. "*Mother*. Either you tell me what you did with no detail spared, or I cut off your milliner allowance forever."

"Bonnet blackmail is decidedly unbecoming for a duke. As is that scowl...oh, very well. The birds in the trees told me when you first arrived here, you were visited by three ladies from St. Mary's in Charlton Kings. Miss Lacey, Miss Kinloch, and their much younger friend, Miss Blair. Then you were seen at the Cheltenham fair talking and laughing with these same three ladies, but most especially Miss Blair. As I am thoroughly invested in your future happiness, I decided to invite Miss Lacey and Miss Kinloch for tea to learn more, but they drove a hard bargain: secrets for premium French brandy. Thankfully, there was an unopened bottle in the drawing room..."

Bloody hell.

"Are you telling me you got two elderly ladies intoxicated to interrogate them?"

Lavinia snorted imperiously. "I beg your pardon. We are not elderly, but sparkling silvers. All enjoying life, able to hold our brandy better than most young bucks, and only wanting what is best for those we hold dear. In conclusion, I left Miss Lacey and Miss Kinloch happily ensconced in the gold parlor while I went and abducted Miss Blair—"

"You did *what?*" he croaked.

"In my defense, abducted is the wrong word. She threw *herself* into the carriage to flee that awful father of hers. Good grief, I've never heard a vicar bellow like that."

Jasper pressed his fingertips to his forehead. At least there was one aspect of this bizarre conversation his mind had managed to partially comprehend. "Ada is here?"

His mother nodded. "Oh yes. Safe and well in the parlor with Miss Lacey and Miss Kinloch."

"I must go to her," he said, rising to his feet.

"No, you must think about what you'll say to the woman who has captured your mind and heart. My new friends inform me your effort at the mineral spring was "er, well, good" and *really*, Gil. No one will swoon at that."

"All of you need to mind your own damned business," he bit out. "I would have said more than "er, well, good," but I was interrupted by bloody visitors."

"How rude, people arriving at a popular public venue."

"There aren't exactly a multitude of locations a duke and a vicar's daughter can meet to chat."

Lavinia's smile widened. "Such a shame there are no private places about, like an abandoned gamekeeper's cottage or so forth."

"We don't talk there, we…"

"Play chess," she replied solemnly. "I understand completely. Winny and I do that regularly. For hours."

"Mother, I beg you. Stop."

"I cannot stop until I know you will do right by your true love. A declaration is important, Gil. You only get one chance to do it properly."

"What makes you think Ada is my true love?" he blustered.

"Do you think of her when she isn't with you? Are you happiest when together? Are you a better man with this woman in your life?"

Unable to remain still, Jasper began to pace. There were several reasons why they should not work; he was a duke, Ada a vicar's daughter. They'd only known each other a few weeks. She believed wholeheartedly in love and expressed it easily; his sterling contribution was *er, well, good.* Yet…the answers to his mother's questions were yes, yes, and yes.

Perhaps he had indeed found his true love. Perhaps he needed to march to the gold parlor right this minute and declare his feelings to Ada—

The door to his library crashed open.

His jaw dropped as Reverend Blair and another much younger man stormed in, both dressed in unrelieved black and clutching their hats. Only that cretin would dare, but he'd gone too far this time.

"Vicar," said Jasper frigidly. "Explain yourself or I'll have you removed from my estate in a manner ill-befitting a man of the cloth."

"I think you know," said Reverend Blair, his eyes flashing. "That woman abducted my daughter and I've come to retrieve her—"

"*That woman* is the Duchess of Gilroy and shall be referred to as Her Grace."

Lavinia examined her manicure in a manner that was somehow more menacing than brandishing a sword. "Also, I merely provided transportation. But I do find it excessively rude, Reverend, that you've charged in here without announcement and haven't even introduced your friend."

The vicar scowled. Then without warning, he smiled. "Oh, you wish to know who this most excellent young man is?"

"I wait on tenterhooks," said Jasper.

The young blond man stepped forward and bowed. "Mr. Micah Ambrose, Your Graces. New curate at St. Mary's in Charlton Kings...and Miss Blair's fiancé."

What the bloody goddamned hell?

Jasper stared in utter disbelief. "Fiancé?"

Reverend Blair chuckled. "Oh yes, it is all arranged. I did say Ada was not for the likes of you, did I not? She'll wed an upright man, a godly man, and be most content."

Lavinia stood, her fists clenching. "And what are the young lady's wishes in the matter?"

Both the unwanted visitors looked at her, obviously startled, as though it hadn't even occurred to them Ada might have wishes.

"My daughter wants to wed," said the vicar impatiently. "I found her an appropriate husband who will fit in just so at the vicarage. I'm not sure why any of this is the business of the aristocracy."

Jasper tilted his head. "Let us find Ada and hear her opinion. At once."

Her father had often made it clear that women disappointed him. Her not being a son. Mama dying before producing a son to follow in his footsteps. But she had thoroughly underestimated what he would do to keep a housekeeper for the lowest expense: arrange her marriage to a stranger and storm the estate of a duke.

Ada continued to pace the ridiculously large and lavish gold parlor, not wanting to be at a disadvantage when her father and Mr. Ambrose burst through the door, as they no doubt would very shortly. Not even burly footmen would halt Reverend Ernest Blair in high dudgeon, and he had been furious at her temporary escape. Poor Jasper. Thanks to her, a circus had indeed invaded his home. Thankfully, she'd had time to explain the situation to Ruth and Martha, so they were prepared for the arrival of vicar and curate and had offered her their spare bedchamber to stay in if need be.

"I really think you should start drinking, my dear," said Martha, from where she sat on an embroidered chaise next to Ruth. "Be easier on your nerves. And this brandy is top notch."

Gracious, the thought was tempting. Either that or dumping the entire decanter on her father's head. She might be nearly thirty, without fortune or property, but she had friends, blast it all. More to the point, she knew what love was, and would not be marrying without it.

"Ada."

Jasper's brusque voice carried from the parlor door, and she sighed in relief at his comforting presence, although at this moment he looked understandably irritated, trailed as he was by her father and Mr. Ambrose. The duchess merely smiled and waggled her fingers as she took a seat near Ruth and poured herself a tumbler of brandy from the half-empty decanter.

"Your Grace," Ada replied, dipping into a curtsy. All she wanted to do was run to him, but he should be reward for toil, not her sword arm today. It was one thing to have a man who would stand toe to toe with her father, but she needed to do so as well. "Er...good afternoon."

"Ada dear, would you like a brandy?" asked the duchess innocently, although the glint in her eyes said she understood the provocative nature of the question. The opening riposte.

Her father coughed. "She most certainly would not. That is a beverage suitable only for gentlemen."

"I don't believe," said Ada slowly, "there is any such beverage. And yes I would, Your Grace."

"Here you go," said the duchess, pouring a small brandy and handing it to her.

Ernest's indrawn breath was overloud in the silence and his cheeks darkened to scarlet; a volcano ready to explode. But Ada deliberately held her father's gaze and took a small sip, for she had to start as she meant to go on. Oooh, it burned. Thankfully she'd been sensible and sipped rather than gulped; otherwise she would be a spluttering, red-eyed mess, and that certainly wasn't in keeping with the bold character she wished to portray. "Ah. Much better."

Jasper's lips twitched. "I might have one also, Mother."

"It's not even one o'clock in the afternoon!" burst out Mr. Ambrose.

"A talking clock," said Ruth. "How modern."

Ada looked away briefly, lest she give in to a very inappropriate giggle. Her entire life, she had feared her father and his bullish demands, his insistence on obedience, and complete lack of care for her wishes. And yet today, surrounded by others who truly valued her, he seemed...smaller. A man who could be defeated.

"I am not a talking clock," said the curate, "but I am Miss Blair's fiancé, and I do not approve of this nonsense. We should be on our way."

Ada glanced at Jasper. The tiny inclination of his head, the warmth in his eyes, and the slight weight of his gift dangling from her wrist gave her the last little boost of confidence she needed to say, "Mr. Ambrose, you are *not* my fiancé."

The young man gaped at her. "But..."

"What are you prattling about, Ada?" snapped her father. "It's all arranged. You agreed."

Fury bubbled, and she clenched her fists. But she couldn't hold it inside anymore. No amount of beating a dusty rug or chopping a vegetable with great severity would calm this storm. Thirty years of frustration and resentment, of sorrow and grief, of constant oppression to cater to the whims of one man was about to unleash in a torrent of emotion.

"I most certainly did not agree. You decided, just as you always do, with no care for my thoughts or wishes. I do not love Mr. Ambrose. I don't even know him. But because it suited your plans, you went ahead and offered me up like a fat sheep at the Cheltenham fair, despite the fact that you do not own me. Despite the fact that I am not fresh from the schoolroom, but a woman grown. And I say no. *No.* There is only one man I love, and that is Jasper Muir, Duke of Gilroy."

Jasper smiled. Ruth and Martha burst into applause. The duchess raised her glass.

But her father's eyes bulged. "What flummery is this? You saw the duke for a minute at the stall and a minute at church. How can you be in love with him? A woman grown does not have such missish fancies, daughter."

Ada glared at him. "It is not a *missish fancy*, Father. His Grace and I have been conducting a secret affair, meeting several times at an old cottage on this estate. Jasper is kind, intelligent, and generous and never have I been happier than my stolen hours with him. He makes me feel special. And beautiful. That I *matter*," she finished at a yell, her voice so loud it would no doubt be heard in every square inch of St. Mary's church.

Mr. Ambrose squeaked like an outraged mouse, but her father actually collapsed into a chair, his face pale with shock. "Well I never."

"That was long overdue," said Ruth, her lips twitching. "I'm proud of you, Ada."

"The vicar needs a drink," said Martha, brandishing the decanter. "Take a swig, sir. You'll feel better."

But Ada couldn't look at her father. The only reaction she wanted to see was Jasper's, the man who had probably bitten his tongue and stood on his own feet so he did not heave the vicar out a window. Instead, her lover had once again offered the freedom to make her own decision while standing ready and willing to offer assistance if required. "Your Grace?"

A tender smile curved his lips, one that warmed her to the soul. "I gave you leave to call me Jasper."

"You did," she agreed cautiously. "At the cottage."

"Indeed. Well, everyone knows about the cottage now, so perhaps the boundary needs to be extended further. How do you feel about coronets?"

Ada's breath hitched.

A coronet?

Jasper wanted to marry her?

Unbridled joy surged through her entire body and Ada took his hands in hers before gazing deep into his eyes. "That sounds very much like you wish to negotiate a new contract. In which case we should probably retire to your library."

"I think that best," he replied, nodding. "Plenty to discuss."

Ada glanced back at the others in the room. Ruth and Martha were beaming. The duchess was dabbing at her eyes with a lace handkerchief. The curate muttered about recalcitrant women, but her father continued to stare at the brandy decanter and shake his head. Gracious. The vicar of fire and brimstone certainly could not take a spoonful of his own medicine.

"Do excuse us, ladies," said Ada, curling her arm about Jasper's as they turned and began to walk out of the parlor. "Very special business to attend to."

"Call me Lavinia," said the duchess. "And if you're going to play chess, don't forget to lock the library door."

"Oh bloody hell," said Jasper. "*Mother.*"

Ada could only rock with laughter. She had triumphed over villainy and found happiness.

Mrs. Radcliffe would be proud.

CHAPTER EIGHT

TWO WEEKS AGO, Ada had been bold and brave enough to walk into this library and make him an offer he couldn't help but accept.

Now it was his turn.

Jasper paused and allowed the scent of leather-bound books and his favorite John Constable landscape on the wall to soothe him. Damn it, he shouldn't be so nervous, but he wanted to say this the right way. A *romantic* way. Now Ada had declared herself, the onus was on him to share the stirrings of his heart, to push past the desire for rules and contracts and order and be vulnerable in front of a woman.

"Ada…" he began, feeling like a fool when his throat closed over. Christ, he wasn't a green lad meeting his first young lady!

She patted his arm. "Let me lock the door, like your mother advised. There we go. Please do proceed, *Jasper.*"

It was difficult to imagine a time when he wouldn't enjoy the way she said his name. Lovingly possessive, but with a hint of wicked as well. Truly, Ada was a woman he could both laugh with and discuss the most serious of matters.

"Earlier in the parlor I asked how you felt about coronets. And by that I meant marriage, in case it wasn't entirely clear."

A little grin tugged at her lips. "Well, I did have my heart set on being

Mistress of Peaches and Pastries, but if Duchess of Gilroy is the offer, then I suppose I could accept that. Are you going to woo me? I must say, it will be difficult to best this ghost-repelling dill pouch. That was an inspired choice; how I knew for certain that you saw the real Ada."

Jasper took a deep breath and reached for her hand. Now or never. "I will walk beside you, never in front. Whether here, in London, in church, or the most haunted castle in England. I will applaud your victories, and comfort sadness or when your eyes misbehave and trickle water. While my jests aren't quite as beneficial as peaches and pastries, you'll have an endless supply of both. I will share my thoughts and hopes and dreams with you, although I must warn you, you'll be in them. Frequently. Wearing spectacles and probably naked because I am enraptured with your Renaissance figure. But most important of all...I'll love you. Without condition or clause. From this day forward, forever."

Her eyes shone like stars, and tears trickled down her face. "I'm not crying."

"I know, misbehaving eyes," he replied, lifting her hand to his lips for a kiss. He'd done it. He'd actually managed to say the words in his heart without stumbling or faltering, and he'd made her happy. Perhaps this love business could indeed be easy with the right woman. "Marry me, sweetheart...*please*."

Ada twined her arms about his neck and tugged his head down for a long, desperate kiss. Any notion of it being wholly sweet and tender incinerated in an instant as she rubbed herself against him and whimpered. "Jasper."

Drawing back a little, he cupped her beloved face. "You have not responded to my offer," he said as sternly as possible when his own eyes threatened to misbehave and trickle water.

"How could it be anything other than yes? Yes! I will say it once or twice or two hundred times. The tales are true, bold acts bring great rewards, because never in my wildest dreams did I think hiring a duke to be my first lover would result in forever after."

"Tell me you love me," Jasper said hoarsely. "I find...I need to hear it again."

Ada giggled. "You mean when I'm not in the throes of orgasm or lecturing my father?"

"Tell me," he repeated, blotting her tears with his thumbs. "Minx."

Curling her fingers around his wrist, she turned her head so she might brush her lips across his palm. "I love you, Jasper. So much."

"Even if you'll be a duchess?"

"Even then," she replied. "I fear I won't be a very good one. I've never been to London, and the thought of fancy balls or directing hundreds of staff makes me itch all over. I want to make the lives of others better. That is the responsibility of peers. Too many ignore their tenants, leave bills unpaid, or compromise maids. The stories we heard from town..."

"I know. And we are in perfect accord. You'll be a splendid duchess, caring and thoughtful. But I hope you'll always be my bold Ada, too. Who speaks her mind and revels in pleasure."

"I do so swear," she said, her brown eyes glinting with pure wickedness. "On that note, if I recall correctly, we still have a contract until the end of the month, Your Grace."

Jasper leaned down and nipped her neck. "That is true, Miss Blair. And today, I won't even charge you."

"How kind!"

"I thought so."

"Hmmm. How to reward such a magnanimous act? A-ha! You mentioned that on the day we met, you thought of spreading me across that desk..."

Jasper scooped Ada up in his arms, carried her across the library to the large oak desk, and sat her upon the polished wooden surface. His aching cock urged him to tear the fall of his trousers open and sink into the exquisite, scalding hot tightness of her without delay. But his mouth watered for the taste of her honey on his tongue. It had been *days*, after all.

"Blue gown," he murmured as he unfastened the buttons at the nape of Ada's neck before pushing the sleeves off her shoulders. "You wore this on the day we met."

"So I did," Ada said breathlessly, arching her back and moving her limbs to assist him in the removal of her gown, petticoat, and stays, so she wore only a knee-length chemise. Her eyes grew heavy lidded, then she yanked at the bodice ribbon to reveal her breasts. Holding his gaze, she cupped them and rubbed her thumbs across her jutting nipples. Offering both for sample.

Christ.

Excited beyond belief, Jasper lowered his head and circled one areola with the tip of his tongue. She moaned, curling a hand around his neck to pull him closer, and he abandoned any idea of teasing her. His fiancée needed to come. Closing his lips around her nipple, he sucked hard to the rhythm of her panting cries, while his free hand delved under the hem of her chemise to inch its way up her inner thigh.

"How would you like to come, sweetheart?" he asked eventually, while his fingertips stroked the bush of crisp hair between her legs. "With my fingers in your cunt? My tongue? My cock?"

Ada wriggled on the desk, simultaneously trying to get him to suck her other nipple and touch her clitoris. He adored her unfeigned eagerness, her sensuality, how she didn't hide her curves from him, but offered them to be pleasured, and pleasure in return.

Soon she tugged his head back a little for another fierce, yet tender kiss.

"Would it be terribly greedy," she whispered, "if I said I wanted it all?"

Jasper laughed. "Your wish is my command."

IT WAS EXCEEDINGLY difficult to concentrate when Jasper kissed her, even more so when his fingers stroked her most sensitive flesh.

But one thought remained lodged in her mind: she loved him. And hearing he loved her in return, that he wanted to marry her and make her his duchess...well, nothing could be more magical. Or empowering, for being bold, and most gratifying, being *herself* had brought together a vicar's daughter and a duke for hire, to start a brand new life together.

One she couldn't wait to begin.

Well, after he'd made her come, of course. First things first.

"Do not *tease*," Ada gasped, as Jasper's thumb no more than nudged her throbbing clitoris.

"I haven't heard you beg, sweetheart. Alas, I cannot lick your cunt, or fuck it with my fingers until you ask me very, very nicely."

She quivered with fierce arousal at his uncompromising tone, and the way his fingertips petted the hair between her legs, nearly parting it but not quite. Another thing she adored about Jasper: the way he remembered details. Her likes and dislikes, her erotic fantasies, what brought her the greatest pleasure. He knew she loved to hear in explicit terms what he would do; to be made to beg for it and then have her desires granted. Imagine that, a husband who didn't restrict her curiosity or deny her natural lust, but encouraged it. A man who loved and desired her—flaws, foibles, quirks and all.

How utterly freeing.

Lifting her fingers, Ada smoothed a section of his hair that she'd previously disheveled. "I am so eager to be your wife. Because of the man you are, and the man you'll strive to be. I hope I'll make you as happy as you make me, in bed and out. Now, I'm begging you, my love. Please, please, *please* make me come."

A growl rumbled in his chest as Jasper unwound his cravat from his neck and placed it beside her on the desk. Next, he removed his jacket and waistcoat, and rolled up the sleeves of his fine linen shirt, revealing those strong, hair-dusted forearms. "Lift your chemise, Ada," he rasped. "Show me your pretty cunt."

"Yes, Your Grace."

Slowly, so slowly, she dragged the fabric upward until it bunched at her waist, before lowering herself onto the cool, hard oak, ready and willing to be plundered. Jasper licked his lips even as his hands rested on her spread thighs, holding her open. Then, in a perfect, deliciously wicked movement, he leaned down and kissed her swollen clitoris as two fingers trailed inward, breaching her soaked sheath.

Ada moaned in delight at her fiancé's ruthless and relentless expertise. His mouth sucked and laved her tender flesh while his fingers curled inside her, finding a spot near her entrance that made her hips buck clear off the desk. She tangled her fingers in his hair, and shamelessly, wantonly, ground her pussy against his mouth and chin to increase the pressure, to allow his fingers deeper, anything to tumble over the edge into ecstasy. As though he knew she needed a little more, he swirled a finger from his other hand in her copious wetness, and gently penetrated her backside.

She screamed his name, the intense sensation of his mouth on her clitoris and his fingers nearly rubbing together as he filled both her holes, hurling her toward the stars in an explosion of shaking, pulsing bliss.

While her entire body still trembled, Jasper withdrew his fingers, then tore the buttons of his trousers to reveal his hugely erect cock.

"I'm going to fuck you now," he said, his eyes glittering. "Hard and deep."

"Yes," she whispered, bracing her feet on the edge of the desk. "Oh, yes."

Jasper took his cock in hand, coating it in her honey. An instant later he plunged inside, stuffing her so full she whimpered at the fine and heady line between pleasure and pain. Every thrust seared her to the soul, every withdrawal provoked a protest, and Ada slid her hands under his shirt, loving the feel of his warm, sweat-dampened back, her fingernails biting into his skin each time he buried his cock to the hilt. As though she hadn't just come, that glorious tightening began inside her once more, building and building until it abruptly released, and waves of ecstasy enveloped her again. Jasper groaned, his hips pistoning, until he yanked himself out and spilled his seed across her lower belly.

This time he collapsed on top of her, and Ada held him close, the only sounds their ragged breathing and frantic thudding heartbeats. Eventually he gently extracted himself and sank back into his chair.

"Forgive me," he said with a grin. "I would remain there with you all afternoon, however my forty-year-old back does not appreciate such an angle."

Ada laughed and eased herself into a sitting position. "This was beyond wonderful, but I shall quietly admit to preferring a soft bed to a wooden desk. Or a door. I am nearly thirty after all."

"Ha. Still a way to go until your hair boasts strands of silver like mine. Alas, they will only become more prominent."

"Excellent," she replied. "For I find them most attractive. I am marrying a man, not a lad. But one thing I would like to know...and it is a little delicate."

Jasper raised an eyebrow. "What is it about this library that invites discussion of delicate matters?"

"Possibly the color of the rug. Or the vast array of books. But I must ask how you feel about children."

He hesitated. "Neither here nor there. In the past I was quite content with my brother Tristan as my heir. He and his wife Tabitha will soon welcome their sixth child."

"Goodness me," Ada blurted, recoiling a little. "I was hoping you might be amiable to the thought of one. Perhaps two at the most. I would dearly love to be a mother, and soon, but have no desire to be endlessly pregnant. Too many sights to see and charitable works to undertake. Schoolrooms. I should like to supervise the building of a great many schoolrooms. And hospitals. Healthy minds and healthy bodies...are you...are you *laughing* at me, Your Grace?"

Jasper stood, stepped forward, and kissed her soundly. "I'm thinking how perfectly, splendidly wonderful you are. But really, if you are going to make significant requests like a dozen schoolrooms, hospitals, or a babe in your belly, you should at least put your spectacles on first."

"Duly noted," Ada replied, attempting to nod solemnly when she was about to burst with elation. "I wonder...must we return to the parlor?"

"Sometime soon, I suppose. But I'm quite sure Mother, Miss Lacey, and Miss Kinloch can wrangle a vicar and a curate. At least until the brandy runs out. After that the clergymen should probably start running."

"I agree. And I do so adore this library."

Indeed, the room would always hold a special place in her heart. Here, she had taken the first step in freeing her true self from the confines of her upbringing and society. Today, it had borne witness to the happiest moments of her life outside the old gamekeeper's cottage.

How glorious to know with Jasper there would be so many more.

IT WAS HIS WEDDING DAY.

Jasper peered at the looking glass as he attempted an elaborate arrangement of his silk cravat for the twentieth time. He'd not expected this, then again, he'd never expected to meet a woman like Ada. His sweetheart.

The battle between their families as to how the day should proceed had been amusing. His mother and Winslow had waxed lyrical over a grand ceremony at St. Paul's Cathedral in London with half of society and the royal family in attendance, while Reverend Blair had unbent just enough to insist upon St. Mary's in Charlton Kings with himself officiating.

But Ada had not wanted either option, so Jasper had suggested he travel to London for a special license from the Archbishop of Canterbury at Doctors' Commons, followed by an intimate private ceremony in the drawing room at Gilroy Park. She'd approved of that idea, and invitations had been sent to Tristan and Tabitha, Miss Lacey and Miss Kinloch, Mr. Blair, and his mother and Winslow. Reverend Henry Foulkes, the brisk yet kindly vicar of St. Mary's in Cheltenham for the past fifteen years, had agreed to officiate.

"You're looking surprisingly well, brother."

Jasper raised an eyebrow at Tristan as he sauntered into the bedchamber in his best man wedding finery, top hat dangling from one hand. "I would look better if this damned cravat would sit properly. Did you expect to find me hiding behind a curtain, perhaps? Curled up in the armoire?"

Tristan grinned. "I wasn't sure. You've been disturbingly amiable since meeting Ada—don't scowl, she gave me leave to use her given name—but wedding days can cause the hardiest of men to falter. I was so afraid Tabby would change her mind that I downed an entire hip flask of brandy prior to our ceremony."

"I'm a little surprised no one tried to dissuade me from wedding Ada," he said cautiously. "She is a vicar's daughter, rather than a peer's."

"You are the duke. Marry whom you please. But it's quite obvious to all and sundry that you are madly in love with each other, and that is what we wanted for you. Happiness."

Jasper cleared his throat. "Do I look...well?"

"Hmmm. White silk cravat, muslin shirt, black tailed jacket, black knee breeches, stockings, and diamond-buckled shoes. I might think you lacked a sentimental touch, but the brown and gold embroidery on your waistcoat represent Ada's eyes and hair, do they not?"

"Perhaps."

His brother chortled and stepped closer to expertly arrange the recalcitrant cravat. "You are indeed in love. But I must urge you to hurry, if only for your bride-to-be's sake. Mother, Tabby, Miss Lacey, and Miss Kinloch opened another bottle of brandy, and are now all cooing around her like a flock of mad doves. Mr. Blair is giving advice to Mr. Foulkes on the ceremony. We may in fact bear witness to the first drawing room duel between two men of the cloth."

"Hell and damnation," said Jasper, smoothing his jacket sleeves. "I'm too old for such theatrics."

"If you think that is theatrical, wait until society discovers England's most eligible yet stubbornly unwed duke has returned to London with a village clergyman's daughter wearing his ring."

"Don't remind me. Ada would prefer I not send a notice to the newspapers. She thinks that we should simply stroll into balls and soirees and say lovely to see you, charming decorations, surprise, we're married."

Tristan whistled. "I hope you have plenty of hartshorn on hand. That will cause a mass swoon to end all swoons, especially from Prinny. He so admired your string of short and strict contracts."

"I'm sure he'll recover," said Jasper, rolling his eyes. What the foolish, spendthrift Prince of Wales thought of his marriage mattered not one whit. All that mattered was Ada. "Shall we proceed to the drawing room?"

"We shall. Tabby and I are so happy for you. We'll be even happier when you fill that carved cradle down the hallway with an heir...too soon?"

"Far, far too soon," he replied. That he'd been coming inside Ada at every opportunity in a quest to grant one of her dearest wishes was not something anyone else needed to know. "By the by, I'm not saying any of you were correct...but there might be a grain of truth in life brightening after meeting the right person."

Tristan turned, his eyes glistening. "It's the gospel truth."

"Gah. You want to hug me, don't you?"

"I really do."

Jasper sighed. "Under the circumstances I will permit a brief celebratory embrace for the duration of approximately two seconds—"

His brother enveloped him in a bear hug. And didn't let go.

"Here, now," said Jasper as he awkwardly patted his brother's back. Perhaps hugs weren't the *worst* thing in the world. "You'll undo your effort with my cravat."

A few minutes later, they made their way downstairs to the drawing room. Mrs. Eden and her team of maids had been busy; they'd moved the furniture to fashion a sort of aisle with chairs either side, there was a plethora of flowers and ribbons, and a smiling Mr. Foulkes waited on a hastily constructed wooden dais, bible in hand.

"Good morning, Your Grace," said the vicar cheerfully. "Glorious day for a wedding. Lord Tristan, how is your charge faring?"

"Quite satisfactory. One might even say eager," said Tristan with a wink.

On another occasion he might have politely crushed his brother's instep, but the sound of excited chatter reached him, and shortly afterward, his mother, Winslow, Miss Lacey, and Miss Kinloch entered the drawing room. The others took their seats, but Miss Lacey moved to the pianoforte and began to play a rather jaunty tune.

Jasper relaxed. This boded well for a bride still willing.

Then Ada walked toward him on Reverend Blair's arm, looking nothing less than heavenly in a new white silk gown overlaid with cobweb-fine silver lace and tiny hand-stitched crystals. He'd taken her measurements with him when he'd travelled to London for the special license, promising a hefty purse and future patronage if the experienced Mayfair modiste and her apprentices performed an overnight miracle with the utmost discretion. They had eagerly accepted the challenge, and it had been worth every penny. The smile on Ada's face...

He swallowed hard. Bloody damned misbehaving eyes.

Mr. Blair placed Ada's hand in his with a frosty look to both him and Mr. Foulkes, obviously still aggrieved his wishes had been ignored. But as Jasper rubbed her knuckles with his thumbs, and looked into her sparkling brown eyes, the world narrowed to her, him, and the vicar about to join them together in holy matrimony.

After greeting the small audience, Mr. Foulkes delivered an uplifting sermon on the blessings of marriage. Then it came time to recite vows from the Book of Common Prayer.

"And you, Jasper Louis Benjamin Muir, Duke of Gilroy," intoned the vicar, "wilt thou have this woman to thy wedded wife, to live together after God's ordinance in the holy estate of matrimony? Wilt thou love her, comfort her, honor, and keep her in sickness and in health; and, forsaking all other, keep thee only unto her, so long as ye both shall live?"

"I will," he said firmly.

The rest of the ceremony seemed to pass in a blur, although he distinctly recalled Ada's wicked little smirk during the "with my body I thee worship" part as he slid a heavy gold band onto her third finger. Nor would he ever forget a cheer that nearly raised the roof when he turned back down the aisle, one beloved duchess on his arm.

Jasper and Ada, side by side as they would always be.

Now and forever.

The End.

~

Love hot dukes + hot sex + happily ever after, but craving a full length story?

Try Duke in Darkness!

ALSO BY NICOLA DAVIDSON

Wickedly Wed series

Duke in Darkness (#1)

The London Lords series

To Love a Hellion (#1)

Rake to Riches (#2)

Tempting the Marquess (#3)

Fallen trilogy

Surrender to Sin (#1)

The Devil's Submission (#2)

The Seduction of Viscount Vice (#3)

Surrey SFS quintet

My Lady's Lover (#1)

To Tame a Wicked Widow (#2)

My Lord, Lady, and Gentleman (#3)

At His Lady's Command (#4)

A Very Surrey SFS Christmas (#5)

Surrey SFS - The Complete Series boxset

Regency Standalones

Her Virgin Duke

Duke for Hire (in the anthology Duke I'd Like to F...)

Mistletoe Mistress

Joy to the Earl

Once Upon a Promise

Medieval Highland Menage series

Scandalous Passions (FFM)

Wicked Passions (MMF)

Tudor

His Forbidden Lady

One Forbidden Knight

Contemporary

Ladies First (erotic short stories)

ABOUT THE AUTHOR

NICOLA DAVIDSON worked for many years in communications and marketing as well as television and print journalism, but hasn't looked back since she decided writing erotic historical romance was infinitely more fun. When not chained to a computer she can be found ambling along one of New Zealand's beautiful beaches, cheering on the All Blacks rugby team, history geeking on the internet, or daydreaming. If this includes dessert—even better!

Keep up with Nicola's news on social media or her website www.nicola-davidson.com.

You can sign up for Nicola's newsletter here!

AN EDUCATION IN PLEASURE

EVA LEIGH

CHAPTER ONE

THE STRANGER HAD the most magnificent arse—and his cock was even better.

It was wrong to spy on the unknown man swimming in the pond, yet for all of Cecilia Holme's stern admonishments to herself, she couldn't stop watching him from the bordering shrubbery. He possessed a rangy, muscular body, and sunlight gleamed in droplets that clung to his olive skin. Dark hair curled on his head, on his chest, and in a nest between his legs—surrounding that selfsame magnificent cock. At rest, his penis was already impressively thick and long. She could only fantasize what it might look like hard and eager.

She squeezed her thighs together in a vain attempt to stop the sudden ache within her. Five years. It had been a full five years since she'd had a lover, and the only pleasure she'd received had been from her own hand. As a governess to a ducal family, she had to be sure to keep her character spotless, which meant no dalliances, and though she had missed intimacy, no one had truly tempted her to forsake her reputation—until now.

Who *was* this man? No one she recognized from any of the scores of servants who attended the Duke of Tarrington and his family here at

Tarrington House, and he wasn't from the nearby village. He had the hard, muscular build of a working man, so perhaps he was an itinerant laborer who had snuck onto the estate to make use of its pond.

This place had always been Cecilia's favorite spot to be alone, but she didn't mind just now sharing it with him.

A mad impulse seized her—remove her own clothing and slip into the water, join the stranger in its depths, press her body to his in a wordless urging. She would be like a mermaid or an undine, twining her limbs with his and discovering the feel of his skin, the taste of his mouth. And he would fall under her spell, yielding to her demands. They would fuck feverishly on the pond's bank, nothing but bodies and pleasure and wordless passion.

The man strode from the pond, carving trenches in the water with his taut calves as he climbed up the bank. Cecilia curled her hands at her sides, her fingers aching with the desire to glide over his sleek muscles, including his ridged abdomen and the sharp lines angling along his hips.

For all their devotion to the aesthetics of the classical world, none of her past lovers had ever looked like living statues. Not like this stranger.

She really should go. It wasn't kind to spy on someone, even though he was technically trespassing. Yet her feet staunchly refused to move, as if they knew she'd never again have the opportunity to see another man as beautiful as this, and wanted her to paint a thousand mental portraits to keep her company over the solitary years ahead.

He turned in her direction. Sunlight fell across him just as he pushed his wet hair from his face, revealing him more clearly.

Her stomach clenched.

She knew him.

Had, in fact, known him for five years.

The beautiful stranger in the pond was Owen, the ducal heir. No, he was no longer the heir. Now he was the duke. His father had passed away suddenly two weeks ago in a riding accident, and Owen had left his studies at Oxford to attend the burial in London. Cecilia had learned that the late duke had been interred with great ceremony at Westminster Abbey, as was fitting for so august a personage, but given the youth of her students, she had stayed with the girls here at Tarrington House.

Owen was due back at Tarrington House sometime this week. She'd no idea he would arrive today. The last time she'd seen him had been six months ago, and he'd been dressed, ensuring that his magnificent body wouldn't be a distraction. Ever since he'd come of age, she had been careful to give him a wide berth for her own protection. Not because she feared anything untoward from him. No, it was *herself* she didn't trust.

Here she was, ogling a man nine years her junior. Not only that, he was now her employer, which meant that staring lustfully at him was entirely wrong, entirely forbidden. Abiding by the boundaries between employer and employed had to be respected. Yet she couldn't stop herself.

A dog's bark snapped her to attention. Goblin, the family's black retriever, was extremely sweet and, unfortunately, quite attached to her, and her worst fears were realized when he came bounding up to her. The dog was allowed to roam freely around the grounds, and as he trotted toward her, he wagged his tail and panted with excitement before letting out another happy yelp.

"Shh, shh," she whispered, frantically petting Goblin in an attempt to quiet him.

Her stomach sank when she glanced at Owen and saw him looking right at her—or hopefully where the shrubbery hid her.

"Goblin," he called. "Here."

The dog bolted from the cover of the bushes, heading straight toward Owen. Perhaps he might think that Goblin was alone, and she could sneak away with no one the wiser.

"Hello?" Owen demanded. "Who's there?"

Damn. No help for it.

She crept out from her hiding place, careful not to look in his direction. "Hello," she said with an attempt at bright cheer. "I didn't see anything. Just heard someone bathing in the pond. Nothing more."

"I don't doubt you," he said, though he sounded surprised.

"Perhaps I saw a little," she admitted, still keeping her gaze averted. Then she realized that her comment might have another meaning, and she hastily added, "Nothing *little*, mind you. Everything was singularly . . . impressive."

For God's sake, she was thirty years old, decidedly *not* virginal, and here she was stammering like a girl straight from the nursery.

Owen made a little choked sound, and there was the sound of rustling. A moment later he said, "I've put my breeches on."

She exhaled and looked at him. He *was* wearing breeches now, but they hung low on his hips. He hadn't yet donned a shirt, so he was still appallingly gorgeous and damp as he stood on the grassy bank. How was it possible for anyone to have shoulders that wide?

Uninterested in the human drama unfolding, Goblin trotted off to the pond, nosing around the banks.

"Everything's been made ready for you," she said in the strained quiet. "The kitchen's been busy since yesterday, preparing all your favorite dishes, and your room was given a thorough airing out. The house is in need of a happy distraction."

He grimaced, which barely altered the perfection of his face. He'd inherited his Mediterranean looks from his Neapolitan mother, and resembled a Renaissance prince, with a generous nose and full mouth. His drying hair was as thick and dark as secrets. She'd become aware of his masculine beauty soon after he'd first come home from Oxford for the winter. Until that point, he'd been a gangly limbed yet good-looking boy, and she'd given him little consideration beyond the fact that he was the older brother of her two pupils. But over the course of his time at university, he'd become an impossibly handsome man.

It had been a relief when, at the conclusion of the holiday, he'd returned to university and she no longer had to ignore her base impulses. With him gone, she could return to her usual routine, untroubled by carnal thoughts of her employer's son.

He had been eighteen when she'd first noticed him as a man. That had been three years ago. Now he was twenty-one, yet that didn't do much to smother her shame. A woman of her age shouldn't lust for a man so much younger than herself. That didn't stop her from wanting, though.

"Suppose I ought to have gone straight in," he said with remorse. "I imagine they've been waiting for me. It's only..." He exhaled. "I wasn't quite ready to cross that threshold."

He reached for his shirt and, to her relief and dismay, pulled it over his head to cover his chest.

"I used to swim here all the time," he went on. "When I was a boy. A place to get away and pretend I wasn't the heir. It was only me and the water." His gaze slid away as though he were overcome with shyness. "Miss Holme."

"Your Grace." She curtsied. "My condolences on the loss of your father," she said solemnly. "He was a kind man, always taking your sisters on learning excursions and bringing them books. And he spoke highly of his son. He was quite proud of you, Your Grace."

Owen's gaze lowered, his lashes forming dark fans against his cheeks. "Difficult to believe he won't be there behind his desk, waiting to ask me about my studies. Giving me stones he collected from his travels. He thought it amusing that a duke's heir loved geology."

"'Some noblemen's sons love drink or chasing petticoats,'" she murmured, affecting the late duke's deep voice. "'My son loves rocks.'"

She and Owen shared a chuckle, but there was a catch in his throat.

"Damn, but I miss him," he said, his voice a rasp.

"Your Grace!" someone said in the distance. It sounded like Mr. Fernham, the estate manager. "Are you here, Your Grace?"

"I should let him know where I am." But instead of alerting the estate manager to his presence, he gathered the remainder of his clothing and ducked behind a hedge. Before he disappeared, he tipped his head to one side, indicating with a questioning look that she was free to accompany him into the shrubbery if she so desired.

"Mr. Fernham could use a bit of exercise, sitting behind a desk all day." Cecilia followed him into the protective shelter of the greenery.

Owen gave another grimace. "I've gone from studying the stratigraphic column for my own edification to evaluating the duchy's countless holdings, and a million other tasks that require my attention."

"I'm in search of insect specimens to show your sisters. Perhaps you can join me in locating a few." She gazed meaningfully toward the woods surrounding the pond.

Why had she suggested such a thing? She oughtn't be alone with him, and yet the impulse to help him had arisen instantly.

He shot her a grateful look. After he tugged on his boots, she quietly led him into the variegated shade of the forest. Wordlessly, they slipped between the trees as Mr. Fernham continued his quest for the duke, the estate manager's calls growing fainter as they moved away.

Once they'd put distance between themselves and the pond, she scanned the ground as though she truly wanted to comb the bracken for insects. As she did, a glance from the corner of her vision showed Owen donning his waistcoat and jacket, though he left both undone.

"What are we looking for?" he asked, pitching his voice low, likely to avoid attracting Mr. Fernham's attention.

"I don't expect you to actually collect beetles and grasshoppers, Your Grace."

He shrugged. "Better that than make important decisions regarding field drainage."

Before she knew what she was doing, she closed the distance between them and placed a hand on his forearm. She ignored the pulse of awareness that moved through her body, though the solid, strapping feel of him threatened to overturn all her good intentions.

"Having you home benefits more than the estate's tenants," she said softly. "Your family needs you."

He exhaled jaggedly. "My tutors and professors all said I was intelligent enough, but that was before I had dozens and dozens of things to consider all at the same time. I'm the sodding *duke*. Forgive my language, Miss Holme," he corrected quickly, shooting her a quick look.

She waved off his concern. "I was never *your* teacher. You can speak freely in front of me. Besides," she added wryly, "the austere exteriors of proper, modest governesses are merely fiction. The interior landscapes are much more complex."

It was as close to the truth as she could dare tell him. And it was still too much.

Belatedly, she realized that her hand remained on his arm. Much as she wanted to curl her fingers around him, she let go, and took a step back.

He stared at the place she had touched, and color rose in his cheeks.

How unexpected, to see him respond to her touch...

"Your Grace!" Mr. Fernham called, his voice nearing.

Silently, Cecilia and Owen pushed farther into the shelter of the trees.

"These are monumental changes for you," she murmured. "University student one day, and the next day, a duke."

He glanced toward the direction from which the estate manager's voice had come.

"There were expectations—my own expectations—that when people would call me *Your Grace*, I'd be a much older man. A man of experience." He gave a rueful laugh as he buttoned his waistcoat. "I'm hardly that."

"There will be people around you to help you learn what it means to be a duke. You won't be alone."

"So they told me in London." He dragged his hand through his hair, which formed beguiling, damp curls. "I left Oxford as soon as I heard Father was gone, and Mother and I laid him to rest in London. Then there were appointments—so many appointments with grim men who gave me stacks of books and papers I must commit to memory. It's all so sodding much."

His grief and bewilderment shot directly into her heart. "When all you want is a few more years with nothing but geology. A boy and his rocks."

"Your Grace," Mr. Fernham called. "Are you here?"

Owen tugged her behind a tree. His hands rested on her hips, holding her close as they both avoided the estate manager.

Her breath came quickly as she looked up into Owen's face and felt the length of his body pressed to hers.

A jolt ran through his frame. But he didn't release her.

Given her history, she ought to feel alarm. Instead, something keen and anticipatory gleamed within her. Was it possible...could she dare believe...? *Should* she?

The air between them thickened with awareness.

The wisest thing would be to walk away, ignoring her desire. There was nothing wrong with feeling desire. She had learned this years ago, just as she'd learned it was not always right to act on that hunger.

Yet Owen's pupils were large, and he looked decidedly *ravenous*.

Putting distance between them was impossible.

"Although," she whispered, "you're not a boy any longer. You've undergone quite a metamorphosis."

"So you've said. But some things about me haven't changed."

"Such as?"

His gaze met hers, slightly abashed. "I had been...I was... infatuated with you."

Stunned, she could only stare at him.

"Ever since you came to Tarrington House," he went on doggedly before falling silent.

His silence was familiar as she recalled their encounters over the past five years. They had been infrequent, since he'd been at Eton, and then Oxford, but the few times their paths had crossed, he had been extremely quiet in her presence. She'd reasoned that, as governess to his sisters, there was little for them to discuss, and she had likely escaped his notice. When she had overheard him alone with his family, he'd been far more open and expressive, teasing the girls and talking animatedly with his parents. Then she would enter the room, and he'd go mute.

Because she hadn't mattered to him, or so she'd believed. But now his silences took on another meaning.

Twigs cracked and leaves rustled nearby as Mr. Fernham continued his search. Cecilia clasped Owen's forearm and led him deeper into the forest, careful to keep her own footsteps as noiseless as possible.

Once they'd put more distance between themselves and the estate manager, she asked in a low voice, "You said you *had been* infatuated with me. It's not uncommon for young men to be indiscriminately aroused by any woman nearby. Those feelings change, however, as they age, and meet more women."

His cheeks reddened as he looked at her hand on his arm. "Even if my feelings persisted, it hardly matters. You're in my employ, and I can't abuse my power."

She exhaled in a peculiar mixture of relief and disappointment—there would be no repeat of the experience with her past employer, whose unwanted attentions had ultimately cost Cecilia her position. Yet she still desired Owen.

"When I was leaving for Eton," he continued, "my father gave me this."

From an inside pocket in his coat, he removed a coin and held it up. Its surface shone in a bright circle, as if its owner spent considerable time and effort maintaining its appearance.

"Can't buy much with a farthing," he murmured, looking at it contemplatively. "Almost nothing. A boiled sweet, or a small glass of beer, perhaps, but little of significance or use. Even so, my father said that I should keep it safe, and never spend it. As inconsequential as the farthing was to me, it meant a hell of a lot more to someone else, someone who wasn't the heir to a dukedom. Took me a while to understand his lesson, but as I safeguarded the farthing, I came to understand what it meant."

In her experience, aristocratic men seldom gave such consideration to the implications of their position, and it was even more rare for them to pass those lessons on to their sons. But the late duke had, and her respect for him increased, conjoined with sadness at his passing.

But what did all these signify to his son?

Her gaze remained on the coin between his fingers. "What did it mean?"

"Value is relative, and it's beholden to me not to abuse my status and harm someone with less power."

"An important lesson," she said softly.

"So it is." He flashed her a rueful look as he tucked the coin into his pocket.

Her life abroad had taught her many things, including the fact that the English were not always kind to themselves in their fervent pursuit of decorum. She had been amongst their number—a shopkeeper's daughter was expected to be well-behaved and modest, even if adherence to that role meant crushing the spirit.

It didn't have to be that way. So long as no one was hurt, it was a wonderful thing to be untethered from rigid codes of conduct.

Owen wasn't her pupil, but she could teach him that. She could show him how to free himself, how the bestowing of pleasure could be a gift given to oneself as well one's lover.

Gently, she said, "It might be confining, too."

His brow furrowed as he nodded slowly. "I've been so concerned about not doing harm that I daren't take a step for fear I might inadvertently hurt someone."

"There's caution," she said thoughtfully, "and then there's paralysis. Imposing such restrictions can be binding to the point of suffocation. I know this from experience. Is it possible that this held you back from voicing your infatuation with me?"

"I didn't think a sixteen-year-old boy would hold much appeal to a sophisticated woman like you. But," he added, "I was most troubled by the possibility I might harm you."

"And now? Do you still feel an attraction to me?"

His jaw worked, and with his neckcloth still undone, she could see the flex of muscle in his neck.

"I dare not say," he finally allowed.

"Because you fear that your interest would be unwelcome?"

He gave one clipped nod.

"You have been confined and restricted for a long time," she murmured in sympathy. "I know what it is like to feel so forcibly restrained. As though you're asphyxiating yourself to fulfill someone else's idea of what constitutes propriety. Right now, without anyone here to pass judgment, I would like you to be honest with me."

"My fascination with you burns as strongly as ever," he said, then clamped his lips together as if holding himself back from speaking more.

Though she made herself look calm without, within, she reeled from his revelation. All through her earlier fascination with him, she hadn't been alone. That pull between them continued to throb with life and potential—*dangerous* potential.

She had urged him to be candid ostensibly to ease the invisible iron bands that wrapped around him. There was another motive, however, one she dared not even think, yet it burned within her all the same.

"When you first met me, you likely knew little about sex."

He nodded, the movement stiff at first, but then loosening slightly. "You said I may be honest, and so I shall be. When you initially came to Tarrington Hall, I was a virgin."

"No longer. Now you're a man of experience."

A small, rueful snort escaped him. "You know so much about so many things, but not this. Men of experience don't turn into wordless oafs in the presence of women. They know how to say the right things, how to flatter and seduce."

"Which you do not," she surmised. His candor humbled her, even as she was astonished at what he revealed.

"That farthing is always in my pocket, reminding me of my father's lesson. It's there now, in here"—he patted the place in his coat that held the coin—"and here." He tapped his finger against his temple.

"Confining you," she said.

"Even if I were a practiced rake," he went on, "none of those other women are you."

"I—" She had no answer to this. All this time, as she'd fought against her own wicked needs, he'd had his own secret, one in which *she* had been his focus.

"How many women have you taken to bed?" she asked, even as her heart thudded so hard it was a struggle to speak calmly.

"Two." He blushed furiously as he spoke.

Her mouth went dry, and she could only stare at him. Never had she believed she would have this conversation with him, and certainly not in this context, when she had been salivating over his naked body moments earlier—in fact, she was *still* ogling him clothed. The beat of desire continued to pulse through her as they stood within touching distance.

"With your looks, I would have believed you've had more than two lovers. Did something keep you from bringing more people to your bed?"

"I had a hope," he said reservedly. At her prompting look, he explained, "A distant, foolish hope that *you* would be the one to teach me about sex."

A short, stunned laugh burst from her. "I'm not certain if I should be offended by your presumption. Do you think so little of me?"

His eyes darkened. "Impossible for me to overstate my opinion of you."

She brought her hand to her own throat, her fingers light against her skin, but even this gentle touch roused her sensitized body. "I'd no idea. All this time, I didn't know."

"I remember meeting you when I was home for the winter holiday," he said, his voice low. "You wore a gray dress, as if you were trying to fade into the background. Yet on no account could you fade away to me. I'd come into the parlor and you were laughing with my sisters, and I'd never seen anyone so abundant with life. You glowed with it—all I wanted was to soak you into me, to be inside you."

As he spoke, her breath came faster, and her banked hunger flared brightly. Yet she had to be honest with him.

"I've no recollection of that moment." Thankfully, she hadn't become attuned to him until later.

His laugh was rueful. "Why would you? I went mute as a piece of shale, and hardly spoke more than three words at a time in your presence. Didn't stop me from staring after you, though. From that day forward, I was fascinated by you."

"It was you," she said suddenly.

He looked at her with alarm. "What was me?"

"I had a collection of books. Erotic books. One night I discovered one of them had gone missing. I had always suspected that a maid had nicked it but..." She stared at him. "You took it."

"I—" He cleared his throat, and he shifted from foot to foot. "I snuck into your room, hungry just to see where you slept. And I found those books." A pink stain spread across his cheeks—from embarrassment, or arousal, or both. "I did filch one."

She sucked in a breath, caught on the blades of stunned need.

"That's when I knew," he said hoarsely, "there was more to you than the cool, learned Miss Holme. You possessed wisdom, experience, passion. And a mouth that I desperately wanted to taste. That's when I began to fantasize about what it would be like to have that wisdom, experience, and passion trained on me."

He shook his head. "This is madness, to tell you this, when I haven't a hope in hell that you could ever think of me in that way."

"Owen," she rasped. The whole of her body was hot and shivering, as if she had a fever, and the need to press herself against him trembled through her limbs.

The wisest thing would be to walk away. End this tortuous conversation, head quickly back to her narrow room, make herself come, and go about her life as if none of this had ever happened. She hadn't seen his marvelous body, or heard him confess his desire for her, or begun to entertain the mad, entirely *wrong* idea that she should act on her hunger for him.

And yet...

Here they were, in the shade of the woods, away from the house and all the staid, strict rules it upheld. At her urging, he'd been open with her, confessing his desire. In this liminal space, for this brief moment, they could be fully themselves. From her own experience, and from communication with other governesses, she knew that men of the family often leveraged their power to force themselves on their female staff. Owen had done none of this, even as he wrestled with his attraction to her.

She could repay his trustworthiness and honesty with her own.

"I noticed you," she said breathlessly, "your first winter home from Oxford. I had...thoughts, desires I shouldn't have. That didn't stop me from wishing and wanting. I did then. I do now."

His thick, dark eyebrows rose. Clearly, her revelation surprised him, but she was equally stunned at her own candor.

She swayed closer, and as he did so too, the distance between them narrowed to inches until the heat of his skin pervaded her. His mouth was tempting, and she could not look away.

"If you wish," she went on, still struggling to take in air, "for the next few moments, these woods will be our classroom."

"What will you teach me?" His gaze went dark, and his shyness dropped away.

"The fine art of kissing."

CHAPTER TWO

HIS LIPS PARTED, and his eyes widened.

"I say," Mr. Fernham called. "Your Grace! Dash it, where is he?"

Owen looked toward where the estate manager's voice had sounded, then held out his hand to her. She threaded her fingers with his and together they wove deeper into the forest.

A massive oak offered refuge, with a hollow in the base of its wide trunk. She stepped into its shelter with Owen, thick roots spreading around their feet like jungle serpents.

He faced her, color darkening his cheeks. Then his lids lowered, and he said hoarsely, "Tell me what I need to do."

The simplicity of that request, combined with his deep, rumbling voice, arrowed between Cecilia's legs, centering in her quim.

"Put your hand on my waist," she murmured.

In silent agreement, they stepped nearer until there was no space between them. Her breasts brushed against his chest. His torso was hard as iron, making her bite back a moan at the sensation. There was so much strength and vitality within him—he all but radiated with it.

He obliged, and despite her gown and stays and shift, the heat of him pierced her skin delectably. "Cup your other hand against the back of my head."

His broad palm cradled her, rubbing the strands of her hair, holding her as though she were the most extraordinary creature that ever existed. She slid her arms around his shoulders.

Their breath mingled, humid and eager. The world was so small now, containing them alone and existing only in the minute space between their lips. Her pulse raced as he simply held her. She was balanced on the edge of madness. Once this line was crossed, there would be no going back. There was nothing to blame but her own need, yet she could not stop herself from lifting on her toes, bringing her mouth to his.

Arousal climbed higher as he made a low sound of pleasure—it was the sound a man might make when a long-cherished dream became reality.

"Put your lips on mine," she whispered. "But take your time. Go slow. Learn and discover."

He rubbed his mouth against hers, but soon grew bolder as the exploration shifted into a kiss. It took less than a heartbeat for him to learn what she liked and how she liked it, his need eclipsing any uncertainty he might have had. They drew on each other as their mouths opened, and she touched her tongue to his. He seemed to understand her cue, slicking his own tongue into her. With each stroke, sensation echoed in her breasts and between her legs.

"For a novice," she gasped between kisses, "you're exceptionally talented."

His smile flashed, both shy and proud.

"Surely you've practiced," she whispered.

Beneath her hands, his shoulders lifted. "The practice was only to make certain I got *this* right. I want—" His jaw tightened.

"Tell me what you want," she urged.

"To touch you." He brought his hand up from her waist to hover above the underside of her breast. "Been aching to know what you feel like."

"No need to imagine." She reached down and pressed his palm against her. Long fingers almost completely covered her breast.

He gave another growl and closed his eyes. A shudder moved along his body, resounding in hers. "God, yes."

"Stroke me," she breathed. "My nipple...pinch it."

When he did as she said, the pleasure was so acute, her knees buckled. But he held her snug against him, supporting her.

"Put your thigh between my legs," she breathed. "Rub against my mound—it's where I need you most."

He rumbled as he did so, lodging between her legs and creating impeccable friction.

Instinct seemed to guide him as he bent his head and kissed her again, the stroke of his tongue timed with flicking and pinching her nipple. She gripped his shoulders hard, determined to keep herself upright. It was all she could do to keep from grinding on his thigh in a frantic attempt to soothe the ache building there.

"Tell me," she gasped, "what you need. I want to hear it."

"Words are...difficult." His breath sawed in and out.

"Then show me."

There was a brief pause, and then he took one of her hands and dragged it down his torso. She luxuriated in the feel of him, his body solid and hard beneath his clothing, taut with power. He kept going, taking her hand along his abdomen, then lower, to the straining length of his cock. At the touch of her hand on him, they both hissed in pleasure. Gently, she squeezed his shaft, and the cords of his neck stood out as he threw back his head to groan.

"Know what I was thinking when I saw you bathing in the pond?" she murmured.

"I've wanted to be inside your head for years," he said shakily.

"Nothing but admiration," she whispered against his lips. "Especially for *this*." She stroked him through his breeches. "What are you doing with such a marvelous cock?"

"It's been waiting for you. *I've* been waiting for you."

His words were far too intimate, as though they were more than two bodies seeking pleasure—there was no room for anything beyond this moment. Lust was less complicated, less dangerous. So she gripped his shaft, caressing him, reveling in his sounds of ecstasy.

"Is this better than your own hand?" she asked throatily.

"Much better than anything I've ever dreamt," he said in a low, rough voice.

As she stroked him, he moved his thigh to again rub against her quim. The first golden filaments of release began to gather, and she surged toward them. It had been so long since anyone other than herself had made her come—yet she knew that the release would be all the greater, more devastating, because *he* was the one bringing her over the edge, and she had wanted him for so long.

There were several sets of footsteps nearby, and the rustling of leaves. Damned Mr. Fernham was still searching, and now he had someone with him.

"The groom said he arrived on horseback," a girl said—it was Ellie, one of her pupils. "But he didn't come in the house."

"Where'd he go?" her sister Maria demanded. "I don't want to wait another minute to see him."

"Nash in the stables said he went in this direction," Ellie said. "He's got to be here somewhere. Maybe Goblin can find him—where's Owen, boy?"

At once, Cecilia and Owen broke apart.

After smoothing her hair as best she could, she crossed her arms over her chest to cover her hardened nipples.

"We cannot hide here," Cecilia whispered.

He nodded, his expression tight.

They left the shelter of the oak and headed toward the sounds of Maria and Ellie. The girls stood in a small clearing in the midst of the trees, the dog trotting around and nosing at the underbrush.

"Owen!" Ellie cried out. "You're here!"

Cecilia pasted on a smile—glancing over, she saw Owen do the same— as they approached his sisters. The two girls beamed at their older brother, their voices overlapping as they peppered him with questions.

"When did you get back?" Maria demanded. She was thirteen, approaching maturity but sometimes very much a child. Since her father's death, she'd needed to sleep in a cot beside her mother's bed. Cecilia's heart ached for the girl.

"Which horse did you take?" Ellie asked. At eleven, she was currently fascinated with anything involving horses or murder. She loved a good ghastly tale. And yet her grief over her father manifested in the way she clung to her sister.

"Have you missed us *terribly*?" Maria pressed, tugging on his sleeve.

Fortunately, neither of her pupils seemed to observe Cecilia, which gave her a moment to calm her frustrated, throbbing body.

"To answer your interrogation, I arrived within the past hour, I rode Orion, and I was beside myself with missing both of you ducklings."

"Why did you not come straight in?" Ellie wondered.

Owen's gaze met Cecilia's. She gave her head the slightest shake, though she had little fear that he'd blurt to his sisters that he'd been moments away from making their governess come.

"I had a bathe," he said lightly, "and afterward Miss Holme happened by, and she wanted to find some insects for your lessons, so I helped her."

"Oh, Miss Holme!" Maria turned toward her. Thankfully, she didn't seem to notice that their governess's coiffure was slightly mussed.

"Isn't it wonderful that Owen has come home?" Maria asked.

"Quite wonderful," Cecilia answered as brightly as she could. "I know how much you've been looking forward to seeing your brother again."

Ellie fussed with the jet buttons on her black mourning dress. When the sisters had first put on their somber clothing, they had wept, missing their father, longing for their brother. Cecilia had comforted them both, soothing them with assurances that Owen would be returning soon.

Only a few minutes ago, she'd fondled his cock as he caressed her breasts.

Shame washed through her. Dear Lord, what was wrong with her, that she would completely lose control of herself and drown in her lust for a man nine years younger? A man who was, as he'd said, her employer. There were so many ways that indulging in her desire for him could lead to disaster. She should have learned from her past, but no, she'd been heedless of everything but wanting him.

There was freeing oneself from the cage of propriety, and then there was utter recklessness.

For as long as she could remember, Cecilia had possessed a ferocious sexual appetite, but short of marriage, sating that appetite had been impossible. There had been no man that had tempted her to trade her freedom for access to cock.

If she had stayed in her small town, her path would have been set. Marriage to a man who would likely take over her father's shop, then she would become a mother, and creep from middle age to dotage with barely any life experience beyond the mile marker at the edge of town.

Instead, wanting more for herself, she'd taken a position as a governess to a couple who lived on the Continent.

When she had been abroad, employed by Sir Kenneth and Lady Juliet Whelan, the unconventional, broadminded couple had encouraged her to pursue her own amours. Cecilia been surprised there was even a possibility that an unwedded woman could take a man to her bed. Lady Juliet had explained what was required to prevent pregnancy—as well as pointed out the hypocrisy in permitting men the freedom to pursue their sexual desires, while women were shamed for it.

With that knowledge, Cecilia had truly learned what it was to be fully in command of herself, taking lovers from the Whelans' circle of similarly open-minded people. She'd done so with the gusto of a woman finally liberated from an unreasonable double standard.

But she was in England now, not the Continent. Things were quite different here. And Owen was her employer. She did not know if he would abuse his power, as Sir Kenneth ultimately had, but she could not take that chance.

Ellie chirped, "Mother's inside and she has told Cook to prepare all your favorites for supper. Chicken pie, and roast asparagus, and strawberry flummery."

"My mouth's watering," Owen answered, but he looked at Cecilia as he spoke.

In response, Cecilia's stomach leapt. It didn't seem to matter how much she lectured herself, she still wanted him—and he wanted her. Resisting that pull would take all her strength.

Ellie's recitation of the menu reminded Cecilia that she hadn't shared a meal with Owen. Before their father's passing, the girls took their meals in the nursery, with Cecilia joining them. But since the late duke's death, the duchess did not want to sup alone, and so her daughters and Cecilia ate with her in the dining room.

"No more lessons for today, Miss Maria, Miss Ellie," she said.

"Surely you could find time for another lesson." A blush tinted Owen's cheeks as he spoke.

Ellie and Maria groaned, clearly uninterested in more schoolwork. Cecilia took no offense at their reluctance. Who wanted to spend more time learning when the day was fine, and their brother was home?

Of course, the kind of lesson their brother referred to was a very different sort.

Cecilia pasted on another smile. "Spend as much time as you want with your brother. I'll see you tomorrow."

She rushed away to the house before she said or did something incredibly foolish—like instruct Owen on how to finish what they had started.

CHAPTER THREE

OWEN SLAMMED an accounting ledger shut and dug his hands into his hair. The room's walls loomed over him, capturing him, confining him. Air was scarce, and he fought to draw it into his lungs.

He used to love being in his father's study. The rows and rows of book-laden shelves promised adulthood, while the smell of leather and paper was redolent of maturity. The large and heavy mahogany desk was where all knowledge concentrated, helmed by his father—who, to Owen's young mind, was a man of infinite comprehension and wisdom.

The late duke hadn't been much older than Owen when he'd married Owen's mother, and within two years of that marriage, became a father. Of course, when Owen's father had married, he hadn't yet inherited the duchy, so there had been more time to ease into the role and learn from Owen's grandfather what was expected of him.

If only there had been more time with Father. If only the late duke hadn't gone riding alone that day, so someone could have been there when he'd fallen from his horse. They could have fetched a physician in time. If only. If only.

Owen touched the black band on his sleeve as if he could somehow touch his father's hand once more, but all he felt was the strip of crepe.

His attempt to temporarily escape the weight of responsibility and grief yesterday had become something far more surprising and wonderful than anything he had a right to feel.

Miss Holme had encouraged him to release the tether of propriety that kept him pinned in place. Still, he would have said nothing had he not sensed her attraction to him. The way her gaze remained on his body, his mouth. How her touch had lingered on him.

He had been prepared to immediately apologize to her for harboring such thoughts and laying them bare before her. Instead, the most remarkable thing had happened. She admitted her own attraction to him.

He'd been granted one of his deepest, most cherished wishes.

To kiss Miss Holme. Touch her. Feel her become aroused *for him*.

His body responded at once to the memory of her. She'd guided him and he had been her eager student, discovering things she desired. And as he had made those discoveries, he'd felt something within himself that he hadn't anticipated—*he* could give her pleasure. It was intoxicating and heady, and he craved more of it, even as it unsettled him.

He'd had to frig himself three times last night as he relived those moments with her in the woods. He had pumped his hand furiously on his cock over and over. It hadn't been enough, but at the least, he'd been able to dull the gleaming edge of his hunger, and managed to tumble into a few hours of sleep.

For five years, he'd fantasized hearing her say that she desired him. The reality had far outpaced the dream, especially seeing the desire in her hazel eyes. Desire for *him*. Fate had bestowed a cruel sort of torment, to grant him this long-held hope in the midst of his grief and confusion. But she'd given him something else besides physical pleasure, and by turning toward their shared hunger, she had eased the crushing weight of his loss.

His fever for more broke under the chill of reality. What happened at the pond could never happen again.

He hadn't told Miss Holme everything about his father's farthing. It had come with another warning: a duke's personal life was *everyone's* business. With the title came tremendous responsibility, and that included his romantic affairs. Many men of rank abused their female servants and social inferiors. Some of those aristocrats believed it was their right to do so. But his father insisted that being the Duke of Tarrington carried *more* accountability, not less. As the duke, Owen could not, would not, hurt anyone in his employ—especially women.

That included his sisters' governess. He had known it yesterday, but desire had overridden sense. In the aftermath, he'd faced the truth that he'd done something terribly wrong, and had to make it right.

A tap sounded at the door.

"Enter," Owen said, hoping he sounded properly ducal.

Vale, the butler, appeared. "You asked me to remind you that Mr. Leaton and Mr. Sulham would be arriving by this afternoon, Your Grace."

Owen glanced toward the clock. It was just after eleven in the morning. He'd spent the hours since breakfast reviewing the mountains of paperwork requiring his attention in preparation for meetings with Leaton and Sulham. They were part of his army of men of business, and had met Owen already in London. Those had been only for preliminary discussions.

I'm just a geologist, he wanted to shout.

"Very good, Vale," he said. "How is my mother?"

"She is well, Your Grace. Currently she is in her parlor, reviewing correspondence, I believe. Would you care for me to summon Her Grace?"

"That won't be necessary." Then, "My sisters?"

"Having lessons, Your Grace. Though I believe Miss Holme usually permits them to take some exercise in the hour before luncheon."

That could be right now. "Does Miss Holme usually take exercise with them?"

"On occasion, Your Grace. Other times, she remains in the schoolroom and plans her lessons for the afternoon and following day."

A fine film of sweat coated Owen's back, and his shirt clung to his skin. He should not appear too eager, not where the governess was concerned. "I'll want Orion saddled once Mr. Leaton and Mr. Sulham and I have concluded for the day."

"Yes, Your Grace."

"That will be all, Vale," Owen said.

The butler bowed and retreated, leaving Owen alone again in the study.

He glanced at the desk, with its towers of ledgers, letters, and other papers. The wisest, most ducal thing to do would be to sit himself down and apply himself to a serious and studious examination of all the documents.

The need to simply *see* Miss Holme drummed through him, urging him toward the door. Scenes from yesterday reverberated in his mind and body. The feel of her in his arms. Her hands upon his skin. The taste of her mouth. The assured, instructive words she'd spoken, guiding him in the ways to bring her pleasure. Even now, he shuddered with need.

Miss Holme had pulled the truth from him and revealed her own. She'd said that she wanted him—yet full consent was not possible if she was in his employ.

The thought of forcing her into doing *anything* churned in his stomach. He'd sooner tear the flesh from his body than make her act against her will.

He ought to ask for her forgiveness. He had to. But that wasn't enough. She needed to know that he'd put his mother in charge of Miss Holme's employment to ensure the governess's security.

His mother had thought it odd, but he'd explained that as the new duke with new demands on his time, he would not be able to devote adequate attention to his sisters' education. Fortunately, his mother had agreed.

Suddenly, he was in the corridor, and then up the stairs, climbing higher and higher to the schoolroom on the second story. On the way, he passed a few servants, who bowed or curtsied, reminding him that he was the master of this home. The care and protection of all his staff and tenants fell to him, and he'd never abuse that.

He nearly turned around to return to the study. Yet he could simply poke his head into the schoolroom, talk briefly with Miss Holme, offer his apologies, and then go back to the tasks that required his attention.

The door to the schoolroom stood open, revealing a small but sunlit chamber that contained two desks for students, and a larger desk for the instructor. Miss Holme sat at it now, the sunshine turning her light brown hair into a soft wheaten color that gleamed. She wrote in a notebook as she studied a volume, her pen scratching pleasantly as it moved across the pages.

For the briefest moment, he permitted himself the pleasure of watching her, unobserved. She had a habit of rubbing her bottom lip when she contemplated something—the gesture had fascinated him as a boy and enthralled him as a man. He could study her face forever, following the angular lines of her cheekbones, learning the shaped of her eyebrows lowered in thought, skimming his gaze across her wide mouth. His gaze went lower. Her figure was abundant—now he knew what her breasts felt like, as well as the generous span of her hips.

He squeezed his eyes shut as he took several steadying breaths. At this rate, he'd come barreling into the schoolroom with a raging erection, and that went against his purpose for being here.

Despite his attempts to calm himself, he must have made some small noise, because she looked up from her book and spotted him hovering in the doorway.

The pleasure on her face made his own heart spin like a top. But she seemed to catch herself and schooled her expression into something far more reserved. He wasn't certain how to interpret this change, so he made his own countenance friendly but not excessively intimate.

"Your Grace," she said, rising.

"I'm not used to it." He moved farther into the room, glad his cock-stand had subsided. "Hearing you call me *Your Grace.*"

"Everyone else does," she noted.

"It sounds different on your lips."

Their gazes held at the word *lips.*

Uncertain, he moved toward the bookshelves and ran his finger across the spines. "I don't recognize all these titles. They're different from the ones my tutor had me read." He pulled out one of the books and regarded its cover. "*A Guide to Mathematics For Inquisitive Girls.*"

She pushed her chair back. He felt her presence draw nearer and nearer until she stood beside him. Other than yesterday, it was the closest they had ever been to each other, and he could smell soap and camellia flowers warmed by her skin. It was remarkable that his hand didn't shake as he held the book up for her inspection.

"That one is a particular favorite of Maria's," she murmured. "She will make some important discoveries in that field one day."

"There's a difference between how girls and boys should be educated about mathematics?"

"For this particular text, no. I took pains to find the books that did not condescend to its readers. But some other treatises have no such scruples. They discuss things such as mathematics within a *domestic* framework."

"The look on your face shows precisely what you think of such peda-gogical approaches," he said wryly.

She smiled at him, and it shot through him, gleaming like metallic veins through stone. "I've been employed as a governess long enough to know what particular methodologies I prefer, and which yield the best results. Particularly in my female students."

He could only nod, too unsteady from having her so near. His attention was fixed on the delicate bend where her neck met her shoulder—at present modestly covered by a woolen shawl, yet the fabric gently draped in such a way that he could readily imagine the sweet, sensuous curve. His fingers twitched with the desire to pull back the soft cloth and press his mouth to the revealed skin.

He needed to speak to her, but words slipped from his mind, and he was caught in the current of his old hunger for her—now sharper than ever after his first taste.

Awareness of his own status caged him, as it had since his father had given him the farthing. Every day for the past ten years, the coin sat in his inside coat pocket, reminding him that he had to recognize and honor his responsibilities.

He hated the thought of hurting anyone—especially Miss Holme.

"It's fortunate that you've come to the schoolroom," she said.

He snapped back into the present moment. "How so?"

"We've something to discuss, you and I." Her tone betrayed nothing, but that didn't stop his heart from pounding, or his palms from growing damp.

After clearing his throat, he said, "We do." He dragged in a breath, preparing to humble himself before her, but she spoke before he could.

"The girls' schooling," she said crisply. "As head of the household, it's now on you to make decisions regarding your sisters' education. Her Grace deferred to your father, so the responsibility falls to you."

He exhaled, relieved it didn't sound too serrated. "Whatever it is you have been doing—mathematics for inquisitive girls—you can continue on as you have. I trust you."

She laughed, a short, ironic sound. "Surprising that you'd trust me, given what I did at the pond yesterday."

He could immediately taste her, feel her, and this time when he let out a breath, it came out rough and serrated. Still, he could not ignore what she said, or what that meant.

"It is not an equal distribution of fault," he insisted. "So long as you are in my employ, the culpability is completely mine."

"Dukes are never culpable," she murmured drily.

"This one is," he said. "And you should know that your position as governess to my sisters is secure. I've given my mother complete control over your employment. I told her I would be too preoccupied with my new duties to be at all useful in the direction of their education. She was initially reluctant, but ultimately, she agreed to accept the responsibility. Anything I say to her regarding you or your work has no bearing on the security of your position."

Miss Holme inhaled sharply, and her eyes went wide in surprise. "I'd no idea."

"She and I conversed yesterday evening. I came up to the schoolroom today to tell you. And to apologize."

He steadied himself. "I didn't want you to think that your employment was at risk because of yesterday. You're safe. You will always be safe here." The farthing seemed to burn in his pocket as he spoke.

"Governesses surely lead precarious lives," he continued lowly, "as women who earn their livelihoods far from home, vulnerable to employers and..." He swallowed. "Predatory men. But I will not be one of those men."

He held his breath as she regarded him. She was in so many ways an enigma—one that continued to fascinate him, but he would hold true to his resolve not to hurt her.

Her chest rose and fell, and she seemed to wrestle with something. Finally, when he was on the verge of bolting, she asked, "Do you realize what you've done by taking me out of your employ?"

"Protected you," he answered. "That was my intention. Was that not the result?"

"The result," she said, taking a step toward him, "is that you've opened the door for more."

Hope surged like a high tide. "More. Between us."

She inclined her head, regal.

But he needed to hear the words. "Is that what you desire?"

"Desire is a wayward thing. It never obeys, the obstinate creature, and no matter how I command it, desire has a strong will of its own." A corner of her mouth lifted. "For so many reasons, I shouldn't want you. Yet I do, God help me. The idea of giving you an education in pleasure is... exquisite." Her words were breathless, her cheeks were flushed.

"An education..." He flexed his hands. "Then I will be your student." Just as he'd been yesterday in the woods. This time there would be no interruptions, no distractions. No imbalance. Only her, instructing him and giving knowledge.

She walked to the entrance to the schoolroom, shut the door, and turned the key in the lock.

The sound shot straight to his cock.

Her finger trembling, she pointed to one of the student desks. "Sit there for your first lesson."

He rushed to sit quickly. It was a relief to take a seat because he was certain either his legs would give out or they'd turn into Roman candles and shoot him into the air.

"Do I take notes?" he asked. Excitement throbbed as loud as his heart-beat in his ears. He had not believed he could ever touch her again. Yet he would, and at her urging—freed from the constraints of *should* and *should not*.

Her chuckle was low as she moved to drape her shawl on a nearby chair, then stood in front of the desk. "This must all be committed to memory."

"I'm a most attentive student."

"To begin with, sex is more than simply sticking your cock into some-one." She lifted a brow. "But you've read one of my books—this shouldn't come as a revelation."

"Not quite a surprise," he admitted, aroused beyond belief that they should be here, in this room where he'd once had his boyhood lessons. Now he would receive a man's lessons.

She crossed her arms over her chest. "You said you've gone to bed with two women."

He was riveted by the sight of her full breasts swelling against the neckline of her gown.

"At Oxford, there are...courtesans who frequent the students' rooms." He knew nothing of flirtation or seduction.

"How involved were you?" she asked. "Did you do anything else besides put your cock in them?"

His face heated. "It was rather fast..."

"So you didn't touch their quims? Or even look at what lay between their legs?"

His arousal battled with embarrassment, a mystifying combination. "As I said, it was done quickly and with a minimum of...of anything additional."

He tried to read her expression to see if she was in some way disappointed in him for his utter lack of finesse. Yet if anything, she looked slightly pleased.

She moved to stand beside the desk, then bent and kissed him. He responded at once, relearning the taste of her, cupping his hands around her jaw. Remembering that she enjoyed it when he'd stroked his tongue against hers, he did it again. She moaned into his mouth, making his body clench in need and pleasure. Her fingers wove into his hair.

The kiss built, grew deeper. Something huge and hungry grew within him, demanding more, and his grip on her tightened—before he made himself loosen his hold. He couldn't give into that internal creature, the one that craved dominion. This was her lesson to lead.

She broke the kiss and straightened before settling her arse on the wooden top. To his astonishment, she swung around to sit facing him, her legs bracketing him.

"Next part of the lesson," she said, voice throaty.

He could not look away as she took handfuls of her skirts and began to raise them, uncovering her calves, knees, and thighs. Finally, her skirts bunched around her waist.

Miss Holme's quim was right in front of him, a triangle of darker brown hair curling above the most gorgeous pink slit. Already, a light sheen of moisture glossed her lips, and his nostrils flared as he caught the scent of her desire.

Of its own volition, his hand reached for her.

She swatted it away, smiling as she did so. "Not yet. You need to learn the geography before you go exploring."

"Show me." His cock was as hard as it had ever been, so upright it pained him, but he leaned into the ache as the sensation merged into something altogether new and wonderful.

She brought her hand up to stroke between the outer lips and made a soft gasp. He reveled in the fact that she was as aroused as he was.

"Touching this part is nice," she said, "but what's within is even better."

Her fingers dipped down to spread herself, revealing luscious, slick flesh, including the raised bud. His mouth watered to see this part of her, so beautiful, and so real.

"Sometimes," she murmured, "I like to be touched here with rough authority, but especially at the beginning, I need gentleness. I like the lips stroked, yet I'm even more sensitive at my opening, and on my clitoris. Watch me."

He nodded mutely. He couldn't have looked away if the house burned down around him.

She caressed and rubbed herself, her breath coming faster and faster, especially when her fingertips circled her bud. He kept thinking he couldn't be more aroused, but watching her touch herself turned his need into a raging fever burning through him. He studied her movements, carving them into his heart so that if—when—the time came for him to touch her, he could do it exactly the way she wanted.

"Now you," she gasped, taking her hand away.

His hand shook as he brought it up to her quim. The first brush of his fingers against her damp, tender flesh made him growl, and her moan.

"Christ," he said through gritted teeth. He clamped down on his own need to free his cock and pump himself to a fast, hard climax.

He touched her, stroking, caressing, paying careful attention to her clitoris and her opening, just as she'd instructed. Whatever he did clearly pleased her, because her eyes closed, her head fell back, and the points of her nipples stood out in relief beneath the fabric of her bodice.

"God, Owen." She canted her hips, giving him even more access to her. "Just like that. But I want more. I want you to fuck me with your fingers."

"Yes." He'd read about it, and if he couldn't have his cock in her right now, he could give her that.

"Slide your finger into me, following the curve of my body."

He did so, and was immediately surrounded by her slick, hot passage. Nothing in the world felt as silken. He added a second finger, and she cried out—but when he moved to pull away, afraid that he'd hurt her, she stayed his hand.

"It's good," she gasped. "It's good. There's a place inside me, a swollen spot. Can you feel it?"

"This," he said, gliding his fingers over it. In response, her breathing came even faster, quick and shallow. Emboldened, he stroked his finger in and out of her, and she pumped her hips against him.

"Put your mouth on me," she urged.

He squeezed his eyes shut. Ever since he'd read about the act, he'd wanted to do it, and now he could—and with *her*.

Owen lowered his head and, after inhaling her fragrance, slid his tongue along her folds. She was slick and delicate, and her musky, rich taste filled him, making him dizzy with pleasure.

"Yes, yes," she panted. "Suck my clitoris between your lips."

He did as she instructed, loving the feel of her sensitive, swollen flesh against his mouth. All the while, he continued to fuck her with his fingers.

"How do I taste?" she gasped.

"Spiced and sweet." His words were torn from somewhere deep within him. "Delicious."

His words seemed to drive her over the edge, and her body bowed up. She clamped her hand over her mouth, muting her cry of release.

That should have satisfied him, but the thing within him burned for more.

Was this what she wanted? Was this what *he* wanted, to give free rein to the ravenous beast? Would he lose himself if he did set it free?

"Keep going," she urged. "No hesitation. Give in to what you want. *Do what you want to me.*"

Untethered, he went on plunging his fingers into her. Impulse guided him to use the tip of his tongue to flick her clitoris until she went taut with another orgasm, and another. Watching her face as it twisted in ecstasy was the most beautiful thing he'd ever witnessed.

She rested a limp hand on his head, but had enough strength to lightly urge him back. He stopped at once, resting his own shaking hands on her trembling thighs.

"You've a...natural...talent," she murmured. Her eyelids were heavy, her expression one of profound satisfaction.

"Is it wrong to feel pride?" he whispered. "Pride in knowing that *I* have been the one to help you feel good?"

She lifted a brow. "The kind of pride that makes a man go boasting to his friends?"

"God, no." The idea appalled him. "This is for us alone."

Her smile was like honey warmed by the sun. "A bit of conceit is good for everyone. And you've earned it."

Miss Holme's praise made his chest swell with gratification. He stroked his hands along the silk of her legs.

"I want to kiss you again," he said.

She leaned down and put her mouth on his. He would have thought the taste of her still on his lips might have repelled her, but no, she drank from him deeply. Reaching up, he cradled the side of her jaw with his palm, running his thumb back and forth over the down along her cheek.

"Our lesson isn't done," she murmured against his mouth. "You've been such a very good student. I think you've earned a special privilege."

He had no idea what sort of privilege she meant, but the throaty note in her voice made his throbbing cock jerk in response.

"Tell me what I need to do."

"Lean against the front of my desk," she said in a low but firm command.

He was on his feet in an instant, though moving around while sporting a furious erection made him slightly less agile. As he took his place, planting his arse on the edge of the desk, he smiled to see how unsteadily she got to her feet, and how her hands continued to tremble as she smoothed her skirts.

She went to a wooden chest and opened it. He knew that chest, since it contained several hornbooks and an out-of-date globe which had been used to teach *his* father geography. The world had changed quite a bit since then—God knew that the world had completely altered for Owen within the last thirty minutes.

From the chest, she removed a plaid wool blanket, which she folded into a neat square.

"What's that for?" he asked while she set the blanket on the floor by his feet.

Her lips quirked. "You're a clever man. I'm sure you can hazard a guess." Her gaze flicked to the tented front of his breeches.

Shock and desire tore through him like a seismic event. He growled, "Yes."

"Darling boy," Cecilia said, leaning close for a kiss.

"Not a boy," he rumbled into her mouth. "A man."

"Foolish of me not to remember that." She palmed his cock through his buckskins, and his eyes rolled back. "I have abundant evidence right here."

She bent and nuzzled her face against the length of his erection. Power coursed through her to hear him hiss in pleasure.

"Have you ever had this before?" she murmured.

He shook his head. "Read about it."

God, how she adored leading him on this journey. When she had taken her first lover years ago, she had been the one without experience, learning at the hands and mouth of a man who made his living as a sculptor. Fortunately, Georges had been gentle and patient, explaining the mysteries of desire and bodies. Not all of her lovers since had been as careful or attentive to her needs. Not all of them had respected her as a person, and she had vowed she would take men to her bed only when *she* desired it. There was strength in her sexuality, and she claimed all of that for herself.

She could guide Owen and show him that one could be fully in command and still respect the needs of their partner.

"What did you read?" she asked him.

"That it doesn't just feel good, but it also makes a man feel powerful."

She gave him a knowing smile. "Those books were written by men. You've much to learn."

Her voice was steady but her hands were not as she undid the placket of his breeches, then reached in and wrapped her fingers around his cock.

"Goddamn it," he growled. Another sound, this one wordless with need, tore from him when she sank onto her knees, the blanket beneath them serving as a cushion. A gleam of moisture shone in the slit of his cock.

She held his erection and angled it toward her mouth. "Watch me," she breathed. He needed to know who gave him pleasure, and who could take it away.

His gaze fastened on her as though he could not look anywhere else. She dipped down, her lips drawing the crown into her mouth.

"Oh, fuck," he burst out.

She pulled him from her mouth to say in wry admonishment, "Language."

"I'm sorry, Miss Holme."

She gave him a smile. "I like it. I want to hear how much pleasure I'm giving you. But never forget that your pleasure belongs to me. It's mine to bestow and mine to take away. Your cock in my mouth puts you in *my* power. Do you understand?"

"Yes, Miss Holme."

Her heart pounded at his words, and she reveled in their forbidden roles as teacher and student.

He swore again when she took him fully into her mouth, sucking him deep. With her hand, she stroked his shaft, timing it with bobs of her head, careful that there was no part of him that went unattended.

A steady stream of profane language spilled from him with each swirl of her tongue and pump of her hand. Her student couldn't keep his hips still, thrusting into her mouth. Yet she sensed his hesitation, as though he feared his own untamed response.

He gasped, "I'm sor—"

Before he could finish apologizing for his brutish behavior, she grabbed hold of one of his hands and guided it to the back of her head.

She drew back. "Remember how I'm the one with the power? *I'm* giving you permission to do this—because *I* desire it. Hold my head so I can take you in as deep as I can. Then I want you to fuck my mouth. Do not forget, though, that in this moment, you have never been more vulnerable, which is its own ecstasy. No book written by any man will ever tell you that."

His Adam's apple bobbed, and he nodded.

She felt his control slip away as he did as she directed. He cradled the back of her head, allowing her to swallow the entirety of his cock. His hips moved, steady at first. Then it was as though he couldn't stop himself from going faster and faster. Through it all, she stayed with him, her cheeks hollowing, the small schoolroom filled with the sounds of her sucking his cock.

"Going to...come," he gasped.

She didn't pull away. Her efforts redoubled as she drew on him harder, loving the taste and sensation of his cock in her mouth, and his yielding to her command.

He clamped his jaw tight as he climaxed. Swallowing his seed, her gaze stayed riveted to his face. In his surrender, he was never more beautiful, and more power pulsed through her to know that *she* gave him this.

When his last shudders of release faded, she tucked his softening cock back into his breeches and did up the buttons.

He seemed to struggle to open his eyes. With a voice drunk on pleasure, he said, "I understand the lesson now. The one on their knees can hold power, too."

She chuckled softly, pleased he'd understood her intent. "Good students are suitably rewarded."

"Miss Holme," he said, "I will be the best student you've ever had."

She straightened, and after setting her person to rights, stroked a finger over his chin. Tenderness swept through her, as well as a protectiveness she hadn't anticipated. Inconvenient, those feelings, when they could only be passing amusements to each other. God knew that a governess had no business developing an attachment to her ducal lover.

"Have you ever taught anyone else the ways of pleasure?" he asked.

"Never." Once, she had been the student. With Owen, she could educate him in the ways of being a considerate—as well as skilled—lover.

He'd take some other woman to his bed. A wife, someday. A mistress, perhaps.

Did she educate him for that unknown woman's sake, or his?

Or her own?

The thought made her pause. She could not form an attachment to him, for so many reasons. Yet...he had been so focused on following her guidance. And the way he looked at her now, as though she were not merely an object of desire, but a person who was worthy of care... She battled the call of her heart, the foolish piece of her that wanted more than physical pleasure.

"Would it matter if I did?" she asked, striving for distance. She moved away from him, picking up the blanket and setting it back into the chest, as if that task were vitally important. "Would your opinion of me decay?"

He was on his feet and beside her in a moment. "Nothing could make that happen. But I suppose if there had been others..." He took her hands in his. "I can't deny that I would have been jealous."

She didn't want to be pleased. Jealousy had never been a quality she encouraged in prior love affairs. Even so, there was something gratifying in his possessiveness—that he, too, wrestled with feelings that went beyond attraction.

But she ought to discourage it to protect them both. She had to end this now, before the seed of affection began to sprout roots. The tender growth could not be allowed to flourish and flower.

Footsteps sounded in the hallway. She and Owen froze, both careful to keep from moving lest the slightest creak of the floorboards give away their presence. Her pulse was an anxious throb within her.

"Just left a book up here, the one about the wife who poisoned her husband," Ellie said, her voice muffled by the closed door. The doorknob rattled. "Strange. Miss Holme doesn't lock the door."

"Maybe she left something valuable inside," Maria answered. "Wager we could get Mrs. Baines unlock it for us so you can get your book."

"Good idea. Let's..."

Their voices faded with the sounds of their retreat in the hallway. As soon as they were gone, she and Owen exhaled. Yet he didn't let go of her hands, and she didn't step away from him.

"We should go," she said reluctantly. "It'll take them all of ten minutes to find Mrs. Baines and come back." She started to slide her hands from his. "This can't happen again."

He looked on the verge of protesting. And then he nodded. "If that's what you desire."

Relief—of a sort. Because they would never know what more they could give each other. "We nursed a mutual infatuation and yielded to it. But it's never to be repeated."

She slipped from his grasp and moved quickly to the door. After unlocking it, she paused for a brief moment, her back to his. Then she opened the door and walked out without looking back.

CHAPTER FOUR

CECILIA'S EMOTIONS swung like a pendulum the rest of the day and through the night, alternating between horror at what she'd done and the glow that came in the wake of astonishing pleasure. How could she have crossed that line with Owen, the duke? True, he was no longer responsible for her employment, and he was a grown man—but lusting for him and acting on that lust were still forbidden, no matter how he'd made her feel.

She did her best to avoid him the next day, but cruel and sardonic fate kept putting him in her path.

In the morning, she nearly collided with him in the corridor outside the breakfast room. He stared at her with what seemed like hunger and longing, until he smoothed his expression into one resembling indifference.

"Miss Holme," he said.

She curtsied, praying that her own face didn't reflect her pleasure and agony in seeing him again. "Your Grace."

Before either of them could do something regrettable, she hurried away. Yet she couldn't stop herself from looking back at him.

He remained where she'd left him, standing in the hallway, watching her avidly.

She rushed to the schoolroom, seeking refuge from the pull between them. But it was haunted by the remembrances of yesterday. She could barely look at the desk where he'd eaten her cunt so superbly. And sitting at her own desk only brought back the feel of his cock between her lips, his taste, and how readily and beautifully he'd fucked her mouth.

Still, she managed to collect herself enough to give her students their morning lessons. Perhaps she could conquer her desire for him and go on, as she had before he became the duke. They could live under the same roof and be cordial strangers.

By midday, when the girls were out for their afternoon ride, she fought the impulse to run to his study and demand that he fuck her, kiss her, touch her, *anything*.

She went quickly to the library. At this hour of the day, doubtless he'd be sequestered with his men of business and immersed in the work of being a duke. There would be no danger of running into him in the hallways, or anywhere else.

Stepping into the cool, dim library, she drew in a ragged breath, as if the scent of paper and leather could calm her sensitized body. Moving toward one wall covered in bookshelves, she studied the titles printed on their spines. One of the benefits of her employment at Tarrington House was the liberal policy regarding the use of its vast collection of books.

She trailed her fingers over them, attempting to ground herself in their feel. As she did, she searched for something that could keep her mind from returning to thoughts of Owen. Governesses always benefitted from learning new things, but today none the history texts, natural philosophy treatises, and tales of faraway places could hold her. And she'd no desire to read accounts of fictional people's trials and triumphs.

There was no hope for it. Nothing could distract her.

She was halfway to the door when, unexpectedly, he strode in.

They stared at each other. It had been mere hours since the encounter outside the breakfast room, yet excitement jolted through her to see him again.

His gaze was bright and hungry. Wordlessly, drawn by undeniable force, they narrowed the distance between them.

"I need to see you again," she whispered urgently. It took all her strength to keep from reaching for him and pulling him to her so they could kiss.

Owen's hands flexed as if he, too, wanted to hold her. "Anywhere," he answered, low and fierce.

"Not here in the house." She glanced toward the open library door. Anyone could walk by and see them standing too close, hear them speaking in passionate murmurs.

"The gamekeeper's cottage."

The little house stood some distance from the main house, sheltered by the woods. Mr. Lytton had retired from service five months ago, and once a month the housekeeper dispatched a handful of maids to clean and tidy it for his eventual successor.

"Midnight," Owen said.

Voices came from the hallway—two footmen, by the sound of it. They came nearer.

Alarm shot through her. "Go," she urged him.

"Tonight?" he pressed.

"Tonight." Her heart knocked with excitement and terror. "Now, you *must* leave."

He shot her a yearning look before striding from the library. As his retreating footsteps grew fainter, she pretended to examine the bookshelves on the chance that the footmen might peer into the chamber and see her.

It was imperative to maintain the illusion that she and the duke had simply a polite relationship, yet the truth was she'd never wanted anyone as badly as she wanted him.

CECILIA SLIPPED INTO THE CORRIDOR, careful to shut the door to her room quietly. She shared this wing of the staff quarters with Mr. Vale and Mrs. Baines, as well as the girls' nanny and the duchess's maid, and while none of them kept the later hours of the footmen and kitchen staff, she had to be as careful as possible to ensure no one was about. She had an excuse at the ready—she'd forgotten some papers in the schoolroom—but hopefully she wouldn't encounter anyone while creeping through the house at eleven thirty in the evening.

Her heart pounded with each step, and her stomach fluttered with a combination of excitement and nervousness. More than anything, her feet demanded she run the distance between her room and the gamekeeper's cottage, but until she left the actual house, her steps had to remain sedate and, most importantly, quiet.

I cannot believe I am truly doing this.

Yet she *could* believe, because yesterday's encounter with Owen in the schoolroom had embedded itself deep within her. Her first affair with Georges had ended by mutual agreement, and after they had parted ways, she used what she'd learned from him, including understanding the measure of her power in seeking her own pleasure.

She'd been so brazen, so bold—but even in her most sophisticated trysts, she'd never behaved so audaciously as she had with Owen.

For all their sophistication, the men she'd fucked had still wanted her to receive their amorous, erotic attention, and not be the instigator and pursuer of her own pleasure.

Owen was different. He'd been with her every step of the way, gladly following where she led, and in the process, giving her the most incredible pleasure of her life.

And if their meeting in the library was any indication, he wanted her as much as she wanted him.

She hurried down the narrow back stairs, keeping her footfalls light so the steps didn't creak. Fortunately, her vision at night was good, and she didn't need the betraying light of a candle to illuminate her way. When she finally reached the ground floor, she eased into a hallway. This was part of the house where she might encounter not just staff, but members of the family.

The girls always went to bed early, as they were active young ladies and wore themselves out with their energetic activity during the day. The duchess hadn't lost her Neapolitan habit of keeping late hours, but since the late duke had passed, she mostly kept to her rooms after supper.

Cecilia herself occasionally indulged in a late-night ramble. It was hard to lose the free-roaming habits she'd acquired on the Continent, and she was somewhat familiar with the house at this late hour. But now every spill of moonlight threatened to expose her, and every shadow could hide an unwanted observer.

Finally, she was outside, down the terrace, and onto the long, sloping lawn. Dew soaked the hem of her skirts, and cool air tried to weave its way under the shawl draped over her shoulders. She ignored these slight discomforts as she took long strides across the grass, pausing briefly to look over her shoulder toward the house.

There was no sign of anyone on the terrace, or standing at their window watching her, so she hurried on. A carefully tended wood bordered the lawn, and as she slipped into the shelter of the trees, she permitted herself a sigh of relief. No one would be able to spot her now.

The cottage was quite private, and it took Cecilia a good quarter of an hour to reach it. She caught sight of a single light ahead and headed toward it. When she emerged from the trees, a lone candle burned in the window of the snug little house, and her heart leapt.

He was here, waiting for her.

It was unseemly how much she wanted him. And yet she didn't try to slow her steps as she raced forward, and up the short set of steps. When she reached the front door, she hesitated. Should she knock, or simply go right in?

She opened the door.

He stood on the other side of the threshold. His gaze on her was ravenous, yet he held himself still. Barely leashed excitement poured out of his body in invisible waves.

As she entered, he took a step back. She shut the door behind her.

His chest rose and fell, his hands curling and uncurling at his sides. The force he used to restrain himself was palpable, and she thought of the farthing in his pocket, and the hold it had over him.

"Kiss me," she said. "Show me how much you want this."

Her words seemed to break the tether he had on himself. He pressed his long, solid body against hers. His mouth on hers was hungry and searching, and she sank into the limitless depths of his kisses. She didn't care about the rigid door at her back—all that mattered was the way he kissed her, as if she contained his next breath, and the one after that, and the one after that.

Her hands roamed over him, soaking in the heat of his body and its delicious strength. She could spend hours, days, years learning all the ways in which he was fashioned, discovering taut muscles and how they shivered beneath her touch.

She arched, snug against him, the hard length of his cock curving into her belly. It wasn't enough, not with all the fabric between them.

"I want your cock in my hand," she breathed, and he shuddered with desire.

Their fingers tangled and snared as they fumbled with his clothing. Impatiently, she tore open his breeches and plunged her hand down to wrap her fingers around his cock. Her mouth watered at the feel of him, thick and eager.

He growled in response.

"Touch me," she instructed, gasping with arousal.

He skimmed his hands down to gather her skirts. His fingers stroked along her bare thighs, and he made another animal sound of approval to touch her.

As she pumped his length, he brought his hands higher, one palm curving around her arse while the other hand found her soaking quim. She gasped as his fingers delved between her folds. The smallest smile tilted her mouth.

"You paid attention to our lesson yesterday," she murmured.

"Memorized every word, every touch."

With incredible skill, he caressed her, knowing exactly where she needed softness and where she needed more intensity. He circled her clitoris, sparking sensation, and stroked around her inner folds before sinking two fingers into her. She moaned, hitching her thigh up to give him better access.

There was no hesitancy in him now as he fucked her with his hand. She sensed his restraints falling away, his thrusts sure and demanding. Yet she wanted more. "Fuck me."

He glanced back toward the bed.

"I can't wait," she panted. "Fuck me against the door."

His brows climbed. "Will that be comfortable for you?"

"I'm not seeking comfort, but pleasure."

"And it will be pleasurable for you?"

"Oh, yes. The question we should ask is, are you suitably motivated?"

"I *am* motivated," he said roughly. "Tell me what to do."

"Keep holding my leg like that. Tilt your hips forward and fit the head of your cock at my pussy's opening." Arousal flowed along her body as she instructed him. She loved using plain, coarse language.

He followed her direction, his body strong and purposeful as he positioned them both. She sucked in a breath when he notched the crown of his cock at her entrance, reveling in the feel of flesh to flesh.

"Yes?" he rumbled.

"Please," she said on a shaky exhale, the word tight with wanting.

He gripped her thigh, anchoring her, and then—

With a thrust of his hips, he was in her, seated all the way to the root in a single stroke.

She clung to his shoulders, moaning as her body stretched to accommodate him. He filled her superbly, and for a moment, neither of them moved. They were speared on a fragment in time, completely inside and surrounding each other.

Much as she wanted to lose herself in this moment, she whispered, "We must be careful. I cannot get with child. Do you know what to do?"

"I'd heard of it," he gasped. "Been told that it robs pleasure."

She couldn't stop her rueful chuckle. "Your male friends gave you that information, I'd wager."

He gave a single nod.

"We'll both enjoy ourselves more if we know there's no chance of a babe."

He nodded again. "Tell me what I need to do."

"When you feel yourself on the verge of coming, pull out."

"But...what about my seed?"

She curled her hand around the back of his neck. "We'll watch it spill all over my belly."

His expression sharpened with excitement. "I want to do that. And I want—" He swallowed hard and tremors worked through his body. He seemed to choke back his impulses and instincts, unwilling have faith in himself. She had been the same way, before she'd gone abroad.

"Trust yourself," she pressed. "And trust me. If there's anything I don't want, I will tell you. Now you tell me, what do *you* want?"

"To fuck you," he confessed. "Hard. Against the door. May I?"

Tightening her fingers around his nape, she urged him on. "Do it."

He held her up as his hips drew back, his cock moving magnificently within her. She gasped as he plunged forward with enough strength to lift her higher. He slid almost completely out and then thrust into her, again with blazing power, holding her as each of his strokes raised her up. It was brutal and forceful, the kind of fucking that came from long pent-up need.

She moaned, "Deep—yes."

"Too...much...?" he rumbled with each thrust.

"I love it." To be filled with his unleashed desire was bliss.

He made a sound of satisfaction. "Hold tight."

She wrapped her arms securely around his shoulders and, to her gratification, he cupped his hand against the back of her head, protecting her from the hard, wooden door. And then...

He fucked her ferociously. Quick, powerful strokes that filled her completely and robbed her of the ability to do anything other than lose herself to ecstasy. She clung to him for support as he drove them both relentlessly toward release. She'd never had anyone give her so much intensity, such purpose. Her climax loomed, teasing her with its explosive possibility.

"Touch my clitoris," she gasped. "I need that. Time it with your thrusts."

He gave a low growl and delved his hand between them.

She came with a long, high cry, safe to give voice to her ecstasy in this remote place. He anchored her as her climax stretched on and on, pleasure suffusing her in unending waves.

Then he pulled from her and snarled with his own release. As she had promised, they both watched as his seed coated her stomach.

His forehead tipped forward, resting against hers, their heaving breath mingling in the tiny, intimate space between them. She was boneless, holding onto him to keep from sliding to the floor. Yesterday, in the schoolroom, she'd come harder than she ever had in her life. But this had been even more intense, her body robbed completely of strength, yet also bright with energy.

"Volume one, lesson one," he murmured, nuzzling her neck. "Make your teacher scream—in the best way."

"Exemplary work," she answered in a haze of lingering pleasure. "Especially as we haven't even made it to the bed."

He pulled back enough so she could see him smile crookedly. "That must be volume one, lesson two."

The press of his hips against hers revealed that, incredibly, his cock was already hardening again. How wonderful to have a young lover.

"We've all night," she said, and pressed her lips to his endearing, sensual smile. "And there's so much material to cover."

~

"The privileges of being a duke," Owen said to her as they delved into the basket he'd brought, "is that I can tell Mrs. Baines I'm raiding the larder for a hamper full of food, and she won't press me for an explanation."

They sat at a small table next to the cottage's diminutive hearth, where a fire blazed, illuminating the many delicious items he'd procured. There were pork pies and wedges of sharp cheese, as well as apples from Tarrington House's own orchards. And, to Cecilia's delight, no fewer than three plum tarts. Owen had also brought an earthenware flagon filled with cider from the selfsame orchards.

In the wake of a mind-altering orgasm, no meal had ever tasted better.

"Just because Mrs. Baines didn't ask for a rationale," she noted, "doesn't stop her from gossiping that the duke has suddenly developed a late-night appetite."

"Growing up, I *did* eat an awful lot," he said with a smile. "All the time, especially after bedtime. By the time I was coming home from Eton, she grew used to me nosing about the larder at all hours."

That was some relief, knowing the housekeeper wouldn't find anything suspicious in his behavior. And the cottage had been cleaned only last week, so there was no chance of anyone discovering that someone had recently occupied it—not for a little while, at any rate. Cecilia would be certain to clean it thoroughly, just in case, including removing the ashes from the hearth.

"Before this," she pointed out after taking a drink of cider, "you were the heir, so you *still* didn't have to explain yourself."

He flashed her the smile that made her stomach flutter with awareness. Incredibly potent, that smile.

"But I used to offer rationales for my behavior anyway." He brushed back a lock of black hair that had fallen across his forehead. "Father used to admonish me about it. Said dukes weren't supposed to be deferential."

A shadow crossed Owen's face, and silence fell, broken only by the pops of the fire in the grate.

"It's a difficult thing, to lose a parent," she said quietly. She reached across the table and took his hand, giving it a gentle squeeze. "I lost my mother in childbed when I was about Maria's age. The babe died as well, so I never had a sibling."

"Was it hard to recover from her passing?" His eyes were dark and imploring, and while it would have been easy to mouth a meaningless platitude, he deserved better than that.

"Everyone tells us that the best way to face grief is to put it behind us," she said, her voice soft. "But then I had to wonder, best way for *whom*? Certainly, it makes other people more comfortable if we're stoic, or cheerful, or don't let anyone know that we're in pain or full of sadness. Yet for us, the ones who are hurting—it's not good at all. We're supposed to choke down our feelings and then pretend we haven't poisoned ourselves."

He rubbed his free hand across his jaw. "All the people I met with in London, the solicitors and men of business and Father's old associates, they would look at me with stony faces and give me approving nods, saying things like, 'Good man. You're holding up well. It's what your father would want.' But," he went on, his gaze beseeching, "*is it* what he'd want? For me to simply put him in the earth and then walk away as if suddenly he was no longer my father? To forget about the rock samples he'd bring me, or the way we used to take rambles through the estate and talk about a book he'd just read?"

The anguish in Owen's voice resounded within her, and she ached for him.

Slowly, she said, "Grieving for him, missing him, it all speaks to how much you cared. And that is never a bad thing. He must have loved you very much."

His smile was small, but heartfelt. "I'm trying to be a good Duke of Tarrington. Theoretically, I've been preparing to be the duke my whole life—yet it feels sudden. I thought I'd have more time to learn what I need to do in order to fulfill my obligations. I want..." He struggled to speak, as if searching for the right words. "I want to bring honor to the title."

"You do," she said without hesitation.

"How do you know?" he asked wryly.

"I've faith in you." She gave his hand another squeeze.

He exhaled. "Glad one of us does." Firelight played across his face, and shadows dipped between the furrow in his brow. "You said your mother passed away when you were Maria's age."

"Yes," Cecilia said quietly. It hadn't been fast or gentle. Her mother had screamed for hours, but attempts to save her and the child were in vain. "They said it wasn't supposed to happen like that. It was supposed to go easier than that—but then, there was well over a decade between me and the next child, so..." Her bones felt rusty as she lifted her shoulders.

"I'm sorry, Miss Holme," he said, his voice genuinely regretful.

She accepted his condolences with a small nod. "I'd been hoping for a baby sister, or even a brother, and thought for a bit that it was my fault, wanting something that turned out so dangerous to my mother's health."

"Of course it wasn't your fault," he said vehemently.

She gave him a little smile. "I know that now. But thirteen-year-old girls are less inclined to understand the world from a position of cold logic. With her gone, though, it made me take a long look around at my life, at the little world of my town that was to contain the whole of my existence. I discovered something about myself."

"What was that?"

He poured her more cider, and she took a drink, savoring its tart taste.

"I wanted more than to take my place beside my father at the shop counter. I wanted more than marrying someone I had known my whole life. So when I was old enough, I advertised my services as a governess." She laughed ruefully. "To say my father was displeased vastly diminishes the scale of his fury."

"He should have been proud of his daughter's spirit," Owen asserted.

She sipped at her cider in an attempt to wash away the bitterness caused by her father's anger. "A spirited daughter was not one of his objectives. And he was doubly furious when I revealed to him that I was going to be a governess on the Continent. But I could not resist the opportunity to learn so much about the world."

She had learned about herself, as well. Her father had insisted that she choose: be a governess, or be welcome in his home.

She missed Edgar Holme—he never answered her letters—but she valued herself more.

"Regarding our lessons," she said, guiding the conversation back to more comfortable territory.

He straightened, ever the attentive student.

"Taking into account that you've already given me several shattering orgasms," she continued, "I think you can call me Cecilia, rather than *Miss Holme*."

"Does anyone else call you Cecilia?" he asked.

"You'd be the first in a long time."

Ah, that smile of his, warm and bright and genuine. "It's just for us, then."

"Just for us," she repeated softly, then crooked her finger at him. "Kiss me."

CHAPTER FIVE

THE FOLLOWING NIGHT, Owen stood at the lone table in the gamekeeper's cottage. As he waited for Cecilia, he arranged and rearranged the plates of food into a display he hoped would please her eye. Perhaps he should slice the pears rather than leave them whole. There was the worrying possibility that she didn't like pears—he couldn't very well ask anyone in the house if she had a fondness for them, or any other dish, without arousing suspicion.

He moved the pears back into the basket, which he then tucked under the table. If she didn't prefer the fruit, he wouldn't give it to her. All he wanted was to give her exclusively the things she loved.

He drummed his fingers on the small, paper-wrapped parcel he'd placed at her seat. A single sprig of cornflowers was tucked into the string tied around the gift—he'd picked it earlier today when out for a stroll with his mother and sisters, and had tried to keep it fresh by setting it in a small bottle filled with water. As he'd hurried to the cottage tonight, his thoughts had been circling over all his preparations, including fretting as to whether or not the cornflowers would retain their freshness and vibrancy until she saw them.

Owen let out a small, rueful laugh. "Christ, look at me," he muttered. Since parting company with Cecilia last night—after an hour of delicious fucking—he'd been in a frenzy to see her again, and not just to see her, but to make her smile, hear her laugh, run his fingers through the mass of her dark honey-colored hair as it spread on a pillow.

His fantasy of her far surpassed the reality of who she was. Her boldness, her quickness of mind, her humor. There was so much of her he didn't know, and what he had glimpsed had been, in all ways, exceptional.

Merely thinking about the waves of her hair made him bite back a growl of desire. God Almighty, there wasn't a part of her that didn't arouse him.

A glance at his timepiece revealed it to be five to midnight. He'd been early, too early, but he wanted to make sure everything was perfect for her.

He went to the bed and smoothed his hands over the blankets, where he'd scattered fresh green herbs that would release their scent as he and Cecilia lay atop them. The heat of their bodies would also bring out the herbs' fragrance.

She taught him so much, but he had other means of learning. This little gambit with the herbs, for example, he'd read about years ago when a secret book about seduction had made the rounds at Eton.

He'd taken many of the lessons to heart, but never until now acted on them. Before Cecilia, he'd been too diffident, too hesitant. There had been a few girls who had intrigued him, but he had remained locked inside his own apprehension. Yet with her, she gave him both knowledge and freedom, urging him to liberate that dark, surging need within him.

His father had alluded to the fact that he and Owen's mother enjoyed robust bedsport. Distressing as it was to have the image of his parents' amorous life in his head, it had encouraged Owen to believe that perhaps someday, he might have a wife whose fierce desires were equal to his.

At Eton, and later Oxford, his friends taught him something altogether contradictory—that exciting sex was for courtesans and mistresses, but intercourse between husband and wife was dull and dutiful.

He didn't know who to believe.

He *did* know that he wanted Cecilia. To the point of madness.

His wildness last night hadn't frightened her. She had...*enjoyed* it. He could still hear that gorgeous sound she made when she came from his rough, hard thrusts against the door.

And hell, there went his cock again, already hard from imagining her.

His heart rammed into his throat when he heard a soft tread on the wooden stair outside. For a brief moment, he considered waiting by the bed, or perhaps sitting in the armchair by the fire to prove he wasn't entirely besotted and overeager.

The doorknob turned, and in three strides, he was there, ready for her.

Cecilia stepped into the cottage, eyes bright and smile wide. Remembering how she'd guided him last night, he took her in his arms without hesitation.

She wrapped herself around him. Their caressing hands were feverish, their kisses ravenous. Her taste was of sweet, spiced brandy, a flavor he would forever link to her and the feel of her mouth against his.

"Impatient for your next lesson?" she asked throatily.

Last night proved that she seemed to like it when he spoke to her, especially if he used coarse language. "Been hard for you all day."

In response, she kissed him greedily.

"I could barely concentrate on giving the girls their lesson," she gasped when she pulled back. "All I could think of was you—teaching *you*." Her hands slid down his back, then lower until she gripped the cheeks of his arse. She purred as she dug her fingers into him. "My God, you're delicious."

He let out a huff of laughter. "Thought squeezing arses was strictly the prerogative of men."

"Thankfully, you and I are far more enlightened to believe such nonsense." Then, cautiously, "Do you dislike it?" She moved to take her hands away.

Quickly, he urged her back against him. "Let me show you how progressive I am." He leaned down and kissed her again, their tongues meeting.

Need built, fast and hot, and he ached with the desire to be inside her. But it had to wait.

He pulled back and stroked his thumb across her lower lip. "I've something for you."

"I can feel it," she murmured, her hand cupping his iron-hard cock.

A growl rose in his throat, and he wanted nothing more than to press himself into her touch. But he had another purpose, so he took a reluctant step back. Holding his hand out, he said, "Come with me."

She frowned in curiosity, but laced her fingers with his, allowing him to lead her to the table. A smile lit her face as her gaze fell on all the details he'd been so meticulous in arranging, from the array of food carefully placed on pretty plates, to the beeswax candles throwing golden light across the small banquet.

He held his breath as he waited for her to see the gift. Her smile widened when she spotted the wrapped parcel.

She brushed her fingers over the cornflowers—they hadn't wilted, and were as vividly blue as when he'd picked them—before undoing the string. Fastidiously, she unfolded the paper, as though she was loath to tear it.

"A fine book," she said, holding up the slim volume. It was, in truth, rather plainly covered, the spine minimally adorned, which was by design. "Looks familiar…"

"It should. It was once yours, and now it's yours again."

Her eyes widened, then she opened the book and read the title page. "*The Scoundrel's Willing Captive.*"

"The one I nicked from your collection of salacious novels," he confessed, suddenly shy.

"You kept it all these years?"

Heat crept into his face. "Read it too many times to count. I used to sniff at its pages, hoping that I'd catch a hint of your scent. I'd hoped—" He swallowed. "I'd hoped that you'd touched yourself, and then turned a page, so that your fingers fragranced the paper. Just thinking about it, I'd hold the book in one hand and frig myself with the other."

She sucked in a breath, her own cheeks stained deeply pink. Her tongue darted out to moisten her bottom lip. He stared at it, fascinated.

"Do you want to keep the book?" she asked, her voice breathy. "For…inspiration?"

"I want you to have it back. I want to picture you holding it, thinking of me with my cock in my hand."

Her lashes fluttered. "For someone with limited sexual experience," she murmured, "you seem to know precisely what to say."

"Instinct," he answered. "And…I never thought myself the sort who felt things like inspiration—I'm a man of the sciences. But with you…" He struggled to locate the right words, to give them shape and set them free.

She was silent, allowing him to find his way on his own.

Drawing confidence from her, he said, "You inspire me. You always have."

She held the book close to her chest, which rose and fell rapidly. Her face upturned, she stepped closer to him. "I never knew. I almost believed you didn't like me—whenever I'd come into a room, you wouldn't look at me or speak to me."

"Hell, all I wanted to do was stare at you," he admitted. "You were so lovely, but more than that, I could feel it within you. This...*will*. Something wild and strong and beautiful, but you wouldn't let it out. Perhaps it was to protect yourself. Maybe it was to shield my family from your spirit, powerful as it is."

Her gaze dropped. "You sensed this from seeing me across a drawing room?"

"If I'm wrong—"

"Not wrong." She shook her head. "Here I'd congratulated myself on successfully playing the role of demure, proper governess. And I didn't fool anyone."

"But you did. Whenever my parents spoke of you, they always praised your propriety, that you were a good example for my sisters."

A wry laugh broke from her. "And yet a sixteen-year-old boy saw through all that."

"Not *a* boy." Small flares of irritation flickered, because he was not a child, and she needed to know that. "*This* boy—who's no longer a boy."

"A man," she murmured. After setting the book down, she stroked her hand along his shoulder, up his neck, and wove her fingers into the hair above his nape. "Kiss me—slow and deep."

"I want to. God, how I want to." He clasped her wrists, feeling her pulse beneath his fingers, trying to memorize her by touch. Because once he said what he needed to, she might push him away and walk out the door. Yet he had to give her the full truth before they went any further. "There's something you need to know. Something that might make you end this now."

Her hands dropped and she took a step back. "You're affianced."

"I've no bride awaiting me," he answered, but had to add, "yet."

She said nothing, her face still and unreadable.

"That farthing's meaning far outpaces its monetary value, because it contains another of my father's reminders."

"It holds a great deal of weight for such a small coin."

He gave a soft snort. "And I carry it with me always."

"What is this other lesson?" she prompted him.

"Every part of a duke's life is woven into the larger world," he explained. "None of his decisions affect merely himself, and that includes his choice of wife."

"Ah." She inclined her head, but he needed her to understand him completely.

"There is no bride picked out for me, but when I marry, I'll have to consider more than just what my heart wants."

"It must be an advantageous match," she said crisply, "in every regard. Wedding a governess is not advantageous."

He spread his hands. "When I was born, I entered a realm where I was merely a player in a larger scheme."

"Yet you still reap the advantages of your position."

"No denying that. There's a price to be paid for everything, however."

"Such as the selection of the woman who will bear your heirs." She leveled a smile at him. "Your meaning is taken. Rest assured that I've no designs on becoming the next Duchess of Tarrington. I've never had ambition to become one of the nobility, or even the gentry. In some ways, gently born ladies have even less freedom than those of us who are commoners."

There was relief at her understanding, yet he could not completely suppress his disappointment that they could never be more to each other than two people sharing physical pleasure. It would be all too easy to care deeply for her. Judging by the way he hurried here tonight, and the care he'd taken in making everything ready for her, he already walked that path.

"Even so," he went on, determined to give her the choice, "if you decide that this is as far as our affair goes, I won't stop you from leaving."

She lifted a brow. "Do you want to end this?"

His chest squeezed tightly. "You're all I think about."

"And your ducal duties," she added, her smile thawing.

"Those, too. But when I'm not considering petitions and reviewing mountains of documents, I am consumed with thoughts of you. I want you, Cecilia. So bloody much."

His breath came quickly, his hands loose at his sides as if he needed to make ready to reach out and seize hold of whatever was offered him.

"I *am* a duke, and powerful beyond all reckoning, but you..." He swallowed hard. "You are so much more formidable than I could ever hope to be."

"You underestimate yourself," she said, swaying closer.

Pleasure and relief coursed through him when she looped her arms around his neck and brought her body close to his.

"There's a matter of a kiss I requested," she murmured. "It has yet to materialize."

He brought his mouth to hers, taking his time as she wanted. There could be pleasure in crashing together, but it could be even greater with a gradual build of hunger.

She pressed closer to him, her hand gripping his shoulder tightly. His senses were afire with her, blazing with her taste and touch. Soon, they were both panting, hips snug together. Though layers of fabric separated them, he loved the feel of her shifting against him. It was as if she tried to push past the barriers and join flesh to flesh.

"I'm returning the book, but there's a condition attached." When she pulled back to look up at him questioningly, he explained, "Tell me what part of the story you liked best."

Her smile was wicked. "You remember the part where they outrun a rainstorm, and take shelter in an abandoned farmhouse?"

His heart thudded erratically—he'd read that section of her erotic novel many times. It never failed to inspire his fantasies. "She rides him as he sits on a chair beside the fire."

"Never done it that way, and I've always wanted to."

He followed her heated gaze over his shoulder to the armchair tucked into a corner of the cottage. His cock twitched in anticipation. "Get undressed."

"The student commands the teacher," she said with a hint of humor. "In this instance, I'll permit your insubordination."

"And if I make a habit of such wayward behavior?"

She lifted onto the tips of her toes and lightly bit his bottom lip, jolting arousal through him. "I don't punish my pupils—but we'll find something suitable for a recalcitrant student. For now, however, I will take your suggestion under advisement. Are you ready for another lesson?"

"Please," he rasped.

"How to undress a woman."

He sucked in a breath, his whole body tightening in readiness.

She turned around, presenting him with a row of tiny buttons that marched down the back of her bodice. "Undo these—and you're welcome to take your time."

"Prolonging the pleasure makes it even greater."

Smiling over her shoulder, she murmured, "Such an excellent pupil."

He glowed at her praise. He might not be able to give her promises of a future, yet he could give her the pleasure they made together. As he reached for the buttons, he could not stop himself from stroking a hand down the length of her nape, where her skin was all suppleness and silk.

"A most outstanding student," she said, sounding slightly winded.

He was graceless as he struggled to slip the buttons free, his hands shaking. It was like uncovering the universe's greatest mysteries as he revealed her, her warm scent rising when her skin was uncovered.

"Help me remove my dress," she instructed, lifting her arms.

"I feel like an ungainly lout." Holding the soft fabric of her gown in his big hands as he guided the garment up and over her head only emphasized the differences between them, and the contrast stoked his desire.

"You don't touch me like an ungainly lout." She took the dress from him and hung it on a peg on the wall. Now she stood in a long white shift, and he could catch a glimpse of her stays beneath. She was closer to nakedness, but still too garbed for his liking.

"How do I touch you?"

"Like a man who wants to revel in his pleasure."

"Wants to," he noted. "But doesn't." She saw him in a way that no one else did—including himself. He was coming to adore this perceptiveness of hers. With each of her insights, the ground beneath them levelled, and they met as true equals.

"There's more to your passion than you're allowing free. Yesterday, when we were against the door, I felt it. When you finally do trust yourself to slip from your tethers entirely..." Her smile was slow and carnal. "Which brings us back to your lesson in stripping your lover. Next is my petticoat."

Turning around once more, she gestured to the ties of the long white garment. He was only slightly more adept at undoing them than he was the buttons of her gown.

"Handling tiny geological samples presents no difficulty," he muttered. "But now my fingers feel like sausages."

"Desire can make anyone clumsy." She pulled off her petticoat and put it with her dress, so that now she was only in her stays and shift.

He lost his breath at the sight of her, her lovely bare skin dotted with tiny golden freckles. Her breasts rose above the top of her stays, barely covered by the sheer shift, and he loved that she stood still and magnificent as he drank her in with his gaze.

He exhaled, torn between frustration and arousal. "Who's responsible for putting women in so many layers of garments?"

She chucked low. "No one benefits, except the mantua makers. Now, the laces on my stays."

It took far too long to undo the ties—he ached for her naked flesh. And yet it was over too quickly— he wanted to savor the experience of undressing her. Soon, she stood before him in only her shift. The sheer fabric barely concealed the hardened tips of her nipples, and he could just make out the triangle of curls between her legs.

"Talk to me," she murmured. "There's something delicious in hearing your lover's thoughts."

"I want inside your body, *and* your mind," he said on a rasp.

"Then let me into yours."

"You're so lovely." It wasn't easy to speak or give shape to the raging need within him. Yet as the words left his lips, her gaze grew both aroused and soft. Perhaps she'd expected him to say something crude. "If you only knew how many times I'd tried to picture you like this."

"Why stop here? Take off my shift."

He helped remove the flimsy garment, his breath rough. Now she was clad in nothing but a knowing smile, and as she plucked the pins from her coiffure, her hair tumbled over her shoulders.

He sank down to his knees as he beheld her—full breasts tipped with large, tawny nipples, rounded belly, a gorgeous nest of honey-colored hair between her legs. "By God."

She stepped to him, and he wrapped his arms around her, pressing his face into the softness of her stomach. He rubbed his cheek against her silken flesh, his breath ragged.

"Go lower," she instructed. "Taste how much I want you."

He nuzzled down, and she inhaled sharply as he dipped his tongue between her folds. The taste and smell of her arousal was a conflagration in his blood.

"I want you to—" he began, then stopped himself as that shadowed, demanding thing within him tried to seize control.

"It's all right," she whispered. "Take control. Tell me what you want."

The creature inside him growled in approval. "Widen your legs for me."

She made a soft whimper, and to his delight, she complied. "Use everything I've taught you."

He caressed her pussy with his fingers, then his tongue, and her hands clutched at his head.

"Yes—*yes*," she urged him.

He lapped at her, sucking and licking and devouring her like the feast she was. When he thrust two fingers into her passage—touching her as she'd instructed in the schoolroom—she moaned. Within her was the secret place, swollen with need, and he stroked against it as he flicked his tongue against her clitoris.

She came with a cry, holding him tightly to her as she ground against his unrelenting mouth. He gripped her trembling thighs to keep her standing, and her knees wobbled.

Kissing his way up her stomach, he kept her upright while he rose to his feet. Her fingers still wove into his hair, and she tilted his head to kiss him.

"You liked that." He'd pleased her—the fulfillment of his greatest wish.

She stroked her hand along his jaw. "When natural talent meets a willingness to learn, the benefits are boundless." Before he could preen, she went on, "Still haven't given me everything I want."

He glanced toward the waiting chair, then back at her, and her smile was replete with sensuality.

Reluctant though he was to let go of her, he had to in order to take off his clothing. He pulled everything from his body in a frenzy of movement, the task made difficult by the avarice in her gaze as she watched him disrobe. He was grateful for the work he did to maintain his condition—if only to see how much his form pleased her.

When he was finally nude, he strode to the chair and brought it beside the fire. His limbs were electric with energy and need, the chair weighing nothing as he placed it precisely where it had to be to fulfill her fantasy. He was rewarded by her approving nod. Her gaze flicked to the chair in a wordless command. At once, he sat down to wait for her.

She walked to him, a timeless siren swaying her hips with each step. Though she seemed breathless with eagerness, she took her time crossing the distance, as though she savored not just their joining, but the delicious tension that stretched out in the space between sex. Here again, she taught him. There could be enjoyment in the delay of pleasure, and in cultivating anticipation.

Yet she was no goddess. She was as much a mortal being as he, and that made his need and admiration for her expand like the corona around the sun, engulfing them both in heat and radiance.

By the time she stood in front of him, his chest heaved and his cock ached as it strained up toward his navel.

"Are you ready?" she asked throatily.

"Fuck, yes." Perhaps he should have been more eloquent, but it was impossible to find pretty words when he was dying with want of her.

Before she could instruct him, he opened his arms. He could show her that he'd taken her lessons to heart, and that he was becoming the powerful man she believed him to be.

She came to him right away, positioning herself. The chair was amply proportioned. Following her lead, he helped arrange her limbs so that she straddled him. Their bodies fit together snugly, surrounding them in heat of their own making, even as the fire sent out its own glowing warmth. He clasped her rounded hips, loving the softness beneath his palms.

They both hissed at the press of her pussy against his cock.

On an impulse, he dragged his shaft through her folds, coating himself in her wetness, and teased the head of his cock against her clitoris. Her moan was his reward, thrumming over his skin like a deep melody.

She lifted herself up slightly, but when he reached to angle his cock to meet her, she gasped, "Let me."

He held his breath as she gripped his shaft, and could not look away as she positioned him where she needed him, with the head of his cock tight against her entrance. He adored how bold she was, how in command of both of their pleasure. A glance at her face showed that her cheeks were flushed, and she bit her bottom lip as she made certain his cock was in precisely the place she desired. Slowly, she lowered, beginning to fill herself with him.

Much as he wanted to see his cock slide into her, her expression enraptured him even more. Ecstasy filled her face as she leaned back to watch herself take him into her body. Pleasure doubled, both from the sensation of being surrounded by her tight passage as well as seeing how their joining affected her.

When he lifted his hips, she said throatily, "Not yet. Let me sink onto your cock, inch by inch."

It took all his strength to keep still and not thrust up, plunging into her entirely. Sweat slicked his back as he held himself motionless. As she had said, she lowered slowly, moaning when he was in her to the hilt.

"This is what you desired," he rumbled. In this position, *she* was in control.

"Yes," she said, almost panting. "Yes, this."

For a moment, neither moved—which was a blessing because she felt so wondrous he could have climaxed without a single stroke.

"Touch my breasts," she instructed him. "Pinch my nipples with those gorgeous fingers of yours."

He did so, cupping her breast with one hand and lightly squeezing the nipple. Her head tipped forward as she let out a pleasured cry.

"There are two of us here." She gripped his shoulders. "Tell me what you want, Owen."

With her surrounding him, he was more himself than he'd ever been. It was reckless and untamed and he gave himself over to the freedom without fear. He growled, "Ride me now, Cecilia."

She lifted and lowered her hips slightly, the barest movement, yet her lashes fluttered with each subtle motion. Then she began to rock with greater heat and speed. He held her hips tightly as she found the angles she required, matching her pace so that he lasted. With every thrust, she ground her clitoris against him.

A command rose in him, and he hesitated for a moment, troubled by what his wild impulse demanded. Yet, looking into her ecstasy-filled face, he found courage. She believed in him, in the pleasure he could give her, in who he was as a man.

"Open your mouth," he commanded hoarsely.

She seemed faintly puzzled by his demand, but parted her lips.

Sliding his thumb into her mouth, he rasped, "Lick."

Her tongue swirled around his thumb, and then, with a wicked little smile, she sucked on it.

He pulled his thumb from her mouth, then brought it to her clitoris. His gaze held hers as he stroked over and around the sensitive flesh, matching the rhythm of his strokes within her.

"Oh, God. *Owen.*" She cried out, her hands clutching his shoulders, her passage squeezing around his cock as she came.

He continued to play with her, lavishing attention on her clitoris as he thrust. She came again, her body taut with the force of her release.

Growling, he pulled from her as his own climax struck, the force as great as a tempest. She draped against him, pressing her face into where his shoulder curved to his neck, and he held her. They both shuddered and gasped, descending from the heights of pleasure. He loved the feel of her damp body against his. Stroking his hand along her hair and down her back, he cradled her close as a golden haze settled around them.

She brushed her lips against his throat. "Based on the book, that wasn't how I thought it would be."

Alarm pierced his fog. "I—"

"It was better." Her voice was low and drowsy, the voice of a satisfied, sated woman. "Much, much better."

He relaxed with a chuckle, even as strength surged through him. He had done that. *He* had brought her pleasure and exceeded her dreams.

"The bed now," she murmured.

Gathering her up, he stood and carried her there. She smiled when her gaze fell on the herbs strewn across the linens, and when he lay her down, she took a few green leaves and rubbed them between her fingers to release their scent.

"How *are* you so good at this?" she murmured in wonderment as he joined her beneath the coverlet.

He flashed her a smile.

Wryly, she said, "Here I thought I had so much to teach you."

"Far different to read about something in a book, versus putting it into practice."

She stroked her hand down his chest, and he purred when she raked her fingers through the hair that curled there. His own hands were not idle, caressing along her neck and arm, touching her because it was impossible *not* to touch her.

"Whereas my knowledge of geology is surely less than yours," she said.

"I promise I won't bring any samples to bed and describe their chemical structures as my chosen method of seduction."

She laughed, full and unrestrained, and it sounded different from the way she laughed when she was with his family. There was so much she kept hidden, so many layers, all far more complex than anything he'd encountered in his studies. He tried to push back against a wave of resentment, knowing he could never have more of her than this, tried to shove aside the bitter knowledge threatening to break apart the pleasure of merely being with her.

"One subject of which I know little," he said. At her questioning look, he explained, "You."

Her mouth formed a line. "Your cock was inside me minutes ago."

"Fucking you isn't the same as knowing *who* you are." He wove their fingers together, his palm pressing to hers. If his words could not convince her, maybe the truth of his body could.

"Trust me—please."

"You are very dangerous. Not intentionally so," she added when he started to object. "But there is much about you that could cause me harm."

"I swear," he said, words firm with resolve, "that though I can't offer you marriage, I will do everything in my power to protect you and shield you from any hurt. Your employment is not controlled by me, and I will never impel you to do anything you don't desire. I'll keep you safe."

"I know you believe that." With her free hand, she traced the angle of his jaw. "Yet unlearning my wariness does not come easily."

He leaned closer so he could see all the colors in her eyes, the enthralling green and brown and gold. "Perhaps there are lessons we both can learn from each other. I've given you my honesty, but you must only provide what you are comfortable in bestowing."

She was quiet for a long time, yet she did not pull away, and he tried to take assurance from that. After many moments, she said quietly, "This is only my second post as a governess. My first was for a couple who were known for their artistic, progressive ways. It was...much freer than my life had ever been before. The rules and dictates that govern society weren't much regarded with them."

Her voice was rich with pleasure, and her eyes shone with fond remembrance.

"They traveled throughout the Continent," she went on, her gaze far away, "and I traveled with them, teaching their daughter. When I wasn't occupied with my duties, my employers gave me free rein to do as I

****

****

pleased, and so I saw all the beautiful, glittering capitals, living as a local, discovering things about the world I had never known before."

She continued. "I took lovers. Sophisticated, unconventional men who helped me see that physical love, that sex, was a thing to be celebrated and enjoyed not just by men, but women too. Women could crave pleasure and seek it out absent of shame. And so I did."

"Sounds incredible," he murmured. He battled with a tiny, jealous demon—no doubt those lovers she'd known had been men of experience, unlike himself. Yet those men weren't here with her now. *He* was, and only moments before, she'd said he had surpassed her fantasy. In the absence of marriage, he could at the least give her ecstasy.

"It was." A shadow fell across her face, and she stared down at her hand, still holding his. "Then my employer, the husband, took an interest in me. Said that my eyes and body were opened now, and he'd been waiting for the right time to bring me to his bed."

"You didn't want to become his lover," Owen said, reading her expression of dismay.

"In the absence of my own family, I'd begun to think of him as kin. A brother, or an uncle, but never anyone I desired. Not the way I desired you." She sent him the tiniest, fleeting smile.

He squeezed her hand, torn between pleasure to hear her attraction to him, and dreading what came next in her tale.

"When I told him so…" Her look turned bitter. "He threatened me. Said I would lose my position, and he'd turn me out without a character, and without paying me the wages I was owed."

Owen swore. "Bastard."

"His wife was no help. Just laughed when I told her and said it would be wisest to indulge his desires that way everyone got what they wanted." Cecilia's mouth twisted. "The freedom they'd offered me was no freedom at all, not when it came at such a price. Thus, I left. At the least, my employers provided me with a character and enough money to return to England, both which enabled me to find work here, at Tarrington House."

He tamped down on the fury he felt on her behalf. She did not seem to want righteous anger right now. So he leaned close and kissed her. But she seemed less in need of defending than validation. Quietly, he said, "Your courage humbles me."

She nodded, but her expression was soft with gratitude.

A lull fell, interrupted only by the sound of the fire and the wind ruffling through the trees.

"I see now the reasoning behind your initial reluctance for us becoming lovers." His father's farthing contained only a fraction of what there was to know about how power functioned, who had it, and what it signified.

He held it, and he could not abuse that privilege. There was a way he could wield so it helped others, rather than merely shoring up his own position in the world.

"You're a far better man than my prior employer could ever hope to be."

"Small praise, given what a son of a bitch he revealed himself to be."

She gave a low exhalation that might have been a laugh.

"You returned to England," he prompted gently.

"For all the liberty of the Continent, I missed my home."

"And you continued on as a governess. Despite what had happened at your prior post."

Her smile was genuine. "For all that man's poison, I still *liked* being a governess, and wanted to get away from London. I applied for the post to teach your sisters. It was conditional, my employment, since I had only the one character, but I suppose I did well enough for them to keep me."

She kissed him briefly, then slid out from his arms to rise from the bed and move to her clothing nearby. Her body glowed in the firelight, yet he couldn't take pleasure from watching her walk away.

"Help me dress." She donned her shift and pulled on her loosened stays before presenting him with her back.

He padded from the bed to her and began tightening the laces down the back of her stays. "I far preferred removing this."

"Staying here for more than a few hours is risky." She exhaled, smoothing her hands down her torso as if assuring herself that her armor was fully in place. "We cannot afford to be forgetful of who we are. In the house, I'm the governess, and you are the duke."

He hated the reminder of the gulf between them, but it was an uncontestable fact.

She slipped on her petticoat, and while he remained nude, she put on her gown. Wordlessly, she gave him her back, and the row of buttons on her dress.

"In this cottage," he said, doing up the fastenings, "we're neither of those things."

With her gown fully secure, she faced him, her expression set. Was the sadness in her gaze an invention of his yearning heart, or was it real?

She reached up to cup his jaw. When he leaned into her touch, rubbing against her palm, she sucked in a breath. Longing shone in her eyes before she quickly banked it.

There was a strange comfort in how she fought against longing, as though he was not the only one who ached for more than they could have. Yet it was no comfort at all because no matter what he and Cecilia wanted, it would always be thwarted.

"Here," she said evenly, "we're the teacher and the student. That farthing tells us that anything else is impossible."

CHAPTER SIX

"Examining samples is the best way to understand the growing structures of plants," Cecilia explained to Maria and Ellie. Since the day was so fine and mild, and since it would be nigh impossible to get her pupils to focus on their slates when a whole sunny world awaited, the three of them sat on a blanket spread upon the massive lawn behind Tarrington House's east terrace. "Which means gathering samples."

The girls shared a smile.

"May we, Miss Holme?" Maria asked.

Her sister all but vibrated with excitement at the prospect.

"Only if you promise not to destroy any creature's home to do so," Cecilia instructed.

"We promise," the girls said solemnly.

"Then go, but don't stray too far. If you're not back within half an hour, I'll be forced to search for you—and then we'll take the remainder of today's lessons in the schoolroom."

"Half an hour," Ellie repeated as she got to her feet. She pointed to the small timepiece pinned to her sister's bodice, which had been a recent gift from their brother.

The mere thought of Owen made Cecilia's face flush and her body shaky with remembrance of last night's tryst.

Fortunately, the brim of her bonnet not only protected her from the sun, it also hid the heat in her cheeks, and Ellie and Maria were mercifully unaware of the fact that their governess was turning pink from lustful thoughts of their brother.

"Go on, then," Cecilia said, waving them toward the trees fringing the lawn. "And stay together."

With avowals that they'd stick close to each other, the girls ambled off toward the woods. Cecilia followed their progress, waiting until they had moved into the arbor before she stretched out on the blanket and picked up her book. She needed to review tomorrow's lesson on the great kingdoms of Asia. There was a considerable amount of material to cover, and it would be a disservice to the topic to rush the lesson, but she had to determine the best starting point for a rich and fascinating subject.

Despite the absorbing topic, her lids were weighted, and keeping them open became a losing battle. A warm breeze blew across the lawn, abundant with the green scents of late springtime. She plucked at the ribbons of her bonnet, then tugged it from her head and set it beside her.

After she had returned to her room last night, she'd been unable to sleep. Though her body had been sated by the pleasure she'd shared with Owen, their intimate conversation afterward kept her mind spinning. Sharing her history with him—and his acceptance of that history—had touched her, making her long for things that could never be. In a different world, a better one, they could mean more to each other than a few stolen moments.

With her past lovers, she'd been content with assignations that promised only physical pleasure. Those relationships had been temporary, nor had she wanted more from any of those men. They were pleasant enough, and skilled at fucking, but none of them desired learning who she truly was beyond that night's amusement. In truth, there hadn't been anything about any of them that made her crave something beyond their bodies. When it came time to part, she was as ready as they had been to end things.

With Owen, there was lust, and she enjoyed guiding him on his sexual journey. Watching him discover himself and being the lucky recipient of his developing erotic skill delighted her. Yet he kept revealing his hidden depths, the tenderness of his heart, and his burning need to do right.

The way he looked at her stole her breath. No one had ever regarded her with such care or respect. She wasn't an object to desire, or something to be manipulated or used. Nor was she seen as a symbol of impossible virtue.

To Owen, she was... She was *her*.

How long could this go on? At some point, his sisters would be old enough to no longer need her.

And she had her own dream of a school for girls. If she were careful over these next few years, she could begin investigating properties to lease, other teachers to hire.

There was no place for Owen in her future, nor she in his.

Yet what if, her thoughts had pressed all night. *What if...?*

If she could catch more air on her face, she could stay awake now. But she'd be more comfortable if she lay on her side as she read. She would merely shift her position a little and then return to her reading.

"Given that this bonnet is in possession of all its ribbons," a woman's voice said with humor, "I can only assume it belongs to you and not one of my daughters."

Cecilia's eyes flew open. Sitting opposite her was the duchess, wearing a gentle smile as she held Cecilia's bonnet.

She lurched upright, mortified to the roots of her being to be caught napping by her employer. "My sincerest apologies, Your Grace. The girls went off to gather botanical specimens and I was reading tomorrow's lesson. I honestly have no excuse for my indolence—"

"Apologies are unnecessary, Miss Holme." The duchess held up a hand, and her expression was mercifully mild. "This is precisely the sort of day that one takes a little al fresco pisolino. When I was a girl at my parents' villa outside of Amalfi, I loved nothing more than dozing beneath the leaves of a lemon tree, with my own governess fast asleep beside me."

Cecilia dipped her head. "You're very kind. Not many employers look benignly on their staff napping."

"So long as you do not make a habit of nodding off when you are supposed to be educating my children," the duchess said, her tone still gentle, but there was no mistaking the iron beneath her words.

"I won't," Cecilia vowed, burning with embarrassment. "I never sleep during the day. Today was anomalous."

"You have been looking rather exhausted these past few days." The duchess's dark eyes, so very like her son's, regarded her thoughtfully. "Are you not sleeping well?"

"I..." She couldn't explain to her employer that, for the last two nights, Cecilia had been busy shagging her son, and worse, entertaining dreams of things that were impossible. "The weather has been so warm, it sometimes makes it difficult to sleep deeply."

The duchess gave a small laugh. At Cecilia's questioning look, she explained, "The difference between what is considered a warm day in England and what we call a warm day in Napoli is vastly different. You poor, pale creatures do not understand what it is like to have the sun truly beat down on you as though you were in the boxing ring, and the sun the favored champion. Oh, but you've been abroad."

"I was in Napoli," Cecilia said with a nod. "I experienced the baking heat there for myself. The coolest day there was like the height of an English summer."

Smiling, the duchess offered Cecilia the bonnet. "I found this tumbling across the lawn."

"My thanks." She took her hat and returned it to her head, tying the ribbons firmly beneath her chin. Noting the black trim on the duchess's bonnet, and the dark circles beneath her eyes, Cecilia asked gently, "Forgive me if I am impertinent, Your Grace, but if you are feeling weary, you're welcome to have a piccolo pisolino here. The girls aren't due back for..." She consulted the timepiece in her reticule. "A quarter of an hour. I can keep watch while you nap."

A corner of the duchess's mouth turned up in a wry half-smile. "It is not so easy to sleep without my husband beside me." She shot Cecilia a look. "Perhaps in England it is not so usual to discuss with one's governess one's sleeping arrangements."

"It may be somewhat unconventional," Cecilia allowed. "However, there's many a custom in England that isn't entirely useful."

"How true, Miss Holme." The duchess exhaled as she smoothed out her black skirts. "We are all learning to exist without the duke. Mi scusi, without my husband. We have a new duke—my son."

Attempting casualness, Cecilia said, "Your Grace must be pleased with how he's assumed the role." Merely speaking obliquely about Owen made her heart pound. It wasn't typical conversation to discuss one's lover with his mother—at least, not amongst the British aristocracy.

The duchess's smile was bittersweet. "Povero bambino, though he is no longer a bambino. He is, as my father would say, un uomo forte."

Quite forte, Cecilia thought.

"My boy is not a boy," the duchess went on, and Cecilia was relieved that the older woman did not have the ability to read minds. "He compares himself to his father and tries so very hard. I think he will be a fine duke."

"He isn't one yet?"

"He is on his way—he requires experience, yet already in the last few weeks I sense a difference in him. A confidence, and though I am glad of it, I cannot say what has given it to him." The duchess's lips quirked. "I would say that it is precisely the sort of swaggering a man possesses when he has a new lover, but Owen has not left the estate since he returned, so that cannot be a possibility. Unless it is someone on the property."

Cecilia bent her head over her book and ran her hands across its pages, as if she could read what was printed there with her fingers. Every nerve in her body tightened in preparation to flee, yet she made herself sit calmly as though her paramour's mother wasn't discussing the probability that her daughters' governess was sleeping with her son. Granted, the duchess was not English, and did not have the English's rigid, narrow views about propriety, but even someone used to more lax ideas of respectability would condemn Owen and Cecilia's affair.

"Though," the duchess continued, glancing back toward the imposing manor house, "he leaves for London tomorrow, so perhaps there he will find a fine widow or courtesan. Young men have so much fire, you know."

A strange buzzing filled Cecilia's head, and with it combining with a sudden, peculiar hollowness, she could barely hear herself say, "Leaving for London?"

"Later today," the duchess answered. "There are more appointments and meetings, which is the lot of a duke. He has not the luxury of sequestering himself in the country, but I am certain the change of scenery will be good for him. He will have the chance to be amongst people his own age, and though his father is recently gone, he might attend some of the Season's smaller gatherings."

"That will be most beneficial," Cecilia said, manufacturing enthusiasm.

She ought to have known that there would come a time when Owen would leave Tarrington House, and he would seek out the company of his contemporaries. After all, she was nine years older than him, and she was not of his class. A wide chasm divided them, and it was better to keep reminding herself that nothing would bridge that divide than persist in some foolish fantasy that things could continue in perpetuity.

Everything changed. She was mature enough to know that.

Still. She hadn't anticipated that two nights were all she and Owen would have. After revealing her history to him, he'd been so open, so accepting, when many others would not have been. It showed her the support he'd offered had been genuine, that she could trust every part of herself with him. It had been a long time since she had been able to be vulnerable. Yet she'd done so, secure in the conviction that he wouldn't hurt her.

Though the physical pleasure they'd shared had been beyond anything she had ever known, the bond growing between them made her anxious and unsettled.

She shouldn't confuse their affair with something more meaningful and lasting. The present moment was all they had, and entertaining dreams of a future together was an exercise in frustrating, heartbreaking futility.

How long had he known that he'd return to London? Why hadn't he told her he was leaving? Did he fear her response, or worse, did he think she didn't merit telling?

She stared at the book in her lap, though reading it was impossible.

A shadow fell across its pages.

"Am I intruding on a lesson?" a deep, familiar voice asked.

"Give me a kiss, il mio ragazzo," the duchess said affectionately.

Cecilia glanced up to see Owen bend and press a kiss to his mother's cheek. His neckcloth hung in loose folds, as though he'd picked it apart. She could picture him absently undoing the starched fabric as he reviewed one of the many letters he received daily.

As he straightened, his gaze touched on her. She must have appeared upset, because a small crease appeared between his brows.

She looked away, ruffling a hand across the grass.

"You have fled your work?" His mother's tone was lightly jesting.

"Petitions. So many petitions, all of them asking for funding. Granted, they use different words but the meaning's the same." He made a noise of aggravation. "Giving people money isn't at issue—we've plenty to spare."

Cecilia asked, turning back to him, "Then why are you looking like a wolf about to chew off his paw to free himself from the trap?"

"Cramming at Oxford was a pleasant idyll compared to this." He dragged a hand down his face. "I'm contemplating running away and becoming an itinerant tinker."

"Il stagnaio?" his mother said in alarm. "Perché?"

"Banging on pots and pans seems positively tranquil by comparison."

"The first tinker with a family crest," Cecilia murmured.

"Pfft." The duchess waved her hand. "A fine use of your excellent breeding so you could fix someone's soup pot."

The reminder of Owen's distinguished bloodline—and that he was tasked with protecting that pedigree—made Cecilia's stomach clench. Shopkeeper's daughters-turned-governesses would never be suitable for a duke.

He glanced warily at her. "In lieu of taking to the open road, might I join you?"

"The master of the house need not ask for permission," his mother said.

He smiled, which, to Cecilia's dismay, made her heart leap. "I'm supposed to do what I please with no care for the consequences?"

"Of course," Cecilia said tightly. "That's what men do. Especially men who are dukes." Realizing that she had spoken rudely to him, and in front of his mother, she pasted on a smile. "I am jesting, of course. But I'll leave you two. Surely you want time together as a family before His Grace leaves for London."

She began to rise, and he held out his hand in a staying motion.

"Do stay, Miss Holme. It's a beautiful day and I'd hate to deprive you of it by chasing you inside." Contrition flashed in his eyes.

Settling back into place, she tried without success not to look at him as he stretched his long body out on the blanket, but it was difficult with the sunlight turning his black hair glossy, and the sleeves of his shirt billowing in the gentle breeze.

"Is everything prepared for your journey?" his mother asked.

"Mostly," he answered, "though I think Chalmers is slightly displeased with me for such a sudden departure."

The word *sudden* caught Cecilia's attention. It seemed deliberately spoken. As placidly as possible, she said, "Mr. Chalmers is remarkably adaptable and resourceful."

"Fortunately for me," Owen said, "given that I only learned I was leaving for London after breakfast, and have been sequestered in my study since then."

She glanced at him, but was careful not to look too long, lest she attract the duchess's notice. "Did someone dare summon a duke?"

"I must make my first appearance in Parliament as the Duke of Tarrington. There's a bill my father was particularly invested in defeating, a bill regarding increasing the number of prison hulks. My father was against the idea. He favored less punitive measures for minor crimes. One of the bill's other opponents, the Duke of Greyland, has requested my support and so I must go immediately to appear tomorrow afternoon."

Anger fell away, replaced by remorse. "Understandable that you would need to make a hasty return to London."

His warm gaze met hers, as though he was grateful she appreciated his reasons for leaving so suddenly.

"But as long as you are back," his mother said, patting his hand, "you will take advantage of the Season, sì? Perhaps find yourself a fine girl from a fine family, someone you can court."

The small measure of peace Cecilia had grasped slipped away, and her limbs filled with restless, unhappy energy.

Color darkened Owen's cheeks. "Cara mamma, I'm not in the market for a bride."

"It is too soon after the passing of your dear father," the duchess said with a small nod, "but there is no harm in, how do you say, getting the lay of the land?"

"We can discuss this another time," Owen said, an edge in his voice. He shot Cecilia a quick look.

"If not now, bambino," his mother pressed, "when?"

"Try me in a decade."

Cecilia pressed her lips together to suppress an unbidden laugh. The situation wasn't amusing, yet she needed some way to release the tension building within her.

The duchess frowned in displeasure. "Owen—"

"Madre, no." His words were firm as he sat upright. "Give me time to learn what it means to be a duke before forcing me into the role of husband."

His mother opened her mouth, clearly about to give him a tart reply, but Cecilia got to her feet before anything could be said. As she did, Owen politely stood, which, to Cecilia's distress, caught the duchess's attention.

"Do excuse me, Your Graces," Cecilia murmured, gathering up her book. "I'll meet the girls back in the schoolroom."

She curtsied before hurrying away, striding across the grass as rapidly as possible. The house grew nearer, and she quickened her steps to reach the shelter it offered. Her throat burned with the need to weep. Though Owen had rebuffed his mother's attempts to make him court a potential bride, the very fact that it was a possibility was an acrid burn deep within Cecilia.

Don't you dare lose your heart to him.

"Miss Holme."

She spun at the sound of Owen's voice and dipped into another curtsy. "Your Grace." When he was close enough, she made sure her expression remained neutral, and she schooled her voice to sound dispassionate. "It's unwise to talk to me on your own, especially if someone might observe us."

"I told my mother that I intended to ask you if you required any books for my sisters."

"It was still a risk that should not have been taken."

His dark eyes were warm and beseeching. "I couldn't leave without speaking to you alone. Cecilia, tesoro." He lifted his hand as if to take hers, but dropped it before they could touch—but she could not let anyone see how this broke her heart.

"The moment I learned I had to leave," he continued, "I wanted to tell you. But there wasn't time."

The longing in his gaze pierced her. "You plan on remaining in London, I imagine."

"There's so much that needs attending to." His jaw tensed.

"Naturally." She gazed at the house, a handsome structure of warm stone that had been built shortly after the Restoration and sat grandly atop a long, gently rising hill. It was the sort of home that proclaimed the family's ancient lineage, the care and continuation of which would always be attended to by its lord. Which included preservation of the bloodline through the getting of legitimate heirs. Precisely the reminder embodied by the farthing Owen's father had given him.

She was a governess, while he, the duke, existed in the highest echelon, swathed in power and significance. What was she to him?

Transitory. She was transitory—there was no alternative.

"I've heard London is delightful during the Season," she said.

"I wish it all to the Devil," he said fiercely. "If you aren't there, it doesn't mean a goddamn thing."

Her heart clutched. "What you and I have—it's fleeting."

"I know," he said broodingly.

More than anything, she wanted to close the distance between them. Her palm throbbed with the need to feel his cheek, and she craved the taste of him on her lips.

She remained precisely where she stood. A tall hedge served to shield them from his mother, but someone in the house might see.

"Go to London," she said. "Live your ducal life and surround yourself with the kind of people you are meant to. We've known from the beginning that this was finite."

He looked agonized, his expression tight as he gave the barest of nods. Which fractured her heart, just a little, because even he, a duke, could not fight several centuries of tradition and responsibility.

She took a step toward the house, her every movement away from him a source of agony. As was proper, she curtsied again, showing respect to her better. "Have a safe journey, Your Grace."

CHAPTER SEVEN

AFTERNOON LESSONS CONCLUDED, Cecilia headed along the corridor leading to the narrow servants' stairs. Hopefully, the glorious early summer weather would lift her mood, though given the way her humor had steadily plummeted in the past week since Owen had gone to London, the chances of anything stirring her emotions was close to nil.

She passed a housemaid and tried to smile at the girl. It was important to maintain some semblance of good cheer for everyone at Tarrington House, yet the cost was far higher than she would have believed.

Missing him was a palpable ache, yet it was the scope of the loss that surprised her the most. She walked Tarrington House straining to hear his footsteps. On her solitary rambles, she drifted past the stables, hoping to see Orion in his stall as proof that Owen had returned.

Never with other lovers had she wished for more, or yearned for what might have been. Yet with Owen gone—likely flirting with dewy, genteel debutantes—pain took up residence in the hollow of her chest.

There were no letters, naturally. He couldn't write to her without arousing suspicion, and she feared what such correspondence might contain. Either he missed her as much as she longed for him, or in the whirl and excitement of the Season, he'd forgotten her.

He'd sent letters to his mother and sisters—she'd known because Ellie and Maria sometimes chatted about him as they'd come in for their lessons—and once, when Cecilia had admired Maria's new coral necklace, the girl had said it was a gift from her brother. For Ellie, he'd sent a book called *The Tower of London's Most Blood-Curdling Executions,* which had made Cecilia smile. He knew his sisters well.

She'd been unable to question any of his family for information about Owen, partly out of fear that they might grow suspicious of her interest in him, and partly because she didn't want to know if he was having a grand time, whirling from private ball to theatre box to dinner party. She didn't want to learn that young and eligible girls were paraded in front of the new duke, hoping to secure his attention.

Continuing down the empty hallway, her steps slowed as her body turned leaden. It was a relief not to have to pretend her entire being was suffused with longing, if only for a few minutes.

She straightened her slumped shoulders when quick, heavy footsteps sounded behind her. Thinking that it was one of the footmen dispatched on an errand, she manufactured another smile and turned to offer a greeting.

Words shriveled and her face froze when she found herself looking at Owen.

He was windblown, slightly disheveled. Tiny flecks of dirt marred his breeches and boots, and his neckcloth was rumpled. Dimly, she recognized that the state of his person revealed that he'd just come from the road—he hadn't been in his carriage, but on horseback.

She could only stare, riveted by the sight of him. God only knew what expression she wore, but he looked fevered, almost wild.

"I need more lessons," he said gruffly.

She took a step closer. Her hand rose of its own volition, heeding the unrelenting call of her body to touch him.

He reached for her, and his fingers wrapped around her wrist. This small touch sent pure heat pouring through her.

Her gaze fell on the door to a diminutive closet, then back to him. "In there."

In an instant, he'd opened the closet door and stepped inside, tugging her in after him. He had the presence of mind to shut the door softly behind them.

The closet's darkness enfolded her, turning her sightless, but she barely noticed as Owen pulled her against him. Their lips found each other, desperate with desire. She moaned into his mouth as his hands roamed over her body, cupping her arse, molding to her breasts, devouring her by touch. She caressed him, skimming her palms across his wide shoulders and down the sinewy length of his arms. The heat of him scorched her and she let herself be burned after an interminable week without him.

A low cabinet bumped against her back, and suddenly he lifted her, sitting her atop it.

He stood between her open legs as they kissed and stroked each other. When he rocked his hips into hers, despite the barrier of his breeches and her skirts, she felt the ridge of his arousal sliding snugly against her quim.

He gathered her skirts, gliding up her legs, past her knees and thighs. She bit down a cry when he glossed through her outer lips before swirling deeper, where she was wet and aching, and when he plunged two fingers into her, she clamped her jaws shut to keep from wailing with pleasure. His thumb moved back and forth over her clitoris as he pumped into her. His jacket's woolen cuff brushed against her thighs, and the feel of the fabric only heightened urgency.

Her climax struck hard and fast, and she bowed up with the force of it. Her throat was aflame from stifling her sounds of release.

He moved her, pulling her to her feet but turning her so that her hands braced against the top of the cabinet.

"Yes?" he growled as he bared her.

"Yes," she answered.

And then he said nothing, only made a feral noise as she heard the sounds of him unfastening his breeches. His fingers caressed over her arse, dipping lower to her trembling pussy. She widened her legs and held her breath as he fit the crown of his cock to her opening.

One hand on her hip, he thrust into her, thick and full. She couldn't keep from crying out in bliss, then his other hand came up to cover her mouth.

"Shh," he breathed against her neck.

Breath sawed in and out of Cecilia's nose as he continued to fuck her. She jolted with the force of each superbly rough stroke, writhing with ecstasy as she fought to keep from making any sound to alert passersby in the corridor. His own breath came in short, hard pants that gusted across her nape.

Owen's hand moved down from Cecilia's hip to her clitoris, rubbing it as he thrust into her.

Cecilia came so powerfully she saw bright constellations behind her closed eyes. It was a mercy Owen's hand covered her mouth, else she would have screamed so loud as to bring the whole house running.

A moment later, he pulled from her, and his hot seed spattered across the dip just above her arse.

Owen slid his hand away from her mouth, and she sagged forward as their gasps mingled in the tight confines of the narrow closet. Sex and lavender scented the air.

Soft cloth stroked over her behind as he cleaned her.

She turned, and he was there, pulling her to him as they kissed deeply. Every swipe of his tongue against hers made her hum with pleasure.

"I wonder if there's anything left to teach you." She shivered in the afterglow of how he'd been so commanding, so driven with need that he'd forgotten all his reticence. "You won't need me anymore."

"Never say that," he said insistently. "There's so much I have to know —and you're the one to guide me."

Only when his fingertip brushed against her cheek and spread wetness across her skin did she realize she wept.

"Vita mia," he murmured, "why are you crying?"

She hadn't cried in years. "I...missed you."

His lips found hers. "Every moment we were apart was torture. Here, with you, is where I belong, and to hell with the consequences."

"Parliament?"

"I voted as I was supposed to. Now that's done and I'm here again."

She wrapped her arms around him tightly, loving the feel of him.

"Amore mio," he said hoarsely, "I don't want to stop what we have. I think of what it would mean to never kiss you again, never touch you again, and it shatters me. But I'll do what you want, only tell me." His voice rasped. "I need to hear it from you—do you want me to stay?"

A shudder ran through her as she pressed her heated face against his shoulder. "I know this cannot last. I know this and yet...and yet..." She swallowed in an attempt to collect herself, but her efforts were futile, and her voice shook. "I will take what I can get."

He sucked in a breath, then rubbed his lips against the crown of her head. "Tonight. We'll meet again at the cottage."

"Midnight, at the cottage."

He was hers and she was his—for now. She could not ask for more than that, even as she ached with wanting more, with wanting him to be hers forever.

CHAPTER EIGHT

D IVING beneath the surface of the pond was like diving into midnight itself. Water black as the sky surrounded Owen, and with a few strokes of his arms, he drove himself through it as though swimming through his own dreams.

He surfaced, taking in air, and sleek, wet arms immediately encircled him.

Pulling Cecilia closer, his lips found hers. Her slick body pressed close to him. Wrapping his arms around her waist, he held her close as he used his legs to propel them through the water. They were one creature, buoyant as they glided together.

He rolled onto his back, his hold on her secure so that she lay partially atop him. Lazily, he kicked his feet, keeping Cecilia and himself at the pond's surface. He loved the feel of her with him in the water, where peace came so readily. Though he swam and sculled at Oxford, it was never as wonderful as it was here, in Tarrington House's pond, with Cecilia in his arms.

"There's almost nowhere to swim in London," he murmured.

Moonlight traced the curve of her cheek and down the length of her wet hair. "The Thames is hardly fitting for a bathe."

"The best I was able to find were the Highgate Ponds at Hampstead Heath, but the demands on my time ensured I was only able to go once in the whole week."

"How fortunate you've returned to all the pleasures of Tarrington House." She rubbed her breasts against his chest. In response, he cupped one of his hands around the curve of her arse. A startled but pleased laugh escaped her. "Such boldness you've cultivated in your time away."

He could do that now, touch her without the hesitation and second guessing that had so hindered him.

"If I've become bold," he said, moving his legs to push them toward the shore, "it's because I have received excellent instruction."

"No teacher could ask for a more receptive student."

They reached the banks of the pond, and he lifted her up so she could stand. Joining hands, they strode through the silt and reeds until they reached the grass. They stretched out side by side on the blanket she'd taken from the cottage. The air was thick and sultry, barely stirred by a breeze, ensuring that neither he nor Cecilia would be chilled as they lay together in the depths of a warm night.

He stroked his hand lazily up and down her back, and they were quiet together. As they'd arranged earlier—after they'd furiously, clandestinely fucked in the closet—they had met in the cottage. There, he'd showed her exactly how much her lessons had taught him. Her teeth left marks on his shoulder from where she'd bitten him during her climaxes. Thank God he preferred to dress himself rather than rely on his valet, even though Owen was reasonably certain that Chalmers wouldn't go tattling to other servants. Still, if he could keep the gossip mill quiet about the new duke's amorous life, all the better.

"You've talked little of London," she murmured.

He shrugged. "Buried in meetings and engagements. There was hardly time to enjoy it." There had been a sophisticated, pretty widow he had met at a dinner party—they hadn't sat beside each other, but the lady had made eyes at him throughout the meal. When they had gathered afterward in the drawing room, she'd offered him nights in her bed for the duration of his stay in the city. He had politely declined.

"Though," he said, "I met with MacCulloch, the president of the Geological Society of London, in the relatively new headquarters on Bedford Street. We discussed new classification systems. He's some theories on mineralogy that—" He stopped at her laugh.

"This the first I've heard you speak of London with any enthusiasm."

She propped her chin on her fist. "And it's absolutely perfect that it relates not to the theater or an assembly, but rocks and minerals."

"Can't find good examples of chalcocite next to the punch bowl."

"And cucumber sandwiches aren't copper ores," she added.

His brows climbed, and he was momentarily stunned into silence.

She laughed again. "It was worth it to research the minerology of Britain, if only to see the look on your face."

"You researched...? Why?"

"It's important to you." Her gaze dropped, and he didn't know what surprised him more, the fact that she had taken the time to learn about geology because it mattered to him, or her sudden shyness. She was never shy, yet here she was, bashful as a girl fresh from the schoolroom.

Leaning close, he kissed her.

When they pulled back many moments later, they both breathed heavily. He said in a gravelly voice, "I wish I'd brought you something from London—jade hair combs, or ruby ear bobs."

"Such things are pretty, but I've no need of them. How's a governess to explain why she has jewels hanging from her ears and costly ornaments in her hair?"

"A fair point. Dispiriting, but fair. But," he added, brightening, "I do have books for you. They're arriving tomorrow with my luggage. Travel accounts of far-flung places, and the latest by the Lady of Dubious Quality."

She stroked her fingers down his arm. "How well you know me."

"I wish to know you as deeply as anyone can know another."

"Why?" she asked with genuine curiosity.

"You have seen and done so much," he answered. "Survived so much. There are worlds and worlds inside you."

"I'm a resource to be exploited?" She lifted an eyebrow.

"You are a person to be known and cherished. For as long as I can have you in my life, that's what I desire."

It gnawed at him, that goddamn farthing, always reminding him of his duty and the pressures of his position.

Now and again, he wished to throw that fucking coin into the ocean. Guilt washed over him—he couldn't push away the lesson his father had been so careful to impart. But hell if it wasn't a burden that he sometimes wanted to flee.

Stories of kings and princes disguising themselves to live amongst the normal people sounded damned appealing.

"Keep speaking such things," she said softly, resting her head on his shoulder, "and I'll open for you like a vault."

Where to start? "What do you like best about being a governess?"

She was quiet briefly. "There's a moment, a beautiful moment, when I give one of my pupils some knowledge. The fact that Elena Lucrezia Cornaro Piscopia received a doctorate in philosophy from the University of Padua in 1678, making her the first woman to receive that degree—in the West, at any rate. Or that the oldest library in the world was founded by Fatima El-Firhi, at the university she also created. These jewels are placed in my students' crowns, making every one of them into empresses."

Her eyes glowed as she spoke, and her smile was as radiant as any queen's diadem.

"You give them the power to believe in themselves," he murmured.

"It's a beautiful power. One I wish every girl in every land could possess. That is my ambition, you know."

"As a governess?"

"Not forever. I hope to save enough that I might start a school for girls and give them the gift of learning."

"What a wonder you are," he said softly.

She chuckled. "A conduit for learning, nothing more."

"*Everything* more." He turned onto his side to face her. "There's an art to teaching, and while there are many poor practitioners of that art, there are those with prodigious gifts. Not just of knowledge, but of this." He rested his palm between her breasts, and her heart beat steadily beneath his touch.

She kissed him, then leaned back, her expression melancholy. "Being the headmistress of a school carries with it its own responsibilities and considerations. Including the fact that whomever is in charge of a school must possess what society considers faultless moral character."

He exhaled, understanding like a vise squeezing the air from him. "Romantic affairs are not part of that faultless moral character."

"When I eventually leave Tarrington House," she said, her voice low, "we can have no more contact with each other."

His lips pressed into a tight seam. Because he had been on the verge of asking her to be his mistress, for as long as she was willing. To the best of his knowledge, his father had not kept a paramour. Owen had planned to remain faithful to his future wife—yet the thought of parting from Cecilia had been a spear through his heart. Keeping her as a mistress wasn't an ideal solution, but it had been the best he'd been able to grasp.

Even that could not be.

"I'd never stand between you and your dreams," he said at last.

She stroked a hand down his face, and her silence confirmed what he suspected. Theirs was an affair that could not last.

"Ellie's only eleven," he added. "So we have considerable time ahead of us before we need to contemplate any of this."

"Many years," Cecilia said with a gentle smile.

The night's sounds surrounded them, crickets and frogs singing in the darkness, forming a protective barrier between them and the world.

"Was it very terrifying," she asked, "casting your first vote in Parliament?"

The change of subject was a momentary relief from pondering saying goodbye to her. He admitted, "I had expected to be shaken to my marrow. Easily, I was the youngest man there, green as a summer hayfield. And yet...When it came my turn to speak, the most curious thing happened." He rubbed his thumb across her bottom lip. "You were in my head."

"Me?"

"What you taught me."

She made a small, alarmed noise. "On the floor of Parliament, you demonstrated how to lick a woman's quim."

He laughed. "You also taught me how to own my authority. It was there, the strength you showed me how to responsibly wield. I looked into all those men's faces, some of them friendly, many of them hostile. The young man fresh from Oxford would have been afraid to make his opinion known—might have even caved to the pressure to vote against his conscience. But I wasn't that inexperienced lad anymore. I felt confident in my strength, because of you."

"Because of *you*," she said, tucking a lock of his hair behind his ear. "You were already heading toward your destination, I merely guided you to the road that would get you there a little more directly."

Threading his fingers with hers, he lay on his back and looked at the night sky spread above them. He hadn't been able to see the stars in

London, yet it made sense that if he *could* see them, it was with her beside him.

"It was a difficult thing to give a boy," he said softly, "that farthing."

"A considerable responsibility to lay on a child's shoulders," she murmured.

"Not every boy would be weighted down with it."

"You aren't *every boy*," she pointed out. "You're you—someone who feels deeply, and that is a wonderful quality."

He snorted. "Not to Englishmen, it isn't." He'd held himself apart from the other aristocratic boys at Eton and Oxford, the ones who had felt entitled to their privilege, which meant that his circle of friends had been small. Small, but valuable.

"What Englishmen value is not precisely the apotheosis of significance," she said drily. "I do hate to disabuse them of the notion that their opinion is not all that matters."

A laugh burst from him. "I don't think you hate disabusing them of that. You enjoy it."

"Perhaps I do." She wore an adorably smug smile, but it faded. "Are you angry with him for giving you that farthing?"

He turned the thought over again, considering it from all angles as though it were a piece of obsidian—one that was darkly beautiful, but could also cut deeply.

"Sometimes," he admitted. "He had his plans for me, and the kind of duke I would become one day. Truth is, I can't *be* him. I want to, but I can't."

"I want you to be yourself," she said firmly. "No one else. You're simply, brilliantly Owen. Beneath all your ducal splendor, that's who you are."

Reaching up, he cupped her jaw, soaking in the feel of her skin against his. "With you, I am more myself than I am with anyone. And I thank you for giving me the gift of *you*. I wish—"

A corner of her mouth lifted sadly. "As do I. But they're only wishes, which have a terrible reputation for not coming true."

CHAPTER NINE

THE NEXT DAY, Owen examined another document related to a tin mining operation that required additional capital. He was careful to give it his full attention. People's livelihoods were at stake, and regardless of how little sleep he'd had last night, the mining scheme deserved thorough concentration and consideration.

He'd gone over the cost estimates as well as projected income potential, making notes to review with his men of business tomorrow. With that accomplished, he set the proposal aside and stood to stretch his cramped muscles. A good swim later in the day would help relieve the tightness, though nothing eased and centered him as much as Cecilia.

His fingers brushed the black crepe around his arm, and a barb of guilt pierced him. It was wrong, somehow, to experience such happiness in the wake of losing his father, yet he couldn't stop himself from being with Cecilia, and living for their stolen time. Existing in a double life, rife with secrets, gnawed at him. He could say nothing to his mother, and would never write of it in his letters to friends from Oxford.

But he wanted to shout it from the roof of Tarrington House: he'd found a woman he cherished beyond reason.

No one could learn of their liaison. Masters of the house could indulge in affairs with governesses, receiving nudges and winks and approving thumps on the back from their fellow aristocratic men. The risk was hers, and hers alone.

He would be praised for his manliness, but society would condemn her for immorality. It was the worst kind of hypocrisy that, though they were both willing participants in their affair, *she* would be the outcast, losing her employment and rendering her unable to find any other work. The school she dreamed of would never come to be. He had to shield her from that fate.

Even though Cecilia deserved far better than stolen moments, that was all he could give her.

He oughtn't brood over the future, and should accept gratefully what he had now. Yet he wanted more. He wanted her always, to fall asleep beside her and wake with her in the full light of morning, perhaps someday to start a family, and walk hand in hand in full view of the world.

Until yesterday, he hadn't known what he truly meant to her, and now that he did, his chest tightened with the futility of his wants and wishes. The best he could hope for now was holding off his mother's push to see him married. He hated the thought of taking any woman who wasn't Cecilia to his bed.

There was a tap at the door, disrupting his thoughts.

"Enter," he said.

Vale stepped into the study. "Forgive me for the interruption, Your Grace, but there is a current matter which requires your attention."

More accustomed now to being the person the staff turned to for direction, Owen asked, "What is the current matter?"

"A caravan of genteel individuals was en route to a gathering in the country when one of their carriages developed an issue with its axle. They were not far from Tarrington House when this situation arose and, knowing you were in residence, it was suggested they stop here and prevail upon the household for assistance."

Owen frowned. "Much as I'd like to provide aid, we're in mourning and not receiving anyone."

"So I explained to them, Your Grace, but I was asked to relay to you the fact that the individuals in the damaged carriage are Lord and Lady Sulgrave."

"You might have told me that first, Vale," Owen said, though there was no reproof in his voice. The viscount was an old friend of his late father—

in fact, the two had been in the same block of boys at Eton many decades ago.

Though it wasn't the custom to entertain guests so soon after a death in the family, for such an unusual situation, an exception could be made. Besides, it would be a fine way to honor Owen's father by playing host to his friend.

"My apologies, Your Grace." The butler dipped his head in dignified contrition.

"Of course, they are welcome to make use of our staff to repair their carriage. While they wait, we'll need refreshments for Lord and Lady Sulgrave and their companions. The day is quite pleasant, so see that the company is brought out to the terrace. And inform the duchess that we are to have visitors. She can determine whether or not she'll want to visit with them, and if she deems it appropriate for my sisters to greet our guests. How many of them are there?"

"I believe there are two other couples with them, as well as three unaccompanied gentlemen, a widow, and her companion."

"Be certain that the cook prepares enough food and drink for everyone."

"Yes, Your Grace." Vale bowed before retreating.

Once he was alone, Owen walked to the pier glass over the fireplace and tried to retie his neckcloth into some measure of tidiness. He had a habit of picking at the fabric around his neck when reading, which helped him focus, but also had the unwanted consequence of making him resemble a wild-eyed poet of the Romantic bent. As the heir, he could afford to appear slightly less than ducal, but now that he *was* the duke, he needed to look suitably distinguished.

Half an hour later, he stood on the terrace with Lord and Lady Sulgrave, as well as their companions, partaking of tea and a bewildering array of pastries and sandwiches. It never ceased to fill him with wonder how adept Tarrington House's cook was, with her ability to provide a bounty of refreshments in such a short amount of time.

The company was on their way to Viscount Sulgrave's country estate, some fifty miles north, and brought with them tales of London. Most everyone had cleared out of the city as the summer heat had descended, but a handful of the ton remained to complain about the weather and ennui.

"You were quite right to flee the moment Parliament was in recess," Sulgrave said before taking a bite of scone. "What a decided bore London is until September."

"His Grace is especially fond of rural life," his mother said from beneath her parasol. She had opted to join the guests, which came as no surprise. Owen's father used to jestingly complain about the number of galas the duchess insisted on hosting throughout the Season, as well as house parties during the summer. "Lately, he is happier here. It is the fresh air that agrees with him."

Smoothing his expression, Owen sipped at his tea. His mother had no idea that, though he did enjoy being in the country, his happiness had one source: the woman currently ensconced in the schoolroom.

"Yes, the countryside is so good for one's health," Sir Kenneth Whelan said from his place by the stone balustrade. He was a hale man who appeared to be in his mid-forties, with fair hair and tanned skin. "When Lady Juliet and I were raising our daughter on the Continent, we kept her away from unhealthy cities as much as possible."

"We *did* compromise," Lady Juliet added with a laugh. She wore her dark brown hair in an artistic arrangement, with fresh flowers tucked in amongst the combs. "A few weeks in a city here, and then a month in the country so we could all restore our constitutions. There's nothing like a good ramble to balance one's humors."

"Very true," Owen said noncommittally. This company was pleasant enough, but how much better it would be to sit on the terrace with Cecilia, unafraid as they enjoyed their tea in the summer afternoon. He could see the sunlight gilding her hair, watch with overt fascination as she brought her cup to her lips, and run his fingers back and forth over the softness of her wrist.

"My own daughters often take exercise in between their lessons," his mother said. "Their governess believes it is important to strengthen their minds as well as their bodies, and I agree with her progressive stance. Difatti, I think we are just at the hour when my girls will take a pause in their studies to for some air. I will tell their governess to bring them out to us."

She waved a footman over to her and conveyed her instructions. At her directive, the servant bowed and left the terrace.

"I always loved it here at Tarrington House," Viscount Sulgrave said, looking around. "One of the finest estates in England, and the best fox hunting too."

"We don't hunt foxes here anymore." Owen tried to keep from sounding too cool, but he'd always abhorred the practice of chasing a defenseless animal on horseback, with hounds eager for blood.

"Since when?" one of Sulgrave's older male guests asked.

"Since I became the duke," Owen answered. Going through the duchy's many holdings, Owen had been pleased to confirm his understanding that when *his* father had inherited the title, he had divested from the Caribbean, and withdrew financial support to shipping lines making their fortune through repugnant practices. Sadly, his father had neglected to end the custom of fox hunting on the estate's grounds, but Owen had seen to that.

Conversation continued, and though he participated as much as would be expected of him, in truth he had little interest in discussing London gossip. He had too much work awaiting him to spend with these relatively genial people, and if he wasn't going to work, taking a quick nap would refresh him so he could give Cecilia all his energy tonight. Last night, she'd whispered that the scene in *The Scoundrel's Willing Captive* involving a blindfold had always intrigued her...

He straightened and smiled with genuine warmth when Maria and Ellie appeared at the French doors. They came forward, looking at the glamorous visitors with interest. His sisters huddled close to their mother, resting their heads on her shoulders and accepting the duchess's maternal caresses.

"What darling children," Lady Juliet cried. "They remind me so much of my Lisbetta."

"She's in finishing school," Sir Kenneth said.

Owen's restless gaze moved toward the French doors. Pleasure filled him when he saw Cecilia stepping out from the house and onto the terrace. Seeing her again banished any impatience he'd felt from entertaining the London visitors.

A governess would not ordinarily join in conversation between the family of the house and their guests, however, which was a damned shame —she had far more interesting things to say than the entire nobly born lot.

Her expression was reserved as she hovered at the periphery. The urge to walk to her and take her hand was so strong he curled his fingers into fists.

"Miss Holme," the duchess said genially. "I trust you do not mind a change in your usual schedule for the girls."

"Change is always welcome, Your Grace," Cecilia answered after curtsying. "It keeps the mind from calcifying."

"Miss Holme is your governess?" Sir Kenneth asked.

Color drained from Cecilia's face, leaving her ashen and waxy. Owen fought with the urge to go to her side, hating that he couldn't show the depth of his concern for her.

What could have shaken her so badly?

SOMEHOW, Cecilia managed to hide her shock well enough to answer with an even, composed voice. "Sir Kenneth, Lady Juliet."

Owen's mother looked from Cecilia to the Whelans. "Oh, that is right! You were her prior employers, and provided her with an excellent character."

Cecilia managed a faint smile. From the corner of her vision, she saw Owen take a step toward her, yet when she held up a discreet hand urging him to stop, he remained in place.

She had prayed she'd never see the Whelans again. With their preference for living on the Continent, and with her in the English countryside, she'd believed it almost impossible their paths would ever cross.

Yet here they were. A single word from them could obliterate her reputation, and end her dream of establishing her own school.

That was all it would take...a hint, an insinuation, and she'd be ruined.

Owen turned to his mother. "Madre, Miss Holme looks tired. She ought to have some rest, and making her stand outside in the hot sun is unfair."

"Bensì." The duchess waved her hand. "You may go, Miss Holme."

Cecilia curtsied before turning and disappearing into the house. God above, if only she could simply run and run. It offered no true solution, and yet the instinct to flee snapped at her heels. With each step, she choked back tears.

Owen caught up with her on the first floor as she made her way to the back stairs that led to the upper servants' quarters.

"Miss Holme, wait," he called softly.

She stopped, but didn't face him. He pulled open a door to a small, seldom used parlor, and motioned for her to go in. She did so, her movements stiff, unable to look at him.

Because she knew the terrible truth now. She'd tried to remain blind, yet there was no denying it now. If Sir Kenneth so much as suggested there had been some impropriety between her and him, everything was lost. And if by some grace he didn't speak of her past, she had her future to consider.

Once the door closed behind her and Owen, he stepped nearer, reaching for her. She slid away so that his fingers grazed her wrist.

"I could tear his fucking throat out," Owen growled.

"You wouldn't hang for his murder," she said lowly, "but you'd be imprisoned, and he's not worth the loss of your liberty."

"Damn it, Cecilia, will you look at me?"

She turned. Surely her eyes showed the depths of her hopelessness.

His expression was tormented. "Tell me how to make it better."

"Dukes can do many things, but they have no ability to change the past," she said without emotion. "I feel no shame in it, but no one can ever know."

"Stop referring to me as a duke," he snarled.

Her gaze lifted to meet his, and for the first time, she took no pleasure in the depths of his dark eyes—because he would soon be lost to her. "That's what you are. A duke. And I am only a governess. The world will always see us as that—a man with power, and a woman who can be used and discarded."

"You are more than that to me." He took her hands in his. "And I don't care what the world thinks."

"That's your privilege, while I have far less of that privilege." She squeezed his hand, as though trying to grip tightly to the feel of him. "Long ago, I thought I was done with illusions, but that's not so. I've been deceiving myself, gulling myself into believing that you and I could go on like this. I was wrong, though. Terribly, terribly wrong."

"Cecilia," he rasped. "No."

"We must stop this, Owen." She spoke with surprising firmness. "Now.

All of it. No more meetings at the cottage. The Whelans reminded me of the truth. If I am to have any possible chance of opening that school, I cannot be your lover. The risk of discovery only increases the longer you and I continue our affair."

"I don't care if we never fuck again," he said fiercely. "I only have to hold you, and talk with you."

Her eyes were hot and damp. "That is worst of all. Because it fools me into thinking that I am yours, and you're mine, when we both know that we must be nothing to each other."

To say it hollowed her out like a cave. Within, she was empty and howling.

"You will never be nothing to me." He ran his thumb over her cheek, catching a falling tear. "You're...you're *everything*."

She shook her head. "Stop. I implore you. Don't say another word, and for the love of God, don't be kind to me. My heart can't withstand that torture."

"Cecilia—"

"It's *Miss Holme* now," she said, "or, better yet, never speak my name again. Please." With a sob, she pulled away from him and stepped to the door. Placing her hand on the wood, she said without looking at him. "They'll be wondering about you downstairs. You need to see to your guests."

Before he could stop her, she wrenched the door open and dashed into the corridor. Behind her, he took three strides in pursuit, then he stopped.

They had begun as instructor and student, yet it went so much deeper than that now. She'd taught him about his power, and he'd learned how to wield it, but had taught her, too. She learned from him how to fully inhabit her own capability. In so doing, he had shown her something no one before ever had. She could be celebrated for her strength.

She needed that strength now, when she'd lost him forever.

CHAPTER TEN

OWEN DREW a breath before knocking on the open door to his mother's private study.

"Entra," she said.

He strode into the chamber just as his mother looked up from her ornately carved escritoire, a pen in her hand. A faint smile curved her lips.

"How you walk now," she murmured. At his puzzled frown, she explained, "With the confident steps of a man. The time you spent in London changed you, I think."

It was not the city that had altered him—that had been Cecilia's doing. Once, he might have entered his mother's study diffidently, but there could be no room for hesitation where Cecilia's future was concerned.

"If there's any resemblance between me and the person I was last month," he answered, "it is purely external."

His mother regarded him, her dark eyes almost exactly like his, from the shape to the color. Right now, her gaze was unreadable.

"Do you recognize this?" From his pocket, he pulled the farthing. "Babbo gave it to me a decade ago."

She rose from her escritoire and walked to him. As she peered at the farthing, her mouth formed a wry shape. "He told me of it, that night. What he hoped to teach you through such a small coin. He wanted so badly you to become a fine man."

"He may be disappointed," Owen said grimly.

Instead of offering him placating murmurs, she tilted her head and said, "It is not for the dead to judge us. The most important judgment comes from within."

"The world judges us, too, cara mamma. This farthing tells me so. It tells me nothing I do is for my sake alone." He held the coin tightly between his fingers. "It tells me of the weight of my responsibility—and that includes who I choose to be my wife."

His heart thudded, but he was not afraid. "Were there objections when babbo married you?"

"So many voices raised," she said with a wry look. "All the pallid English protesting that it was not proper to marry a girl from Napoli. But your father and I, we loved each other too fiercely to heed them." Her expression softened, and grief flashed like a dark banner against the sky.

He took her hand, so much smaller than his, and just beginning to soften with the advance of age. Yet there was nothing weak or fragile about his mother, even in her sorrow.

"I *have* changed," he said. "I've learned things in the wake of losing babbo."

"A lesson from Signorina Holme," his mother noted.

His surprise flared, but could anything have escaped his mother's keen awareness? Firmly, he said, "There's no blame for her. Know this, and take no action against her."

"When you came to me and asked me to take responsibility for Maria and Ellie's education, I knew. I had to trust that my son was a man, a man who could make his own choices. And in tasking me with Signorina Holme's employment, I saw that you would not harm her."

"I care about Cecilia, mamma." Saying it aloud to his mother made the truth resonate within him. "She has my heart."

His mother raised one eyebrow. "Do you have hers?"

"I thought I did." Her face haunted him, hopeless and sorrowful as she ended their affair. "She is convinced that we cannot be together—in any way."

"What are *you* convinced of, figlio mio?"

He let go of his mother's hand and walked to the framed portrait on the wall. It was of him and his sisters, painted shortly before he left for

Eton. Maria was in her simple white frock as she clung to the leg of his breeches, and Ellie was snug in a cradle.

His sisters were now on the verge of becoming young women, and he had left boyhood behind. Every moment brought new understanding, new maturity.

"A lesson changes its meaning depending on whoever is receiving it," he said as he stared at the portrait, "and that includes how *I* interpret what babbo told me."

Turning back to his mother, he said firmly, "To me that farthing means that in loving whom I want, I'm telling the world that love is more important than artificial social barriers. Love surpasses *everything*."

"Love," his mother said, her brows climbing higher.

"Yes, mamma," he answered levelly. "L'amo. I love her. And if she'll have me, I want to be her husband."

Energy filled him to speak it aloud. He hadn't allowed himself to think of the depths of his feelings for Cecilia and what their future might bring, but there was nothing to fear. Precisely the opposite. He was never stronger, never more powerful than when he gave full rein to his emotions and led with his heart.

"She has taught me so much, mamma. She helped me learn what it was to be unafraid."

His mother clicked her tongue. "Do you want a governess or do you want a wife?"

"I want a partner, an equal. She's all of those things, and more. So much more."

His mother walked to him. She possessed an imposing beauty, yet beneath the cool hauteur of her exterior, one glimpsed a tempestuous, passionate being.

"If it is amore," his mother said, "vero amore, then that is all I truly wish for you, figlio mio. And when the time comes, any whey-faced English family who will not wed their sons to my daughters, how do you say, can go hang."

~

THE POND'S surface reflected the midnight sky, a shard of moon floating atop an expanse of liquid ebony. At this late hour, the water was no doubt hold enough chill to steal Cecilia's breath, but that would presume that she had enough breath left after hours of weeping.

Before walking out to the pond tonight, she'd glanced at herself in the small mirror perched atop her washstand. She'd never been one of those women who cried prettily, with a single crystalline tear tracing down a smooth cheek. Instead, her nose was red, her eyes were swollen, and her entire face was mottled.

It only meant that she possessed strong feelings. Some days she was grateful to feel as much as she did, but tonight, with her heart open and ragged, she wished she could have been the porcelain ornament her father had wanted her to be.

Yet denying how she felt about Owen, and what it meant to give him up, was a grave and terrible wrong. He had been—no, he *was* the best part of her life because he'd rejoiced in every part of her.

She would have to learn to live with the pain of not having him as hers. She might survive, but it would be a hard and barren existence.

There was no breeze tonight, and the pond's polished surface remained unbroken. Had she the physical strength, she'd take one final swim in it, regardless of the water's temperature. But she was limp with exhaustion, so she remained seated on the banks, immersing herself in memories of her and Owen frolicking in the water, and how they'd spoken of their innermost selves in the secret depths of a summer night.

She ought to get up and leave, go back inside and prepare herself for the next chapter. Yet she remained where she was, too tired and too weighted with sorrow to do anything beyond wishing that the world was a different place, and that history had been kinder. They were futile wishes, but that didn't stop her from making them.

She stiffened at the sound of the rustling grass behind her, then moved to rise.

"Don't go," Owen said. He approached slowly, as if wary that she might bolt like a doe. "Can we just...sit here, together? I won't do anything without your express permission."

What was one more injury in an already mortally wounded heart? She lowered herself back to the grass, and after a moment, he eased down beside her. The night kept him mostly in shadow, but she knew his form anywhere—especially in the dark.

"Didn't expect to find you out here," he murmured into the silence.

"This place is special," she said softly. "It's where I first saw you when you had returned to Tarrington House as the new duke."

"Spying on me as I swam." There was a smile in his voice.

"It wasn't spying. I accidentally saw you."

"And didn't draw attention to yourself," he teased, "or look away. A myth in reverse—Diana watching Acteon."

Only when her cheeks ached did she realize that she, too, was smiling. It was always so good between them, so comfortable and full of potential.

Her smile fell away as bitter truths confronted her.

"That myth didn't end well for Acteon," she said quietly. "Torn apart by his own hounds."

"Cecilia—"

"I have something for you." She held out a folded piece of paper before he could say anything more and completely obliterate her with his beautiful soul. "It's for the duchess, in fact, but if you could give it to her, I'd be most grateful."

He took the paper from her. "What is this?"

"My resignation." She had written the letter in the gamekeeper's unlocked cottage, surrounding herself in wonderful, tormenting memories.

He hissed, as if in pain. "No."

"I cannot remain here any longer." It was an agony to keep speaking, to tell him what she had to, but there was no alternative.

"Sir Kenneth is gone," he objected. "The whole party left this afternoon. There's no danger."

"The danger is living beneath your roof, knowing that you're so close, but completely out of reach. It's like living just beyond the boundaries of Paradise, looking in and seeing what's been lost. I'm a strong woman," she continued, her voice catching, "but not strong enough to endure that kind of pain."

"Where will you go?"

"It will be far from here, I know that much."

His hands were suddenly on her shoulders as he knelt in front of her. The shadows concealed his expression, but even in the dark she felt the intensity of his gaze.

"Marry me," he said, those two words reverberating with strength. When she said nothing, only stared at him in stunned wordlessness, he went on, "Be my wife, and we'll never have to be apart."

Her heartbeat was a thunderstorm within her. "Impossible."

"It doesn't have to be," he said fiercely. "It can be you and me forever, all you have to do is say yes."

Hope was a terrible, monstrous creature within her, threatening to devour her. "You're so young," she said, mostly to remind her of all the obstacles between them. "You haven't truly dedicated yourself to the bride hunt and finding your perfect duchess."

"I've already met my perfect duchess," he said hotly, "and she's right here in front of me."

God, how she wanted so much to reach for what he offered. Yet— "What about your mother and sisters? The scandal of marrying the governess? There *will* be a scandal. If the Whelans talk—"

"Whelan and his wife will be made to understand that if they don't keep silent, I'll buy up their debts and dun them into oblivion."

She gaped at him. "Would you do that?"

"I'm a duke." His smile was pure, cold arrogance. "I'll do as I bloody well please."

Pressing her fingers to her lips, she said in half horror, half admiration, "You inhabit that role so completely now."

"You gave me that strength. And I will use it to face anyone with how I feel about you."

"What of the duchess? Neapolitan mothers are fierce in defending their children."

"And their sons are fierce in defending the women they love."

She inhaled sharply. Surely she hadn't heard him correctly? Surely his love couldn't be hers, could it?

"None of it matters," he went on. "All of my oaths and promises and vows mean nothing unless..." He swallowed. "Unless you love me, too."

Shaking, she brought her hands up to cup his face, feeling the delicious abrasion of his stubble, and the dampness of his cheeks. He was kindhearted, and loyal, and both his mind and his heart contained profound depth. And she was important to him, truly important.

"I do love you, Owen. I love you beyond reason."

He kissed her, fiercely, and she kissed him back, losing herself in the passion that rose so readily between them.

"That's all that matters," he rumbled when they broke apart to breathe. "Everything else are details we can overcome together. And I've already spoken to my mother."

Aghast, Cecilia stared at him. "Why has she not run me off the estate?"

"Because she knows that where you go, I go."

Wrapped around her, his arms were strong and secure and sheltering. They would hold her up when she needed support, and be there when she stood on her own.

"Your dream of the school belongs to you," he whispered, nuzzling her neck, "but I would love to help transform it from a dream to a reality."

"Oh, yes, Owen." She pressed her lips to his, trembling with unbound joy. Still, she could not help but ask, "Are you certain? That it's *me* you want for your wife?"

His smile flashed. "I didn't want an education in pleasure for any other woman, Cecilia. I wanted to learn how to please *you*."

She leaned close, breathing him in, this wondrous man who had, with his courage and passion, gifted her the world.

"You've done it." She pressed her lips to his. "Never has a teacher been so pleased with their student."

"They say that education is a lifelong process," he said between hungry kisses. "I'm ready to learn everything you can teach me."

She had never believed anyone could fully accept and celebrate who she truly was, or that she could find someone to believe in her dream as much as she did. Owen was all those things, and so much more. He was the finest person she knew. There was no one like him.

"We'll teach each other," she murmured. "Our first lesson as an engaged couple starts now."

The End.

～

Looking for more appallingly hot Regency romance by Eva Leigh?

Check out Would I Lie to the Duke, featuring a dirty talking, sexually submissive duke and the woman who brings him to his knees...

ALSO BY EVA LEIGH

The Union of the Rakes:

My Fake Rake

Would I Lie to the Duke

Waiting For a Scot Like You

The London Underground:

From Duke Till Dawn

Counting on a Countess

Dare to Love a Duke

The Wicked Quills of London:

Forever Your Earl

Scandal Takes the Stage

Temptations of a Wallflower

ABOUT THE AUTHOR

Eva Leigh is a romance author who writes novels chock-full of determined women and sexy men. She enjoys baking, spending too much time on the Internet, and listening to music from the '80s. Eva and her husband live in Central California.

You can sign up for Eva's newsletter here!

evaleighauthor.com

THE DUKE MAKES ME FEEL...

ADRIANA HERRERA

CHAPTER ONE

"I NEED to speak to Marena Baine." What was it about men who could not take no for an answer?

"Sir, I've already explained to your footman that the potency tinctures are back-ordered," she informed the man who had entered her shop. The authority in his voice—and the immediate request to speak to the owner —told Marena he was probably the employer of the extremely persistent individual she'd just sent on his way. This was tiresome, and she was not in a mood to placate men with too much money and little manners.

It had all started when she'd given a sample of her tinctures to one of her most faithful patrons after she'd complained that her husband had been unusually deficient in their amorous pursuits. After a couple of tries, the earl in question had taken to the mixture of ginseng, ginger, and white oak bark. Within weeks, half of the ton was trampling into her little apothecary in the hither end of Haymarket, demanding she sell them the "miraculous elixir." It had been a boon for business, but this level of demand had its drawbacks. Such as aristos interfering with her end-of-the-day routine.

"*Potency tinctures?*" the man finally asked, his voice hoarse with what sounded like suppressed humor. "I can assure you I don't require any assistance with my stamina." He said the last word with obvious amusement.

She almost blurted, "That's what they all say," but even if her current mood had her feeling uncharacteristically pugnacious, Marena was never reckless. Attending to the maladies of London society's upper crust meant one had to cultivate a monastic level of patience and master absolute emotional disengagement. Marena had sturdy walls protecting her from the harsh words, condescension, and ludicrous requests tossed daily in her direction. A man trampling into her shop and making demands, unfortunately, did not even achieve the label of being remarkable.

She gathered the final reserves of her patience and turned around to explain one last time that she did not have tinctures to sell. But the words died in her throat. She recognized that mouth and those entrancing blue eyes.

"There you are," he said pleasantly, his eyes fixed on her, a small smile tugging at his lips, as if they'd been playing a game of hide-and-seek.

What was the Duke of Linley doing in her shop?

"Could you fetch Ms. Baine for me, darling?" he asked idly, his gaze roaming over the shelves on the walls which were lined with neatly labeled ceramic canisters. He appeared to be completely unconcerned, as if he were guaranteed to get anything and everything he asked for.

This man was truly testing her restraint. The nerve. She was nobody's darling. She didn't care who he was. This was the plight of dealing with London's high society—one could not toss them out on their ear for behaving insolently.

"Sir, I—"

"Tell her Arlo Kenworthy would like a word, won't you?"

She felt unsettled by his presence, and not with the mix of irritation and exhaustion that seemed be an essential part of any visit from the nobility. No, this was a flutter in her belly and a warmth in her chest that truly had no place while she was alone with a duke. She was about to open her mouth to tell him she was aware of who he was, but the fact that he used his family name, and not his title, gave her pause. In her experience, dukes, did not miss an opportunity to assert their importance.

Well-bred in England meant specific things, and brawn and vitality were not typically what she associated with the expression. But this man was a *presence*. Even his hair was arresting. She'd never seen that particular shade of brown, almost like burnt copper, making for a striking contrast with his piercing blue eyes. A face that demanded a second glance, as her mother would say.

He was so tall his head almost reached the frame of the door. And he had the shoulders and chest of a man who worked with his hands, not one who spent his time in the House of Lords. But that was only one of the reasons that made Arlo Kenworthy one of the most talked-about peers. One could somehow resist falling under the spell of his presence, and perhaps even defend against the effects of his strapping physique. But that mouth was where the battle with all common sense was lost. Sinful. Absolutely sinful. He was almost too much to take in at once. And what could the man possibly want with her?

She'd seen him at a salon organized by Lady Barbara Smith Bibichon, where he passionately spoke his support for women's enfranchisement. He'd impressed her, but she never imagined she'd see him again, and certainly not in her shop. Not only did he look to be in exceptionally good health, but even if he did need her services, he did not seem the type to do his own shopping.

He cleared his throat, bringing her musings to a stop. "Am I to wait much longer?"

That haughty tone should've irritated her, but instead prompted an irritating pulsing in her chest. After years of dealing with all kinds of ill-mannered patrons, Marena had trained herself to maintain a veneer of placid detachment. It usually worked, but occasionally there would be someone who would walk in and pique her curiosity.

On the rare occasions she felt that urge, she'd play a game she'd invented. She would take the person in slowly from head to toe, and imagine the labor of the many hands involved in dressing a grown, capable, and able-bodied adult. Usually by the time she got down to the lustrous leather-clad feet, she could scarcely come up with anything more than tepid disdain. The problem was it did not seem to be working with Arlo Kenworthy.

She stayed behind the counter, feeling reassured by the solid wooden structure that kept him at a distance, and finally revealed herself. "I'm Marena."

He widened his eyes, probably surprised that the proprietor of the apothecary was a Black woman. Or maybe it was the way she'd said her name. She'd pronounced it in Spanish, surprising herself. She usually gave shop patrons the anglicized version, turning her name into a harsh sound for the benefit of British sensibilities. That, and it was a better alternative than subjecting herself to hearing her given name be butchered a dozen times a day.

Marena guarded her real name like a treasured secret. It was a fanciful combination of the words for sand and sea her mother had come up with, and felt like a tangible connection to the tropical beaches that shaped her childhood. She never uttered it for people she didn't think would treat it kindly, but somehow for this stranger, she had.

After another moment of charged silence, Linley dipped his head, eyes still unnervingly focused on her face. "Marena."

He came as close to a proper pronunciation as she'd heard from a Brit in the fifteen years since her family had touched upon the shores of Bristol. And no, that absolutely could not be a shiver of pleasure running down her spine. It was exhaustion and exasperation, because how dare he get it right on the first try?

"How may I help you?" she asked brusquely. In response, he offered her his hand, which was unexpectedly personable...and discomfiting. One thing she'd learned in the time since her store's popularity had surged was that to London's high society, she was the help. "Your Grace."

He raised an eyebrow at the deference. He hadn't revealed his title, but it wasn't like he was an unknown. Arlo Kenworthy was notorious. The son of the accidental Duke of Linley. Fifteen years ago, Hubert Kenworthy had come into a duchy when a distant cousin died without an heir. Before his rise to the very top of the nobility, he'd been a career foreign office man who'd married an American woman—a Quaker, of all things—and, for the most part, avoided Britain as much as he possibly could. The man had been an unorthodox aristocrat in every way possible except when it came to his penchant for excess.

After his son Arlo took the reins of the estate ten years ago, the dukedom had flourished and was now one of the most prosperous in the Commonwealth. To the befuddlement of every landed aristocrat in England, Arlo had achieved this feat by working. He was a financier, a cunning investor, an advocate for workers' rights, and a suffragist. He brazenly spoke out against archaic, redundant systems. He was thoroughly despised by most of his peers and he seemed to thrive because of it. His father's passing had made him duke less than a year ago, and to the ton's dismay—and morbid fascination—Arlo continued to be as irreverent as ever.

"Ms. Baine." She jumped at the sharpness of his tone, not that she could blame him. She'd been gawking at the man like he was a showpiece at a museum.

"My apologies," she said, flustered, her face hot from embarrassment. "The shop is closed for the day, but if you'd like to place an order, I can have a messenger see it to you once it's ready." She was proud of managing to sound mostly normal. "We would, of course, make sure that your privacy was guarded."

His eyebrow rose slightly further up on his forehead at that, and she swore he was biting back a smile. "There seems to be such a furor for your products I am almost curious to try them."

"I'd be happy to put your name on the list," she informed him as she stepped around the counter, ruthlessly ignoring the fluttering in her chest. She almost brushed against him before reaching the door. She locked it before realizing she was now alone in the shop with a notorious nobleman.

"I require a bit more from you today, Miss Baine." His voice was warm and rough, and his eyes on her made every piece of clothing on her body feel constraining. As she usually did at the end of the day, she had already taken her apron off and slipped the pins out of her hair. He was seeing her without her armor.

"My sister is about to return," she blurted out untruthfully.

"Your sister? Lluvia Baine, the physician?" His mention of her sister's name brought Marena's back up.

"How do you know my sister?" She sounded defensive, but she was tired of whatever cat and mouse game the man was playing. The end of the day was no time for subterfuge.

"I don't." He let that sit for a breath, then a second one, and she was ready to scream in frustration by the time he opened his mouth again. "Know her. That is."

"Your Grace, with the utmost respect..." After deciding there was no polite way to say it she muttered, "Get on with it."

To Marena's confusion, her rudeness seemed to elicit an amused glint in the man's eyes. "I'm looking for your friend, the midwife Delfine Boncouer." The words razed through her weariness, and instantly she was completely alert. She almost wished he'd come to see her about a prick potion. He cleared his throat again. This time, the sound was one of discomfort. "I need to find her."

Judging from the set of his shoulders and the furrow on his brow, the Duke of Linley was not here for a social call with Delfine, and this could only mean trouble. "I'm not certain how I can help you. Delfine doesn't live here."

"I'm aware of that. She lives with Lluvia Baine, your sister, who has also disappeared. I've been looking for Delfine for almost a year, but she seems to have left London without a trace. Since Delfine has no family, I wondered if you had information on her whereabouts."

"It's 'You-be-ah,'" she corrected sharply, irritated by the way he mispronounced her sister's name. "It means rain."

"Lluvia," he repeated, pronouncing it perfectly, while Marena hastily tried to deduce what the man wanted.

A year ago, Delfine had to leave London in haste after the family of a young woman who'd come to her for treatment almost managed to have her thrown in gaol. Apparently, emboldened by the understanding and validation she found under Delfine's care, the young woman had gone to the police and accused an older and powerful male family member of rape.

In response, the family sent her to an asylum for the insane and asked a judge to charge Delfine with manslaughter for performing an abortion, even though Delfine had only stepped in after the girl had miscarried. The whole thing was an unholy mess. If this man was here looking into their whereabouts and expecting Marena to betray her friend, he would be sorely disappointed.

"I'm sorry, but I can't help you, Your Grace."

Your Grace.

Arlo had heard those two particular words directed at the men in his family for a good portion of his life. First, at his father and, in the last year, at himself. He sometimes marveled at how, depending on who was proffering the deference, it could be infused with regard, respect, adulation, and on occasion, even anger or disdain. But he had never heard them uttered as an indictment on his person.

Despite Marena's obvious unwillingness to cooperate, Arlo did feel marginally better knowing Delfine had people who stood up for her. Formidable people, at that. In the few minutes he'd had with her, he could see this woman was a firebrand. The look the herbalist was levelling at him was not merely defiant; it was menacing. She would do whatever was necessary to protect her friend and her sister.

He'd heard about the Baine sisters, of course. The daughters of a retired foreign officer who'd gone to the West Indies on a short assignment, only to come back from Hispaniola twenty years later with a wife and two daughters. Even before his death, Connor Baine had been a legend in the Exterior Office, a skilled diplomat and respected botanist. He'd opened this apothecary upon his return, and his wife, who had been a root worker back in her homeland, was the one who had mixed the remedies and salves. Now his daughters ran the place—or more like the youngest one, Marena, did.

Despite his feigned ignorance, he'd also been be aware of her tinctures which could supposedly restore any man's stamina to that of a young buck. What he did not know—what no one had mentioned—was that Marena Baine was the most beautiful woman in London. If he would've known, he would've prepared for her. For the mass of chocolate brown curls streaked with honey cascading over her shoulders. For those lips, which even twisted in an unhappy expression, were lush and inviting.

The more his eyes took in, the more he wanted to touch and taste. And this...had to stop. This was where his similarities to his father became dangerous. Arlo could get his head turned in a second and forget what he was about. This was not the time, and this was not the woman...no matter how beguiling she was.

With great effort, he lifted his eyes from her lips to brown eyes that were looking at him with a distinctly unfriendly expression. "I'm aware Delfine isn't here, Miss Baine. I'd like some assistance discovering *where* she's gone." In the years since he'd been at the helm of the Linley estate, he had gained a reputation for his keen eye for investments. He'd become excellent at detecting what others could not. He would not get anything from Marena Baine that she was not willing to give. "And I see that you're protective of your sister. It's admirable and I respect it. But I assure you, I mean neither of them any harm."

"*Torres.* My full name is Marena Baine-Torres," she corrected him, her back still pressed to the door. His man had not told him they used their mother's family name as well. That was the kind of detail that could've been useful. Now he had to make amends. This woman wasn't just a pretty face; she was brazen. Unafraid. She knew her place in the world, and she was not about to let anyone, not even a duke, deny her what she was due.

"Miss Baine-Torres," he conceded with a nod. "I assure you the business I have with Miss Boncoeur will be of interest to her. To her benefit, even."

She narrowed those winsome brown eyes at him again before she spoke. "Forgive me for not taking your words at face value."

With that, she pushed from the door of the shop and walked behind the counter. It wasn't a big space, so she brushed past him, giving him a whiff of lemon and something spicier he couldn't quite place. Then she gave him a view that had him wondering if it would have been a better idea to send his grandmother on this particular errand.

The woman's bottom was...distracting. A perfect peach he desperately wanted to take a bite out of. Her dress was simple—cotton in light yellow and white stripes—but made by someone skilled. The fabric hugged every line and curve, highlighting her lush figure perfectly. No bustle, but still her waist flared out to hips and an arse that beckoned him.

He was tongue-tied. Like a damn schoolboy.

He, Arlo Kenworthy, once the most unflappable man in the House of Lords, struck speechless in the presence of an ...herbalist. An herbalist who was beginning to look at him like she was going to chuck him out of her shop if he didn't "get on with it." He didn't blame her for being tight-lipped; he knew why Delfine had left London. The private inquiry officer he'd hired to find his half-sister made short work of uncovering that. What he had not been able to find out for love or money was where she'd gone.

He breathed in and exhaled. This was the first time he would tell a stranger that his late father, the fourth Duke of Linley, had fathered a child with a Haitian woman while on a diplomatic two-year expedition to Hispaniola, and then had left her and the child there. His father, who had spent most of Arlo's life lecturing him about maintaining a moral compass and who had called him to task hundreds of times for not upholding the respectability of the family name, had seemed to lose his own morality when it came time to face his responsibilities. Now it was up to Arlo to make this right.

"I'm looking for the whereabouts of Delfine Boncoeur because she's my sister." Arlo had been taught by his mother about the impact of words. He'd heeded that lesson always, mindful of what he said and how it could make people feel, but he'd rarely ever thought of the impact his own words had on him. His confession to this woman in this small space, redolent with warm fragrances, had his heart galloping in his chest.

"Your sister?" Disbelief tinged Marena's voice, and he could not begrudge her that. She angled her head to one side, studying him. At least this part, the distrust and the scrutiny, he'd been ready for. *That* he had anticipated.

"My father named her in his will." The expected onslaught of anger and confusion coursed through him at the thought of what his father had done. The frustration of never knowing why his father had hidden his sister from him, only to leave him with the responsibility of finding her. Why did he claim in death the child he'd forsaken in life? Arlo would never know. "I'd like to see her get what belongs to her." He breathed through too much feeling, too much that he did not want to think about, and looked at Marena again. And her face soothed him in a way that would surely bring about another set of problems eventually.

"I've known Delfine my whole life and lived with her since I was twelve-years old," she scoffed incredulously. "I would've certainly heard if she were the daughter of a duke."

"Delfine may not know," he explained. The private detective could not find out if Delfine was made aware of who her father was. "I only learned of her existence on my father's death. She has a right to claim what is hers."

The truth was more than that. Arlo wanted to know if, like him, Delfine yearned for a sibling. But that was not something he was ready to share. So he told Marena the other thing he'd come to say. "I want to help her with the situation that forced her to leave the city." She barely blinked at his words. "I will put the family's name and influence behind that help, if necessary."

Marena's tightly crossed arms suddenly fell to her sides, and her sharp eyes assessed him once again. A thaw, a minor one, but still it was there. "I have to think about what you're saying," she said. "I need to talk to my mother..." She paused, lifting a hand in the air, palm out. "Not that I know where Delfine is."

He knew *that* was false, but he would take this minimal concession as a win.

"Do you have a calling card?" she asked, clearly flustered, which brought an enticing red tint to her cheeks.

"Here," he said, plucking one from his breast pocket and handing it over.

She looked at it for a long moment, then placed it face down on the counter. "If I have anything else to say, I will send word, Your Grace." With that, she lifted a hand in the direction of the shop's door. "I will unlock it for you," she offered, already moving toward him.

It seemed he'd been dismissed. He should be glad he'd gotten closer to finding out where his sister was, but he felt unsettled. Like he'd opened a door which could not be closed, and it all had to do with the woman who was presently ushering him out of her little shop.

Marena Baine-Torres was not what he'd expected. Arlo's life rarely offered thrills these days, but as he stepped out of Baine's Apothecary, he could barely keep himself from asking her when he would see her again.

CHAPTER TWO

MARENA HAD BEEN TO MAYFAIR, of course. The herbalist of Haymarket made house calls when high society patrons did not want their peers to suspect them of needing assistance with certain ailments. The women especially would send their carriages with footmen and ladies' maids to fetch her.

She'd been in these homes dozens of times. Houses with names recognized by Londoners as if they were city landmarks. She had been in them, but she had never done so for a personal reason. The short distance between the end of Portland Place, where she lived, and Hyde Park might as well have been the Atlantic Ocean. Mayfair was not Marena's world. But that would not stop her from doing what she needed to.

After a long and stilted conversation the night before, her mother had confirmed that the late Duke of Linley was in fact Delfine's father. He had not been the duke when he'd been in Haiti. He'd been the dashing Hubert Kenworthy, a colleague of Marena's father. And after a short and furtive affair with Delfine's mother, the thoughtless prick left her with child and sodded off back to England. Before her death, Delfine's mother had told her the truth about who her father was, but it scarcely mattered since the man had never acknowledged her.

So now here Marena was, ready to be cordial and polite as was required of her. This man could be the key to bringing Delfine and Lluvia back home, and if that meant dealing with the likes of Arlo Kenworthy, she would do so. She stopped at the half-open gate leading up to the door of the Kenworthys' townhouse. Then reminded herself it was actually called Linley House, and *she* was about to go see a duke. A vexingly handsome duke with eyes exactly the color of the Caribbean Sea, who had burst into her life twenty-four hours ago and was still lingering in her thoughts.

She stood back to take in at the stone monstrosity. It was on Park Lane, and if she turned, she'd get a view of the flurry of activity in Hyde Park. She'd looked the house up in the Cunningham's guide. She knew the name of the architect who designed it, and even who built the stone gate. Having some piece of information that made her feel like she wasn't completely in the dark put Marena at ease.

She supposed it was from those first years in London when everything and everyone felt like a mystery she would never unravel. When it seemed her accent and the color of her skin gave away her status as a foreigner before she got a chance to utter a syllable. She loathed feeling out of sorts, not knowing what to expect. And Arlo Kenworthy had her feeling extremely out of her depth.

Marena marched up the stairs, clutching her handbag so tightly she feared she might snap it in two. She was barely at the door when it opened to reveal a tall and handsome man dressed in uniform.

"Miss Baine-Torres," he said in the accent she'd learned to connect to Jamaica. Every Caribbean island had its unique blend of West African, native, and colonizer languages. It was comforting to find a familiar sound in this house where she was about to do something that would surely be unpleasant.

Just speak, *Marena.* "I'm here to see His Grace."

"Certainly. He's in his study." He lifted a hand to gesture beyond the foyer toward a pair of massive wood doors. "Please," the man said, and Marena began to walk. Her heart was beating fast. She needed to get herself under control. Meeting a man who was used to getting his way while feeling peevish could only lead to trouble.

The butler walked and talked as they made their way through the house. "It's through here," he explained as they passed a large round malachite tabletop with a crystal vase full of hothouse roses.

He came to a stop when they arrived at the double doors, and promptly knocked as Marena held her breath.

HER HAIR WAS UP. The mass of curls he had not been able to stop thinking about was now coiled into a crown of braids. A damned travesty.

Still, his skin prickled from the sight of her. *Open your mouth, Arlo. Speak.*

"Miss Baine-Torres," he finally said with a terse nod, moving aside for her to pass. She gave him a look he could not quite decipher and stepped in. "Cyrus, would you be so kind to bring us a tray of tea?"

She raised an eyebrow at that, her shoulders straightening as if she expected to carry out this conversation while standing in the doorway of his study.

"Your Grace. I don't mean to stay long." She followed that with the most insouciant curtsy he had ever seen. He had to press his lips together to keep from laughing because the woman was truly irreverent and, blast it all, that only made her more appealing.

"Miss Baine-Torres, p—"

She held up a hand at him. "Please, call me Marena." She shook her head, something resembling humor pulling at her lips. "I commend you for trying, but you butcher the Torres."

His face heated and a sensation he could not quite identify pulsed in his chest, making him want to scold and ravish her all at once. But then she smiled, and the pulsing transformed into a different thing altogether. "Don't fret, Your Grace. It was a valiant attempt. I find the Scots are the only ones who can do the Castilian rolled *r*'s any justice. Marena will do."

Arlo could only be grateful she was the sole witness to the way his voice shook when he finally said her name. "Marena, please come in."

He'd been expecting her, but he'd not expected her effect on him. No. That was a lie. He had not stopped thinking about that yellow dress or her brown eyes. And her mouth...the mouth was the biggest obstacle when it came to behaving like a human being when it came to this woman. As they made their way into the room, he noticed how the sage green dress she wore contrasted with her gold and brown hair. He was riveted by a few curls that had come loose from her braid to frame her face. He'd never been a gawker, but he could see now how people could fall into the habit. Life in the nobility oscillated between stodgy to maddeningly boring, and for Arlo, the only thing that seemed to provide any excitement was finding ways to scandalize his peers. He'd spent years wondering if anyone could spark a fire within him again. And here she was, glaring at him like he was a sodding fool.

She stood in the middle of the room, he supposed, waiting for him to tell her where to sit. There was his desk, but it seemed impersonal to sit with about a meter of solid oak between them. Usually that type of advantage appealed to him, but once again this woman's presence was wreaking havoc on his instincts. He looked to the small settee, decided so much proximity would be ill-advised given the situation, and finally settled on the two armchairs on either side of the hearth.

"Please." He extended his hand and bowed his head, and after a moment of observing him and probably surmising—accurately—that there was something seriously wrong with him, Marena took a seat.

As he sank into the dark blue velvet cushions, he heard Cyrus's light footsteps as he wheeled in a tea cart. The next few minutes were consumed with cream and sugar specifications, and debates between scones and slices of ginger cake. But Cyrus was exceptionally efficient at his job, and soon they were alone again, with their teacups acting as shields between them.

He considered what to say for a moment, then another, and decided to go with what had always worked for him in business: bluntness. "I'd like to pay you for your assistance in finding my sister." She widened those bewitching brown eyes and gave a miniscule shake of her head.

"No." It wasn't even a protest, just a statement of fact.

"Yes." He could issue edicts too.

She shook her head again, eyes on him. "This is important to me, to my family. Delfine is like a sister. More than that." She lowered her eyes so that her eyelashes seemed to kiss her cheekbones.

He was a fervent admirer of every part of a woman. Over the years, he'd taken pains to learn the best places to make them fall apart with pleasure. Yet he'd never noticed eyelashes. How they curved into a cheek, fluttering over the skin...

For fuck's sake, Arlo. Focus.

"We want her back safely. She should not be hiding like a common criminal when all she did was save that girl's life." Her voice hardened. "All Delfine has ever wanted was to heal people."

From what he'd seen yesterday, he knew Marena would defend Delfine, would be a true friend, and yet the barely restrained anger in her words cracked something in him. This kind of loyalty was not something he came across often in his world. He looked at her for a moment, sitting tall, her head high. A queen, not because of the finery in the room, or the luxury surrounding her. But because she had the heart of one.

"We can discuss money later," he said roughly, eliciting an unfriendly look. "I know you have no reason to trust me," he offered coolly, suddenly self-conscious of what she might think of him. "I also know I have a certain reputation of being irreverent within the peerage, but I assure you my intention is to see...Delfine back home safely." He almost said *my sister*, but something held him back. The way she was looking at him made Arlo feel like he had not earned that right yet.

"I don't care what people think," Marena responded with a shake of her head. "and I don't usually take the nobility's word on anyone's charac-ter, especially someone who challenges their hold on power. If I heeded what society said about my own right to exist..." She scoffed. "Well, let's just say I would not be running my shop. I don't pay attention to any of it." Her tone was impatient, like she had no time for such nonsense as societal norms.

"Then why won't you let me compensate you for the help you're providing?" She pursed her lips—clearly irritated he'd used her own words to get one over her—and bloody hell, he wanted to kiss her. More than that. He was becoming increasingly fixated on finding out how she tasted right at the juncture where her neck and shoulder met.

"I don't want your money." She paused, as if realizing her tone had been more than a little pointed. "Your Grace." He smothered the laugh bubbling up his throat at the grumbling deference.

"Arlo," he said. "It's only fair."

She harrumphed and shifted in her seat, her eyes everywhere but him. Marena Baine-Torres had opinions on the nobility. And that thought brought an image of her hissing her less-than-favorable assessment at him while he made his way down her body, kissing and licking every inch of that flawless skin.

"Arlo," she said, bringing him back from his lustful thoughts. "If you insist on me calling you by your name, the least you can do is respond when I do," she griped. His cock pulsed in his trousers.

"I find myself distracted today," he said, looking at her mouth again.

That red tinge from yesterday appeared on her cheeks. He put down his teacup, just to have something to do. The air practically crackled between them, and he lost the thread of the conversation altogether.

"She's in Paris," she offered jolting him back to the matter at hand.

He considered the answer for a moment. France. "She must've been fearful if she'd fled the British Isles entirely," he said, and Marena quickly nodded in agreement.

"Things were grim, and it seemed like the best option."

"I need you to accompany me to Paris."

She looked at him, unblinking. "I can't do that."

"Delfine has no reason to trust me, but if you are there with me, it may be easier," he reasoned, but Marena's expression was completely shuttered.

"*I* don't have any reason to trust you."

He pressed his lips shut to keep from growling the command on the tip of his tongue. "I will make sure your business suffers no loss. If you know where she is, we should not be gone more than a week. It's—"

"No. And my business is none of your concern," she informed him, outrage coming through in her voice. "I can't travel on my own with you. What will people think, I—"

"I thought you didn't care what people thought."

"I don't," she snapped, her eyes focused on his face. "But I do care about aristos hearing I'm letting noblemen take me on holidays to Paris, and then having them in my shop thinking they can take liberties. I deal with enough already." He didn't miss the barely repressed shudder that coursed through her, and fury ignited in his chest.

"Liberties," he ground out, barely able to keep himself from demanding she tell him the names of every bastard who had harassed her. He felt bloodthirsty, reckless with the need to hurt anyone who had pestered her. Then he remembered he belonged to the very class of people who'd done that to her. He felt shame settle in his gut like sludge. He needed to stop wasting this woman's time.

"Delfine needs to know I am who I say I am. I can bring them home, Marena."

He could see the moment she relented. Her shoulders drooped and she closed her eyes, taking deep breaths. When she opened them, they were flinty. "Four days. Two for travel, two in Paris. And you can keep your money." She stood then, and ran a hand over the skirt of her dress, her gaze everywhere but on him. "I'll need the next two days to arrange some things."

"Do you have a passport? We will need it at Calais."

She gave a sharp nod in response and with a grimace muttered, "Yes, and I will use it to get to Paris *on my own*."

Her tone brooked absolutely no argument, but blast it all, he would not let her steamroll over him. He didn't want her taking the train and ferry on her own.

"Your job is not to protect me," she protested, as if she could read his thoughts. "I lived in Paris on my own a few years ago. I can get myself there without your assistance... Your Grace." She opened her mouth and then closed it. Her lips pressed together, ensuring whatever almost slipped out, didn't.

"If you will not travel with me, then allow me to make arrangements." He could talk down even the most fastidious lords in Parliament, and yet this woman continued to run circles around him. "I would like for you to get there safely and in comfort. It is the least I can do."

"Fine. Send me the information by messenger." She crossed her arms and decreed.

"I will see you there, Marena." The satisfied thrum in his blood from getting his way was heightened by the prospect of spending more time with this querulous herbalist.

She lifted a finger and pointed it directly at his face. "We're not friends, and this will not be a social call. We are getting Delfine and Lluvia back, and parting ways the moment that's done." With that, she turned and left the room.

This woman reminded him of who he used to be. Of the passion with which his grandmother lived. He wasn't sure if the effect Marena had on him would be positive or disastrous, but he was eager for more of her either way.

CHAPTER THREE

GARE DU NORD, PARIS

"It is fortunate that I adore those two as much as I do, because otherwise this would be the most foolish thing I have ever done," Marena muttered under her breath as she gathered her things from the private train car Linley had reserved for her trip to Paris. Two days. That's what she'd agreed to, and even that felt dangerous.

Arlo Kenworthy had an extremely adverse effect on Marena's common sense, and this jaunt through Paris would probably prove to be her doom. But it could not be avoided. The man *was* Delfine's brother. *El duque*—as she'd been calling him in her head—had not been pleased with her request to meet him in Paris, but he'd conceded. Not that she would've agreed to travel with the man.

She would not be compromised by boarding a train in London with a notorious aristocrat and be labeled his mistress. No. It had taken a lot of effort to finally convince her mother and their patrons that at five-and-twenty, Marena could operate Baine's Apothecary on her own, and four years later she would not lose her hard-earned reputation over a man she wasn't sure she liked.

Arlo Kenworthy had a purpose to serve in her life: to help get Lluvia and Delfine back home to London. Once that was done, she'd be happy to

see him only if absolutely necessary. But now she'd arrived, and the anticipation was like champagne bubbles in her blood. She loved Paris, and fool-
ishly, the idea of walking some of her favorite streets with Arlo Kenworthy
made her heart skitter in her chest.

Too much feeling was a dangerous thing. Letting a nobleman be the
source of excess emotion was downright perilous, and Marena had always
been excellent at self-preservation. As she stepped on to the platform, she
thought of the next part of her journey: find her way to the lodgings Linley
had arranged for them in the Place des Vosges. The tony square was not
anywhere she'd frequented in the short months she'd lived and studied in
Paris. She'd admit, if only to herself, that the thought of staying at such a
fashionable address was another reason for her excitement. She walked
with purpose to where her small trunk would be delivered, looking around
to spot where the fiacres would be lined up to take newly arrived passengers to their Parisian destinations.

There were hundreds of people milling about, but her French was
excellent, and she knew Paris well enough to get around. She slid a hand
into the pocket of her skirts in search of the note where she'd written the
direction to the apartments.

"They've already got your bags. They'll take them to the townhouse." A
voice from behind startled her, but Marena didn't have to turn around.
After only two meetings she'd recognize his voice anywhere. The Eton
accent in that baritone was unmistakable. But what was he doing here?
He'd left a day before she did. They'd agreed she'd see him at the Place des
Vosges.

She squeezed her eyes shut for a moment, still with her back to him.
Perhaps she'd embellished her memory of him. The man's arrival in her life
had been a whirlwind, and now her memory of his looks superseded the
real thing. No one was that handsome. Bolstered by that thought Marena
turned as people walked around them, her narrow skirts brushing against
his trousers. He seemed to be everywhere. The base of his throat was so
close that if she leaned forward just an inch she could press her lips to it—
and what kind of reckless, pernicious thought was that?

Someone rushed by, jostling her, and a strong arm gathered her at the
waist. "I have you," he assured her, tightening his arms so that his body
shielded her. His voice was husky, and she wondered if she was imagining
the flush of color at his neck. She leaned into him, and he gathered her

closer. Her own blood rushed through her veins like wildfire. When Marena finally looked up so she could see his face, she came to the troubling conclusion that her memory did not, in fact, hold a candle to his beauty. And what was she doing, falling into the man's arms not even a minute after she'd stepped down from the train?

"What are you doing here?" she asked shakily, stepping away from him. He raised an eyebrow at her less-than-friendly tone. He towered over her, and everyone around. If not for the finery he wore, he could be an East End bruiser. All of it made her short of breath and exceedingly ill-humored. It was not fair for anyone to look this dashing so early in the morning.

"I'm here for you." Her stomach dipped at the words. Her nipples tightened when his roaming gaze paused just a moment too long on the area of her mouth, then her neck. She had to clasp her hands to keep from covering her face. Her bonnet was askew, and her skirts rumpled. Still he looked at her like he was ravenous and she was the only thing that could satisfy his hunger.

"You came for me?" She sounded winded.

"Yes, you." His mouth quirked. Bastard. "I'll take you to the townhouse." He was scrambling her senses, and she resented him for that. Resented that perfect sable curl on his forehead that made him look young and roguish all at once. Resented that the emotions she had kept safely locked away wanted to burst out of her the moment he was near. And most of all, she resented his blasted good humor. She couldn't turn him down just to be contrary. Then she would really seem unreasonable, and they did have to spend the next couple of days together.

"Fine." She harrumphed, narrowing her eyes at the elbow he offered her before stomping off in the direction of the street. "Where's the carriage?"

He chuckled, seemingly delighted by her irritation. "Right outside. The staff at the townhouse is very competent. There's breakfast waiting." She almost pointed out that she had no idea what made a competent staff, since she'd never had one. Even when they were in Santo Domingo, most of the folks that worked in their house were some kind of family. In London, they had day help, but never anything like the army of servants a duke might have.

"Why didn't you send someone? You didn't need to bother," she said, walking fast enough to stay out of his reach. After a few steps she realized her mistake. There were too many people, it was easy to get swallowed up by the crowd, and she had no idea which one of the almost dozen cabs waiting by the road was Arlo's.

She'd also lost him. Panicked, she looked through the crowd, trying to get her bearings. Then the smell of bay rum announced his proximity before he reached her.

"You haven't lost me," he whispered close to her ear. She dearly wished that the frisson coursing through her spine was due to the chill of the early morning. "We're in the green right in front."

She would not shiver. She would not tremble from the man's chest barely brushing against her shoulders. "Thank you," she bit off, but when she tried to run, he wrapped an arm around her waist.

"The crowd is too dense. Let's get to the carriage, and then you can tear my arm off." Damn the man for sounding delighted at her foul mood. She would not smile, because there was nothing at all charming or funny about this situation.

"All right." She conceded, begrudgingly, as they walked with his hand firmly on her waist. She could not deny that once he took charge, the crowd parted before him. Fleetingly, she had the thought that people would see her getting into the carriage with him, and then remembered in Paris that was much less likely.

"Your room is ready in case you want to rest for a couple of hours after you eat."

"I have some errands to run this morning." She realized her tone was bordering on rudeness and softened it by offering an explanation. "I have to buy some things for the shop."

He nodded, then pulled an envelope out of his jacket pocket and handed it to her. "This came early this morning." The humor in his voice from a moment earlier was replaced by something cautious.

She slid her gloves off, and then, self-conscious he'd see the dryness there, almost put them back on again. Working with herbs and acidic substances day after day took its toll on the skin. Even if she rubbed them with cacao butter and aloe, her hands were not soft. Not a lady's hands.

And why did she have to dwell on that? Why was she dwelling on anything Arlo saw or thought of her? She stopped herself from answering because that information felt entirely too dangerous to grapple with now.

She ran a finger under the seal of the envelope and quickly read the short note, aware Arlo had looked away to give her privacy. Still, she could feel the tension emanating from him as he waited for her to share news from his half-sister. She'd sent a couple of long telegrams, advising Delfine of their arrival in Paris and the news of Arlo's desire to meet her. Her friend had agreed to the visit, but there had been no opportunity for Marena to share details other than when they would arrive and where they would be staying. They were not in hiding in Paris, but Lluvia and Delfine asked to come to them instead of bringing Arlo to where they lived, and that was still the plan.

Marena smiled at the eagerness in Lluvia's note, filled with hope that Arlo would really help them return. They liked Paris well enough, but it wasn't London. It wasn't home. And it had been almost a year. Maybe he *was* the answer. Marena hoped he was.

"Delfine needs a day." She said, studying his profile. "She's attending a birth that will probably go well into the night. But she and Lluvia will come see you tomorrow in the early evening."

His shoulders relaxed at news he'd be able to meet Delfine. Then he turned to face her, and a truly terrifying thing happened. Arlo Kenworthy, the fifth Duke of Linley, really smiled at her. Not the rakish smile he'd proffered freely from the moment they met, which involved a curled top lip and a raised eyebrow. Or the amused one that showed straight teeth and made a dimple appear on his left cheek. No, this smile was...radiant, and it could be deadly for her. Because this man, the one whose eyes shone at the idea of meeting a sister he didn't know existed a year ago—this man would be far too easy to fall for. To make matters worse, she had a full day and night with him before they could complete their mission.

"That's good. We will have to keep ourselves occupied until then," he said, and the way his mouth curved up when he spoke felt like a proposition she very much wanted to accept. Her hands itched to trace his lips, run the pad of her fingers across their edges. She wanted to know what else could turn those lips up. She wanted too many things, and she would need to dedicate the next thirty-six hours to remembering she could not have a single one of them.

"WHAT ARE YOU DOING?" Marena asked Arlo in surprise when she found him standing by the entrance of the townhouse, seemingly ready for an outing. Mere minutes ago, when she'd gone to her room to freshen up, she'd left the man sitting in the parlor enthralled by the Parisian paper in his hands.

"Doing the shopping with you." That was uttered like a statement of fact as he reached for the basket she'd procured from one of the kitchen maids. She sidestepped out of his reach, shaking her head.

"You most certainly are not," she retorted, placing the basket behind her back. "I'm not going to the Rue de la Paix for gowns and jewels. I'm going to the Marais, where common Parisians do their marketing." When that statement didn't seem to dampen his eagerness, she sighed again, then explained, "There are some herbs I need for the shop that I can't find in London."

He tipped his head and stood to his full and exasperating height. "Excellent. I'm quite good at doing the marketing."

"A duke doing the marketing." A grin formed on her lips as she spoke. The man was entirely too much.

"I wasn't always a duke, you know. For most of my life I was just Arlo Kenworthy." He winked—*winked*—at her. Carajo, but the man was handsome. Almost aggressively virile. So much energy in that large body.

She appraised him from under her lashes. The trousers that fit his strong legs like they'd been sewn on, with his jacket and matching waistcoat. The perfectly appointed four-in-hand silk tie. Bowler hat in hand. He was every inch the duke, and definitely not dressed for a day of walking and marketing.

"The covered market is hot. You'll suffocate," she warned, pointing at his collar.

"You're wearing twelve layers of cloth," he quipped back, and curled that damned lip again. She wanted to bite it. Then suck on it, perhaps, her arms around his neck... *For heaven's sake, Marena.* It wasn't that she was a prude, or even a virgin. It was that letting this particular man get under her skin like this was absolute madness.

But he wasn't wrong. Women's clothes were a true travesty, and though there was no point in disputing it, she still did. "I'm wearing linen."

He took in her skirts, without frills or embellishments. He inspected her jacket, with only simple pleats at the hem, her unadorned straw bonnet—and he made a small appreciative sound, as if he were looking at the most sumptuous gown from the House of Worth.

"It's a lovely shade of blue." The way he said *lovely* felt like a caress, making something inside her flutter. Although she should not have, she let him stare, reveling in his appreciation of her. The way his eyes roamed over her neck, her chest, her waist and hips, all the way down to her sensible boots, with their wide heels and soft leather—it would be easy to forget who she was under that admiring gaze.

"I'm wearing cotton and walking boots," he finally said, patting the breast pocket of his light gray jacket. She really ought to say something cutting to swipe that flirtatious smile off his face, but what was the harm? She wouldn't mind the company, and this wasn't London, where half the people they encountered would know who he was, and the other half would know her.

Here, she could be another Marena, and he...well, he'd still be a duke. But here, the distance between their worlds seemed less vast. Paris was always a good place for escaping or reinventing oneself, for indulging in fantasies, no matter how foolish and reckless they were.

"I presume you will come no matter what I say." He was so achingly beautiful, with his mouth set in a sardonic smirk, and those soft, eager eyes telling a different story.

"It's quite impressive how fast we've learned to understand each other." This smile made the dimple appear, and Marena almost chastised him for the audacity of being fetching to the extreme. "I let you win for the trip from London, but I will be a tougher negotiator here."

She narrowed her eyes. "I already explained—"

He raised a hand in concession, smile still firmly in place, but there was a tension there she could not quite decipher. "Yes, you did not want to be seen with me. And you explained your very sensible reasons. I only wish you'd tell me who these bastards were, and I could knock some heads as soon as I set foot back in London."

A warmth spread in her chest at how furious he looked on her behalf. Marena valued her independence more than anything. Her parents had raised her and her sister to be self-possessed, to stand on their own two feet. But having this man ready to brawl with the gentlemen of London for her awakened a yearning that surprised her.

"Are you going to slay dragons for me?" she asked, and the way his eyes widened and nostrils flared made her breath catch.

She kept her eyes on him as he stepped closer. So close that if she raised herself on the tip of her toes, she could kiss him.

Bringing his lips to her ear, he whispered, "I'm tempted to, but for now I would be honored to carry your basket to market." If the man kept this up swooning was eminent. Marena had to close her eyes and breathe as she gathered the strength to step away from him.

"I will carry my own basket, thank you very much," she muttered, congratulating herself for drawing some kind of line in the sand. She attempted a scowl, which only seemed to delight him more.

"Excellent." He lifted an elbow for her, and her scowl deepened. As if thinking better of it, he opened the door for her instead.

"Don't you have a footman or valet who needs to know your whereabouts at all times?" she asked, looking around the well-appointed room.

"I answer to no one. And besides, it's Paris. Indulgence and spontaneity are the entire schedule."

She raised a doubtful eyebrow at him. "This expedition will be on foot, Your Grace."

His lips twitched at the heavy dose of scorn she injected into the last two words. "I can barely contain my anticipation."

CHAPTER FOUR

"How long were you here for?" Arlo tried not to smile at the dubious look Marena sent his way at the question. They'd been doing this all morning. He'd ask questions, and she'd provide as little information as possible.

"About six months. I was studying under a root worker from Port-au-Prince named Marie Lemba. I'd come to the market with her every week."

No wonder she'd so effortlessly brought them to the market. They'd come out the townhouse, and Marena had swiftly led them through cobbled streets lined with shops and eateries. After about a mile of twists and turns, she'd veered into an enclosed alley and brought them to a building full of market stalls, which she explained was the *petit marché du Marais*.

As soon as they walked in, he was thrust into an overwhelming sensory experience. There were dozens of stalls offering every comestible one could need. Fruits, vegetables, cheeses, chocolates, wine. Marena expertly guided them through the narrow paths between the rows of stalls, pointing out the vendors she remembered. She let him know the cheeses she loved or the grocers who had the freshest produce as he walked alongside her.

Since they left the townhouse, her demeanor had been lighter. This was obviously her world. She smiled freely at the many people they encountered in the market, negotiating prices down while somehow making the sellers laugh in delight. She was a marvel, this woman. Fierce, competent, and with an air of regal dignity that he wanted to breathe in until he was drunk off it.

And now she was buying fruit. She moaned and cooed over a little bundle holding fresh figs, which he found absolutely erotic. Then, as if they'd done this a thousand times, she raised her hand in the air, passing him the fruit, still talking to the woman running the stall. Something possessive and hot ran through his body at the idea of having this kind of intimacy with her. To be the man a woman this self-sufficient could depend on.

He was trying to focus on the conversation, perhaps ask more questions about what she'd studied. But Marena Baine-Torres sucking on raspberries with red-stained lips was astonishingly distracting.

"Do I get a taste, or am I only here to carry them?"

She rolled her eyes at him and snatched the basket from his hand.

"Here," she said, offering him a few raspberries and taking one for herself. "You keep looking at me," she commented as she popped another plump berry in her mouth.

"Do I?" he asked huskily, his gaze unable to leave the vicinity of her lips.

"Yes. You did the same thing at the café."

That, he could not be blamed for. She'd eaten an éclair. A mess of chocolate and custard that she'd licked off her lips and fingers until he was so aroused, he feared he'd have to sit there for the rest of the day. As he handed over some coins for a bottle of wine, he considered what to say. Her mood was so different from any he'd seen from her thus far.

Light, humorous, eyes open and curious of everything they saw. With another woman he'd consider his words, not wanting to offend by being too forward. But he wanted to mean every word he said to her. "I'm finding it exceedingly difficult to look away. I am helplessly drawn to beauty. And there are few things worth admiring more than a woman taking pleasure in something delicious."

They were walking again, she in front and he behind, between the narrow walkways of the market, but he could see a flush of red on the deep brown skin at her nape as he waited for her response. After a moment, she tipped her head up, her long, elegant neck taut from looking at him. At this angle, he could see a smattering of freckles along her collarbone. He'd put his mouth to every one of them if he could.

Her eyes twinkled at whatever she was thinking. "Did that actually work on all those unsuspecting debutantes you supposedly deflowered?" She was teasing him. Suddenly, he was overcome by an urge to explain himself, and that stopped him in his tracks. This was a feeling he couldn't even recall. Being with someone who he wanted to think positively of him.

He looked down at her as they moved, tempted to put a hand on the dip at her back where the curve of her delicious bottom started. "For your information, Miss Baine-Torres, I've never deflowered anyone."

She gave him a doubtful look, but he shook his head, needing to be clear on this. He pulled her into a more private corner of the market so they could be face-to-face for what he'd say next.

She seemed confused, but went along with it, holding the half-empty basket like a shield between them. His heart was racing now, the moment turning into something volatile and crackling with energy, like a summer sky brewing a storm.

"I have never deflowered anyone," he repeated, his eyes locked with hers. "I prefer to leave virtuous flowers on the vine." He sounded ridiculous, and yet he could not seem to stop.

"I thought gentlemen valued purity above all things." She sounded breathless, her lush curves distracting as he tried to muster up a response.

He wanted her, that was undeniable, but with every word exchanged between them, his lust careened into something far more perilous. He wanted to impress her. He wanted her to see Arlo Kenworthy, and not the Duke of Linley.

"I find it hypocritical that women's purity is held as proof of their value, while a man can do as he pleases. If the sexes are truly equal, then why would I expect something in a woman when I wouldn't of myself?"

"Hmmm." She made the sound as she licked her lips. He hoped it was not because of the lingering taste of raspberries, but because she, like he, was craving a kiss. And he would give it to her...if she asked.

"That's quite commendable of you." With that, she turned on her heel and pushed into market again. But she wasn't fast enough for him to miss the flush on her cheeks.

They didn't speak again until they arrived at the next stall of interest.

The vendor recognized Marena and quickly, they began exchanging a warm greeting in French.

"This is Phuong," Marena informed him. "She has the best herbs and tisanes. Her family has a farm in Marseille and they bring products from Vietnam."

Arlo bowed to the woman and introduced himself in passable French. Marena appeared to find his efforts amusing and turned back to Phuong, a smile still on her lips. Soon she was back to the business at hand, listing things from a piece of paper as the seller moved around her miniscule stall, pulling out jars and scooping things out of barrels.

Marena's face lit up when Phoung handed her a bundle of yellow and green stalks tied together with string. "Merci," she said with pleasure in her voice, and again his treasonous cock twitched in his trousers as he watched her press the stalks to her nose and inhale with her eyes closed.

"Citronelle." She lifted the stalks to him, and he obliged by taking a whiff. It had an intense citrus smell that reminded him of the lemon verbena his grandmother used, but spicier. "In Santo Domingo we call it limoncillo. My grandmother used it for teas and remedies," she explained, piercing the tip of a stalk with a fingernail, coaxing out a more intense aroma. "It's good for digestion and excellent for the teeth." She revealed her own gleaming teeth, and once again he was tongue-tied merely by seeing Marena at ease.

He, who was used to sitting in rooms with the most powerful men in London and speaking his mind. He, who was known in the House of Lords for always delivering the right words at the right time, could not produce a single one which did justice to this woman, who had brought him here to this little corner of Paris and showed him her world.

"You can't find it in London?" he asked, voice hoarse from whatever was afflicting him.

She gave him a curious look as she placed the packaged goods Phuong prepared for her in the basket. "I can find it on occasion, but it's expensive and not freshly cut like these. Other things like the lavender and chamomile I grow in my hothouse."

"What do you use it for? The lavender?" He was suddenly hungry to know how she'd use each purchase.

"Lavender is good for swelling joints. And the oil with chamomile helps settle the nerves. But I just like how it smells." Marena beamed as she pressed a bundle of lavender Phoung had handed her to her nose. "French lavender is the best." She said it in French, offering a smile to Phuong, and all he wanted in that moment was to see her naked and amorous, sitting in a tub fragrant with flowers. He'd run a soapy cloth over those generous breasts and bend down to take one of the sweet peaks between his teeth.

"Is it too hot?" Marena's concerned question snatched him out of his improper musings. It appeared that when it came to the Caribbean herbalist, even a mundane conversation about lavender somehow ended with him having lustful fantasies.

"I'm all right." He pulled on his collar with an ungloved finger and tilted his head toward the jar that Phoung had just passed to them. "What are those?"

"Preserved bitter orange. Those are *much* harder to find, I usually replace them with other ingredients if they're called for in a poultice or salve." She secured the jar in the basket, moving it around until it was in a nook where it would not get jostled. "It's what I came here to study. How to adapt my family's recipes to what I could find outside the tropics."

She angled her head to look at him. "Are you sure you're interested in this?"

"I am."

She gave him a doubtful look but continued her explanation. "Root work, is about using what the earth yields, and letting it give you what you need for healing. The problem is, the soil here is very different. There is only so much I can do to reproduce what was available in the islands."

Arlo was not a romantic. He could be cynical and was decidedly jaded on love. And yet, the image of Marena as a Caribbean Demeter—reaping what she liked from the cold earth of Britain and warming it with the sunshine from her hands—came to him as clear and solid as a memory. And before his good sense could catch up, he spoke.

"You're here. You've brought the sun with you." Her expression softened at his words, and he almost added something ridiculous like, "I felt the warmth of you from the second we met. I miss it whenever you're not near." But a growl from his stomach saved him.

She smiled, and he blushed like a blustering schoolboy. "You probably need feeding constantly to keep all this upright," she joked, waving a hand up and down his torso. "Let me pay Phoung and we can go find some nourishment for you."

"No, no, no. I will pay for this." Her eyebrow rose, and he realized he'd spoken in an imperious tone, and softened the next part. "Please. I said I'd pay for all your expenses while we were here. You are helping me connect with my sister. It's the least I can do."

She held a finger up to him and turned to Phoung. "Would you excuse me a moment?" The woman nodded and gave them both a knowing smile, as if they were quarreling lovers. "You *are* paying for my expenses. You paid for my train and ferry. And we're staying at your townhouse. You also refused to let me pay for the coffee and pastry at the café, for heaven's sake." She gestured to the basket he was holding and shook her head. "This is not part of the arrangement. This is for my work."

"But—"

She held up a hand, her gaze pinning him in place as she spoke. "I cannot accept it. Please."

He wanted to push until she let him do this for her. Some unreasonable part of him wanted to give her everything she needed. But he was starting to understand this woman. She was protective of certain things. Her work; the safety of her loved ones. There were places where she would not give in, where she would stand her guard until he'd earned the right to be there. He could only guess at the reasons that had made her that way.

He sighed, accepting defeat. "Only if I can buy your lunch...and your dinner." She rewarded him with a shy smile and nod, which he was certain made his chest grow a size.

"You are very lucky I'm in a compliant mood, Your Grace."

Instinctively, he stepped closer and tried to suppress the possessive growl trying to escape. "I'd be lying if I didn't say I'm extremely curious to learn just how compliant of a mood you're in." He knew the exact moment when the words and their meaning landed. He saw it in the way her chest moved up and down, and how she met his gaze.

"Don't be fooled by my giving mood, Arlo. I bite." Her tone was placid, but her eyes burned him. Everything about Marena burned through him like fire. Arlo would probably associate street markets with a heightened state of arousal for the rest of his life.

"This information has done nothing to decrease my curiosity," he said as he followed her away from Phoung's stand and back into the fray of the market. His words felt like a promise. This was certainly one of the most foolish things he'd done in a long time, but he wanted Marena Baine-Torres in his arms more than he had wanted anyone in a long time. He could scarcely remember when in the last fifteen years anything had felt this vital. This woman was careful, with good reason. He had to remember that. And yet, he found himself wanting to bend all the rules to make her his.

CHAPTER FIVE

PARIS ALWAYS HAD an adverse effect on Marena's good judgment. It was the only reasonable explanation for why she was currently strolling down the Rue de la Paix on the arm of Arlo Kenworthy after an entire day of shopping and flirtatious conversation.

They'd roamed the stalls of the Marais where he'd asked her a thousand questions, seemingly fascinated by the intricacies of root work. She'd explained, at times going into extensive detail, and instead of glazed-over eyes, he'd wanted to know more. Marena didn't know what to make of this man. The nobility in England had a mold, and Arlo Kenworthy fit it, but it seemed that only on the surface.

"I'd seen you before. At Lady Bibichon's house." she said, and immediately felt like she'd revealed too much.

He raised a hand to point at a window farther down the street. "I'd like to get something there."

She nodded, wondering if he'd intentionally ignored her comment. She always did this—second-guessed herself whenever she shared something intimate. Which was silly because his visit to Lady Bibichon's house had not been a secret. But the way his words impacted her that night, ought to have been one. And now she felt exposed. She distracted herself by pulling out her spectacles to get a clearer look at the storefront he'd mentioned.

"Maison Maquet?" She perked up at the suggestion of visiting the famous stationery store, her spirits buoyed at the possibility of purchasing some letter paper.

"You wear spectacles?" He followed the question with one of his rumbles of appreciation. She decidedly ignored the flutter the sound elicited in her lower belly.

"I do. They're fairly new and I keep forgetting I have them," she said, feeling dizzy under his scrutiny.

"They suit you." He said it matter-of-factly, like him offering a compliment was nothing unusual between them—which only made it that much electrifying. And then he pointed in the direction of the store. "I meant the Gaillon Sisters. But we can stop at Maison Maquet if you like." Her gaze shifted to the storefront next to Maison Maquet, which housed the famous—and exorbitantly expensive—shop known for their delicate lacework and embroidery. The Gaillon Sisters' creations had been part of the nobility's wedding trousseaus for decades. The pang of irritation flaring in her chest at the idea of Arlo buying a delicate lacy undergarment for some paramour was confirmation that Marena had indeed shed all her good sense.

Still, her lips parted, and words exited. "Buying something for someone special?" Her mouth was becoming a serious liability.

Another grunt. This one had an undertone of amusement. He looked at her, the smug smile on his face making her consider a vow of silence, and whispered, "Curious about the special women in my life, Miss Baine-Torres?"

"No," she said grumpily, unable to suppress a huff of annoyance that had the cad laughing so hard it made some passersby turn in their direction.

In response, he tightened the hold he had on her arm, and gave her another of those exceedingly devastating grins. She looked away, but he stayed close.

"What did you think about that meeting at Lady Bibichon's?" She snapped her gaze back to him in surprise. She should've known the man would go at the inflammatory topic head on. Marena considered how to reply. She'd been *advised* she could become overzealous when this subject came up. Even the men who were in favor of women's suffrage seemed to like the females in their midst docile and only marginally opinionated. But perhaps speaking her mind would finally provoke a reaction from Kenworthy that would dampen her extremely foolish attraction to the man.

"I was nonplussed, in all honesty. I was not expecting a peer to speak so passionately about women's suffrage. In my experience, the House of Lords is more interested in serving those who already have power." He hummed in apparent agreement. "I was surprised by the fervor in your words," she continued, not bothering to keep the admiration from her voice. The way he spoke that night, advocating for suffrage, for *expanding* the rights of women to leave marriages in which they were harmed, was... earth-shattering. "I didn't know that there were those in the ton with that kind of clarity about the place of women."

He didn't respond for a long moment. His face was serious, brows furrowed, mouth pursed as they passed artfully decorated store windows. "I told you before. There was a time when I was not a duke, nor even a duke's son."

"Yes," she said softly, wondering if he was about to tell her of his family's ascent to the highest echelon of the aristocracy.

"My father was not supposed to be duke. He was of the gentry, but his family had not much wealth to speak of. The assignment in the Foreign Office was a respectable alternative to finding a wealthy relative to support him, as many of his peers did. That's how he met my mother; he was in America for a few years."

"Ah." Marena nodded, recalling that she'd heard about Arlo's mother being from a famed abolitionist family in America. "Did you go with him? On his travels?"

"We're here," he said, startling her as he stopped in front of Maison Maquet, but she found that stationery was no longer as appealing.

"I want to hear the rest."

He nodded, pulling her into a side street so they were out of view, and continued to talk. Fleetingly, Marena thought the crowds of fashionable Parisians strolling along the sidewalk would notice a man tugging her into an alley, and decided that in this moment, she didn't particularly care. She pressed her back to the brick wall and lifted her face to Arlo.

"After they married, my mother went to England with my father. A few years later he left again for the Caribbean." Marena tried to listen for what he wasn't saying, but his voice was devoid of emotion. For a man who seemed able to imbue everything with humor, this flat and unaffected tone told her these were not happy memories. "My mother died when I was five, and my grandmother, who was widowed by then, came from New York to raise me. My mother was her only child."

She opened her mouth to say something, but he looked at her with a small twinge of his lips. "I'm getting to the duke part, darling."

Marena's chest filled with air at seeing a hint of that ever-present humor, and her face heated at realizing how close they were. Leaning, as she was to the side of a building, and with him right in front of her, his mouth so close to her ear—she was more than a little breathless. Still, she was eager to hear what he'd say next. "Get on with it, Linley. There is more shopping to do," she said haughtily, eliciting a grin.

Oh, that grin, that flash of teeth promising enough mischief to scandalize and thrill her. "When I was fourteen, my father's cousin, the Duke of Linley, died without leaving any heirs." The grin turned flinty. "And my father finally had a reason to return to England."

"That's quite a story." She felt unsteady, ready to tumble down wherever this moment would take her.

"Hm," he grunted as he ran the back of an ungloved hand over her cheek. "Your mouth keeps stealing my focus." He shook his head, as if he were vexed by that epiphany. "I've been captivated by it from the moment I saw you. Wondered how it would taste."

There were so many things she should have said in that moment. Reminded him they were mere feet from a busy street. That this was a compromising position for her. That she would be the one to lose in this game. But all the shoulds were razed to nothing by the flames of a singular thought in Marena's mind.

Kiss me. Kiss me.

She felt the material of her bonnet scrape against the bricks as she pushed up to where Arlo's mouth was waiting. "There's only one way to know, Linley."

He didn't give her a chance for second thoughts. He wrapped her in his arms and pressed his mouth to hers. His lips felt as soft as she imagined, lush and warm on hers, parted just enough that she could feel his heat. She opened for him and his tongue came searching for hers, the glide of it on her lips making her tremble. Her stomach dipped as if she were barreling down a steep hill and her desire spiraled further up every passing second.

"I could devour you," he gasped, and between hungry, mind-addling kisses, Marena thought to herself, *I might just let you.* She brought her hands up, scraping her nails over the nape of his neck, an action which rewarded her with a lusty hiss.

He nipped at her and she returned the favor, exploring him, greedily running her hands over his wide shoulders while he cradled her face and kissed her in earnest. Then she carded her fingers through those curls she'd been wanting to touch for days.

He slid a hand to the bodice of her dress, fingers searching until he found her nipple. "I've almost gone mad thinking what is hidden under all this," he said hotly as he tweaked the sensitive peak between his fingers. Even over three layers of cotton his touch singed her. "My mouth dries any time I look at you."

"Arlo," she gasped, trying to suck in the air that would not return to her lungs.

"I will stop now," he said, and she almost protested, not caring they were practically in plain view. "Not because I don't want to ravish you right here. But because when I finish the job. I'd like to have you on a bed, naked. Take my time with you."

The mention of taking things to a bedroom finally broke through the madness of the moment. What in the world was she doing? She could not be on a bed with Arlo Kenworthy. The man was a duke, and what's more, her best friend's brother. Mortified, she slid away from him and tried to set herself to rights.

"I should not have let that happen." She was panting, which significantly lessened the stern tone she was attempting, but after a long, considering look, Arlo nodded, stepping back.

"It's a shame. I enjoyed that immensely and would very much like to do it again. For an extended period of time." Her breath hitched under the heated look he proffered her. "I'd taste every inch of you. Feast on your body." She should turn and walk out to the street, to the safety of the crowd on the Rue de la Paix. Instead, she stood, riveted by his sensual promises. "Hours, Marena. I'd kiss, and bite and lick you for hours. Then I'd make my way down—"

That finally propelled her to move. Learning about what he'd was too dangerously enticing. She heard his husky laugh as he followed her onto the street. "The offer is there, if you would like to avail yourself of my mouth or any other parts you may require. We have a whole day of wait-ing, after all. And there is only so much shopping to do."

She ignored him, turned on her heel, and walked into Maison Maquet. Buying expensive paper would have to do for Parisian indulgences.

CHAPTER SIX

"AND WHAT IS THIS?" Marena asked her empty bedroom as she walked out of the bathroom, wrapped in Turkish towels. They'd arrived from their day out an hour before and had gone to get ready for dinner. Arlo had been secretive about the evening's dining plans. And she could admit it only to herself: she was not only curious for where Arlo would take her, but craved spending more time in his company. The man was a walking, talking implausibility. He was direct, thoughtful, and funny. So unexpectedly real. She could not recall the last time she'd laughed as much as she had while walking the streets of Paris today. And what's more, he made her *feel* things. From irritation to consuming lust, Arlo had brought it all up in Marena this day. It had been a long time since she'd let her emotions run wild like this. Since her return to London from Paris, really.

The arrival in London after those few months of freedom in Paris had been a rude awakening. She'd left for France a girl of twenty-four, eager to learn. What she'd found was a place where she could be more herself. She'd had trysts, felt free in a way she never had in London. She'd been happy here. And in the past five years she'd lost that. Since the first day she began managing the shop, the cutting comments about her age, her knowledge, her expertise and even how she styled her hair were an everyday occurrence. So, she'd closed herself off to all of it.

She'd poured herself into the salves and the tinctures and kept everyone else—and their effect on her—at a safe distance. Her dedication and focus had fueled her success, but it had been lonely. Now Arlo Kenworthy, in a matter of hours, had infiltrated her carefully guarded walls. Instead of heeding the danger of that development, she found she was taken with the man, and now he was sending her gifts. *Bedroom gifts.*

A heavy pulse beat in her chest as she approached the light blue box on her bed like it was an open flame. Her eyes narrowed as she inspected the thing. She recognized the packaging. She had a much smaller one on top of the dresser in the room. It was from the Gaillon Sisters' shop, which was puzzling since they could not have been there more than fifteen minutes. While there Arlo purchased two dozen ladies' handkerchiefs, which he requested be monogrammed with the letters BB. Marena had glared hotly at him as he placed the order—if he noticed her pugnacious looks, he did not say—but he did casually inform her BB was Beatrice Brooks, his grandmother. Then he launched into a story about defective pocket squares that made her grin from ear to ear.

On a whim, she purchased some gifts for her mother, while Arlo offered commentary on everything she glanced at. He liked to tease her, and she would rather cut her tongue out than admit she deeply enjoyed his ribbing. The man was infuriatingly witty, and he'd somehow devised the precise way to making her laugh and annoy her at the same time. He had something to say about gloves, mantillas and every other garment that piqued her interest, except for one. An item large enough to need a box about the size of the one on the pristine white coverlet.

She reached for it, pulling it to the edge of the bed where she was standing, and lifted the lid. The Gaillon Sisters exclusively made accessories and undergarments, so this could only be something extremely inappropriate. The man was shameless, scandalous, utterly disreputable, and still her breath quickened at the idea of him discreetly purchasing it while she wasn't looking.

She pinched the paper between two fingers and lifted it, revealing the chemise she'd seen. The garment which when she'd picked it up, had elicited one of those sounds from Arlo that made her stomach clench and her heart race. It was a simple thing. White satin, linen, and Valencian lace. No long sleeves, like what one usually saw in London. But narrow straps, lined with the same lace on the hem and the edge of the bodice. She'd imagined herself sleeping in it. The sensation of the smooth, slippery fabric, cool against her skin, had called to her, but it had been obscenely expensive. Far beyond what she could justify spending.

This was not a simple gesture. This was a proposition.

She pulled it out of the box to put it on, a thrill unfurling in her belly as the buttery texture of the satin slid against her skin. It was as decadent and luxurious as she'd imagined. Even the small buttons were perfect, shiny pearls.

After fifteen years in Britain, many of which she'd spent in the family's shop catering to the gentry's ailments, she'd learned more than a few things about men like Arlo. They either looked right through her or viewed her not as a woman to know, but to possess. Some of it was class, of course. Aristocrats existed in a world of their own making, and they seemed to go through life unaware of the humanity of anyone not part of that world. It was a privilege she did not have, and she never put herself in a position where men like that could use her for their temporary entertainment.

Still, Arlo had surprised her. He'd let her lead him around the Marais searching for supplies before more walking in the Rue de la Paix. At some point, between sharing raspberries and him talking about his past, she had lowered her defenses. No, she'd done more than that. She'd kissed him and she'd flirted. *Shamelessly* flirted. And she'd enjoyed it. She wanted another kiss, wanted more time in his arms.

Marena had long ago accepted that her independence and having a mind of her own in English society meant spinsterhood. It meant keeping who she was and her ideas about the place of women to herself. So she'd been careful. Distant, her mother and sister said. Unfeeling.

Except now she yearned for a night of heedless passion. It was a complicated thing, being a woman who had no intention of marrying, but who also wanted to experience pleasure occasionally. She imagined Arlo peeling this chemise off her, pulling with urgency as she melted in his arms. And need slammed into her like a tidal wave. It had been a long time since she'd let herself contemplate a liaison. Since she'd allowed herself to feel desire.

A knock on the door startled her out of her heated reverie, and she shook her head as if she could dislodge whatever had been swirling in there since she'd kissed the Duke of Linley in the alleys of Paris.

"Entrer!" she called, eager for some distraction. Still with her back to the door, she walked to where her dinner gown hung. The chambermaid, Colette, had drawn her bath and promised to return to help her dress. "Ça va, Colette?"

The appreciative grunt that came in response to her greeting made her miss a step. "I came in to ask if you wanted to have a drink before dinner, but now I'm contemplating the idea of completely adjusting our plans for the evening."

Marena took a breath, crossing her arms over her chest. She was in her chemise, a man—*a duke*—was about to see her in a most scandalous state. She should care. She should yell at him that she was not that kind of woman. She would do none of it. It wasn't as if she had forgotten the reasons why doing this with Arlo was dangerously reckless. It was simply that at this moment, she could not find it in herself to care.

She turned slowly, trying to snap the thread of excitement coiling around her. Good heavens, but she wanted him. She took him in—tall, muscular, with that wicked ocean gaze focused on her. He was dressed smartly, as always. Matching trousers, jacket and waistcoat in a charcoal gray. His four-in-hand perfectly knotted, this time in a deep burgundy. The precise, strong lines of his face, and those lips. Those sinful lips she could still feel on her skin, turned up in a smirk of appreciation, like he was exceedingly pleased with himself for barging into her room unannounced.

"Do you make it a habit of storming into ladies' rooms, Your Grace?" she asked placidly, forcing herself to drop her arms to her sides, giving him the view he'd come to see.

He made a sound that could've been yes, but might have actually been tits. It was hard to decipher, but as he took a step closer, his gaze landed right where the edge of lace of the chemise kissed the top of her breasts. He bit his bottom lip, eyes still focused south of her face. "I have all kinds of deplorable habits."

She huffed, something cutting ready to leap off her tongue. Possibly some epithet about the need for decency and restraint. But Marena didn't make a habit of lying to herself. At least, not when it was clear there was no more avoiding the truth.

"So you thought after one kiss I'd be so entranced I'd let you have your way with me?"

"Only if you are offering, sweetheart." Every word out of his mouth made her soften and heat up at once.

She turned, giving her back to him, and reached for her dress. "I am not having this conversation half-naked."

"But that's the ideal state for the topics I'm interested in discussing."

She narrowed her eyes as she extended a hand to pick up her corset. "I need help with this evil contraption, and since you seem so keen on bursting into rooms when women are trying to dress, you might as well make yourself useful."

Turning to face him, she caught the amused twitch of his lips as she bit back her own smile. "And what compensation will I receive for my labor? I would think a kiss would be a fair price."

She scoffed as she worked on the hooks of her corset. The way his nostrils flared at the sight of her breasts pushed together indicated this game might not end as she anticipated. Or more like exactly as she'd hoped.

"I cannot in good conscience help you conceal these two beauties from the world." He sounded genuinely affronted, and she had to bite her tongue not to laugh. "I regret to inform you, darling, that my expertise is in helping women free themselves of corsets, not get into them."

"You are a scoundrel," she said, marveling at how much she enjoyed this man, especially in these outrageous circumstances.

He'd said he was not Linley here, just Arlo Kenworthy, a man of means on some business. And who was she? Marena, a woman trying to help her family, one more of the thousands of foreigners who walked the streets of Paris every day. Her family had always been comfortable, well-off, never wanting for anything. But this was opulence. The high ceilings and elaborate molding, the enormous four-poster bed covered in the finest damask, extravagance beyond anything she'd experienced everywhere she looked. This was not the life she would go back to when she arrived at Charing Cross Station. This moment, this place, was a fantasy, and she felt compelled to luxuriate in it. To indulge in it. In him.

Marena let the corset drop to the floor, and as if she'd tugged on a string, he closed the space between them. He stood there, eyes hungry, chest moving fast. Waiting.

"I've been considering your offer." She circled her arms around his neck.

"Have you?" he asked, voice low and seductive, the vibrations melting her core. She shivered at the strength in his hands, the way he dug them into her skin, one at her hip and the other with a tight grip on her bottom.

"You are correct. We have an evening and a day before our meeting with our respective siblings."

Another grunt was accompanied by a brush of lips to her neck.

"So," she whispered, letting her own lips travel from his neck, to his jaw, smelling the scent of his freshly shaved face. "I'm pondering on how to best use our time."

"I have many suggestions," he offered with enthusiasm as he undid the buttons of her chemise and exposed her breasts, eyes boring into her, and yes...this was what she needed. Heat pooled at her core as he brought his mouth level with her breast. His hot breath making her nipples harden, as the throbbing between her legs intensified. He touched her so lightly, lips brushing over her collarbone. His thumb grazing the valley between her breasts until she was panting. Still he would not put his mouth where she wanted him.

"Arlo, please."

"Do you need something, love?" He ran the tip of his tongue over his bottom lip, and she swore she could feel it on her own skin. He opened his mouth, making her gasp, desperate to have it on her. "May I?" he asked, the tip of his finger flicking the aching tip of her breast.

She responded by grabbing his head in both her hands and bringing his mouth exactly where she needed him.

THIS WAS A DELIGHTFULLY surprising outcome for his impulsive gift of undergarments. Marena had too much of a spine to recriminate him, or feign offense, but he had not expected this, an aroused, impassioned Marena offering him what he'd been aching for from the moment he'd laid eyes on her. And he'd known it would be like this. No demure double-entendres or half-heated insinuations. It would be a fevered, demanding whirlwind that would quite possibly ruin him forever.

"If I'd anticipated this would be the reaction," he muttered, as he cupped her breast and ran the flat of his tongue over a hardened nipple. "I'd have had your bed filled with boxes from Gaillon this morning."

She let out a sound somewhere between a scoff and a moan. "I would've thought giving you something to do with your mouth would prevent me from listening to nonsense, Your Grace." She moaned lustily as he added teeth to his efforts. "This happened because I want you, and I've decided that between now and the moment we fulfill the reason for this adventure, I shall have you."

He looked up from his work on her breasts, which were even more magnificent than he could've imagined, unsettled by her words. And he must really be a fool, because she was giving him something every man wanted: the chance to quench his lust without attachments. He should take this without hesitation, ask how he could please her, inquire about her most dark fantasies, and set about making them true in the next twenty-four hours. If there was a tightening in his chest at the idea of only getting her for a day, then that was something he'd have to deal with on the train to London. Tonight and tomorrow were for pleasure. "What changed your mind?"

"You made some very lofty claims after that kiss, Your Grace." Something about her playful tone felt false, like she was keeping her true self hidden, and he wanted all of her here with him.

"Arlo," he demanded. "Say my name."

"Kiss me, Arlo."

Something feral and primal burned in his gut. His head spun, drunk on his desire for this woman. She turned her face up to him and he brought their mouths together, his tongue stealing into her mouth with barely contained hunger. He had always prided himself on his restraint, but the onslaught of Marena Baine-Torres, lusty and wanton in his arms, had easily undone him.

Some men of his station liked to be the ones to own a woman's innocence for the first time. Found pleasure in demure inexperience. But there was something about a woman who knew exactly what she wanted, a woman who understood herself enough to demand her pleasure, that had always excited him.

The way she moved against him. Hips rolling seductively as she kissed him without restraint. He wanted to know what it would be to have those same hips crashing against him as he surged into her. To have her lithe limbs wrapped around his waist as he took her. The idea set his blood on fire. His hands went back to undo the last buttons on her chemise, while still kissing and tasting her mouth. She smelled like the citronelle and lavender from the morning. He wanted to inhale her, press his nose to the secret places that held her scent. Lick into her until he knew every inch of her body.

"I want to taste you everywhere," he said as he fumbled with her chemise.

"Bloody hell, these buttons are more effective than a chastity belt." He growled, ready to tear the thing off her. For all his experience, he felt like a fumbling arse, he was that eager for her.

She laughed, bringing her hands to meet his, and efficiently undid the rest of the buttons, exposing her enough to give him a peek of the nest on brown curls which hid the place he most wanted to taste. "You were supposed to be helping me get in my gown, not out of my undergarments," she teased as he reached for her.

"How could I? With these two beauties calling me. All I want is to lay you on that bed and play with them for hours," he said before he swirled his tongue around a pebbled peak, making her gasp.

"More," she demanded, and in that moment, he would have given her anything. He took one breast in his mouth, his hand playing with the other as she writhed against him. Breathy moans of pleasure escaped her lips, tearing at the very fabric of his sanity.

"I don't think there is anything in the world that could keep me from tasting you," he said heatedly as he pressed openmouthed kisses on every inch of skin he could reach.

Soon he was moving down her body—dinner trousers be damned. He needed to get at the core of her. He traced a path with his lips, kissing the underside of each breast and every inch of her until he arrived at seam of her cunt. Once he was on his knees, he looked up at her, and his breath caught at the sight. That mass of wild curls almost to her waist. Her deep brown skin tinged with red from the heat of the moment. Her mouth was open and a little swollen from his kisses. Her eyes wild and her body wanton. He'd never seen anything more perfect.

"You are vision." He whispered against her skin, unable to hide the emotion in his voice.

Some things were undeniable. Some people were inevitable, and Arlo had learned long ago that shrewd men didn't resist change, but embraced it. He could see himself rearranging his whole existence to have more of her. From the moment in that shop when she'd turned those heated brown eyes on him he'd been adrift, every new moment with her displacing the ideas he had about himself. He'd told himself a million times that he'd never attach himself to anyone. Would not open himself to more liaisons that further tied him to his duties in the nobility. He certainly never planned to take a wife. But with Marena every touch, every kiss revealed a different truth. One night would never be enough.

"Marena." It was a supplication, a question with no answer. He pressed his nose to the apex at her thighs, breathing in her scent as she ran her hands through his hair.

"Please. I need you," she pleaded, her voice hoarse, and he felt addled by it. His control edged out by the need to possess her. He had no idea what had caused her change of heart, but he would not be foolish enough to question it. With his eyes locked on hers, he slid up the chemise, over her knees, then her thighs, until the fistfuls of linen, lace and silk were bunched up against her waist. He pressed his nose into the soft brown curls and inhaled deeply, drunk on her.

Arlo enjoyed sex and could draw satisfaction from giving and receiving pleasure, but this urgency, this all-consuming need, was a revelation.

"I want to do unspeakable things to you with my tongue," he muttered, lips already pressed to the thatch of hair at the juncture of her thighs.

"I'm very keen to let you," she gasped. "I'm curious to know what skills a gentleman rake acquires to earn that title."

He didn't speak another word, already engaged in the task at hand. He grazed his lips to her mons. Something between a moan and a hiss escaped her lips as he explored her.

"You're torturing me," she groused, tugging on the hair at his nape.

He clicked his tongue as he used his thumbs to lay her bare to him.

"Beautiful." His mouth watered with the need to taste her. "And so wet for me."

She glistened, beads of liquid beckoning his tongue. He applied himself to the work of tasting her as if he were aiming for the highest marks. He lapped at her cunt like it was coated in honey. The tip of his tongue circled and flicked her hardened nub until her moans turned into frantic cries. Her hand was fisted in his hair, keeping him pressed to her pussy. God, but he loved how demanding she was.

"More," she begged, and he obliged, desperate now to taste her crisis, the nectar of her passion flooding his mouth and his senses. He used one hand to hold her open to him, tongue lashing into her, and pressed two fingers inside.

"Ahh...yes, fill me up." Arlo thought he'd known passion, that he'd done all there was to do. But that was before Marena. He thrust in his fingers as she demanded more of him. Her hips undulated, seeking her climax.

"Yes, use me, love. Take your pleasure," he coaxed, circling the pads of his fingers against her clitoris.

"I'm so close," she hissed, making him redouble his efforts. He used his thumb on that little button, making her keen against him. He tasted and caressed her until she was too sensitive for his touch. His mind swirled with a million thoughts. He wanted to pick her up and take her against the wall. He wanted to stay right here until she let him worship her with his mouth again. He wanted... more. More of her body, of her time.

But Marena had already told him what she was protecting herself from, and he would not be his father. To have more of her would mean changing the rules he'd set for himself. It felt like too much, too soon, and yet he could not stop himself from wanting it.

When he felt her nails softly scraping his scalp, he looked up, and the satisfied smile on her lips melted away his fretting. He had her here now.

"I hope I lived up to my reputation," he said, feigning a smugness he did not quite feel.

"So far, I am moderately impressed." She smiled mischievously at his sound of protest and bent for a quick kiss. Arlo had always wondered about men who lost their heads, squandered fortunes, ruined their names, lost their lives chasing after a woman. He'd thought them foolish and callow, but now he knew he'd engage in unmitigated recklessness to keep those blazing brown eyes on him.

"Moderately," he muttered as he gripped that backside which was already an obsession. "That kind of cheek will only achieve making us even later for dinner." She laughed, and it quickly turned into a breathy gasp when he began applying small bites and kisses to the soft skin of her belly before making his way up to her breasts. He kissed one, then the other as she made encouraging sounds. He placed his lips to the hollow of her throat, going higher and higher until he could taste her mouth again. After a moment, she pulled back, chest heaving up and down.

"I may need a few more demonstrations."

"You're requesting an encore then." There was no hiding the satisfaction in his voice, so he did not even attempt it.

She laughed in his arms and a rare jolt of joy flared in his chest.

"I would say it's more like I was intrigued by the first act and would like to experience the rest."

"I am exceedingly happy to oblige." He picked her up in flurry of lace and crumpled linen as she screamed in delight.

"Your Grace, *put me down.*"

"I am willing and able to take you through the second and third act with no further intermission."

She shook her head, barely able to speak from laughter. "Absolutely not. We are going to dinner. I have a gown and an appetite. I will be fed," she demanded imperiously, a queen who would have her every whim fulfilled, and Arlo wanted to satisfy all of them.

He could lose every ounce of sense for this woman. He had already started to.

"All right. But I reserve the right to skip courses and possibly chewing," he teased, already wondering how he could accelerate the five-course dinner he'd planned and get her back here in his bed.

CHAPTER SEVEN

THEY MANAGED to arrive at the restaurant after only a few minor delays. Marena recognized the white façade as Café l'Anglais, one of the most exclusive eateries in Paris. Without asking, he had brought her to the one place she would've picked in all the city. She had not eaten here during her months in Paris; the prices were exorbitant. But she'd walked by the popular restaurant many times. She felt a frisson of delight at the idea of eating here with Arlo.

"You're staring, Your Grace...again. I thought rakes were aloof and uninterested once they slaked their passion," she said as he helped her out of the carriage. She was having too much fun with this man, and this time when he offered her his arm, she took it.

"I am nowhere near satisfied, and I assure you, sweetheart, neither are you." If the last hour had taught her anything, it was the Duke of Linley could absolutely see that kind of promise through, and it was probably best not to provoke him in a public place. No matter how her body tightened, or her core ached at the mere suggestion of having him "satisfy" her again.

"I'm afraid to ask." She turned her face up to look at him, and he returned the same giddy expression she was sure she wore. Like her, he had refreshed his appearance, and was looking every inch the Duke of Linley. The man was imposing, almost aggressively male, and now that she knew what he could do with his hands, resisting the full effect of his heated gaze on her was a test of endurance. Marena knew this dalliance would have its consequences. No longer being the object of Arlo Kenworthy's attention would be a deep hole to crawl out of, and yet she had no regrets. She was enjoying him too much to fret about what, at this point, was inevitable.

"I assure you will enjoy every second of it." The man was too arrogant.

"Promises, promises," she said, mouth twitching as the corners turned up into a grin. She could feel him looking at her, but she kept her eyes on the massive door in front of them. Before they could knock, it opened, and they walked into a low-lit foyer covered in gleaming dark wood and gold-plated fixtures. The man who greeted them had a generous mustache, which was meticulously clipped and oiled.

"Bonsoir, monsieur," the man said politely as he discreetly looked through the list in front of him.

"My man arranged for a table. Linley" Arlo informed him, and instantly the man's face lit up at the name.

"Your Grace," he said reverently. "I am Guillaume Benoit, the maître d'hôtel. We are very honored to have you and your guest with us tonight. Welcome." He snapped his fingers, and the effect was immediate—like the staff had been hit by a bolt of lightning. Everyone moved in a flurry to accommodate the duke.

Arlo quietly observed the flurry of activity as he placed a possessive hand at her back, and her stupid, reckless heart did a somersault in her chest. "This is Mademoiselle Baine-Torres."

"Of course, Mademoiselle Baine-Torres." Another bow. Marena suspected Monsieur Benoit would've had the same reaction if Arlo had announced he'd arrived with Satan's spawn on his arm. A little voice in her head wanted to fuss about people linking her to Arlo, but she reminded herself she was in Paris and she could hide in plain sight.

Benoit extended an arm toward the door on the far side of dining room. "We have prepared the cellar for you."

The cellar? Marena's back stiffened as she tried to figure out what Arlo had devised.

"They have prepared a table for us in the cellar. It's cooler there." He was so close she could feel his warmth as they crossed the room. "And more private. I was promised we would not be disturbed by other diners. I'm of a mind to test how soundproof it is down there."

It was a travesty how she found the man's filthy mind tantalizing. "That does not seem particularly sanitary."

That brought out a husky laugh, accompanied by a devastating smile. "I'll make sure to take all precautions." And with that, he pulled her to him and helped her down the stairs.

"Arlo!" She exclaimed in surprise once they reached to bottom of the stairs. The cellar, which Monsieur Benoit had explained was one of the biggest in all Europe, was indeed enormous. There was an alcove in one corner where a table for two had been set. Candelabras stood off to the sides, illuminating the place settings, which were edged in gold. All around them, rows and rows of wine bottles covered the walls. Whatever food was being prepared was pleasantly filling the room with the aroma of butter and herbs. "How did you?" Marena asked, still admiring the many beautiful details.

"You like it?" His voice was rough, as if the moment were affecting him as well.

"It's magnificent." This would've never been possible in London, where only in the last few years could men and women dine together in a restaurant, much less have a private room for two.

He made one of his sounds. By now, she'd heard enough grunts from Arlo Kenworthy to know they were a language of their own, and the man was thoroughly pleased with himself. "A friend mentioned one could get a private table with a special menu here, and this afternoon it occurred to me I'd very much like to bring you. Have you all to myself." Why did he say things like that? She wondered if she would find the courage to tell him he was giving her the kind of evening she'd dreamt about for years.

Every passing minute with Arlo showed her he was not the kind of man she imagined him to be. And the more he said, the harder it was to keep her feelings at bay. These twenty-four hours of freedom would have long-lasting consequences because Arlo could steal her heart.

Marena looked at his handsome face, with his strong jaw and tender eyes. Without caring that Monsieur Benoit was puttering around them, regaling them with details about the dinner, she lifted up on her toes and kissed him. And as if he has been waiting for her, Arlo immediately took her in his arms, those strong, capable fingers tightening on her back as he tasted her, slow and sweet.

"Mmm." She leaned into the pleasure of being held like this, being kissed with barely contained hunger. After a moment, she pulled back, lightheaded. He ran a thumb over her bottom lip, and for a second, she caught it between her teeth, making him grin. "I might have to devise more cellar dinners in the future."

The future. The word was like a splash of cold water. She pulled back until she was free from his embrace, feeling unsettled.

"Are you all right?" he asked, brow furrowed in concern at the change in her mood. Everything felt tight and confining. Her dress, her thoughts, her life, but mostly the little bit of time they had left.

There would be no more dinners, not in cellars or anywhere else, and there would be no future. Not one in which they were like this, at least. Even if Delfine and Arlo managed to have a relationship, it would not involve Marena, and this would certainly not be part of it. No, a man of Arlo's station would never marry a woman like Marena. And why was she thinking of marriage, something *she* didn't want. But that felt like a lie too when she was in his arms.

"Marena." He called her name, bringing her out her stormy thoughts. She opened her mouth to offer some kind of platitude, but Benoit—who she'd forgotten was in the room—saved her from answering.

"Your Grace," he discreetly called from a corner. Marena quickly added mortification to the barrage of emotions coursing through her. "Your table is ready." The host gestured, and they walked over, Marena slowing to admire the luxurious trappings surrounding her. Arlo, on the other hand, was solely focused on her.

"Allow me." He hovered over her as she arranged the skirts of her dress. When she was seated comfortably and had a crisp white linen napkin on her lap, he bent and kissed her. A brush of lips to the bare skin of her neck, as if he could not resist the temptation of her.

"Thank you," she whispered, offering him with the best smile she could muster, too full of perilous emotions to trust herself to say more. He gave her a long, serious look. His gaze was different, softer, as if he knew she was feeling fragile.

At the precise moment Arlo sat, servants appeared from a door on one side of the room and began placing platters on the sideboard behind their table.

"Your Grace," Benoit said, demanding their attention. "The chef has prepared five courses for you and mademoiselle." A young man with a mop of red curls and a homely face stepped forward to place handwritten cards with their special menu in front of them. "And for boissons..." Benoit nodded, and another member of his tiny army came forward with a tray laden with bottles of wine. "Our sommelier has chosen the perfect varietals for each of your courses. We have a Coteaux de l'Aubance recently arrived from the Loire Valley that will go perfectly with the foie-gras in your first course." He smiled widely, making the curled tips of his mustache almost reach the corner of this eyes.

Arlo barely acknowledged Benoit's efforts. His eyes were only on Marena, as if the sumptuous dinner he'd arranged was of no consequence. She pulled her spectacles from her small handbag and read over the menu.

"I am looking forward to the famous pommes Anna," Marena told Benoit, excited to try the dish made of thinly sliced and crisp potatoes gratinéd with Gruyère, for which Café l'Anglais was known.

Benoit grinned widely, as if she'd complimented one of his children. "You have heard of pommes Anna. They are the perfect companion to the caneton à la Rouennaise." He pressed two fingers to his lips in a flourish. "The duck breast is stuffed with truffles and our special sausage. And the sauce is made with the Bordeaux wine and bone marrow, with lots of butter, of course." He beamed at her.

"Sounds heavenly," she replied with her own smile. She had missed the way the French made eating an experience for all the senses. She was looking forward to seeing Arlo Kenworthy savoring the dishes.

"I'm sure everything will be delectable." The heat in his eyes made Marena wonder if Arlo was referring to the meal, or other things he'd already sampled this evening.

Within seconds they each had a glass of champagne, accompanied by a small mother-of-pearl spoon laden with caviar and topped with crème fraîche. After that, they were left alone, with the promise of returning shortly with the first course.

Marena wanted to say something silly or droll about the caviar, or Monsieur Benoit's mustache, but Arlo's mood seemed to have shifted, his expression more serious now. Marena found she desperately wanted the smile that had been appearing constantly on his lips to return.

"You brought your spectacles."

"I brought my spectacles so I could read the menu. Everything looks so delicious," she said, pointing at his menu.

Arlo looked at the card on his plate with disinterest and returned his focus to her. Marena was no stranger to stares or close examinations. Being the child of a Black woman and a white man seemed to be a source of endless fascination and scrutiny for Londoners. She'd learned to ignore it, dismissing it as ignorance for which she had no time. But that was not how Arlo looked at her.

Arlo's eyes caressed her, like he could see right through her clothes and find all the places that warmed to his attention. He shifted in his seat, his back pushed against the chair, as he distractedly ran his index finger over the stem of the champagne coupe. With every passing second the beating of her heart increased until she felt a thrumming at her temples, and still the man would not speak. Finally, after taking another sip of wine and licking his lips in that way that made liquid heat gather low in her belly, he opened his mouth.

"I'm looking forward to feasting on you, darling. I'd take you right here if you'd let me," he said darkly, voice like gravel scraping across her over-sensitized skin. Her hands tingled and her breath quickened until she had to hold the sides of her chair to keep from listing. "I should've tried harder to skip dinner, because right now all I want to do is put my mouth on the places I didn't get to yet."

"I appreciate your candor." She kept her gaze locked with his as she leaned forward, enough to flaunt a bit of the attributes on which he was so riveted. "And *I* look forward to once again seeing you apply yourself to such a worthy task."

He shifted in his chair, predatory blue eyes on her, but before he could ravage her on the spot, Benoit and his assistants marched in with the first course.

CHAPTER EIGHT

DINNER HAD BEEN EXQUISITE TORTURE. Arlo's upbringing at the hands of a loving but practical woman had taught him to harness impatience and relish anticipation. Beatrice would always remind him that waiting meant a deeper satisfaction when the thing he desired was finally his. And for most of his life, he'd considered his composure one of his most valued attributes. He could keep a cool head and a steady hand in almost any situation. It had served him well a decade earlier, when his father's poor judgment had put the substantial holdings of the duchy in dire straits, and had required Arlo—with the help of his grandmother—to bring them back from the precipice of financial ruin.

It had also been a valuable skill in the past year when he tried to appeal to the peerage to pass bills that expanded rights for and improved the living conditions of women, children, and the poor. Arlo could wait anyone out. He'd seen far more dignified men than he work themselves into a frenzy while he remained calm and collected. But that was before he, the man known to the peerage as "that unflappable stone-cold bastard," had to sit through a full hour of Marena Baine-Torres licking her lips and moaning in ecstasy as she made swift work of three courses of the best gastronomic offerings in Paris.

"You never told me how you became involved in women's suffrage." Her voice was redolent with the smile that had been on her lips through the meal, and it blessedly pulled him out of his fevered thoughts. Arlo was not a fanciful man, but something possessive and not a little primal pulsed in him with the need to keep this woman glowing. The thrill he felt from knowing he'd been the one to do this for her, to feed her, fill her senses with things that delighted her, was a revelation. And now she was looking at him like she wanted to know him, the distant, wary woman of mere days ago replaced by a whirlwind of curls and bright smiles.

Arlo usually kept his past, his true self, close to his chest. He'd learned early on that being the Duke of Linley could erase who he was completely. So he kept the two Arlos separate. The grandson of Beatrice Brooks, and son of Clarice, only appeared for those who had known him before the move to Linley house. That Arlo needed to be hidden from the world into which he had been thrust, lest the peerage recall he was not one of them.

Not because he was afraid of losing his title; if there was something aristocrats were good at, it was making sure their kind could do and say what they wanted with absolute impunity. His fear was that he'd gotten so good at wearing that mask, he wasn't sure he could take it off. But for the past day he'd been letting *her* see him. It felt like he was finding his way back to a place from which he'd strayed, and to which he yearned to go back.

"My grandmother grew up in a Quaker family." She nodded as if that meant something to her and leaned in slightly. "Her parents were abolitionists and believed in the equality of the genders and races. They were wealthy, owned the biggest newspaper in Boston, and they put money into the cause." Arlo never had many reasons to feel proud of his family's legacy, especially when it came to his father, but he was proud of this.

"That's—" Marena paused, lifting her gaze to the ceiling for a moment as if searching for the right word. When she looked at him again, her eyes were bright in a way he had not seen before. Curiosity perhaps, but Arlo hoped it was more than that. "Your mother's family sounds very unusual."

"If you mean unusually aware of the world for a lot of rich tossers, you're right." He smiled at her horrified expression. "Those are my grandmother's words. She never misses a chance to remind me that the least we can do is work to uplift others when we have been handed so much. Even as a child, she was vexed with the ability of the wealthy to ignore their hand in the plight of everyone else. That's partly why she never went back to America. She arrived in England with the plan to take me back to New

York with her, but then decided she could do more here," he explained. "When my grandfather died, he left her a very wealthy woman, but it was 1850 and slavery was still a fiercely protected institution. She stayed and continued to support efforts there, helping advocates for the cause visit England and gain supporters. My father was always away." He shrugged, noticing that the ever-present sting of his father's abandonment, felt somehow less acute tonight. "I spent my formative years sitting with some of the most brilliant free thinkers of Britain and America. By the time my father fell into this dukedom, I had already been steeped deeply in my grandmother's beliefs."

"She sounds like someone I'd like to meet," Marena said in a low but serious voice. The thought of it made the blood rush to his ears. He wanted that. Would love to watch them together. Talking passionately. Speaking freely.

"I think she'd love you," he said, certain of that fact.

She raised an eyebrow, considering him. "Why are you revealing this to me?"

Why was he? Was it an attempt to impress her? Show her he wasn't like one of those cads that walked into her shop and disrespected her? No, it was more than that. He looked at her now, and for the first time in what felt like an eternity he saw things clearly. He could surmise how a person's sense of themselves or their future could be changed in a moment. Because to him, now in this cellar, Marena felt like answers to questions he'd never thought to ask. And he wondered if she might see him the same way too. After a lifetime of glancing at people, Arlo had finally found someone who compelled his complete focus.

She was still waiting for his answer. "I'm not sure," he said ruefully. "I look at you and the things you need to consider about your reputation, your name, your business. And I look at how things are for me, how they've always been, even before I become duke, and I feel like I've been spared having to become an adult in fundamental ways. How unfair that is." He shook his head. He was making no sense. "This is coming out all wrong."

"I don't think it is." She sounded alert, and her eyes were lit with anticipation. Marena wanted to hear where this went. This conversation mattered.

"To be ignorant of what occurred before you were born is to remain always a child." It was out of his mouth before he could think about it, but instead of confusion, her eyes widened and her lips parted into a grin that made him feel like they were sharing a secret.

"For what is the worth of human life, unless it is woven into the life of our ancestors by the record of history?" she said, finishing the phrase that his grandmother had repeated to him his entire life.

"Cicero." They said the name in unison, and he saw his own smile on her face.

"That is the sum of it." He said, reaching across the table for her hand, needing to touch her.

Of course she'd know. Of course. He lifted the glass of Burgundy wine they'd been served with the duck and took a sip before asking. "And what about your family? How was it to arrive in gray and dreary London after a childhood in the sunshine of the tropics?"

She looked at him from under those long eyelashes, a shy smile on her lip, but when she answered, her voice was strong and self-possessed. "Different." She shook her head, almost like she was sorting memories to share with him. "It's funny to think it now, but until our parents told us we were going to England, I never really thought about it as a real place." She smiled longingly at whatever she remembered. "We were in Havana at the time and had been there for a few years. It was after my grandmother passed away. My mother wouldn't come to England without my grandmother, and *she* would not set foot outside of the Antilles. So we stayed until after."

Her face crumpled a little, and he brushed his thumb across her palm, which he was still clutching. "Were you close to your grandmother? I couldn't imagine losing mine," he said sincerely.

"I was." She smiled radiantly. "My grandmother, Azucena Mejia de Torres, was the one who introduced my father to botany. She was a famous root worker, you see? People would come from all over the West Indies to learn from her. That's how I knew Madame Lemba. She had been my grandmother's apprentice. Once I started working at the apothecary with my father, I had to learn about doing root work in England. My mother didn't have the passion for it." She sighed at the mention of her mother, but her wistful smile remained on her lips. "And my father could only teach me so much, as the work gets passed from woman to woman."

"We both were taught about life by wise women with very strong views," he said, feeling too much at once.

"We were," she said thoughtfully, her eyes distant for a moment. Like they were fixed on a faraway memory. But when her gaze returned to him, there was heat in those gorgeous brown depths. "You have a breadth of hidden passions, Your Grace." Her tone was enticing, and so warm the blood in his veins thrummed at the sound of it.

Arlo had garnered the reputation of being unflappable for good reason. He'd forgotten what it was like to let his guard down for anyone but his grandmother. Even the lovers he occasionally took never got much more than a few fucks and a goodbye. The world in which he lived put him in contact with women who never seemed to hold his interest for long. But for Marena, he wanted to bare himself.

"I'll be glad to demonstrate how high my passions can run, darling," he said, diverting the topic. Taking things back to the familiar grounds of seduction seemed like a safer alternative. Even if he hated himself for ruining the fragile, intimate moment. But then she made a small surprised sound and shifted in her seat, a tinge of red on her cheeks, and he was bowled over by need. He pushed his chair back, eyes locked on the mouth that now seemed to be all he could see, and stood.

"Arlo," she warned as he tossed his napkin on the table and came to her.

"Marena." He hardly recognized his voice, roughened by desire as he pulled her to standing. He didn't know what he was going to do. The world could burn in the next minute, but right then his whole life whittled down to making this woman moan with pleasure. He bent to kiss her, their lips brushing. "I love those sounds you make, but if you stay very, very quiet, I imagine I can make you come before dessert arrives."

He felt her mouth tip up. "You're an astonishingly bad idea, Arlo Kenworthy."

"The very worst," he asserted as he kissed her, sliding his tongue into her mouth. She opened for him and his world again tipped on its axis. A man of thirty-five ought to have more composure when it came to a simple kiss, and yet his control ripped at the seams. "I'm very close to tearing this room apart or ruining your gown when I tumble us both to the floor."

"Don't you dare. My mother worked on this dress for months. She'd kill me, and don't think she wouldn't come looking for you in Mayfair." He wished he could store the sound of this particular laugh in a music box so he could listen to it—happy, a little wicked and very, very aroused—when she was gone.

"I'm impressed by your mother's skills," he said, pulling back to admire the bright blue raw silk and tiny black seashells embroidered along the sleeve caps of the dress. The contrast against her skin was truly breathtaking. "And I thank you for advising me on this being her handiwork, else I would've done some damage. Now, let's see how fast I can undo this row of buttons."

At that moment, he heard footsteps at the top of the stairs, and without taking his hands off her, he lifted his head and bellowed, "Whoever you are, *do not* come down those stairs!"

The scrambling was immediate, followed by the sound of the cellar door closing in haste. "I was looking forward to the dessert," she protested weakly as he ran his teeth over her neck. "I didn't come to be debauched in a cellar. I came to enjoy the best food in Paris."

He groaned in agreement as he diligently kissed the crook of her neck, swiping his tongue just enough to make her shiver. "And I've enjoyed watching you enjoy it. I nearly maimed myself at the sounds you made over that Bordeaux sauce."

She huffed a laugh as she held on to his shoulders. "In my defense, it was made with a large quantity of cream, as is the glacé that I will now be deprived of." He felt the vibrations of her delighted laugh as he made his way down to her collarbone, kissing warm skin until he reached her breasts. He smiled against the warmth of her, almost overcome by the devastating pleasure of having her in his arms.

"I'll buy you whatever sweets you'd like tomorrow. I'll have Cyrus raid every patisserie in Paris."

"But this glacé is famous and it's topped with raspberries. And they have chocolates." Even though Arlo was not certain on the whether her amorous moan was due to his attentions or Marena's penchant for chocolate, his cock still made a valiant effort to break through the placket of his trousers.

"I'll send him to the Marais for berries and then to every chocolatier in Paris," he said, his hand cupping her sex over the many layers of her dress. He pressed two fingers to the seam, making her gasp. He wanted to fit himself in between her thighs and bury himself inside. He was vibrating with the need of it. "I'll have him come here and get you the blasted ice cream. I need to touch you. Can I touch you?"

"Yes, please," she said ardently, and he made short work of lifting her onto the sideboard.

"You are a miracle in silk and spectacles." He pulled back to look at her.

"The things you say, Your Grace." She was smiling at him, amusement making her eyes sparkle, and again he felt things shift in him. He wanted more, so much more.

"Spread your legs."

"For a man that claims to not fit well into the nobility, you are certainly good at barking out orders." The expression on her face as she leaned back to consider him, provocative and brash, was a sight to behold. "Are you certain there's something there you want?" With that, she crossed her legs, taunting him. Good God, he wanted to ravage her.

He punched his fists into his trouser pockets and offered her the same heavy-lidded look she was giving him. "More than I have wanted anything in my life." He tried to grin, as if this were a bit of fun, but he felt those words in a forgotten corner of his heart. A place that had been closed so firmly he scarcely knew it.

"When I know what I want, I make sure I get it."

"And what you want is to have me in this cellar." Very slowly, her legs moved under her skirts until they were parallel to each other on the sideboard.

"What I want, with your consent, of course, darling," he said, hands itching to touch her, "is to spread your legs, slide the necessary layers of fabric off you, and avail myself of that sweet little cunt I can't seem to stop thinking about." He licked his lips for good measure, and he heard the tiniest hitch of breath.

"If only you'd said so from the beginning." She teased and obliged by giving him access between her thighs, a secret smile on her face.

He slid the dress up and went to his knees with his heart hammering in his chest, cock painfully hard. "You've been bare all night," he groaned, feeling his control being edged out by powerful need. He placed his hands on the inside of her thighs, opening her to his view.

"I decided it was sensible planning," she said voice tight. "I seem to have left every ounce of sense back in London." His chest rumbled in a appreciation as she tipped her hips forward, giving more access. "It felt like the practical thing to do."

"Practical, of course," he said, entranced. He quickly wet two of his fingers, then knelt so his mouth was right at her core. He could see beads of liquid forming there already, and he used his digits to go searching for the little nub. "Have you been ready for me all night, sweetheart?" He flicked the little peak with his tongue as he pushed a finger inside her, and was rewarded with a gasp for his efforts.

"I've been like this since the moment you walked in my shop." Her voice trembled as he feasted on her. He placed his lips around her clitoris and sucked while she moaned and writhed for him. He had her reaching her crisis in minutes, her walls clamping on his fingers and her pleasure rushing onto his tongue.

"Arlo." When she said his name like that, he felt like he could raze the world to have her like this always.

"Tell me what more you want," he pleaded.

"I want to touch you," she said, her eyes hot, and he thought for a second that he saw more than just lust there. There was a softness, a warmth he had not seen before. His heart drummed in his chest at the possibility of it. She reached for him, and he stood.

Soon they were kissing again, her hands fumbling with the placket of his trousers. Her hands rubbing over the fabric, fingers sliding over the shape of him until he was painfully hard.

"Mmm," she hummed as she opened the placket of his trousers and pulled his cock out, the sound making him impossibly harder. "This is impressive. You certainly don't require my vigor tinctures." she purred, surprising a bark of laughter out of him. But soon he was holding on to the edge of the sideboard and fucking into her hand in earnest. He shivered as she used the beads of liquid gathering at the head of his cock to ease her strokes with one hand and tugged on his balls with the other.

"You are impressive in your own right, sweetheart," he said, barely containing a moan when she tightened her grip on the head of his cock. He bent down to kiss her and pulled down the bodice of the dress, looking for her breasts, needing to have his mouth and hands full of her.

"Ah," she gasped as he tweaked a nipple between his fingers and kissed her jaw, the side of her mouth, and finally her lips. She sucked on his tongue as she redoubled her efforts, stroking him like her hand had been made solely for that task. Fire licked at his spine, pleasure building and building as he slid his fingers into her heat while he thrust into her hand.

"I want to hear you come apart again, beauty," he demanded between kisses, his head fuzzy. He felt his orgasm coming, that exquisite pressure before the release. "Your hands are a marvel, Marena."

"I like how you say my name," she confessed, as his climax barreled into him, and in that last second, he thought, *This is what bliss feels like*.

"Marena." Her eyes were still bright, but there was a bit of uncertainty there, and that would not do. He took her chin between his fingers and gave her the sweetest kiss he'd ever given anyone. "Would you say that was at least as good as the finest dessert in Paris?"

Her lips turned up and his heart drummed in his chest.

"No raspberry sauce, but delicious in its own way." She smiled against his mouth, their foreheads pressed together. He'd never been callous with the women he'd taken to his bed, but he was not one to crave closeness after lovemaking. To press in instead of pulling back. Except now, he could not seem to stop touching her.

"You're delectable and addictive. The more I taste, the more I want," He tried to sound casual, but the pressure in his chest at having the words out in the open told a different story. She let him work to put her skirt to rights in silence, and when he finally helped her down from the sideboard, he was sure she would distance herself from him.

But instead she ran her hands over his chest, straightening his cravat. Pressing her palm gently to his cheek. "Thank you for dinner." Her eyes were still soft and vulnerable, and he practically vibrated with the need to ask her if she wasn't feeling it too. That everything was changing. Instead he tucked an errant curl behind her ear because the other things he wanted to do felt too precarious.

When he could speak again, he took her hands in his and drew her toward the stairs of the cellar. "Let's go."

"We're leaving?" She paused to grab her gloves and handbag.

"Yes." Soon they were climbing the stairs, his eyes and hand on that delicious bottom. He intended to see her gloriously naked and in his bed within the hour. "I'm already craving seconds, and I'll need a lot more privacy for that."

CHAPTER NINE

THE CARRIAGE RIDE HAD BEEN...FRENZIED. They hardly could keep their hands off each other, and by the time they arrived at the townhouse, their clothes were in an extremely sorry state. Arlo was utterly shameless, and Marena was smitten. No, smitten made her think of wallflowers, ballrooms and longing glances across crowded rooms. What Arlo had started in her was far more explosive than that. Since that morning at the market when he'd looked on with fascination at everything she purchased, to when he kissed her and made her forget every kiss that had come before that one, she'd known. This man was a storm passing through her quiet life and there would be wreckage after he was gone. But Marena had allowed herself this night, and she would have it.

They'd arrived at the Place des Vosges and, after the usual formality of handing off hats and capes to his valet, they'd each gone to their rooms. Arlo had promised he'd come to her, and now she was waiting and feeling like she was on fire. Anticipation thrummed through her blood. It had been some time since she'd done this. Her sexual appetites were varied, and she wasn't a novice. But she was cautious, not wanting a pregnancy or an illness. Nor London's gossipmongers arriving at her shop's door.

She was particular with who she took as a lover. She had to be. A Black woman running a business that served the rich had to be beyond all reproach, a guileless vessel with no opinions of them, of their lives...of their idleness. Or any life of her own. She loved her work, but it could be a lonely existence. Especially when you were ambitious. She worked at her craft, strived to master it. And in the years since she'd been running the apothecary, she'd discovered competent women tended to encounter at best disinterest and at worst scorn from men.

Not Arlo. The Duke of Linley seemed fascinated by every detail she shared about herself, and not once had he implied what she did was not important. He intrigued her so. He had no reverence for his title, yet cunningly used the power it gave him it to pursue what he felt was important. Damn the man for having morals.

Arlo was dangerous. Too handsome and imposing, too much like everything she'd never wanted. But in him, she could not seem to get enough of. A man who could satisfy her body and her mind. With all that power, he could decimate her, which was why she had to walk away. Because even after one day, she knew if he asked her for more—if he asked to see her in London—she wasn't sure she could turn him down. As if he were waiting for the exact moment when her defenses were at their lowest, she heard a knock on her door.

"Come in," she called as she walked to the table by the balcony doors where she'd placed the small silk pouch she'd brought with her from London. Proof that, despite everything she'd told herself about how things would be with Arlo Kenworthy, before she boarded that train in London, she'd already known the truth.

The door clicked as it closed, followed by footsteps. He was quiet too, and she wondered if he'd had his own reckoning in his room and was coming to tell her this had all been a mistake. After only a few days, she already knew he was the kind of man who would not take a woman to bed for the wrong reasons. The kind of man who would do the honorable thing.

She didn't think he'd put her reputation at risk. Not if he wasn't willing to face the consequences with her. She wondered if he'd go as far as offering marriage just so he could have her in his bed. Not that she would consider the offer. She had never been a fool, and letting herself get swept into a world that would despise her would be madness. But then she felt his hard chest against her back, and sensibility fluttered up and out the window into the Parisian night.

"I was hoping you'd still be dressed."

"Mmm?" Enveloped in his touch, his voice, his heat, she let herself drift. This man could become an addiction, and she could not fall. "Are you going to take the place of the chambermaid again, Your Grace?"

"Call me by my name," he demanded, his hands already possessing her. He palmed her sex over her dress and placed his other hand on her neck, the two places where he could feel her pulsing for him.

"Arlo. Are you going to undress me?" she asked, and brought her hands to cover his, his touch filling her head with things she ought not want. She'd spent so many years mastering the art of keeping everyone at a distance, yet with Arlo she craved closeness.

"Out of respect for your mother, I will mind the buttons," he said, his hands sliding from under hers. He stepped back and she missed his warmth immediately, but soon he was making quick work of the buttons at her back. "The curve of your neck," he said as he ran a finger on that very spot, "is why artists go back to the same model again and again." He punctuated the last word with an openmouthed kiss at her nape. His hot, dark caress in such a sensible place made her tremble. "If I could paint—if I had the talent—I'd spend decades on your body. The lines and curves of it. How does a man attend to the demands of life once he'd had this?"

"I'm already letting you bed me," she said unsteadily. He made a gruff noise at that and slipped the dress off her shoulders.

"I must invest in endeavors of the rational dress movement," he said with appreciation as he removed the front clasps of her corset, then her narrow petticoat, until she was in her chemise. "I will become a fervent advocate of the cause if it allows for such brisk undressing. Turn around, love." The word pierced her. She had to take a breath before facing him. And she was not prepared for what she saw.

"Arlo," she breathed out her eyes landed him. He loomed large in front of her, all brawn and barely contained power. He was barefoot, his shirt unbuttoned, cuff links removed, revealing smooth skin like sculpted marble. She didn't know where to touch first. "You are a beautiful man."

His lips quirked up. "You think me beautiful, Marena?"

She nodded, hands busy removing his shirt. "I do." She pressed her lips against the skin that was in front of her. The silky hair on his chest tickled her palm as she lapped at him.

"I've been dreaming about your mouth, and would like a lot more of that very soon, but I need to see you." With that, he stepped back again so there were a few feet between them. "Bare yourself for me, Marena."

Her skin felt fevered as she undid the buttons on the front of her chemise. This was madness, and yet she could not stop herself from looking at him as the garment slid down her body to the floor.

"Like this?" she asked, her skin tight, burning for his hands.

"Tell me where you'd like me to touch you first. I can still taste you, and I want to bury my tongue inside you again."

"Dios mío," Marena whispered, the Spanish coming to her when she had no words left in English to voice what she was feeling. She had not taken many lovers. She'd had two, to be exact—Jean-Pierre, a Haitian poet who she'd met here when she was studying under Madame Lemba, and Lily, who had left England looking for a place where she could be who she was more openly.

Marena knew what she liked. She'd learned from both Lily and Jean-Pierre the places where she liked to be touched and the parts of her lovers' bodies she most enjoyed. She appreciated a woman's softness and delighted in the rough planes and angles of a man's body. But she'd always been able to keep her head; she'd been the one in control, the one who beckoned. With Arlo Kenworthy, she felt like prey. And more concerning was the fact that she ached to be caught.

He moved closer, taking her into his arms. His touch at once gentle and rough on her body. "Did you know that most of peerage hates me?" he asked as he slowly slid his big hands down her back to her bottom. "They think I'm too common. That I'm too stoic. But really what they hate is they can't find a weakness to exploit. I've seen firsthand what happens to men who let their passions dictate their actions."

Perhaps this was when he'd let her know that this was just a convenient tryst, that he, too, had a life where none of this could fit. Except it seemed to Marena that with every graze of his hands, every brush of his lips, it became less clear why they should ever stop.

"But," he said before kneeling in front of her, his hands already searching for that little engorged peak of pleasure that he seemed to know so well. "You've turned my head and I can't stay away. It should feel like weakness, but all I feel when you're in my arms is powerful." He licked at her then, his tongue circling her clitoris until her entire existence became the pleasure radiating from her core. "I could spend the rest of my days right here." He pointed the words by using to fingers to spread her folds, opening her to his eyes, to his mouth. And yet she was the one who felt consumed by hunger. "Lost to making you scream my name."

His hands, she thought, would be why she finally succumbed. Working with the earth, Marena had learned to appreciate a person who had good instinct for touch, and Arlo had the gift. She pressed herself to him, showing him without words where she needed him most, and instantly his thumb was right where she ached. She circled her hips, looking for that perfect friction, and he tightened his fingers on her thighs exactly where she needed to feel him.

She could get lost in him. She already was.

"Más," she demanded, and he obliged. He ate at her, flattening his tongue so that he could lap her up. She felt her climax coming at the very moment he inserted two fingers, which felt like too much and not nearly enough, because what she wanted, what she *needed*, was all of him.

She'd barely come back to herself when he was on his feet, picking her up. "I am afraid we've arrived at the moment when I thoroughly ravage you on this bed."

For all his rough talk, he laid her on the mattress like she was made of spun sugar, his hands quickly looking for her heat again. If he started that, she'd be begging him to take her within seconds, and she needed her cervical cap. "Arlo, wait."

The reaction was immediate. He pulled back, his hair adorably ruffled. It gave his almost masculine face a boyish demeanor. That paired with a not-quite petulant wrinkle on his nose tugged at something in her.

"Is something wrong?"

She shook her head at his question, her lips quirking up of their own volition.

"Nothing's wrong." She ran hands up his powerful shoulders, marveling at the way looking at his body made her feel. But she'd always loved to look at beautiful things, and this man was certainly that.

"How did this happen?" she asked, pressing her fingers into hard muscles. She softly raked her nails over his hard chest, coaxing out a hiss of pleasure. He closed his eyes as she continued to touch. "I thought the peerage spent their days lounging around White's, eating bland food and sipping brandy."

He threw his head back to laugh, his blue eyes glinting with humor.

"That is not an inaccurate assessment." He grabbed one of the hands she was running over his chest, and playfully bit the tip of one of her fingers. "Idleness is a virtue for many in the ton. But not for me. I fence, I ride, I swim." She lifted an eyebrow when he mentioned swimming. "Linley House has an indoor pool. We keep it heated so I can use it year-round."

"An indoor pool," she said, unable to hide the wonder from her voice.

"I had it put in for my grandmother," he said, bending to kiss her. "I hired the architect who builds them for the Cambridge Swimming Club."

"Swimming in warm water," Marena marveled. She hadn't done that since she'd left the Caribbean at fifteen. Growing up, she'd gone early in the mornings with Lluvia, and they'd swim at a little private beach a mile or so from their family's house. There were swimming clubs in London and public pools, but decent ladies would never appear in public in any attire fit for swimming.

"There are days when I feel stifled by this title, but the idea of you naked in my pool may have made it all worth it." He ran his big, warm hands on the insides of her thighs as his eyes singed her. "I would like to see that."

She was about to tell him that could never happen, that there would be no swimming or anything else between them once they were back in London, but the words died in her throat when he covered her with his body. His chest hovered above her, hands on either side of her head until all she could see was him.

"I'd sit you on the ledge, spread your legs and lick you. Then I'd fuck you so thoroughly." He licked his lips as if the taste of her were the most sinful delicacy. "Mm, for days I'd do nothing else." Before her brain could produce a response he came in for a kiss, licking in to her in that way he did. His tongue gentle but his every move focused and determined. By the time he pulled back, she had her thighs bracketing his waist and was ready to move on from conversation.

"I want to have you." he said, his mouth hot as he spoke next to her ear, hips thrusting against her. "I want to be deep inside, feel you clenching against me." Her head was swimming with need, her legs scissoring against the ache there. Her core pulsed with the echo of those words, *I want to have you*. She'd never thought possessive demands would evoke such yearning in her, but she wanted to be his.

"I need to do something first," she said, pushing him off her and climbing out of the bed.

Once she'd reached it, she held up the cervical cap, almost certain she was about to ruin the moment. But this was something she would not compromise on. She had everything to lose if she did not keep her head. And she would finally see what kind of man Arlo Kenworthy was. If he was the type who spoke about women's rights as long as it never hindered his ability to indulge himself. She raised her gaze as she spoke. "Contraception."

His smile faltered for a moment, and her heart sank, but then his face split into a grin that practically reached his ears.

"You *were* planning to ravish me before you even left London."

CHAPTER TEN

"You're an insufferable sod, and I like to be prepared." She groused, an impressive feat considering the grin on her face.

"Prepared for my prick, you mean. And for the record, I brought French letters, as I too like to be prepared." This earned him a pinch on the arm, which only made him dissolve further into laughter. He was being an enormous arse—and quite possibly ruining his chances of getting to put said prick anywhere near her—but the woman was a delight to incense.

"For a man who is just a step from the monarchy, you use very crude language." It would be easier to take Marena's growl more seriously if she were not currently naked and holding up the contraception device she'd brought from London, which she had obviously planned to use while in Paris.

His cock gave a slight jump for joy at that new development as he made his way to her. "You look extremely tempting leaning on that dresser," he said, taking her in. "I'd envisioned fucking on the bed, but now I'm reconsidering." He licked his lips as she squirmed. "If I seat you on the edge, I can see your tits bouncing as I thrust into you, suck on them while your sweet little cunt tightens around my cock."

"You are a reprobate."

"Of the worst order," he teased, putting his hand out for the pouch which she lifted over her head.

"You are not touching it with dirty hands."

"But my hands have only been…in you," he said innocently, eliciting another frustrated growl from her. And then a second one when he effortlessly lifted her until she was seated on the dresser. Instead of trying to convince her to hand him the cap again, he did what any reasonable man who had a pair of luscious breasts at face level would do. He popped one in his mouth.

"This is unseemly, Arlo. I am trying to be serious." Her breaths were coming more quickly, so he continued his efforts. Suckled on one nipple while his thumb and index finger tweaked the other. He used his tongue and teeth, as he had noticed Marena enjoyed, and soon she was panting, legs spreading for him. Her arms came to her sides and she fumbled with something between her legs.

He came up for air to ask if she needed assistance, but a hand at the back of his head pressed him right to the nipple he'd abandoned. "The more you do that, the easier it is to put this in place, and then I can finally experience this legendary cock for myself." She sounded winded, but right under that there was amusement, and that was what undid him. This woman who had been so distant, so cold with him, was now playful. She had no qualms in showing him that she wanted him as much as he wanted her.

It overtook him again, the greedy feeling, that urge to manipulate and cajole until she agreed to see him again once they were back in London. He just might make commitments or marriage offers if it came to that, just so that he could continue to have this.

"I'm ready," she whispered, her voice suddenly small and fragile. "Now you get ready."

He moved fast, making quick work of finding the condom in his pockets and sheathed his cock. Within a moment he stood to his full height, pressed between her thighs, already poised to enter her.

He kissed her as he spread her folds. He stroked her, their tongues gliding together. Her small moans of pleasure enticed him until his hips rolled against her. He was at the edge of a precipice, and once he jumped would never be able to find his way back.

"Please, Arlo."

"What do you need?" he asked through clenched teeth as he held the base of his cock, the wet tip rubbing against the little nub that brought out those delicious sounds out of her.

"You, I need you." She rocked her hips closer, and they both gasped as he entered her. He forced himself to stay perfectly still for a breath, for a heartbeat. then slid in until he was fully seated in her.

No. There was no coming back from this. He already knew the truth. He would want more, much more from Marena Baine-Torres.

"You are..." Perfect. Irreversible. Essential. "Tell me how I feel inside you," he asked with an urgency he could not recall feeling with anyone ever before. He needed hear her to say this was obliterating her too.

"So good and I'm so full," she cried, her arms tightly wound around his neck as he surged into her. "Don't stop. Please," she begged, her hips thrusting to meet his, as if their bodies had been made for this singular purpose. He lowered two fingers to the tight space between them and circled her clitoris, making her keen from pleasure. Soon, he felt her walls gripping him until he, too, was gasping for breath.

"You feel so good, sweetheart. I want to be inside you forever." Even in the heat of this moment, those words struck true. He would never get enough. He kissed her hungrily, luxuriating in how freely she screamed her climax against his lips. She gripped him like a vise, hot and perfect, and soon he felt his orgasm crash over him. He braced his legs on the floor and held onto her as their breathing evened out. Once he could make his limbs move again, he scooped her up and brought her to the bed.

"You seem to favor these gratuitous displays of strength," she mumbled against his neck.

"Not carrying you would've meant letting you out of my grasp, and I can't let go quite yet." He was being possessive, but that would linger as long as he still had the taste of her on his tongue.

Once she was on the bed, he got a damp towel from the water closet and cleaned them both up. Then he covered them with the light linen blankets that felt cool in the warmer June night. He took her in his arms, her hot, damp skin already feeling essential. And she went to him, still amorous and pliable. She rested her head on him and sighed contentedly. He already wanted to demand more time with her. In business, no one could outmaneuver him; he could wait any competitor out. But when it came to Marena, urgency felt like a fever under his skin.

"This has been an evening of exquisite pleasure, Your Grace," she whispered as she peppered him with kisses.

"*You* are a pleasure." There was a rumbling in his chest as he stroked her wild curls and felt her warm hands against his skin. "I enjoy you very much." His heart galloped inside him from all the things he wanted to say but didn't know how to voice. She murmured something, a sleepy, soft sound, and tightened her arms around him while he warred with himself.

He had not been prepared for this. Then again, the world he lived in, the peerage and its silly rules and inconsistent behaviors, its morally vacuous sensibilities and puritanical nonsense, could not produce a magnificent being like the woman in his arms. Maybe that was why he'd been content all these years with the idea of remaining alone. If he'd imagined someone like her was possible, he would've been running for the altar years ago.

"I want to see you when we're in London." The words were out of his mouth before he could stop himself, and just as quickly the fragile perfection of the moment was shattered.

Marena sat up, her eyes wide and skittish. "Arlo. We agreed."

"That was before we—" He gestured a hand in the space between them.

She closed her eyes, her chest moving up and down as she breathed through her mouth. "Please, don't do this. Arlo, I can't." She scrambled out of the bed as she spoke, rifling through the room in her luscious nakedness. His chest tightened at the unhappy look on her face and he wondered what, if anything, he could say to make her stay.

"I know you feel it too. I know you want more."

She was already sliding the chemise back on and turned a watery gaze in his direction.

"I want a lot of things I can't have, Arlo," she said miserably as she pulled the lace-trimmed straps on her shoulders. "I want to be able to own a business without having every person who walks in demand to know where the man in charge is. I'd love for people to not look at me and assume they can touch my hair." She threw her hands in the air, clearly frustrated. "I'd love to live in a world where me wanting you was reason enough to let myself have you. But I can't be anyone's mistress, Arlo. And certainly not the mistress of a duke."

"I never said you'd be my mistress." Arlo was always painstakingly restrained, but his control felt close to shattering. He was angry. Not at her, but at the whole fucking world. "I am ready to talk about conditions, tell me what you want, and—"

"You're a duke, Arlo. I'm a merchant. A half-Black merchant." She laughed then, and it was a hollow, bitter sound. "If I take up with you, everyone in London will know and I will be the one ruined. You'll just be another lord who wanted to try something different for a bit." Every word she said was true, and he despised himself and his kind in that moment, as much as he ever had. "Also, Delfine is *your sister*."

"But we could—"

"There can't be a *we*, Arlo. We said we could have this one night. Please don't make this harder than it already is." A lone tear ran down her cheek, and when he moved to go to her, she ran to the water closet and closed the door. She left him there, stifled by this blasted title he had never wanted. And which now, for the first time, truly felt suffocating.

CHAPTER ELEVEN

"GOOD MORNING, YOUR GRACE." She was a coward, so she didn't look his way.

Arlo grunted something that resembled a greeting as Marena stiffly perused the breakfast table. Every meal so far had been delicious, and she'd been looking forward to the petit dejeuner offerings from the chef. In the mood she was currently in, some bland English gruel would've been more in order. She could feel his eyes on her as she focused on cutting a wedge of the Saint Marcelin he'd bought at the Marais after she'd said it was her favorite. As soon as they'd returned to the townhouse, he'd handed the cheese to his valet and informed the man it would be for their breakfast. He'd been so proud of his market purchases. All of this would be so much easier if he'd fulfilled her expectations of the nobility and behaved like a cad.

Alas, he'd been nothing but decent. More than decent. Last night he'd been...too much of everything she wanted and could never have. Too good, too clever, too charming, too wicked. *Too tempting.* Arlo made Marena forget the rules she'd set for herself. And when he'd told her he wanted more, God help her, she'd wanted to fling herself in his arms and tell him she felt the same.

But she didn't live in a fairytale. She lived in London. He was a duke, and she would not throw her life and business by the wayside to be a rich man's temporary fancy. Because that's what she would be. A man like Arlo could afford to indulge in fantasies, but women like Marena could not. And so, despite how much she'd preferred waking up to Arlo making his way down her body with his mouth, she'd have to settle for buttered croissants.

When she'd arranged her plate to her liking, she chose the seat at the end of the eight-person table, at least twelve feet from him. He raised an eyebrow, but continued to cut the piece of bacon on his plate. She smothered the pang of disappointment at his silence and reminded herself that she'd asked him for this distance. Now she had to live with the stark reality of no longer being the object of Arlo Kenworthy's attention.

"Any word from Delfine?" she asked, grasping for something that could make this excruciatingly awkward meal bearable. She looked up from her own investigation of the omelet on her plate to find Arlo's impassive gaze on her. He *was* a bit disheveled. His usual perfect appearance a bit off-kilter. Perhaps like her, sleep had not come to him until almost dawn.

"No."

One word. No humorous inflection. No flirtatious repartee. She straightened her back, her eyes on the window behind Arlo that, in the French style, went from the floor to the ceiling. It was a beautiful day, with barely a cloud in the bright blue sky. She could see the tops of the streets of the square at the center of the Place des Vosges. But her attention kept returning to the copper streaks in Arlo's hair. She could almost feel the coarse curls between her fingers, remembering how she'd gripped them as his mouth feasted on her sex.

The crash of the fork slipping out of her hand sounded like a gunshot in the suffocating silence of the room.

"Mierda!" she hissed, jumping up from the chair as flecks of coddled egg splattered over the lovely toile tablecloth.

"Are you all right?" Arlo asked with concern. She wanted to scream. Just scream in frustration that she could not even give herself twenty-four hours with this man without thinking she could be ruining her entire future.

"I'm fine." Her face was hot with embarrassment as she tried to blot out the grease stain already soaked into the fine linens. "I can't believe I did that. So clumsy," she said, frantically rubbing a wet napkin on the spot.

"It's all right. It can be replaced." The casual dismissal of the ruined tablecloth, which probably cost what she made in a week at the shop, made everything worse.

"Of course," she scoffed. "What was I thinking? I'm sure there are a dozen more pristine ones ready to take it's place." The caustic tone in her voice made him pause as he reached for the bell, presumably to summon a brand-new tablecloth and place settings. Meanwhile, an ugly, sharp wretchedness slithered inside her chest. She wanted to say horrid things, dismiss everything she'd learned about him. Give him a reason to stop looking at her like he could see her misery. Maybe then she'd be rid of the frantic need she felt for him.

"Is that what you think?" He sounded hurt. "That I toss things out when I have no use for them?" He was at her side in an instant, towering over her. He smelled like leather and bergamot oil and she loathed every one of the perfectly good reasons swirling in her head which told her getting close to this man was a mistake.

"What does it matter what I think, Arlo?" She looked away. He was wearing light gray trousers and a matching waistcoat and jacket. A crisp white shirt and cravat completed the ensemble.

"Because it does."

She shook her head and averted her gaze, not wanting to let the yearning in his voice affect her, unable to stare into those blue eyes that had already gotten her in so much trouble.

"Marena, please." He reached for her, and she backed away. If she gave in, she'd be lost. She had only the morning and afternoon to get through, and this evening they would see Delfine and Lluvia. She'd be on her way back to London in the morning.

Marena was not one to run away. Her parents had raised her to stand tall in a world that sometimes didn't see her at all, but this felt too risky.

"I have some things I need to do before this evening," she said hastily, and made her escape.

As she reached her room, she told herself it was for the best. He would think her rude and not worth the trouble. When he did, she would lie to herself again and pretend that was exactly what she wanted.

"WHAT ARE YOU DOING?"

He could not decide if it was anger or exhaustion in her voice. Like the previous day, they were at door of the townhouse with Marena glaring at him. But if he had not let London's high society get the best of him yet, he could surely navigate an afternoon with a surly Marena Baine-Torres.

"I'm coming with you," he said pleasantly as he reached for his hat. He'd recognized the turmoil in her eyes at breakfast because it was exactly what was wreaking havoc in him. Arlo had expected the morning to be awkward, but he refused to be one of those men who let a bruised ego turn him into a brute. He'd been clear last night that he wanted more. She'd declined, and for now he had to accept it. He had only one alternative left—let her see for herself that what was happening between them was worth exploring.

"I don't require a chaperone, Your Grace." He raised an eyebrow, genuinely impressed she could make sounds when her jaw clenched so tightly.

"I'm not offering to chaperone. I enjoyed our outing yesterday and was hoping you'd let me accompany you again." He was proud of himself for not alluding to the other things he'd enjoyed doing with her and kept a very friendly, respectable distance. His efforts did not thaw Marena in the slightest.

She looked at her clothes, avoiding his gaze. Inspected them from the tip of her toes to the waist of her skirt, taking her time before she answered him. "I'm not going shopping," she said, still not meeting his eyes. "I thought I'd walk to the river and spend some time at the Jardin des Plantes." A flush stained her cheeks, and the urge to lift her chin and kiss her senseless was almost overpowering. "It's my favorite place in Paris."

If he didn't already have a dozen reasons why he should be captivated by this woman, the fact that the old medicinal garden of Louis the XIII was her favorite place—in a city where one could find any indulgence possible—would've have left him hopelessly infatuated.

He had never seen anyone more enticing than this woman in a practical, unassuming morning dress, ready for a day of walking in the sun. She was in light green today, with a simple embellishment at the hems and waist, the cuffs at her elbow of a darker green filigree embroidery. She'd said she didn't use long sleeves because she worked with tinctures so much and would always stain them. He looked at her hands—which she'd mentioned made her feel self-conscious because of their dryness—and felt an irrational urge to take each one and kiss her palm.

She wore no bustle as usual, not that she needed it. Marena made Botticelli's beauties pale in comparison. Her hair was up, half covered with a bonnet, the rest coiled in intricate braids. An image of her with her hair down puttering in a garden, made his chest tighten with unbridled longing. He would upend his life to see that. To have the chance to walk in on her, hands dusty from her work, her face sun-kissed and warm.

"I'd love to see the garden again. I haven't gone in years." He couldn't remember the last time he'd sounded this tentative. Or the last time something so simple felt so enormously important. Yesterday, he'd felt content walking through that market. Happy in a way he had never felt with anyone but his grandmother. Despite how things had ended last night, he wanted more of that.

"It's a long way there, and I plan to walk. It may get warm."

"I'm wearing my walking boots." he tipped one foot up. "And I am happy to perform basket-holding duties again," he said as amiably as he could manage.

"No baskets today," she said, a shy smile quirking her lips. "We'll be back in a few hours. For when Lluvia and Delfine arrive."

"Of course." His heart pounded in his chest, giddy. He was giddy for a walk in a garden. Maybe this woman *was* a sorceress.

"Don't you need Cyrus to..." She twirled a finger in the vicinity of his head.

"I've sent him on a special mission. Shall we?" he asked, thrusting her parasol at her. It was best to keep the purpose of the mission as a surprise for a later time, when he needed more ammunition for Ms. Baine-Torres's resistance.

She considered him for another moment. This time, the smile reached her dark brown eyes. "There are going to be lots of bugs there."

"I'm a devotee of gnats and all manners of flying insects," he said matter-of-factly as they stepped out into the street.

"That is a lie if I've ever heard one."

"Possibly," he admitted as they walked, his chest expanding with every step he took by her side. "But I'd suffer through more than a few gnats for a little more time with you." He was pushing, he knew that, but when he offered his elbow, she slid her arm into it. And in that moment, Arlo realized that if marriage were the only path forward, he would do it. If it meant keeping this woman long enough to convince her they made perfect sense together.

CHAPTER TWELVE

"FOR A LOUSE ENTHUSIAST you gripe in excess over a small bee sting," Marena teased as they walked into the townhouse.

"It was a remarkably robust bee. The blasted thing practically blinded me."

"It stung your *cheek*," she exclaimed, barely able to talk through her laughter.

He grabbed her by the waist and pressed his mouth to her ear. "I thought I was going to get some tending to for my injury."

"Arlo, someone could see us," she said weakly, letting him turn them around so they were half-hidden in a small alcove by the entrance.

The visit to the gardens had turned into a picnic, and then some kisses in the shade of some horse chestnut trees. She should've resisted, but she hadn't wanted to. Besides, their time was almost over. Once they saw Lluvia and Delfine she'd stop, she promised herself as she brushed her lips to the angry red welt on his face.

"I may have some lavender oil I could put on this tiny welt," she said, feigning annoyance. "For such a big and strong man, you need a lot of coddling." At that, Arlo turned his face and kissed her.

A kiss, and a taste of the blackberries they'd eaten still on his tongue. "I may be taking advantage of the fact that I have the most famed herbalist in all London to help heal my battle scars." His mouth was already leaving a trail of kisses along her neck. "But may I request you thoroughly inspect for more bites or stings? I suggest we go to my bedroom and get undressed so you can properly investigate."

She huffed a laugh even as she gave him more access to her neck. "You do not need to take off your clothes for a bee sting on your face, Arlo."

"I meant undressing you," he said, laughing so hard his entire body shook.

"Swine." She could nor the life of her infuse the word with any rancor. She was hopelessly smitten.

"I love when you use pet names, darling."

That elicited another bout of laughter, so that they were more heaving against each other than kissing.

"Marena! I thought that was you—"

Her sister's voice made Marena jump back as if she'd been scalded. She frantically looked at Arlo as she righted the collar of her dress. Her face was hot with mortification.

This was a disaster. Her sister had caught her *kissing* Arlo. Kissing Delfine's brother. Kissing the *duke* who was Delfine's brother.

"Sweetheart," Arlo whispered, reaching for her, but she stepped out of the way before he could touch her.

"No, please," she begged, not able to meet his gaze. She took a deep breath, her eyes closed. Tremors coursed up and down her body from embarrassment. Right under it was the regret of knowing her time with Arlo had come to such an abrupt ending. It cut to the bone. She'd lied to herself over and over about being able to walk away, but before she'd even started, she'd known it would hurt. And she'd been right.

When she faced Lluvia and Delfine, she found matching expressions, which were a mix of open curiosity and embarrassment. But there was something else more devastating—a glint of hope. Over the years, Lluvia had made it her mission to let Marena know she needed to let her guard down, that she should find someone who would make her shed her aloofness, and Marena has always told her she was not interested. She knew what her sister was thinking. That maybe someone had finally broken through Marena's defenses. Unfortunately, it didn't matter how effectively Arlo had done just that—he was not a man she could have.

"Lluvia," she said, tears suddenly brimming in her eyes. She embraced her older sister, who was as different from her in temperament as she was in appearance. Where Marena was curves and voluptuousness, Lluvia was tall and slim, planes and angles, with straight black hair that fell flat down her back when she let it down. It had only been a few months since Lluvia had been in London. She'd come back three or four times in the year since she'd moved to Paris with Delfine. But seeing her now shook Marena to her core, as if in the last twenty-four hours she'd drifted out of the world she belonged in and seeing her sister had jolted her back.

"I've missed you, Mare." Then, in a stage whisper, Lluvia added, "and I have many questions, but those can be reserved for later."

Marena shook her head helplessly. Lluvia could always make her smile, even in the direst of circumstances. Then she noticed Delfine and Arlo standing a few feet away, staring at each other with open curiosity.

"Delfi," she said, pulling out of Lluvia's arms to embrace the other woman, also a sister by the ties of friendship and family. "Are you ready?" She didn't have say for what. The man who had brought them together was patiently waiting his turn.

Delfine nodded, a shaky breath escaping her full lips, which Marena noticed bore a keen resemblance to the ones she'd become so fond of in the past few days. That thought was ruthlessly smothered and stored where everything else about Arlo Kenworthy would go. She turned to him and saw too much emotion in those stormy blue eyes. He'd found his sister after so many months searching.

"Your Grace," she said with formality, as if everyone in the room was not aware she'd let the man bite her neck only minutes ago. "This is Delfine Boncouer, and my sister Lluvia Baine-Torres." She turned to her friend, whose face was crumpling from the emotion of the moment. "Delfine, this is the Duke of Linley." To her mortification, she had to choke down tears. "Your brother."

Delfine was petite, but she cut a stalwart figure. Her arms and back had been made strong from delivering children into the world. Her skin was a deep brown, a contrast to Arlo's fairness, but their faces gave them away as family. They bore the same proud forehead and stubborn chin, and puzzlingly, identical eyebrows.

"Sister." Arlo's voice wobbled, and Delfine's throat convulsed as if she were trying to speak. After a moment, she gave up and threw her arms around his shoulders.

It was almost too intimate a moment to witness. A whirlwind of conflicting emotions raged through Marena. Longing, yearning, regret. But in the midst of that was gladness. She felt a hand reach for hers and looked up to find Lluvia gazing at the love of her life embracing her brother, a beatific expression on her face. Like she could physically feel Delfine's joy coursing through her. For the first time in her life Marena yearned to have what Lluvia and Delfine shared.

After a moment, Delfine stepped back from her brother's embrace and glanced up at him with a bright smile. "Arlo, my brother."

"I am so glad to have found you." Arlo smiled widely and nodded, then turned to Marena. "I'm grateful for Marena's kindness in agreeing to bring me to you, sister." Their eyes locked, and the naked affection in them made her look away.

Lluvia who had always been the boldest of their trio, stepped forward. "It's a pleasure to meet you, Your Grace." She gave a little curtsey, a bright smile on her lips. "I'm Lluvia."

"My sister's companion. It's my pleasure to meet you." Marena's heart thumped in her chest at the revelation that Arlo had known all along the nature of Lluvia and Delfine's relationship and didn't think anything of it.

Lluvia and Delfine exchanged a look. After fifteen years of being in love, in a world that repudiated their devotion to each other, they'd learned to have entire conversations without saying a word. And since Marena had been there for a lot of it, she immediately understood they wanted to continue this discussion, and wherever it might lead, in private.

"Your Grace—"

"Arlo, Marena, please."

She dipped her head in concession as she avoided looking at Lluvia and Delfine. "Arlo, it may be best to move to the study. I can ask Colette to prepare some tea for us? Did you have time to eat?" It was highly inappropriate to give directions to Arlo's staff, but she desperately needed a moment to compose herself.

"I can always eat." Lluvia said enthusiastically, to which Arlo responded with an appreciative grunt.

"I very much approve of the Baine-Torres women's voraciousness."

Their gazes met as he spoke, which only flustered Marena further. She looked down, afraid that if she kept her eyes on him a second longer she would give herself away. She needed to get herself under control, and for the second time and two days she escaped before her feelings for the Duke of Linley finally got the best of her.

CHAPTER THIRTEEN

"It's settled, then." Arlo's voice already held genuine affection for Delfine. Marena smiled as she watched them. They'd spent a few hours getting to know each other, sharing details of their lives. In the end it seemed Arlo would fulfill his promises. Delfine, if she wanted it, would be a very wealthy woman.

Lluvia and Marena had not been excluded from the conversation, and Arlo had turned to them for opinions and thoughts on how to handle the return to London, which seemed imminent. Apparently, in the few days she'd been preparing for the trip here, Arlo had retained the best law firm in London to resolve the misunderstanding.

Delfine, not fully convinced the legal issue that had kept her away from home for over a year could be taken care of in such a short time, looked at her brother incredulously. "And you're sure we can go back without risking me going to gaol?"

Arlo stiffened at the word, his face assuming a mutinous expression. "My solicitor has already been working on investigating what these supposed charges were. None of the Beaton's claims hold any water." Fury tinged his voice as he mentioned the family who had caused so much strife for Delfine when she had only helped an innocent girl. "Not to mention that deviant, Richard, has done this before." He scowled again, and Delfine's face hardened.

"I suspected as much."

Arlo sighed. "This morning I received a telegram confirming that in a week's time everything should be finalized. Which is why I will be here in two weeks to fetch you." Lluvia and Delfine's eyes widened and immediately Arlo clicked his tongue, as if he just remembered something important. "Forgive me. I didn't consider you may both have patients that need you."

Lluvia spoke first, her hand comfortably holding Delfine's as they sat opposite Arlo. "Two weeks should be enough time for me to end my rounds at the hospital. How about you, amor?"

Delfine considered for a moment, then smiled at her brother. "I have only a couple of patients in the final trimester, and I can pass them to a midwife I work with. We should be ready to go when you return."

Arlo dipped his head and smiled brightly at his sister. "I'll make the arrangements." After a moment, he stood and turned in Marena's direction. He sent her the same guarded and concerned expression he'd been giving her through dinner. "I imagine the three of you would like some privacy. Marena, would you still like to return tomorrow? If you want more time here I can—"

She didn't let him finish. "Yes. Tomorrow." Her tone was too sharp and her words too terse for the question. She willed herself to sound more normal, certain that Lluvia and Delfine were staring. "Now that I know these two pests will be back in two weeks, I need to enjoy the last bit of peace and quiet in London."

"Right." His tone was discomfited, unhappy. "I will instruct Cyrus to confirm your reservation for tomorrow morning." He turned to Delfine and Lluvia with a warm expression. "I'll have the carriage ready for you." After giving them each a kiss on the cheek, he left quietly without looking at her. Her heart constricted as he walked away.

As soon as the door closed behind him, both her sister and her best friend flanked her on the settee. Lluvia was the first to speak. "Marena Baine-Torres, I'm impressed. A *duke*." Her sister's voice was brimming with laughter, and Marena wanted more than anything for the ground to open up and swallow her.

"I've no idea what you're referring to," she said sternly, attempting to maintain eye contact with her sister.

"Marena dear, the man had his teeth on your neck and both hands on your bottom."

She was sure her entire face would go up in flames. Neither Delfine nor her sister were above bringing this entire sordid affair to her mother's attention, or worse, asking Arlo about it. "I will say one thing and then will never speak of it again."

The two bobbed their heads at the same time. "Now that the two of you are going to be associating with London's high society, you really will need to curb that penchant for gossip."

Delfine cackled, and Marena sighed in defeat, ready to confess. The truth was, she was desperate to talk to them about it. "I may have engaged in sexual congress with the duke."

A yelp from Lluvia was joined by a lascivious grin from Delfine. "This is a very favorable development."

Marena shook her head at the insinuation it would happen again. "There is no development." Something in her chest squeezed so she could barely breathe as she spoke. "I am not in a position to indulge in fantasies where I can be with Arlo. Women like me cannot afford dalliances with nobles. You both know that. I..." Her denials and protests died in her throat. It was no use to lie to them, it would be like lying to herself.

"You looked happy, Mare." The sympathy in Delfine's voice was almost unbearable. Marena pressed a hand to her breastbone, willing her heart to stop galloping.

"I don't think I've ever heard you giggle." Of course, her sister had to make her laugh even when she felt overcome with regret and frustration. She shook her head after a moment, still stubbornly rejecting that this thing with Arlo could be more than what had happened between them, yet knowing it already was so much more. "It's too complicated. He's your brother, Delfine. And what if people start talking?"

"You're not serious? You're talking to two women who are in a committed companionship that most of society has deemed either an abomination, a mental disturbance, or both. No one understands more about complicated love affairs than we do." Marena's face heated with shame. How could she suggest Lluvia and Delfine didn't comprehend her dilemma when they had faced so many obstacles and still were not able to freely let the world see their love?

"I'm sorry, hermana. That was so thoughtless of me."

"It's all right. It's not like you weren't there for most of it. Without you we would not have had a soul to turn to in those first years when we were afraid of telling anyone," Lluvia reminded her, some of the humor gone from her voice now. "You know what it was like for us."

"And I'd do it all over again," said Delfine, reaching for Lluvia's hand.

"Me too." Lluvia said, her voice so gentle it cracked Marena's heart. "Some things, some people, come into your life and force you to reimagine the dreams you had for yourself." Marena wasn't quite certain who Lluvia was speaking to, but the message was clear all the same.

"All right, all right, you two. I am aware your undying love is the stuff of myth and legend, but could we focus on my deeply injudicious entanglement." That broke the heaviness, and Delfine and Lluvia took each of Marena's hands in one of theirs.

"Is it an injudicious entanglement you'd like to see end?"

That was the question, wasn't it? The instant answer should have been a resounding yes. That would be the sensible response, the typical Marena approach, and yet yearning burned in her belly like a roaring fire. "He's asked me to continue seeing him in London." She shivered at the possibility of having him longer. "He said I could set the conditions." She shook her head. "I don't even know what that means."

"Then why don't you ask him? You deserve to be happy, Marena." Lluvia had always been the risk taker, but maybe she was right.

"I don't want to have my heart broken." She thought of the liberties so many in the ton already took with her when they frequented her shop, and felt wary of what would happen once people found out she was involved with Arlo. "I don't want men coming to my shop thinking they can have me too."

This time Lluvia put her arms around Marena and sighed. "I wish men didn't behave like utter prigs, but even after only knowing him for three hours, I have the feeling Arlo would not let that happen."

"They'd still talk."

"Hermana," Lluvia said, tightening her arms until Marena was close enough to kiss her on the cheek. "Mamí and Da did not raise us to let other people's opinions keep us from reaching for what should be ours. If he wants you, and you want him, why not see where it goes?"

"He wants me *now*, but once tongues start wagging, he'll reconsider, and I'll be blamed for the whole sordid ordeal."

Delfine inhaled sharply, her hand patting Marena's. "I'd give him a bit more credit than that. The man barely batted an eye about the fact that your sister and I are practically married, and"—she pointed a finger at her own chest—"may I remind you that he in no uncertain terms asked us to come to live in his big mansion in Mayfair with seemingly no caveats about our relationship."

This was true. He had taken it all in stride, like he did everything. The unflappable Duke of Linley.

Except, when it came to her, she had seen some cracks in that calm demeanor. For her, Arlo had lost his composure more than once. The man had carried a basket through the Marais, been stung by a bee, and today she'd seen the hurt in his eyes when she rejected his touch.

"The way he looks at you, Mare, that's not something to walk away from."

"But—"

"Was it unfulfilling?" Lluvia asked, as if only now realizing that could be the reason for Marena's discomfort. She once again felt grateful for the family she was born into. "Maybe you don't want hi—"

"No, that is not the issue. On the contrary, it was *too* fulfilling," she said in a mortified whisper.

That elicited a knowing laugh from the other two. "Then see where it leads. Let yourself have this. You know how to take care of yourself, and no matter what happens, we will be home to support you." Delfine's strong voice made Marena almost believe this could be true.

"And we have him to thank for that." That was Lluvia, always the truth teller.

"And don't forget, I'm his sister. I can give him a piece of my mind if he steps out of line." That made them all smile again.

"He does say he believes in the equality of the genders," Marena offered, already feeling like a massive boulder had been plucked off her shoulders.

"We will test that particular pronouncement until we have confirmed its veracity," Delfine stated imperiously, already moving to stand. "We should return home. We are both exhausted from too much excitement and not enough sleep."

Marena stood and looked at the two women who had always been by her side, each so familiar that they were practically extensions of herself. "I'm so glad you're both coming home."

"You and Arlo did this for us—together." Lluvia was never one to take the subtle approach. "Now see us off so you can mend things with the man."

Marena walked with them to the door of the study. "I don't know if I can continue a liaison with Arlo in London, but I will at least make things right with him tonight."

Lluvia and Delfine exchanged frustrated looks at that, but didn't press her on it again.

Within moments the two women were in a carriage and heading home, and Arlo and Marena were on their own once more. She stood on the front walk for a minute, then another, still unsure of what she would say to him. He'd been with her as they saw their sisters off, but when she came back inside, he was nowhere to be found. He'd left her there without saying a word, and he knew she would be leaving in the morning. She was being unfair and unreasonable, but she was incensed that he would not even say goodbye.

She walked back into the study only to find Cyrus placidly looking at her. "Would you be so kind to tell me where His Grace has gone?"

"He's in his bedroom, miss."

"Thank you," she said, turning on her toes and heading up the ridiculously large marble staircase, not caring that the valet knew she was headed to Arlo's private rooms. She stopped in her room for a moment to find and insert her cervical cap. She was angry, not foolish. Or at least not that kind of fool.

It took her exactly ten footsteps to reach his door, and before she had a chance to really think about what she was doing, she was pounding on it. She should have expected he'd answer it bare-chested...and scowling.

CHAPTER FOURTEEN

"MAY I HELP YOU, MARENA?" Arlo was not sure what outcome he was aiming for, but he could not stop himself from acting like an arse.

"Were you really going to let me go without saying goodbye?" she asked without preamble, a wounded expression on her face.

The truth was that he'd been hurt too. They'd come back from the gardens, and things had seemed to shift on their day out. He'd thought that, like he, Marena had seen something worth pursuing, but as soon as Delfine and Lluvia arrived, she'd acted like he was a total stranger, and though he understood why she'd been so startled, he'd hoped she could trust him more.

"I came to say goodnight." She was irritable and a bit disheveled and he wanted more than anything to take her into his arms and make love to her until the tension melted off her body. And he could either keep his pride from stealing the last chance he had to tell her how he felt, or he could let her go back to London and lose the best thing that would ever happen to him.

"I was coming to see you," he confessed.

"With no shirt?" she asked as she glared in the direction of his upper torso.

"I thought you enjoyed seeing me in a shirtless state," he said provokingly, unable to help himself.

She growled, eyes still locked on the area where his chest hair was most prominent. He ran a hand over it and was rewarded with an audible hitch of her breath.

"I know how much you enjoy my pectoral area. I wanted to offer you one last look as a parting gift." She looked positively indignant and again, every base instinct in him bubbled to the surface. He wanted to pick her up and kiss her senseless. Make her laugh until she dissolved into a pile of giggles, then lay her on his bed and make love to her all night. But she wasn't laughing. She looked miserable, and he wished with a disquieting ferocity that he could make every one of her worries disappear. But if he tried, she'd just push him away.

"I..." She paused and wrung her hands. "I'd like to talk to you." A glimmer of hope lit up inside him.

"In my room? Ms. Baine-Torres, is that appropriate? Given the nature of our corresponding positions in—"

"Oh, do shut up, Arlo," she exclaimed as she pushed past him into the room with surprising ease. She shut the door in a huff and stayed with her back pressed against it, her brown eyes roaming over him. "You are infuriating."

"Then we have that in common, love. I don't think anyone in my entire life has perplexed me as you do, and yet I keep coming back for more." He took a step toward her, eyes on the mouth he'd been deprived for what felt like days. "You drive me absolutely mad," he said as he planted both palms to the door, covering her with his body. He leaned down until his lips hovered above hers. "I can't get your taste out of my mouth."

She scoffed, turning her eyes to the ceiling as if pleading to a deity for patience. "I'm clearly having similar issues." She sounded so flustered, and yet she pressed herself to him. The linen of her dress rubbed against his skin.

"My ailment is more precarious than that, Marena," he explained, and brought a hand down, needing to touch her. "No matter what I do, all I want is to be here." He cupped her sex, his mouth watering with the need to taste her.

"Oh, for God's sake," she groused as she grabbed his hand, shoving it under her skirts. He took her lead quickly enough and made his way up her thigh until he found what he wanted.

"Tell me you want this as much as I do," he breathed out, his cock already twitching in his trousers.

She muttered testily, but her arms were already circled around his neck. "Possibly more. It's hopeless. I can't stop wanting you."

He kissed her hard, tongue tangling with hers as his fingers parted her furrows. He licked into her mouth in exactly the way he was planning to lap at her cunt. With two fingers he spread her and ran his thumb over the hot little nub that made her melt for him. She bucked against him, those enticing moans that drove him mad escaping her lips.

"Please," she begged as he pushed down the bodice of her dress to take a nipple into his mouth.

"What do you need, love? Tell me where you ache."

"You know where," she gasped as he worried the hard peak between his teeth.

"You want me to go down on my knees and love you with my tongue, sweetheart?"

"Why do I have to give you instructions?" She sounded absolutely infuriated, but he already knew how to bring out her more docile side. "Mmm yes...Like that." She gasped, as he touched her, his finger moving in tight circles against her clitoris.

"You're so wet for me already. I want to be inside you, but first I want to lick into you until you're screaming my name."

"Yes, that," she said frantically, already working to undo her corset so he could have better access to her breasts. "Kiss them," she demanded, pushing them toward his mouth.

"Mm." He moaned as he sucked on her, making sure he used his teeth, and felt a rush of wetness lubricate his fingers. "I know you enjoy my teeth on your tits, love. I'm going to play with them a bit more, but then," he said as he pressed two fingers inside her, "I'm going to take you right against this door."

"Please." She brought her hands to his head and nudged him down until his mouth was where they both needed him to be.

"You're always ready for me," he said, unable to hide the possessiveness in his voice.

"You are too full of yourself," she said as she gathered her skirts and widened her legs, baring herself to him.

"Oh, that's beautiful." The awe in his voice was not feigned. Her lips were a dark brown on the outside and pink inside. Gorgeous. "This has become my favorite place in the world," he whispered, blowing a bit of air on her sensitive skin. It elicited a long moan from his lover.

"More, Arlo." His heart skittered in his chest from the need in her voice. He wanted to give her everything. Sink into her and taste her skin until they were both sated and wrecked. Until neither of them could come up with a single reason not to keep doing this.

"I could make a meal out of you," he growled.

"Promises, promises," she groused between gritted teeth, and he was caught between almost spending in his trousers from the reediness in her voice or dissolving in laughter at her shameless demands.

"Mmm, I'll give you whatever you want." He flattened his fingers and slapped her clit while his tongue entered her, making her sob from pleasure. He did it again, and a rush of liquid soaked his tongue. Her legs started to tremble.

"I'm coming. Please Arlo, I want you inside."

He scrambled up as she hurriedly undid the placket of his trousers. "But the cap...," he said between kisses as she stroked his cock.

"It's in," she said gruffly. "I know enough to know I can't control myself around you. And don't be pompous about it."

"I would never," he promised even as he struggled to hide the satisfied grin on his face. But soon his attention was back on her. He lifted her and she immediately wrapped her legs around his waist. They gasped in unison as he filled her, rocking against each other. The pressure in his groin built as she met his thrusts in earnest. "God, you're perfect. I could die right here, right now, a happy man."

"Please don't die until I come again," she grunted as she brought her hand to her pussy and started rubbing her fingers in a tight circle.

This woman would be the end of him. He could not lose this. He had to tell her. "Touch yourself, sweetheart, tell me how I feel inside you," he said, as he drove hard into her, the door shaking from their efforts.

"You know you feel perfect and that you've now ruined me forever." Her voice was strained, but devastatingly honest as she brought herself to climax. And soon she was clamping down, making his own orgasm barrel into him. He thrust into her until he was utterly wrung out. Somehow, he was able to get them to the bed unscathed where he laid on his back with her sprawled on top of him like a debauched empress.

"You get a bit too much satisfaction from carrying me around," Marena protested.

"I like your body and I like touching you. I find that I want to keep doing it for as long as you'll allow me," he said, knowing he was risking her running off again.

"Arlo, I don't know," she said weakly, while she pressed kisses to his neck.

"I will let you set the terms. As much or as little as you want," he said as he worked on divesting her of her chemise.

"We both know that between the two of us, I will never be the one setting the terms. You have all the power in this."

"I'd have all the power if I were willing to use it to convince you," he clarified. "But I am not. This is solely up to you." He turned her face, which she had hidden in his chest, and brought her chin up to look at him. "You are the only one who can grant me access to your life, to your body. If you don't want me, I will walk away."

"I'm scared that it'll change everything." He could see how much she wanted to say yes, and he wished he could promise her nothing would come between them, but she was right. Things would not be easy. Even for a duke, challenging societal norms meant certain sacrifices. And yet he was certain he'd be willing to make them, for her.

"Everything's already changed, love. Don't you feel it?" he asked as she buried her face in his neck. "I want to be clear. I am not asking you to be my mistress. I will make you duchess, if that's what it takes to keep you with me."

"Arlo," she wailed, scrambling to sit up, but he kept her tight to him. "You can't say things like that."

"Why ever not? It's the truth." He punctuated each word with a kiss or a caress, and soon she was pressed to him again, sitting astride him, her round bottom against his cock, which was already hardening for her. Perfect. She was perfect. "If you tell me you don't want this too, I will not ask again."

"I can't say that," she admitted. She brought her mouth to his, and he opened, immediately lost in her kiss. Their tongues sparred while he ran rough hands over her delectable back and arse. "I love kissing you," she sighed, burrowing farther into him, her breasts rubbing against him, legs tangling with his. And in that moment, he knew what it was like to be whole.

"I've always been bold when I've needed to be. I've had to be, but this makes me feel afraid," she confessed.

He held her tighter, feeling fiercely protective. "I will slay dragons for you, and I don't mean metaphorical ones. If you and I begin this, I will make it my mission in life to let every man in London know that if they ever walk into your shop with anything other than money to spend and a gracious demeanor, there will be hell to pay."

"I'd be Mayfair's most popular novelty. A duchess mixing salves in an apothecary," she exclaimed with humor. "And besides, you can't scuffle with every aristocrat in London, Arlo."

"If it means I get to have you?" he asked, his voice serious. "Just watch me. And my duchess will be the talk of the town, because she's the most beautiful and brilliant woman in England." He could feel her breath catch at his words.

"Let's sleep," she whispered and peppering kisses to his warm skin. "Let's talk in the morning."

When he woke, she was gone from his bedroom. He sat up, scrambling to find his trousers. He rang the bell for Cyrus, who was in his room within seconds.

"Is she gone?" he asked, his heart beating fast. But he'd almost expected this. She was testing him, needing to be sure he'd meant what he said.

Before Cyrus opened his mouth, Arlo already knew the answer. "I'm afraid she is, Your Grace. She asked her chambermaid to help her slip out early this morning," Cyrus informed him. "She only took her smaller valise and asked we forward the rest."

"She did?" he asked as he paced the room. Then he understood. She'd left him a reason to go to her, if he chose to use it. The time for words was over, and now he had to show what he'd do to keep her. "Have the carriage ready in five minutes." Cyrus was already gone from the bedroom by the time Arlo slid on a fresh shirt.

He was going after her.

He had to prove to her this was not a whim or a matter of convenience. Everyone took Marena at her word that she didn't need grand gestures, that she was fine in her quiet, lonely life. But they didn't know the fire that burned in her. They hadn't watched her become a storm of lust and passion, one she had only given to him. He had to tell her that he would never expect she renounce who she was for him, that he wanted her exactly as she was. He had to reassure her that he didn't expect her to stop doing what she loved. That he would use all his resources to make sure she could continue to pursue her every passion, if that meant he could keep her by his side.

If she left for London before they agreed to what would happen next, he would lose his chance. The possibility of it filled him with dread. He knew, unequivocally that letting Marena slip from his fingers would be the biggest mistake of his life.

CHAPTER FIFTEEN

"Do you need anything, mademoiselle?"

Marena shook her head at the attendant who, for the second time in the last half hour, had popped his head into her private train car to ask if she required anything. She had the compartment to herself. There were three other empty seats and a small table where they would serve her food. There was a sleeping compartment too, with a big, comfortable bed which she would probably use later. At any other moment she would've been embarrassed over such extravagance. But this morning, when she felt utterly miserable and had gotten almost no sleep, she was grateful for Arlo's generosity.

She'd lain in his arms until right before dawn, her stomach in knots, misery rolling over her in waves. She wanted him too much, and that was so utterly mad. But what terrified her was the need for him. Even as she pressed herself to him, she felt the pain of his absence. She could see herself willing to compromise on her hard-won freedoms only to have more time with him. And then end up with nothing. Because there was no future for them, not unless he was willing let her continue her work. A duchess working as an herbalist…that could never happen.

So, she ran.

She'd arrived so early at the station that she'd been the first passenger on the train. But now, the departure time was near. She looked out the window, smothering the foolish hope that Arlo would come running across the platform, yelling for her to get off the train.

She imagined his long, powerful legs swallowing the distance, carrying his frame with ease as he leapt onto the train car and made his way down the aisles, calling for her. Scandalizing all the first-class passengers and not caring because he was determined to declare his love to her. But the platform was almost empty and the train only minutes from leaving the station. She closed her eyes, riddled with doubt, missing him already. She'd known from their first kiss that she would never forget what it was like to be in his arms.

There was a knock on her compartment door again, and this time she didn't have the composure to be cordial. "I don't need anything! Please just go."

Marena laid her head against the window, hoping she'd scared away whomever was on the other side of the door, but after a moment she heard the doorknob turn. She swiveled to give them a piece of her mind. "I said—"

The rest of the words died in her throat.

"Such tone, darling." His face was inscrutable, his full lips in a neutral line, eyebrows and forehead smooth, but those blue eyes were stormy, unsure.

The compartment, which only a minute ago had seemed vast and empty, filled with Arlo. His body—his presence—made the space feel small. And her heart...it was somewhere in her throat, trying its best to leap out of her.

"You're here," she said, standing so that she was only a couple of feet from him. It still felt like he was an ocean away.

"I am." He looked at her for a long time, his back against the narrow door. He was once again impeccably attired, this time in a looser fitting morning suit, the better for a long day on the train. She, on the other hand, was...disheveled. She'd barely paid attention to what she put on, and her hair was almost certainly a disaster. And yet everywhere his eyes landed, they seemed to gobble her up.

She ran a hand over the bodice of her dress, tipping her chin at the box he was holding. "What's that?"

"The sweets I promised you." He offered the parcel to her. She took it from him, giving him a confused look. "The other night at l'Anglais," he said. "I told you I'd get you the best sweets in Paris."

Now her entire face was on fire. "Oh."

"I also brought you some pastries because you missed breakfast." Her lips turned slightly at that, but she focused on gently placing the box of sweets on one of the seat before turning to face him again.

"Why are you always trying to feed me?" she asked, feigning an irritation she did not at all feel.

"Because I like watching you eat, and I like giving you what you need." He took a step toward her at the same time she reached for him. Soon they were embracing, his lips on hers. How could she believe she'd be fine letting this slip away? His hunger matched hers and they only stopped when the train started to move. He sat on the settee, bringing her with him so she was sprawled on his lap. "Were you really going to leave without saying goodbye?"

She closed her eyes, the misery from before coming back in earnest. "I didn't know what else to do, Arlo. I don't want to give up my work and I don't know if I could be in your world. I don't want to be scorned."

He kissed her again, and she succumbed to it, the misgivings of the morning melting away with every touch. "I would never expect you to give up doing what you love. I swear to you, I will see to that. As for us, I can't promise anything more than I want to try. And if you want to as well, I will make a way for us."

"How can you be so sure? It's only been a few days." She hoped he had a perfect answer that could let her believe she wasn't risking everything for something fleeting.

He ran a finger along her hairline, pushing back the riot of curls around her face. His eyes took her in greedily. "I'm sure in the same way you are. Some things are inevitable, and that's how you felt to me from the moment I saw you."

She could say so many things. More reasons why this could end terribly for them both. But she could not deny the truth of his words. He'd made her *feel* for what seemed like the first time in her life. She could turn her back on that, or she could trust it, and right now Arlo Kenworthy was too good to let go of.

"Kiss me," she demanded, and like he'd done over and over in the last week, he gave her exactly what she wanted.

Marena decided it was a very good place to start.

The End.

~

Enjoyed The Duke Makes Me Feel...?

Check out Adriana's latest, American Christmas!

ALSO BY ADRIANA HERRERA

ABOUT THE AUTHOR

Adriana was born and raised in the Caribbean, but for the last fifteen years has let her job (and her spouse) take her all over the world. She loves writing stories about people who look and sound like her people, getting unapologetic happy endings. Her *Dreamers* series has received starred reviews from Publisher's Weekly and Booklist and has been featured in The TODAY Show on NBC, Entertainment Weekly, OPRAH Magazine, NPR, Library Journal, The New York Times, and The Washington Post. She's a trauma therapist in New York City, working with survivors of domestic and sexual violence.

You can sign up for Adriana's newsletter here!

MY DIRTY DUKE

JOANNA SHUPE

CHAPTER ONE

LONDON, 1895

IT WAS the social event of the year and Violet was squandering it. She should have been dancing or chatting with friends. Instead, she was propped against the wall, hiding in plain sight, staring at him.

She could not stop staring at him.

The ballroom was filled with titled lords and ladies, but she was always able to find him. He was tall, nearly the tallest man in any room. Elegantly dressed. Starkly handsome, without frills to pretty up his visage. His features were strong, harsh like a Roman warrior, with dark hair, and eyes like twin pools of midnight. If she could photograph him right now, the caption would read, "Feared by most, revered by the rest."

Once upon a time he spoke to her with kind words, during her parents' dinner parties when she was deemed old enough to attend. That was before finishing school. Before her debut. Violet fell in love with him then, this intelligent and beautiful man who commanded every room.

At the time, she hadn't a clue as to why her stomach dipped and swirled in his presence. Now, at eighteen, she understood. She'd read books and seen racy photographs. Moreover, she'd overheard the maids talking about their beaus. So, Violet knew why her breathing quickened around him, knew the reason for the slickness between her thighs when she thought about being alone with him. Why she possessed this mad desire to have him smile at her again.

He never looked at her, though. Not once. Nor did he visit her father, his closest friend, at their home any longer. Since Violet's debut, he'd not asked her to dance, though most of her father's friends had indulged her at least once. He hadn't even spoken to her during her season. It was as if she were beneath his notice.

But then, most of London was beneath him. He was a duke.

And not merely any duke. His was one of the wealthiest and oldest of the titled families, the Duke of Ravensthorpe, Maximilian Thomas William Bradley III. She once looked his lineage up in Debrett's and learned that the very first Ravensthorpe received the title after thwarting an assassination attempt against Charles II.

"Why are you not dancing?" Her friend Charlotte appeared, her gaze studying Violet's face. "You are forever on the outskirts, observing. You should be having fun."

"I am taking a break."

"Who were you watching?" Charlotte's head swung about, searching. "Was it that newly widowed viscount everyone is talking about? He is scrumptious—and under thirty years of age."

"There is a newly widowed viscount?"

"Have you not heard? Honestly, Violet. What do you do with your time at these things?"

Stare at Ravensthorpe, obviously. "Why should I exert myself to learn all the latest gossip when I have you to do that for me?"

Charlotte laughed. "Fair enough. Tell me, at whom are you staring? Perhaps I can help you get his attention."

"Do not be silly. There is no one here for me. Just a bunch of old dukes and boring dandies."

"The dandies are quite nice to look at, however. Better than the stodgy dukes."

Not all dukes are stodgy, Violet wanted to say. Some were quite glorious.

"I wish I had my camera," she told her friend. "Then I could prove to you how not boring it is to watch."

Her father had gifted her with a camera two years ago and Violet had been taking photographs ever since. She'd converted a space in their attic into a developing room and had been studying photography at London Polytechnic for the last six months. She liked the challenge of photography, of achieving the perfect image. One of her dreams was to someday photograph Ravensthorpe, to capture the harsh angles and pretty features of his face. The cool stare and the haughty lift of his brow. Then she could have the image forever.

Such was the advantage of photographs. They were a way to record an instant, preserve a memory that might otherwise have been forgotten to the sands of time. Who knew what sorts of discoveries were ahead as cameras grew more advanced?

Violet continued to watch Ravensthorpe out of the corner of her eye so as not to alarm Charlotte. Her friend would try to dissuade Violet from her singular purpose this season, which was to somehow get Ravensthorpe to notice her. Again.

Suddenly, a woman walked behind Ravensthorpe and lightly touched his shoulder. The edge of the duke's mouth hitched and he leaned to whisper in the woman's ear. She was a countess, wife to the Earl of Underhill. Whatever the duke said must have satisfied her because she nodded once, and then slipped through the terrace doors.

An assignation?

Envy spiked in Violet's blood, violent and sharp, like she had poked herself with an embroidery needle. Charlotte kept talking, not taking notice of Violet's discomfort, and Violet was glad for it. She needed to gain control over her emotions.

Perhaps Ravensthorpe would not go. He would reconsider and decide—

Her stomach sank as he excused himself and followed the countess out the terrace doors. Definitely an assignation. She could hardly catch her breath; jealousy lodged in her lungs. She longed to beckon him to the gardens where she could touch and kiss him, explore that generous mouth and bask in his stern gaze . . .

Violet fanned herself vigorously as she burned with curiosity. What would Ravensthorpe and the countess do in the gardens, kiss? Fellatio? Sexual congress?

There was so much more she needed to know. For example, was Ravensthorpe a bold and demanding lover? Selfish? Or was he eager to please, as many of the erotic photographs she'd seen depicted? Perhaps if she learned more about what he liked, then she stood a better chance of getting him to notice her.

Charlotte must have perceived that Violet's attention had wandered. "Violet? One minute you are flushed and the next, pale as flour. What is wrong with you?"

She had to go. She had to see what was about to happen in the gardens. There wasn't a moment to lose.

Gripping Charlotte's arm, she kissed her friend's cheek. "I apologize. I'm not feeling well. I think I shall tell my father I'd like to go home."

Charlotte nodded, her expression brimming with affection and concern. "Excellent idea. Go on, then. Rest. I'll call on you tomorrow."

Violet bid Charlotte good night, then wove through the crowd, pretending to search for her father. In reality, her goal was to lose Charlotte and blend into the crush. With a final check to ensure no one was watching, she slipped through the French doors and onto the terrace.

The night smelled of lilacs and fresh dirt. Only a sliver of moon added to the soft torchlight along the edge of the garden path. Lifting her skirts, she moved carefully, desperate to not make any noise. She had been to this house before and knew the garden was designed as a large square, with a fountain at the far end. Tall hedges surrounded the path, high enough to offer cover to any couple. Her guess was that Ravensthorpe and the countess would meet near the fountain, farthest from the house.

She found a break in the bushes large enough to slip through and continued along the outside of the hedges bordering the lawn. Likely her slippers were ruined but she could not stop, not when she was close to discovering more about the duke. Sartorial sacrifices were necessary in the pursuit of all things Ravensthorpe.

Silent, she made her way along, allowing the hedge to be her guide in the dark. Near the final corner, she heard a lady's light laughter and a deep chuckle.

Ravensthorpe.

She crept closer, hardly daring to breathe. She needed to hear and see it all, so she bent and peered through the branches. After some maneuvering, she finally located the perfect vantage spot. Two figures were locked in an embrace, one of them clearly the duke.

Light from the house provided enough illumination to see that Ravensthorpe was kissing the countess, her body pressed tightly to his long frame. He clutched her waist with one hand while his other hand massaged her clothed breast. Violet's own nipples stiffened to peaks under her corset, the crisp air a delicious torture on her hot skin. The couple was ravenous, their mouths attacking one another between gasps of air.

In a flash, Ravensthorpe spun the countess so her back rested against his front, with both of them now facing Violet. He wrapped one set of his long fingers around the woman's throat as he shoved his other hand into her bodice. He lifted her breast out of her dress and undergarments, exposing it before caressing the plump flesh. His mouth slid along her cheek as the countess's lids fell shut, her lips parted with her rapid breathing.

"Look at you," he said, his voice like smooth silk. "A dirty girl with your gorgeous tit out. Ask me nicely and maybe I'll play with you."

"Please, Ravensthorpe," the countess whispered on a groan. "Oh, please."

Violet swallowed, her throat clogged with desire. Could they hear her heart pounding inside her chest? She would give anything to trade places with the older woman. Had the countess any idea of her good fortune?

"How pretty you are when you beg, Louisa."

Using the pads of his fingers, he stroked the taut bud at the tip of the countess's breast, pulling and pinching it. Louisa writhed, rubbing her body along his as he continued to work her, his other hand never leaving her throat.

Blood pooled between Violet's legs, her quim pulsing in time with her heartbeat. He was beautiful and compelling, an angel of sin and lust. Light reflected off the threads of silver at his temples, the effect like a match to her insides. She had never wanted anything or anyone more in all her eighteen years.

"If I lift your skirts, will I find you wet?" he asked.

Yes, Violet wanted to answer. *So very wet.*

The countess panted. "Oh, God. You . . ."

"Yes?"

"I cannot think. Please, do not stop."

"Do you need my cock, Louisa? Shall I place you over the end of that bench there and fuck you?"

Violet pressed her thighs together to ease her aching flesh. Sweet mother of mercy, he was potent. The angles of his face were harsh and unforgiving, his mouth almost cruel in its lasciviousness. Again she longed for her camera, wishing she could capture him in this stolen moment.

The countess shuddered at his words. "I cannot. As much as I crave you, I must return."

"What is another moment when I can make you come so hard?"

"Oh, you devil." She drew in a deep breath and covered his hand to stop his movements. "Unfortunately, I need to get back. I've been away too long. My husband will be wondering where I've gone."

"Hmm." Shifting her clothing, he tucked her breast away. Then he released her. "I suppose we will need to pick this up later, then."

The countess turned and bit his jaw, then drew her fingertip along the heavy ridge in his trousers. Ravensthorpe sucked in a breath, and she smiled. "Tonight, Ravensthorpe. Leave your side door unlatched. We'll play one of our naughty games."

Without waiting for his agreement, the countess hurried along the path toward the house. Ravensthorpe stood unmoving for a long moment, his chest rising and lowering in his evening clothes. A lock of dark hair had fallen over his forehead, a stripe of ink slashing his perfect skin. Violet could not look away, completely entranced.

He finally raised his head—only to pin her with a dark stare. "You may come out now, little mouse."

VIOLET FROZE.

Little mouse?

Was he talking to her? She had been so quiet, completely concealed by the hedges. Heavens, she was standing on the lawn. He couldn't possibly know she was there.

Cold terror filled her lungs as he walked directly toward her. She considered running, but where would she go? He'd see her for certain the instant she took off.

Bending, he came eye to eye with her from the other side of the hedge. "Come out of there, Violet. Now."

The tone was decidedly ducal, one used to being obeyed, and dread and embarrassment washed over her entire body. Violet prayed for the ground to open up and swallow her whole. She'd wanted him to notice her, but not like this. Never like this. She'd only wished to watch him with the countess like a voyeur hidden in the dark.

The hedges parted thanks to Ravensthorpe's arm, and there was soon enough room for her to slip through the branches. She tugged her skirts free, no doubt ripping the delicate silk. Clothing, however, was the least of her concerns.

Ravensthorpe's eyes were like frozen ice, a winter storm that chilled her to the bone. He put some distance between them, and his mouth was set in a flat, unhappy line when he whirled around. "What in hell do you think you are playing at?"

Her mind blanked in the face of his anger. "I went out for a walk."

"A lie. No lady walks on the lawn and risks her slippers." He pointed to her now-ruined footwear. "Again, what are you doing here?"

What happened if she admitted the truth? Would he finally see her as an adult, not some silly child he'd ignored for the past two years? She hated that he no longer talked to her. He acted as if she didn't exist, instead spending time with women who were married to other men, like the countess. What was so wrong with Violet?

"You are trying my patience, little mouse."

The truth fell from her lips. "I followed you."

"That is obvious," he said, the words like icicles, sharp and brittle. "What I cannot fathom is why."

"I was curious as to the type of woman who attracted you." She winced, but there was no taking it back now.

"Again, why?"

God above, was it not obvious? Was he actually going to make her speak it aloud?

You have nothing to lose. You have already embarrassed yourself.

"Because I wished to take her place, Your Grace."

Ravensthorpe dragged a hand down his face. Turning, he went to the iron bench near the fountain and sat, his long legs spread out before him. Violet wrapped her arms around herself, feeling like the world's biggest fool.

"Violet, you must return to the house and forget this ever happened. You must forget *me*. There are dozens of men in there tonight who would gladly share a tryst with you."

"But they are not you," she whispered.

He winced as if struck. "I am far too old for you."

Old? She paused, blinking at him. He was not old. He was male perfection wrapped in a cloak of confidence and swagger. She'd seen plenty of decrepit men and Ravensthorpe was far from that group. Besides, it was nothing for a lord his age to wed a debutante. Such matches happened every season. "You are forty-one. Hardly old."

"No, but I am too old *for you*. I am your father's friend. I've known you since you were born, for God's sake."

"You are two years younger than my father, if memory serves."

He gave a dry laugh. "Christ, Violet. Are you trying to say two years makes a difference?"

"I don't care how old you are." There. She'd said it.

"You should. It would be far better for you to find a man your own age. Or close to it."

She cared little for the men her age. Foppish fools who worried more about appearances than anything else. During dances, they merely stared at her bosom and stepped on her toes.

Besides, how could she ever be interested in anyone other than Ravensthorpe? He'd starred in her dreams for so long there wasn't room for anyone else in her head. "I don't want a man my age." *I want you.*

"You are eighteen. You have a lifetime ahead of you. Find someone to share that life with, someone who makes you happy."

He appeared less angry at the moment and more like the kind man she remembered, so she decided to present him with a reasonable argument. "Many girls my age marry older men. It's common amongst the ton."

"Are you . . . Is this about becoming a duchess?" He sounded horrified. "Even if we were closer in age, I am not interested in marriage, ever. I will never take another wife."

She hadn't known his feelings on marriage, but she didn't care about titles. She wanted the man, end of story. If that was outside of marriage, so be it. "I am not proposing marriage, Your Grace."

"Christ, do not use my honorific in that tone of voice."

Why? She'd called him "Your Grace" hundreds of times. "I apologize, duke." It was a more personal form of address, one he would reserve for intimate members of his circle. She hoped to one day join that inner circle, whispering in his ear whilst they were in bed.

"Fuck, that is worse." Standing, he put his hands on his hips, an imposing tower of disapproval. Something about his scowl made her want to bow and scrape for his admiration. She nearly licked her lips. He said, "You are the daughter of my closest friend. This is inappropriate and needs to end, Violet."

She would not back down, not without answers. "Is that why you stopped talking to me? Why you won't even look at me anymore?"

He glanced away, not meeting her eyes. "I have no idea what you are talking about. I do not interact with children."

"You did. With me. For years and years. And then you stopped like I'd contracted smallpox."

"That was before. When it was harmless."

"What does that mean? Have I hurt you in some manner?" She didn't understand. He was speaking in riddles. She had made her position clear, yet could he not do the same?

A muscle jumped in his jaw. "Before you developed breasts and hips. Not to mention an arse I'd like to sink my teeth into. Have you no looking glass? Your body is made for sin and your face would make angels weep." He dragged a hand through his hair. "You have every man panting after you the second you walk into a bloody room."

Violet's knees wobbled. The air left her lungs and she feared she might faint. This was what Ravensthorpe thought of her? Lord above. She was rounder than most girls her age, with their tiny waists and bosoms that barely peeked out from their gowns. Indeed, she was what her mother called "robust."

But Ravensthorpe liked the way she looked. He said she had every man panting when she walked into a room. Did that mean him as well?

Was this why he no longer talked to her?

Men were so confusing.

"I don't understand," she said. "If you like the way I look, then why ignore me?"

Something dangerous flashed in his gaze. "You must stay away from me, Violet."

"Why? I am not pressuring you for marriage. I merely want . . ."

Heavy, angry footsteps brought him directly in front of her. "To fuck me. Is that it, little mouse? Do you need me to put my cock inside you and make you scream?"

Lust rushed through her veins, heavy and thick, and her lips parted as she exhaled. Lord, she wanted that so badly. To experience all she'd seen in those erotic photographs with the man standing in front of her.

He read the answer on her face. "Have you ever been fucked, Violet? Had a man's fingers inside your tight pussy? Or maybe a thick cock?" When she said nothing, he barked, "Answer me."

"No." She hadn't considered even trying with anyone other than the man standing in front of her.

"Do you even know what it's like to make yourself come? Do you stroke your clitoris under the covers at night, or perhaps in the bath?"

Her mouth dried out, speech impossible. Triumph lit his eyes, as if he'd succeeded in exposing her as inexperienced and unsuitable. "Stay away from me. Do not follow me again. Forget you even know me."

Ravensthorpe stepped around her, his footsteps crunching on the gravel path as he stormed away. She sagged against the prickly hedge behind her, more aroused than she'd ever dreamed possible.

Do you stroke your clitoris?

Was that the place between her legs that she rubbed in order to climax? She might not have learned the proper names, but she had explored her own body. She wasn't nearly as innocent as he thought.

And someday, now that she knew their attraction was reciprocated, she would prove it to him.

CHAPTER TWO

I AM DESTINED FOR HELL.

Not that Max was a religious man, but the Devil himself was certain to come collect him for the dirty thoughts he harbored for Lady Violet Littleton.

He *burned* for her. So badly he could hardly stand to be in the same room with her. And she was wrong—he *always* noticed her. Since the moment she'd developed into a woman, Max hadn't been able to take his eyes off her. If they were anywhere in close proximity, his body remained in a permanent state of readiness, arousal simmering beneath the surface.

That was precisely how he'd known she was behind the hedge, watching him with Louisa. And then he, God forgive him, put on a prurient show meant to scare Violet away.

Yet he hadn't scared her.

Worse, she'd called him *Your Grace* in the high-pitched, breathy tone used by yielding lovers, those who adored nothing more than getting on their knees and taking whatever he was willing to give them.

Fuck.

He straightened his clothing and tried to compose himself. He was forty-one years old. Far too advanced to feel this twisted giddiness, this dark lust for a girl less than half his age. Hell, he had a son who was two years younger than Violet. Max was positively decrepit in comparison.

Not to mention that he'd fucked plenty of women since losing his virginity at the age of fifteen. Even more after his wife died while delivering their son. He had enjoyed a lifetime of debauchery and pleasure, hardly any of which he regretted. Moreover, he had no plans to give it up, not even for a fresh-faced virgin begging to ride his cock.

Jesus, her father would skin Max alive if he knew.

Max would need to adjust his social schedule for the remainder of the season to ensure Violet and he never attended the same event. It was for the best. She was far too tempting, especially now that she'd admitted her feelings for him.

Because I wished to take her place, Your Grace.

The statement had made him instantly, painfully hard, and it had been followed by a deep sense of shame. The girl was eighteen. A virgin. His friend's only daughter.

What the hell was wrong with him?

Max stepped inside the ballroom, not bothering to close the terrace doors. Charles Littleton, Lord Mayhew and Violet's father, grabbed Max's arm. "Ravensthorpe, have you seen my daughter?"

Charles was one of Max's close friends, a man he'd met shortly after arriving at school, long before he'd become Ravensthorpe. They had crossed cities and continents together, growing up in luxury, as many entitled aristocrats did. They knew each other's darkest secrets—well, all save one.

He forced his expression to remain blank. "No." Max held Charles's gaze like the competent liar he was, thanks to years in Parliament. "I was, ah, outside with Louisa." Not a lie.

Charles chuckled. "Of course you were, you bounder. Never one to pass up the opportunity for quality quim, are you?"

Uneasiness slid through Max. He reminded himself he'd done nothing untoward out there, at least not with Violet. "Cannot seem to help myself."

"I've an appointment myself tonight. Going to a little place on Holywell Street, one where they all wear masks. Perhaps you'd like to tag along?"

"I thought you said you were scaling back on your nocturnal activities after the missus discovered that you fathered a bastard."

"Well, what she doesn't know won't hurt anyone. So, what do you say?"

"Afraid I have plans, Mayhew. Have a pleasant time. If you'll excuse me."

Max had to get out of here. His skin was crawling with hunger for a girl he could not have. A woman, he supposed, but barely.

Violet was the type of gorgeous woman oblivious to her appeal, which in turn made her all the more appealing. An angel's face with a siren's body. Lush tits barely contained by any neckline, a round arse that beckoned with every stride. A woman built like a mistress, not a wife. In other words, utterly fuckable.

However, he was no green lad lacking in self-control. He could not pursue her. Even if the age difference did not bother him, there was the issue of his friendship with her father. While Max may have been a scoundrel, he was a loyal one. God knew he would not want his profligate friends anywhere near a daughter, if he had one.

No, Charles knew too much of Max's sordid history. Charles would reach for his pistol the instant after hearing word of his daughter in Max's bed. And Max wouldn't even bother to defend against such an egregious breach in friendship. He would deserve a bullet or two for defiling her.

Do you even know what it's like to make yourself come?

No idea why he'd asked such a crude question, other than to frighten her away, but it was clear by her reaction that she had touched herself. In the bath, perhaps? Or, had her seeking fingers drifted beneath the covers at night to stroke and circle her clitoris?

Blast. He had to stop or else he'd grow hard in the middle of this godforsaken ballroom.

Tonight, he would see Louisa and do all manner of wicked things to her. Moreover, he would forget about the blond beauty that haunted his dreams.

"Ravensthorpe."

Max stopped and found Louisa's husband, the Earl of Underhill, at his elbow. Hellfire and damnation. Was he conjuring these men through his illicit thoughts of the women in their lives? "Evening, Underhill."

Underhill wasn't a bad sort, actually. Louisa had been a penniless third cousin to a viscount before Underhill married her twelve years ago. More to the point, he was aware of Max's sexual relationship with his wife. Underhill might even have been relieved over it, seeing as how the Underhills had stopped screwing eons ago.

And, as much as Max loathed it, his mistresses enjoyed an elevated social status during their time together. It had nothing to do with him and everything to do with his title. Still, husbands had been known to leverage that status a time or two, including Underhill.

Sodding aristocracy.

"Need a favor, Ravensthorpe."

Indeed, here came the leverage. "Oh?"

The skin above Underhill's cravat flushed, and he cleared his throat. "I suppose it is unusual considering the circumstances, but I, uh . . ."

Out of the corner of Max's eye he saw Violet slip into the ballroom. Awareness skated over every inch of him, his flesh hot and itchy under his clothes. He had to leave. Piercing the man across from him with a harsh glare, he barked, "Spit it out, Underhill."

The other man leaned in. "I need you to stop seeing Louisa. Just for a time. I'd like to start trying again for a son and, well, you understand."

He couldn't risk raising a duke's bastard. "Have you spoken to her about this?"

"No, but it is her duty to provide me with an heir."

Max smothered a sigh. He was disappointed, but probably not for the reason Underhill assumed. He needed the diversion of a woman closer in age, one who did not make him randy at every turn. Losing Louisa meant he needed to find another woman, fast. "Of course. There were plans for tonight, so . . .?"

"I'll take care of that. Appreciate it, Ravensthorpe."

"I wish you luck. She is a remarkable woman."

They parted and Max wanted to punch the wall in frustration. All he could do was pray his hand would suffice for tonight.

VIOLET'S FATHER found her almost the instant she slipped back into the ballroom. Papa was protective of her, especially in settings such as this. Perhaps it was because he was a rogue himself and knew the dangers that lurked during these night events. In fact, Mama frowned every time he left the house after dinner, as if she knew the illicitness he would seek out in those evening hours.

Violet and her parents had never been close. She'd never understood her father's philandering. Mama would yell and carry on, demand he stop seeing other women, and he would settle down for a few months. But the cycle soon repeated itself, her father incapable of remaining faithful, apparently. He never cared about the harm he caused, or the burden on his wife in enduring it.

For her part, Mama seemed unhappy, angry with everyone. Withdrawn. She refused to attend large social gatherings, even during Violet's debut, so Papa escorted Violet about instead.

"There you are," her father said. "You had me scared half to death. Where were you?"

Violet caught Ravensthorpe's tall form across the room where he was speaking with Louisa's husband. The duke appeared uncomfortable, his shoulders stiff and straight, looking nothing like the man who spoke seductive filth in secluded gardens.

You have every man panting after you the second you walk into a room.

"Violet," Papa snapped. "I asked you a question."

"I required fresh air. I went out on the terrace for a moment."

"It is unsafe for you to be there alone. Did you . . . see anyone?"

"No," she lied. "Not a soul."

Her father visibly relaxed. Had he known Ravensthorpe was outside?

"Good. Shall we leave, then?"

Ravensthorpe headed to the door, most likely leaving the ball. With the duke gone, there was no reason to stay. "Of course. I've had my fill of heated ballrooms."

"You are looking flushed. Are you all right?"

"I am?" She patted her cheeks. Was Papa able to see the lust on her face?

Lord Patton suddenly appeared at Papa's elbow. Patton bowed to Violet, his gaze lingering on her bosom in a manner that had her longing for a shawl. She'd never liked the man. He stood too close when speaking with her and found excuses to brush against her whenever possible. It made her skin crawl.

"The lovely Lady Violet." Patton reached for her hand, taking it before she could blink, and brought it to his lips. "Good evening to you, miss."

"My lord," she offered with a curtsy.

"Do you mind if I steal your father away for a moment?" Patton asked. "Then perhaps you'll honor me with a dance?"

She said the first thing that came to mind. "We were just on our way out."

Her father nodded. "We were leaving, but I'll only be a moment, Violet. Meet me by the front entrance, won't you?"

She excused herself and sighed in relief over evading Patton. Perhaps a stop in the ladies' retiring room was in order. At least there she could splash water on her face in an attempt to cool herself after the encounter with Ravensthorpe. The man possessed an uncanny ability to send her up in flames at the snap of his fingers.

The retiring room was empty. She took a moment to relieve herself and clean her hands. When she cracked the door, she discovered Louisa and her husband, Lord Underhill, behind a plant in the corridor, embroiled in what appeared to be a heated exchange. Had Lady Underhill's husband discovered her affair with Ravensthorpe?

Violet slowly retreated into the retiring room while keeping the door cracked ever so slightly for sound. Terrible of her to eavesdrop, but how could she help herself? This conversation could provide her with additional insight into Ravensthorpe.

"You will do what I say, Louisa," Underhill said, his voice low and sharp. "You will not see him again—not until I have an heir."

Violet sucked in a breath, then covered her mouth with a hand. So, Underhill knew of the affair and was forcing Louisa to call it off.

"Absolutely not," Louisa hissed. "You have no right to ask me to do so."

"As your husband, I do, actually."

"We've tried for a child twice without success. I have no desire to try again. It's exhausting."

"Understandable, as it's no picnic on my end, but that does not change the fact that we must do it. I've looked the other way on your affairs for years. This is the least you can do. Otherwise I'll be forced to move you out to the country. Try meeting your paramour way up there."

"You wouldn't dare."

"I'll have your bags packed tomorrow if you don't agree."

Violet's eyes widened. Between her parents and this couple, marriage seemed like a nightmare for wives. No fidelity or trust. Just threats and tantrums each way one turned.

"But I may return to him once I give you an heir?"

"Of course." Underhill actually sounded accommodating, as if he were doing her a favor. "Not that Ravensthorpe will wait for you."

"We have a bond you could not understand," she said—and Violet's stomach sank. Were there legitimate feelings between Ravensthorpe and Louisa? The possibility made Violet nauseous.

Underhill chuckled, but not with humor. "No doubt his wife thought the same before he caused her death. Besides, the man has screwed his way through the ton for years. You don't believe you are special to him, do you?"

"Again, you would not understand. I have kept his interest longer than most."

"Even still, do not find yourself surprised when he moves on."

"We have plans tonight. When I see him, I'll inform him that—"

"No need," Underhill interrupted. "I took care of it earlier when I spoke to him."

Violet leaned closer to the door, surprised. Lord Underhill had canceled the assignation with Ravensthorpe. Was that why the duke had appeared so uncomfortable on his way out?

Louisa gasped. "You had no right!"

"I beg to differ. I plan on getting started immediately, Louisa. And no doubt Ravensthorpe is wallowing in a Covent Garden bordello by now."

Was that where Ravensthorpe had gone? Out to visit a bawdy house? Violet's throat tightened, choking on the possibility that she might never be alone with him again.

"He despises those types of establishments," Louisa said. "Which is why I know he'll wait for me."

A group of women came laughing and chatting around the corner, likely headed for the retiring room. To avoid being caught eavesdropping, Violet pushed open the door and walked into the corridor. Lady Underhill brushed by as if headed for the ballroom, while her husband had already turned away, drifting deeper into the house. Violet's mind spun with possibility as she nodded at the blur of young ladies as they passed, not really noticing them.

Would Ravensthorpe return to sit in his house, alone? Or would he find feminine companionship elsewhere?

If he were at home . . . would the side door be unlocked, even with his cancelled plans?

No, she couldn't.

Could she?

He would never allow Violet inside . . . but what if she didn't ask? What if she surprised him? He was attracted to her—he'd admitted it outside—and she might convince him to act on it, if they were alone together. Isolated, where no one would find them.

The moment felt fortuitous. Momentous. Everything she wanted—a chance with Ravensthorpe—was dangling right in front of her like a sweet treat. She merely had to be bold enough to take it.

Was she content to wait around and hope he noticed her again?

Your body is made for sin and your face would make angels weep.

One thing was perfectly clear: he would never come to her. He had ordered her to stay away from him, had pushed her to find a man her age. She would need to take matters into her own hands.

Did she dare?

CHAPTER THREE

MAX LOUNGED in the darkness of his study, legs angled toward the fire as he sipped the most expensive brandy his vast amounts of money could buy. He'd long lost track of the time, the chime of the clock forgettable since he arrived home. His plans for the evening were ruined, and he hadn't been able to do much of anything except sit and brood.

I could be fucking her right now.

He shouldn't think it, shouldn't even let the hint of it cross his mind. He should imagine screwing Louisa instead, with her bold caresses and wicked tongue—not a girl barely out of the schoolroom.

And yet.

The brandy lowered his defenses, and Violet crept into his mind like a vine that burrowed under his skin to hold and drag him down. He couldn't resist wondering and speculating, his mind storing a mental list of all the depraved things he'd do to her glorious body if but given the chance.

This had to stop. Lusting after her like this caused him to feel like a filthy old man. Many dukes in their twilight years married young girls, but Max had secretly sneered at those pathetic louts. Yes, they all needed heirs —Max had already scaled that particular mountain—but there were plenty of seasoned women who could bear children. One need not marry a girl barely more than a child herself.

His eyes drifted to the mound of paperwork on his desk. His nights with Louisa were necessary diversions, an escape from the responsibilities of his life. To pleasure and be pleasured in return, to let his mind focus on something other than numbers.

You're lonely.

He snarled at the fire, as if the voice had come from the flames. The idea was ludicrous. He was invited everywhere, had his pick of bed partners, and there was Will, his sixteen-year-old son and heir. Will was away at school, off to Eton as all young aristocratic males did at his age.

Will had been the center of Max's world for so long. Since the boy's birth, Max had kept his son close and made certain to spend time with him, to show Will how much his father loved him. Then perhaps Will would not hate him when he came to learn the circumstances of what happened to his mother. How Max had utterly failed as a husband.

He didn't want another wife or any more children. Ever. He had an heir and, thanks to Max's proficiency on the Exchange, Will would inherit more money than God when Max died, not to mention a dukedom. Ducal duty had been fulfilled. Max never needed to go through that again.

He did, however, need another mistress. This required an immediate search, though there were some options. Such as the viscountess who had propositioned him at the opera last month, or the Spanish princess he'd flirted with at the palace dinner weeks ago. As well, his former mistress, Georgina, had written recently in the hopes of reestablishing their association.

None of them caused his blood to race, unfortunately.

That's because you want her.

Christ, this had to stop. He downed the rest of the brandy in his snifter and debated pouring a fourth. He had a meeting with his estate manager in the morning and a hangover would only make the bloody business take longer.

The scrape of metal caught his attention. Someone was slowly opening his study door.

No servant would dare to enter without knocking. This could only be one person, and Max's mood picked up considerably.

Louisa. She'd found a way to sneak off from her husband after all. Fortunate that he'd unlocked the side door earlier, despite Underhill's warnings.

Relief flooded him. A distraction was exactly what he needed, and he should reward her a bit for coming. Louisa liked when he ignored her and she had to beg for his attentions. Max didn't mind. What man wouldn't want a beautiful woman begging him to fuck her?

Playing coy, he focused on the glass in his hands, twirling the empty crystal in the firelight. Slippers moved across the carpets, skirts rustling, and lust sparked in his belly as he contemplated what was to come. Louisa rarely wore drawers and kept the hair on her mound trimmed short. Was she already wet and eager for him?

The outline of a black cloak caught the corner of his eye. She'd come prepared like a thief in the night. Underhill wouldn't like this, but one last time as a way to say good-bye properly wouldn't hurt, would it? Max wasn't fully hard, but it wouldn't take much to excite him, not after his encounter with Violet.

Because I wished to take her place, Your Grace.

No, not now. He could not think of her *now.*

Louisa stopped just out of his reach, her face turned away from him, toward the fire. She trembled slightly, anticipating his touch, and he relished the reaction. It made him feel more powerful than any man on earth. "I see you escaped," he said, his voice a low rasp. "Are you here to play?"

The hood moved as she nodded.

"I like that you couldn't stay away from me. Needy little thing, aren't you?"

Another nod.

In deference to Underhill's request for an heir, Max said, "I cannot fuck you tonight, sadly, but I do plan to enjoy you in every other way possible."

She was quiet, but he could almost feel her vibrating with excitement. Normally, Louisa would break character about now with a giggle or urging him to hurry. She was showing incredible restraint . . . and he meant to honor that effort by giving her unimaginable pleasure.

"Bend over that chair," he said, pointing to the plush armchair opposite his. "Fold yourself over the arm."

For a second, she hesitated. Then she walked over and draped her front over the side of the chair, arse in the air, with her face hidden.

"Such a good girl," he praised, unfolding from his seat and rising. "Now, lift your skirts."

She struggled awkwardly with her skirts, almost as if she were shy. Or innocent.

Lust unwound in Max's groin, a slow warmth that traveled along the backs of his legs and through his bollocks. He didn't care to question as to why her performance aroused him—he was terrified of the answer—so he just accepted that it did.

"Higher," he barked when she paused. "Show me."

Damn, it was as if they'd switched and were now catering to his fantasies. His cock lengthened, pushing against his underclothes. Her calves and the backs of her knees were already bared to his gaze, and he saw the lace of her drawers peeking out to tantalize him.

His skin hummed with a familiar sensation, one he'd experienced at the ball, but he forced it away. This was no time to let those thoughts intrude. That particular young woman wasn't here and he needed to focus on the woman in front of him, to continue their games until they were both exhausted and dripping with sweat. "I see you are a tempting little minx tonight," he growled, dragging a finger along her spine.

She moaned softly and he couldn't wait a second more. Dropping to his knees behind her, he shoved her skirts out of his way. "Spread your legs," he ordered, and hurriedly stripped off his waistcoat. Gripping her inner thighs, he pushed her open further. He couldn't see much in the dim firelight, but the lips of her quim glistened with arousal, causing his mouth to water. Leaning in, he dragged his tongue through her folds.

The heavenly taste, a sweet and musky flavor, exploded on his tongue just as bells went off in his head, a clamoring that something was very wrong. The feel of her body was different. The smell of her skin was not the usual vanilla and lavender, but rather lemon. The hair on her mound was longer. The drawers . . .

Bloody hell.

Shoving himself away from her, he fell back on his arse, skittering on his limbs like a bloody crab, desperate to put distance between them.

No, no, no. She hadn't. *He* hadn't. This could not have happened.

"Turn around," he choked out, dread pressing on his chest. "Turn the fuck around, right now."

Legs shaking, she slowly straightened and let her skirts fall. Then she faced him . . . and Max's stomach dropped.

Violet.

"You." Blood rushed in his ears as he stared up at her, unable to believe it. "What in God's name have you done?"

Red bloomed on her cheekbones and she stared at his shoes. "Is it not obvious?"

"Not to me. Spit it out, Violet. Why have you come here tonight, sneaking into my house and making me believe you were someone else?"

"I never said I was her." Her head snapped up and she straightened, almost defiant. "And I thought you saw my face."

Fury raced through his veins like a lit fuse, sending flames to every part of his body. He nurtured it, grateful to replace the other unwelcome emotions from a moment ago. "A lie if I've ever heard one. As far as you knew, Louisa was coming tonight and you tried to take her place."

"I knew she wasn't coming. I overheard her husband telling her that she could no longer see you."

"So you draped yourself in a cloak, thinking I wouldn't know the difference between you and her. One cunt is just as good as another, is it?"

She flinched, but he would not apologize. Just having her taste on his tongue, picturing her bent over his armchair, had him balancing on a precarious edge. He wanted her too badly for politeness.

"You were able to tell the difference just from . . . that?"

God save him from innocent virgins. "We men are simple creatures, but yes. Even we are capable of recognizing the woman we are currently fucking from behind."

"*Were* fucking," she corrected with a knowing smirk. "Seeing as how her husband has now forbidden it."

The little she-devil was entirely too pleased with herself, and he liked this brazen side of her. A lot. Which meant he had to distance himself from this young woman at all costs. "Get out, Violet. Before we both do something we will regret."

"Did I . . ." She took a deep breath and let it out in a rush. "Did I not taste acceptable to you?"

The conscience he'd long forgotten chose that moment to rear its ugly head. He could have cut her down with a few simple words, destroyed her newfound confidence and probably sent her from the room in tears. But he couldn't do it. Nor would he lie, not about this. "You tasted like the sweetest ambrosia. I could spend a week doing nothing but licking you to orgasm and not tire of it."

Desire darkened her eyes and she swayed on her feet, a tiny gasp escaping her lips. Goddamn, she was magnificently responsive. So easily affected by him. More blood pumped to his groin, his cock hardening further beneath his clothing. He wanted nothing more than to dive beneath her skirts once again, hear her cries of delight ringing in his ears.

She is Charles's daughter.

Only eighteen.

He will never forgive you.

You cannot marry her.

With her taste in his mouth and the image of her naked quim in his brain, the usual reasons why he should stay away from her weren't working. He resorted to pleading with her. "Please, Violet. You should—"

"Did I cause that?" She pointed to the obvious erection between his legs.

"Yes," he answered without thinking. "But you should not know of such things, little mouse."

"May I see it?"

Every muscle froze and all the moisture fled his mouth. *Oh, Christ.* What was she trying to do to him? He'd end up in an asylum before the end of the night at this rate. Why was she not fleeing his house in terror?

Because she's far stronger than you've imagined, you dolt.

He swallowed. "If you cannot even say the word, then you are not ready to see it." His voice came out husky and teasing, not the biting tone he'd imagined in his head.

Violet must have sensed his weakness, because she took one step closer. "May I see your cock, Your Grace?"

His lips parted, his breath sawing out of his chest, short and swift. The question and the honorific uttered in her pliant, pleasing voice were his undoing. He'd tried so hard, but he wanted her too badly. Craving sizzled in his veins, like an addict denied his pipe, and Max could deny it no longer, whatever the consequences.

He let his lips curve into a sly smile full of wickedness. "You may, but you must take it out first."

CHAPTER FOUR

VIOLET HAD NEVER BEEN SO scared in her whole life. But there was something underneath the trepidation, an emotion that emboldened her and turned her into a wanton creature worthy of Ravensthorpe. Perhaps it was longing or passion, or the ravenous desire he inspired in her. Whatever it was, he seemed to appreciate it.

Even while angry with her, Ravensthorpe made her feel safe. Protected. Like she could say or do anything and he'd not judge her harshly for it. Which was probably why, despite her inexperience, she wasn't afraid of whatever was happening between them.

He remained sprawled on the study floor, his long limbs akimbo as he studied her, the erection in his trousers enticing her to come and play. Firelight danced off the sharp angles of his face, the glow reflecting off the silver strands at his temples. He was irresistible and shameless, and the darkness only enhanced his appeal.

Ravensthorpe said nothing, his chest rising and falling with the force of his breaths. Though he was on the ground, he was clearly still in control of the room, like a jungle cat taking a momentary break to tease its prey, daring her to approach him.

Did he believe she wouldn't follow through?

Flicking open the clasp on her cloak, she shrugged off the heavy cloth and let it fall. Then she lifted her skirts and dropped to her knees, the carpet soft beneath her stockings. Without a word, he widened his legs, making room for her between them, so she shuffled forward, her heart pounding behind her corset.

When she reached his thighs, he growled, "Unfasten my trousers."

With trembling fingers, she reached to do as asked. Her nail traced the edge of the wide black button before slipping it through the hole. There were more buttons underneath, so she carefully undid each one around his bulging erection. Her fingers brushed his belly, the brief contact making him jump. She pressed her lips together to keep from grinning. *I affect this gorgeous man with a simple touch.*

"Now the braces."

He made no move to assist her, only held perfectly still as she slipped one brace over his shoulder, then the other. When she finished, she sat back on her knees and waited for him to continue with instructions.

"My shirt."

His collar and necktie had already been removed, so she leaned in once more and set to work on the small buttons on his chest. His lean muscles rippled beneath her fingers, the carefully leashed power betrayed by his rapid breathing.

When enough buttons were loosened, she dragged the expanse of fabric over his head, Ravensthorpe lifting his arms to help. The thin garment he wore underneath was of the finest cloth, and it outlined the thick muscle and sinew, the flat planes and elegant grace. Another wave of heat rolled through her, centering between her legs.

More.

She was greedy when it came to this man. Dark need buzzed beneath her skin, a yearning to see every bit of him.

When she stared too long, he said, "The undergarment, Violet."

Instead of unbuttoning the garment at his chest, she reached for his groin. After all, they both knew what she was after, considering she'd asked to see it.

Behind the opening in his trousers, she found small buttons and began working them open. He didn't speak but she could feel him watching, his intense gaze like a caress over her breasts, along her center. Would he lick her again? Because that one swipe of his tongue between her legs had felt like heaven.

Bare skin appeared as she continued, her first peek at the man underneath the polished exterior. She could hardly breathe for all the excitement coursing through her.

"That's it," he said, his voice a silky whisper, and her body shivered under his encouragement.

More.

She purposely paused, just so he would start talking again.

"Keep going. Just one or two more, my little mouse."

Oh. She pressed her thighs together, nearly groaning under the weight of her longing. She would do anything if he kept speaking to her like that and calling her his. Her hands moved faster now, following his direction as if she'd been born to do it.

Reclining onto his elbows, he lifted his hips slightly as she tugged his trousers low on his hips. Fabric shifted on his stomach, and his erection emerged from between the open sides of his undergarment. His penis sprouted proud and thick from a patch of dark, coarse hair, and she stared at it, fascinated by its reddish cap and smooth, tight skin.

Their breathing and the pop of the fire were the only sounds in the room. Was he assuming she'd run screaming from the house? Hardly. The sight of him made her mouth water. If only she had her photography equipment. . .

She licked her lips, uncertain but definitely eager. "What do I do?"

His dark eyes glittered from underneath his long lashes. "You worship it."

Yes, yes, yes. Indeed, that she could do.

He watched carefully, every bit of his attention on her, and she vowed not to disappoint him. She dipped to press a kiss to the head of his shaft, not looking away from his eyes. His lips parted and she heard him give a swift intake of breath. Emboldened, she touched her tongue to the same spot, and he hissed a very creative curse.

He reached down, gripped the base with his elegant fingers, and angled his cock toward her mouth. "Suck."

She wrapped her lips around the plump head and drew him in. His entire body tensed. "More. Take me deep."

Pressing down, she slid him as far back as she could manage. He tasted clean and musky, so firm and silky on her tongue. It was much better than she'd ever imagined. She repeated the journey, noticing how his cock jerked when her tongue glided over the skin underneath the head. The next pass was slower, with more attention paid to that sensitive spot. His muscles clenched, and the reaction felt like a victory.

She worked hard then, moving faster to show him without words how much she wanted to please him. He grunted and rocked his hips, lost in the moment, until he suddenly lifted her up and away from his erection. In a blink, she found herself on her back, Ravensthorpe leaning over her, pressing her into the floor an instant before he sealed his mouth to hers in a punishing kiss.

This was no sweet melding of lips as described by poets and school-girls. No, he devoured her, his mouth immediately opening to give her his tongue. She took it eagerly, widening to allow him in, reveling in the slick heat as his tongue twined with hers. This kiss was a battle, a test. He was showing her all the passion, all the lust inside him, and she had to prove that she could accept it. Prove that she wanted it.

Violet never could resist a challenge.

She kissed him back just as eagerly, with just as much fervor, their lips and teeth crashing into one another as their mouths worked. It was messy, almost angry, and she loved every minute of it. Ravensthorpe kissed as if he could bend the world to his will through this alone, and she wasn't entirely sure he couldn't.

Tearing his mouth away, he slid his lips down the column of her throat. "I might not ever recover from the sight of my cock between your lips, sweet girl."

Her back arched as he bit her skin, his teeth digging deep to mark her, and wetness pooled between her legs. She dug her nails into his back.

Without warning, he sat up. For a moment she worried they were done, but he let his gaze travel the length of her. "I want you naked," he growled. "Here in my study."

"Yes," she breathed, ready to give him almost anything if he'd just continue kissing her.

Relief flashed over his expression, as if he'd feared she would deny him. He made a motion with his hand. "Roll over."

∾

MAX HELPED Violet turn onto her stomach. He wouldn't take things far tonight, but whatever happened, he would damn well ensure that Violet enjoyed it. Nothing else mattered at the moment.

Quickly, he unfastened her bodice and unlaced her corset. Untied her bustle and skirts. He was no stranger to women's clothing, well familiar with the tapes and hooks, and the process took hardly any time at all. Violet remained on her stomach, lifting when he ordered, allowing him to disrobe her.

With the outer layers removed, she was down to a chemise, drawers, and stockings, all white with pink satin ribbons. Perfect skin glowed underneath, the shape of her tempting him, an outline of the curves he'd imagined for months. The tip of his cock leaked, his bollocks aching with the desire to pump inside her. To defile and pleasure her. To *ruin* her.

You cannot fuck her. You cannot marry her.

But he could do everything else.

"On your back."

She turned over, giving him the perfect view of her ample tits. Full and ripe, the creamy mounds spilled out over her chemise, the berry-tipped nipples jutting against the thin fabric. Her chest heaved with her excitement, thrusting her breasts higher, and Max's mouth went dry.

He clenched his fists and contemplated rending the flimsy fabric in half. "Take off your chemise."

She did as he asked, wriggling her hips and shoulders, revealing her bare torso to his greedy gaze. Fuck, she was perfect, with curves exactly where he liked them. His hands shook as he reached for her, his sanity slipping. "If I do something you don't like, tell me and I'll stop. All right?"

She nodded, but that wasn't enough. "The words, Violet. Tell me you understand."

"I understand, Your Grace."

She peeked at him through her lashes, shy but emphasizing his honorific, and he couldn't bring himself to care. He fell on her like a man possessed, kissing her hard and deep, needing her like he'd never needed anyone before in his life.

Before the weight of that thought could bring him down, he moved to take the tip of her breast into his mouth, drawing deep. His hand cupped the supple flesh as he licked and sucked, loving the little whimpers she gave before he moved to the other breast to give it the same attention.

Her nipples were thick, each surrounded by a large areola, and he adored the way they felt on his tongue. When she was writhing under him, moaning loudly, he pulled back to admire her. The suction from his mouth had caused her nipples to puff even more.

Jesus, everything about this girl was so damn arousing.

"You are absolutely gorgeous," he muttered as his hands went to her drawers. "But you still have on far too much clothing."

In a flash, he divested her of her drawers and stockings, marveling that she hadn't yet shied from his touch or tried to cover herself. She seemed to want him every bit as much as he wanted her. Surely that wouldn't last. It couldn't.

It never did. His former duchess had proven that, hadn't she?

So he would enjoy this with Violet while he could.

When she was naked, he sat on his haunches, marveling at the picture before him. Lush breasts, smooth skin, generous hips that would cushion his own perfectly . . . and her mons with its delicate triangle of hair. No man had explored there, and while Max knew he didn't deserve to be the first, he was bastard enough not to refuse it.

"Spread your legs. Show me."

Those pale thighs parted, revealing her pussy, and he couldn't breathe. *Goddamn beautiful.* Arousal glistened on the petals, with more gathered around the entrance. He traced the soft flesh with a fingertip, relishing the slick her body produced for him. "Is all this for me?" She watched him with wide eyes as he brought the finger to his mouth and sucked the sweetness onto his tongue. "Oh, my darling girl. I fear I'll never get enough of your taste."

Dropping onto his stomach, he let his breath tease her until she started to squirm. Then he began licking her, gently at first, getting her used to the feel of a tongue between her legs. The taste was exquisite, tart and musky, and he felt like a fifteenth-century explorer on a voyage of discovery and delight into unchartered lands while she gasped and mewled beneath him. His cock leaked onto the carpet, the skin pulled so tight it hurt, and yet he somehow resisted the urge to hump the floor.

When his attentions focused directly on her clitoris, her entire body twitched. "*Your Grace!*"

He swirled his tongue over that swollen bud, loving it with his teeth and mouth, sucking and laving until she trembled. One of her hands found its way onto the back of his head, where she held him in place, fingers clutching his hair, and nothing made him prouder than his little mouse demanding her pleasure.

She was close, her body stretched like a bowstring, her chest pumping in a desperate plea for air. Max needed to feel her inexperienced walls clamp down, if not on his shaft, then on his finger. He carefully slid the tip of his smallest finger inside her cunt, and her slick walls sucked him inside as if starved. God, how he wished . . .

No. He could not even contemplate it.

Then it happened. Her thighs shook around his head, her cries ringing in his ears as she found her peak. The release went on and on, her body completely his in that moment, and the satisfaction he experienced as she climaxed on his tongue was incomparable.

When she relaxed, he removed his finger and continued to lick her, softer, relishing the additional wetness that now pooled at her entrance. So responsive, so delicious . . . he longed to do this until sunrise. But his bollocks were tight, almost painful, with the need for his own release. He feared he would spend on the carpets if he waited another moment.

Rising onto his knees, he took his cock in hand and stroked, admiring her luscious form the entire time. Christ, she was beautiful. "Play with your breasts," he ordered, little electric shocks of lust shooting through his groin. "Pinch your nipples."

Her hands crept to her tits, cupping them as if offering them up to him. Then she squeezed the tips, her mouth rounding in surprise, as if she'd never touched them so intimately before. Her innocence—not to mention her willingness to do as he said without question—drove him positively wild. "More," he grunted, his hand moving faster along his shaft.

She watched his hand, seeming fascinated, as she rolled and tweaked her nipples, her tongue swiping across her lower lip. Was she thinking of sucking on him again? Swallowing his spend down her throat? God, the idea of it . . .

"Fuck," he gasped, sensation overtaking him, heat sizzling along nerve endings, and spend erupted from the top of his cock to land on her stomach. He clutched her thigh to steady himself, his tight fist milking all the pleasure from his body while his limbs jerked and twitched. "So good, so damn *good*," he gritted through clenched teeth. He couldn't remember the last time he came this intensely, as if his entire body were being wrung inside out in pleasure.

Each blissful pulse washed over him, renewing and reenergizing, breathing new life into his old and tired brain. He never wanted this feeling to end.

Yet it soon did. His faculties returned slowly, and with them came the dawning horror as to how low he'd sunk.

I've debauched her. Touched her when I hadn't the right.

Taken another innocent girl and horrified her with my base ways, just like Rebecca.

He hung his head, unable to look at her. What had he done?

CHAPTER FIVE

"This was a mistake."

Ravensthorpe's words, combined with the remorse stamped on his features, had Violet's stomach churning. This had been the best night of her life. She could not allow him to destroy what had happened between them with recriminations.

Yes, she'd come here in the hopes of seducing him, but she hadn't meant to trick him. Not really, anyway. While she may have tried to keep quiet at first, she hadn't known the room would be so dark, that he wouldn't see her face until . . . well, until it was too late. He'd made it clear at the ball he desired her. She'd planned to come tonight and give him a small nudge, to talk to him in private and convince him to give them a chance.

Of course, she hadn't realized Ravensthorpe would begin orchestrating a seductive play the moment she walked through the door. Not that she was complaining. The man merely had to open his mouth and she was at the ready, waiting like a good little soldier to follow his instructions.

And he believed this was a mistake?

Coming up on her elbows, she said, "I don't regret any of it. I'd do it again, in fact."

The duke dragged a hand down his face. "Violet, you cannot possibly—"

"Stop. Do not dare tell me I cannot understand. I have much more to lose than you by being here, and I am well aware of the possible repercussions."

"I won't marry you."

She flinched. The reminder was meant to put distance between them, and it worked. Pushing aside the sudden ache surrounding her heart, she reached for her stockings and pulled them on. "I haven't asked for marriage, Your Grace."

He mumbled something under his breath.

"I beg your pardon?"

"I said to call me Max."

He was giving her leave to use his given name? That had to mean something, didn't it? "I haven't asked for marriage, Max."

Head down, he began putting his clothing back to rights. She ignored his unhappy expression and studied him instead, from his wide shoulders and strong arms, to the perfectly sculpted flat chest. Even partially dressed, he made her heart flutter.

If she ever saw him completely naked, she'd likely faint from lust.

She was tying her drawers when he moved to still her hand. His gaze was soft, but filled with resolution. "Let me help you."

Her body melted at his sudden tenderness, and she leaned back to let him proceed. When he'd finished tying the ribbons, he ran the silk through his fingertips. "Pink and delicate. I think you wore these to drive me mad."

Before she could ask what he meant, he righted her chemise and dropped it over her head. He smoothed the fabric down, taking extra care at her breasts. "A shame to cover these beauties." One finger traced her right nipple slowly, almost reverently, and the flesh quickly puckered under the attention.

"My God," he murmured. "I do love the way your body responds to me."

Because you are the only man I've ever wanted.

She didn't dare say it, however. Not while he considered tonight a mistake.

She knew otherwise. This evening had proven how much he desired her, how explosive they were together. Nothing about coming here had been a mistake.

They hardly spoke as he assisted her with the corset and bustle, the petticoats and dress. The emotional distance grew as more and more layers of clothing separated their bodies. After he handed her the black cloak, he gestured to the door. "I'll see you out."

The sentence held a note of finality, that this was the last time, and the possibility terrified her.

She dug in her heels. "When will I see you again?"

He sighed and shoved his hands in his trouser pockets. "You won't."

Pain ripped through her chest and settled behind her ribs. "Max—"

"Do not argue with me, Violet. We've satisfied our curiosity and that was that. This is not an affair."

"I am far from having my curiosity satisfied—and it could be an affair, if you'd but allow it."

"You ask the impossible," he said, his voice low and angry. "And one day you'll thank me for preventing it."

"Because you believe you're too old for me."

"I *know* I am too old for you. And your father would never—"

"My father hardly has a moral ground upon which to stand. You of all people probably know that better than most."

Max shifted and did not bother to deny it. She'd hit her mark, then. Indeed, Max was privy to her father's sins. "Nonetheless, he is your father and my friend. An affair between his daughter and me is impossible."

She hated how rational and calm he sounded, as if his mind were made up. What happened to the wild lover of moments ago, the one spewing filth from his mouth and clutching her as if he never wanted to let go? "Are you saying you've never slept with a woman more than twenty years your junior?"

His expression darkened at the reminder of their age difference. Stalking away, he grabbed the decanter on the side table and refilled an empty glass. After taking a large swallow of what had to be brandy, he said, "I haven't, actually. I make a habit of choosing experienced women who needn't be shown how to pleasure a man."

The wounded lion lashes out.

Violet was not fooled. This man had nearly fallen at her feet moments ago, dazed by her kisses and drunk on her taste. His body's reaction to her couldn't have been faked, so she knew her innocence hadn't bothered him.

In fact, she would guess the opposite based on his rabid ardor—that he'd enjoyed instructing her.

Confidence surged through her like a great gust of air and filled her with newfound knowledge and purpose. She lifted her chin. "Perhaps I'll find a young buck to teach me, then. I'll return after some tutelage and you might reconsider."

His gaze, possessive and dark, narrowed on her. "Do not even contemplate it, Violet."

"Or?"

"Or I'll put a stop to it. And beat whomever you've convinced to help you within an inch of his miserable bloody life."

She bit her lip to hide her smile. Oh, yes. This was far from over between them.

"Stop looking so pleased with yourself," he snarled. "I will only destroy you and never marry you. Consequently, you should run from this house and never look back."

"And yet I cannot."

"I do not want you to return. Is that clear enough for you?"

The words were like spikes through her heart, tearing the tender flesh straight through, but she would remain strong. He was stubborn . . . yet so was she. "I think you're lying."

His lips flattened into a thin, angry line. "I've pummeled men for lesser insults than the one you just handed me."

"You won't hurt me. I've known you nearly all of my life."

"You know nothing about me."

Yes, I do. I see you. I've always seen you.

She had observed him carefully during her parents' dinner parties. Well read and intelligent, Max could speak to almost any topic, no matter how obscure. He was also kind and thoughtful. He made certain to escort elderly Aunt Harriet, who had difficulty walking unassisted, and he doted on his son, refusing to ship the heir off to boarding school when William was a young boy.

Now she'd discovered more about the allegedly wicked Duke of Ravensthorpe. His sweetness. His giving heart. His jealousy when she mentioned other men.

He believed he would destroy her, but that was impossible. Tonight she had discovered herself . . . and Max had helped her do it.

"We shall see," she said, cryptically.

"Goddamn it. You must listen to what I am saying."

Yes, she was listening, and one thing was perfectly clear—she could no longer chase him. She had to give Max space and let him come to her instead. Whatever was between them only worked if they were both amenable, both willing to take risks for the other. As it was, she had risked enough for him.

What if he moves on without you?

It was a gamble, certainly. No telling how many women were angling to get in his bed. And yet, everything inside her screamed this was the right choice.

"I'll see myself out," she said and turned to the door.

"You are not leaving until you agree never to return."

She paused and tried to remember this was for the best. Either way, win or lose, she couldn't pursue Max like a hound after a fox forever. "I won't return until you invite me."

Glancing over her shoulder, she gave him a heated look from under her lashes. "Because you will come looking for me, *Your Grace*. And when you do, I'll be waiting."

FOURTEEN DAYS.

It had been fourteen days since the night in his study, the moment when Violet had turned his world upside down, and now Max worried he was losing his mind.

He couldn't stop thinking about her, couldn't stop remembering their night together, and somehow the girl had burrowed under his skin with her shy smiles and bawdy demands. So eager, so brave. Looking up at him as if he were a good man, one capable of solving any problem on earth.

This is a mistake.

Yes, entirely. He could readily admit it, yet he could not stop himself.

For a week he'd held out, staying busy with his accounts and clubs. By day nine he'd begun drinking heavily, fisting his cock as he relived the memories of her kiss and the feel of her skin.

Day eleven had found him at one of the city's high-end brothels, one he hadn't visited in ages. He'd turned around and left before even removing his coat. How could he fuck another woman with the taste of Violet still fresh in his brain?

By the end of day twelve, he was stalking his London home like a starved dog, snarling at anyone who dared bother him. He locked himself in, convinced that Violet was a fever in his blood, one he merely needed to ride out. Then she would be out of his system forever and he could get on with his life.

It hadn't worked.

Now he was broken, unable to concentrate. An utter mess of a human being. A man on the verge of hysteria.

Just once more, he'd promised himself earlier today. If he could touch and kiss her just once more, that would be enough to get her out of his head. Then he could set her free, where she could marry anyone she pleased.

He was doing her a favor, really. Most young women—his deceased wife included—came to the marriage bed completely ignorant and unprepared. Max would leave Violet a virgin but at least teach her about sex and her own pleasure.

God, you're pathetic. You're attempting to justify bedding an eighteen-year-old woman.

Yes, but he was too far gone. He'd beg if necessary. Everything about her had been too perfect, too right. It had been the most erotic night of his life, one he couldn't help but relive every time he closed his eyes.

She was confident for her age, self-assured in ways that had surprised him. When was the last time he'd been surprised? Perhaps his liaisons had becoming boring of late, more rote than exciting, but Violet had energized his existence. She made him feel ten years younger and more randy than a university lad in a bordello.

"Ravensthorpe."

Max froze at the sound of the familiar voice, making sure to wipe his expression clean. He'd avoided Violet's father since the night in his study, uncertain how he could face his friend after what had occurred. The only good part about seeing Mayhew meant that Violet was likely in the room, as well.

He cleared his throat and spun around. "Mayhew."

Charles slapped Max's shoulder. "Haven't seen you in ages. Where have you been keeping yourself?"

At home, dreaming of fucking your daughter.

Instead, he said, "Here and there."

"Heard Louisa gave you the shove-off, my friend. A shame, indeed. Have you already found someone new?"

Max suppressed a wince and adopted an easy smile. "Not as of yet, no."

Charles leaned in closer and lowered his voice. "In that case, I'll happily show you a new place I've discovered. It's in Cheapside and the women are willing to do anything for the right price. And I do mean *anything.*"

After spending so many nights in Charles's company, Max had a good idea of what "anything" might include. "I believe I'm set for the moment, but I'll let you know. Are you here with your wife and daughter?"

"Just Violet. The missus is peeved with me again. Said I came home smelling like perfume too many nights this week."

My father hardly has a moral ground upon which to stand. You of all people probably know that better than most.

How much did Violet know about what went on between her parents?

Max frowned at his friend. "I hope you shelter your daughter from hearing such things. It could leave a damaging impression with her."

"Come now, she's a grown woman. I've got two suitors sniffing around her skirts, so best she learn how marriage works between a husband and a wife." Charles's brows lowered, his expression etched with disbelief. "Besides, you cannot tell me Will isn't aware of your mistresses."

Suitors? A dark cloud rolled through Max, his mood blackening at the thought of some repulsive masher pawing at that lovely girl. Scowling, he said, "Will is a man, not an impressionable young woman. And just who are these two suitors?"

"The young lords Wingfield and Sundridge. I had hoped Surrey would take an interest, but he seems enamored with the Gabriel chit's dowry."

"Wingfield undoubtedly has the pox and a bowl of porridge contains more intelligence than Sundridge. You cannot in good conscience encourage either of those fools."

"How on earth did you come by that information?"

His son, actually, who loved to gossip more than a maiden aunt, but Max didn't say as much. "Just know that I am right. She can do better, Charles."

Mayhew hooked his thumbs in his vest pockets. "Might not have much of a choice. The girl isn't exactly putting forth an effort. She stands against the wall and watches at every event. I never should have encouraged that photography habit of hers."

Photography? Violet was one of those Kodak Girls? He could almost picture her behind a camera, studying and observing. Laboring over her prints in a developing room. He hadn't much experience with photography himself, but he'd love to see her in action someday. "Perhaps you should put it off, let her experience this first season without pressuring her to marry. Then choose her a husband next year."

You are going to Hell, Max. Straight to Hell.

"Can't. I promised the missus we'd marry Violet off this year." Charles lifted a shoulder. "No idea why my lady is in such a rush, but I won't disappoint her—not on this."

Because he planned to disappoint his wife in other ways.

Max shifted on his feet and stifled the urge to say more. He had no right to interfere with Violet's future. After his own disastrous attempt at playing husband, he couldn't marry her—or anyone else—so he should just leave off, turn on his heel, and quit this bloody ball.

Yet he wouldn't. Because she was here, somewhere in this very room. And if he didn't find her soon, he might tear this ballroom apart with his bare hands.

Charles tipped his chin toward the dance floor. "Ah, I see Wingfield's claimed her for another dance. That's the second one tonight."

Max's head whipped toward the dancers, and he spotted her right away, her golden hair gleaming in the gaslight overhead. The breath locked in his lungs and he had to remind himself to breathe as he examined her. She was absolutely lovely in a cream silk evening gown with intricate beaded work covering the bodice. The delicate column of her throat was bare, begging for Max's mouth and hands.

That same sizzle whispered over his skin, like desire had commandeered his flesh, making him burn everywhere. *Once more. That's all I need.*

Wingfield's gaze drifted down to Violet's bosom, where it lingered far longer than was polite, and Max's hands curled into fists. Wingfield would need to be put in his place, it seemed.

"I'm headed to the card room," Charles was saying. "Care to join?"

"I'll pass. Excuse me," Max said, already drifting into the crowd. He moved to the edge of the dance floor, not bothering to hide as he caught Violet's eye. She stumbled when she spotted him—requiring Wingfield to steady her with a hand on her hip—and blinked.

Momentarily setting aside the need to pummel her dance partner, Max tilted his head toward the terrace. She nodded ever so slightly then looked away.

Excellent.

He ignored those who attempted to catch his attention as he strode through the crush. The whole world could wait, as far as he was concerned.

Now was time for play.

CHAPTER SIX

HE WAS HERE.

Ravensthorpe was here and wished to see her. Violet could hardly believe it. Had her plan worked? It had been two weeks since their night together and she'd grown despondent, certain she'd erred in giving him space. So, she'd buried herself in her classes at the Polytechnic Institute and in her photographs. In fact, after so many hours in the developing room, the chemicals had begun to sting her lungs.

All that had been worth it, however, because the handsomest duke in London had arrived . . . and he'd motioned for her to meet him outside.

Her chest worked to draw in air, her corset growing tighter at the idea. Would he kiss her again? Goodness, she hoped so. She hadn't been able to stop thinking about their night together, the way he'd touched her, as if he already knew every part of her. As if they'd been together for years.

He thought he'd ruin her. Destroy her and toss her aside. Violet didn't believe it. She was safe with him, protected. Cared for. He'd pushed her away out of loyalty and an overblown sense of nobility, but perhaps he'd come to realize that he was safe with her, too.

Finally the music ended and Wingfield led her off the dance floor. "Lady Violet," he said, and she noticed the beads of sweat on his upper lip. "Would you do me the honor of joining me—"

"No, thank you, my lord. I must find my father. You'll excuse me?"

Without waiting on a response, she curtsied and then darted into the throngs of lords and ladies as she made her way to the French doors.

To Ravensthorpe.

Giddiness ignited in her chest like flash powder—and then Charlotte appeared in her path, a questioning expression on her friend's face. Violet stopped before she careened into the other woman. "Hello, Charlotte."

"You never finished telling me about your new suitor during our shopping trip yesterday." Violet's expression must've reflected her sudden panic because Charlotte continued. "Calm down. I meant Wingfield."

"Right." Violet exhaled in relief. "Wingfield."

Charlotte's brows lowered. "Who did you think I meant?"

"No one. Just unaccustomed to having a suitor, I suppose."

Her friend drew closer. "I am so happy to see you dancing. Three times tonight! For once you're not standing against the wall, watching everyone else."

Violet had no desire to converse at the moment. She tried to gracefully edge around her friend. "I don't know what's come over me. Perhaps I should get some air."

"Oh, excellent idea. I'm due for a dance, so I'll find you after." Charlotte squeezed Violet's hand and then disappeared into the crowd.

Violet wasted no time in hurrying to the French doors. She slipped onto the terrace, where cool night air washed over her exposed skin like a caress, causing her to shiver. With no torches or lamps outside, darkness engulfed her.

Strong fingers wrapped around her arm and began pulling her deeper into the gloom, helping her down the stone steps. She didn't need to see his face to know it was Max. His presence surrounded her, a feeling of safety and danger, arousal and comfort all at the same time. She went willingly, eagerly, unconcerned with getting caught.

Once on the ground, he tugged her into an alcove hidden underneath the stairs. Before she could see his face, he was on her, the muscular length of him flush to her front, her back against the rough stone.

But he didn't kiss her.

He put his mouth near her ear, his warm breath coasting over her skin. "Happy, little mouse? For two weeks I've tried to forget you. A goddamn fortnight, yet here I am—all because I cannot get the taste of your pussy out of my head."

Her lips parted on an exhale, his words both thrilling and arousing. Wetness gathered between her thighs, her pulse hammering in every bit of her sex. "Very happy, Your Grace," she whispered and slid her hands along the rigid slope of his chest.

"Christ," he bit out, bending to rock his hips into her thigh, his erection large and hard against her. She melted, her limbs growing languid. "I want to fuck you right here," he growled. "Turn you around and toss your dress above your head, bare you and sink inside."

"Yes," she gasped, definitely ready for that. There was emptiness, a place in her soul earmarked just for him, and she needed him to fill it.

"Hold your skirts."

"What?"

But he didn't explain, merely sank to his knees and began pushing layers of silk out of his way. He looked . . . possessed. Wild, like a starving man at a buffet. She moved to help, gathering the skirts in her arms until cool air washed over her stocking-covered legs.

Finding the part in her drawers, he lunged, pressing his face toward her sex, disappearing underneath layers of cloth. Then she felt the bold swipe of his tongue along her seam, and her knees wobbled as sensation jolted through her. His hands cradled her buttocks and lifted her left leg to place it over his shoulder.

"You must remain quiet," he ordered and dove under her skirts.

He wasted no time, licking and sucking until she whimpered. She thrashed her head as he tended to every part of her, driving her higher and higher, and lust tightened her muscles. He feasted, softly grunting in response to her moans, his mouth and tongue unrelenting, unforgiving against her flesh.

Voices suddenly sounded above on the terrace, a few revelers out for a bit of fresh air, no doubt.

Though she was well hidden, she froze, her chest heaving, and stared down at Ravensthorpe. The light of the moon revealed Max's smirk as he appeared from under her skirts. "Quiet," he mouthed, then returned to his task.

Sweet heavens.

She trembled under the onslaught, but her mind was stuck on the fact that they weren't alone out here. What if they were discovered? She tried to dislodge his face from between her legs, but the duke wouldn't budge.

In fact, he doubled his efforts with her clitoris, sucking on the bud, laving it with his tongue.

It was too much.

Her eyes closed, the pressure building as fear and arousal mixed to overwhelm her, and she shoved her forearm into her mouth to stifle her cries as she came apart. Her body spasmed as her walls convulsed, white light exploding behind her eyes. When she regained herself, he gently dipped and swirled his tongue at her entrance, like he was trying to soak up every last bit of her taste.

Finally, he shot to his feet, his dark eyes glazed and hot. Her wetness coated his face and chin, and he licked his lips as he brought her hands to his waistband. "Finish me, Violet. Right now."

Oh, yes. She wanted that desperately. "What about . . ." She pointed to the terrace.

"They left. Hurry."

Swiftly, she unfastened his trousers and moved his shirtfront out of the way. "So many clothes." He made no move to help, staying perfectly still except for the breath sawing out of his chest.

She unbuttoned his undergarment and reached in, taking his shaft in her hand. The soft skin was stretched tight, her fingers unable to meet around his girth.

He dropped his forehead against her temple. "Squeeze hard," he said, giving a little thrust of his hips. "Stroke me. Fast."

Obeying, she tightened her grip and pumped his erection. He sucked in air and placed his hands on the wall behind her head. "That's it, my little mouse. Precisely like that."

He was so beautiful with his chiseled jaw and the few silver threads at his temple, his skin taut with excitement. She reached her other hand down to his testicles, rolled them in her palm, and Max let out a drawn out, "Fuck."

Hot breath hit her cheek as he began to talk. "We haven't long. Your father is in the card room and he'll come looking for you when he's done. I have the taste of you in my mouth. Would you like the taste of me in your mouth, as well?"

Her nipples tightened inside her clothing, and she rubbed her thighs together in a desperate bid for friction. Goodness, yes. She most definitely wanted that.

She started to lower to her knees, but he held her upright. "Wait."

He tore off his evening coat, folded it over, and dropped the cloth to the ground. She lifted her skirts and kneeled on his coat as Max began working his cock, rougher than she had, focusing almost entirely on the head. "Now, Violet," he gritted out, so she pressed forward and opened her mouth. Steadying her with a hand on her crown, he slid the head past her lips and groaned when she sucked. It took one swirl of her tongue and he reached his peak, his fingertips trembling on her scalp as spend coated the inside of her mouth.

"Yes," he gasped and shuddered. "That's it. Take it all."

She did, gladly. Her body sang in self-congratulatory pleasure as he climaxed, and when he finally pulled out she swallowed him down. Resting a palm against the hard stone, he lifted her chin with his free hand. His thumb traced her lips. "I expected you to spit but you didn't, did you?" He helped her stand then pressed his forehead to hers. "My God, Violet. What have I ever done to deserve you?"

He touched his lips to hers, kissing her softly, sweetly, with so much tenderness that she wanted to bottle it and hold onto the emotion forever. "Max," she whispered into his kisses, clutching him tightly. "*Your Grace.*"

When they broke apart, he breathed, "Thank you, sweet girl," before stepping back. He tucked and smoothed her hair instead of righting his clothing. "There. Now you may return inside."

"What about you?"

"I'll go around the side and find my carriage. I've no desire to stand around a stuffy ballroom this evening."

Did that mean . . .? Giddiness flooded her chest, her heart swelling to a ridiculous size. "Did you come just to see me?"

"Go back to the ball." He began redressing, his attention on his buttons.

She shifted on her slippers, the gravel crunching beneath her feet. "When will I—"

"Inside, Violet." His tone was sharp and authoritative, the one he no doubt used when the Duke of Ravensthorpe wished to get his way.

But he was not the duke with her, not any longer. He was Max. He would not push her aside, especially when she still had the taste of him in her mouth. "Not until you tell me when I will see you again."

"We cannot do this." He pushed his shirtfront into his trousers. "It's too risky."

"Then let me come to your home."

"Violet—"

"Max," she snapped. "If you do not tell me precisely when, then I'll show up and surprise you."

"I won't let you in. I'll have the doors and windows locked at all times."

Silly man. She slid her hand up his chest, tucking her body close to his. "No, I don't think you will. In fact, I don't believe you'll last even fourteen days this time."

"Do not try to play games with me. You will lose."

She nipped his jaw with her teeth—and he shivered in response. Moving away, she whispered, "We shall see, Your Grace. We shall see."

MOST DAYS, Max avoided visiting his clubs. They were a waste of time, the rooms filled with brash young men barely older than Will, laughing and joking as if they hadn't a care. They caused Max to feel a hundred years old. Had he ever been so carefree, so jovial?

Not since assuming the title at fourteen, certainly. After a decade of wrangling the ducal accounts into shape, including taking risks on the London Exchange to refill the empty bank accounts, he'd been ready to do his duty. His choice of bride, the daughter of a high-ranking earl, had seemed a good one at the time, but he and Rebecca had been a poor match.

From the start, there had been problems in the bedroom. She preferred he not undress, and refused to let him see her without clothing. She remained perfectly still during the act, not complaining, but not participating, either. Kisses were to remain chaste and he was to leave immediately upon finishing.

Unhappiness had gnawed at him until Rebecca started increasing. Then he'd taken a mistress, relieved to finally enjoy himself with an eager partner. It had been selfish of him, a decision he'd regretted when his wife found out. Hysterical over his infidelity, Rebecca had gone into early labor and died whilst delivering Will.

A year into his marriage, Max was left widowed with a young son. And guilt. Plenty of guilt.

And the guilt hadn't yet subsided, not even sixteen years later.

None of it had been Rebecca's fault. Max should have been more patient, more understanding. He should have tried harder to explain his needs and desires, instead of rushing off to another woman's bed. Young and stupid, he leaped into marriage with the belief that a wife was no different than the other highborn ladies he'd slept with, the lusty widows and bored society wives.

But Rebecca had been different. It was Max who hadn't bothered to adjust his behavior, and he'd caused her death. Not a day went by when he didn't chastise himself over what he'd done, and he would repeat his pledge never to marry again.

Some men were not cut out to be husbands.

Still, he had no choice but to protect Violet.

Brooks's was quiet at this time of morning. After handing his hat and cane to the attendant, Max found his quarry in the main room, nursing coffee. Only a handful of men were spread out amongst the furniture.

Wingfield frowned at Max's approach. "Why must I be here so early, Ravensthorpe?"

Max slid into the chair opposite. "Because I wish to speak with you. And you are at my service, not the other way around."

Wingfield scowled but said nothing as he took another sip of coffee.

After an attendant brought Max a cup, they were alone again. Max came right to the point. "You will cease your pursuit of Lady Violet."

The young man's mouth fell open. "You have no right to—"

"I have every right," Max said icily. "I am a close family friend and have known the girl since she was born. You are not good enough for her."

"Not good enough for her?" Wingfield's voice rose several octaves. "The girl is the unequivocal flop of the season. I am doing her a favor by paying her attention."

His little mouse, a flop? Outrage roared through Max's veins like cannon fire, yet he tamped it down, hiding his emotions behind a bored expression. "You are a drunk and a spendthrift. Also, I have it on good authority that you've had mercury treatments—multiple times, in fact. You are not marrying Lady Violet."

Twin spots of scarlet dotted Wingfield's cheeks. "How dare you? My father—"

Max sighed loudly. "Your father is in debt to the West London Bank for hundreds of thousands of pounds. Would you care to guess the identity of that bank's largest shareholder?"

Wingfield sputtered. "Are you . . . Is this a threat?"

Christ Almighty, how was the world to survive with men this stupid?

"Yes," Max admitted, and then downed the rest of his coffee. "I am threatening you in order to keep you away from Lady Violet. Is that clear enough for you, Wingfield? Shall I put it in writing so there are no misunderstandings?"

Wingfield swallowed hard. "No, I understand. I'll stay away from her."

"Good." He rose. "See that you do."

Wingfield mumbled, "She's a stupid cow, anyway."

Max's entire body clenched and he leaned close to the younger man's face. "What did you say?"

"Nothing."

Max's hand shot out and he jerked Wingfield up by his collar, lifting the younger man until his feet barely touched the floor. Conversation in the room died, every eye turned their way. No one would dare say a word to stop Max, one of the most powerful men in Britain, from doing whatever he liked with this piece of filth.

"How dare you insult her." He tightened his fist, cutting off Wingfield's air supply. "If I hear of you talking about her, I will feed you to the pigs on my estate. Are we clear? You don't breathe her name ever again. If you see her on the street, don't even offer a polite greeting. She no longer exists for you."

Wingfield gasped, his eyes bulging, but Max didn't let up until the other man nodded. He let Wingfield go and straightened his cuffs. "Glad we understand each other."

With that, Max collected his things and strolled onto St. James Street. Instead of taking a hansom home, he decided to walk and clear his head. Rage from the encounter with Wingfield continued to burn through him, and he still had no idea what to do about Violet.

Two days had passed since the night of the ball . . . and he was already weakening. The craving for her lurked his blood, always present and growing stronger every minute.

I don't believe you'll even last fourteen days this time.

How had she known?

She was so certain about him, about *them*. The folly of youth, he supposed, not to understand the whole picture. He was bad for her, too old and too . . . rough. She deserved better. Someone sweet and kind, closer in age. Hell, Max would be lucky to live another twenty years. She needed a man who could marry her, give her children, and make her laugh into her old age.

Max was not that man.

Yet he wasn't certain he could stay away from her. He thought of her nearly all the time, his cock currently chafed thanks to his hand and his memories. Like a teenaged boy, he'd stolen a small jar of oil from the larder to protect his skin while pleasuring himself.

It would be funny if it weren't so mortifying.

As he crossed Piccadilly, he spotted a camera shop in the middle of the block. He recalled Charles mentioning Violet's interest in photography. Did she frequent this establishment?

She'd always been a clever and curious child, asking him questions about Will, the ducal estates, and anything else that crossed her mind during the Mayhew dinner parties. Math and history had been her favorite subjects, as he recalled, but they'd even debated philosophy at one point. Those qualities, along with her current voyeuristic tendencies, likely made her a stellar photographer.

Charles hadn't seemed appreciative of Violet's photography habit, but it was important to nurture hobbies, even for women. Perhaps especially for women, as they were told so often what they could not do, rather than be allowed to express themselves. Max would hate to see any of Violet's creativity stifled.

He was walking toward the shop before he could think better of it.

A bell chimed over the door as he entered. A middle-aged man emerged from the back and his eyes widened at the sight of Max. "Good morning. How may I help your lordship?"

Max didn't bother to correct the form of address. "I am interested in purchasing some photography equipment for a friend. Is there anything new or something you'd recommend?"

"I'd be honored. Has your lordship an idea of this gentleman's level of experience with photography?"

"It is a she, and no."

"I see. Then allow me to recommend this latest Kodak box model, the number one. Most women find it lighter and much easier to operate. It also comes pre-loaded with a flexible roll of film." The clerk pointed to a camera in the glass case. "It is our best seller."

"I'll take that, then."

"Excellent." The clerk withdrew a box from a locked drawer under the case. "Shall I wrap it for your lordship?"

Max considered this while he studied the other items in the case.

Have them deliver the camera with a note saying you cannot see her again.

The black heart in his chest instantly rejected the idea. He needed to watch Violet's face as she unwrapped his gift, see the youthful exuberance that hadn't yet been snuffed out by this harsh life. Drink in her happiness as if it were his own.

He wasn't ready to give her up.

You'll regret this.

Pushing aside his conscience, he handed the clerk his card. "If you would, yes. Have it delivered here."

The man's brows shot up. "Your Grace. Forgive me, I hadn't known. I shall see to it personally."

"Thank you." Max placed his bowler atop his head and left the shop, feeling lighter than he had in two days.

Soon, my little mouse. Soon.

CHAPTER SEVEN

VIOLET WAS in her dark room, developing photographs. She loved swirling the paper in the chemicals, watching the still image slowly take shape before her eyes, preserved forever. Memories that no one could take away, indisputable proof that someone had put their mark on this earth.

It required patience, which Violet had in abundance. After all, hadn't she waited years for Max to finally notice her? And now that he had, she'd never been happier.

What if I cannot change Max's mind about a relationship?

Then life would march forward. Women were more independent nowadays, at least outside of the ton. Perhaps she could convince her parents to let her live over her favorite camera shop in Chelsea in a set of small apartments. She could sell her photographs for money and support herself. Unless she could marry Max, there was no pressing need to find a husband.

I won't marry you.

If she couldn't change his mind, then she would suggest a long-time affair. Better to have Max in her life and suffer the social consequences than to live without him.

She removed the last photograph from the fixer bath and rinsed it in fresh water. Then she hung the paper on a line to dry along with the rest, taking a moment to appreciate it. This image might be her best yet. The light had hit the buildings perfectly, the women in the foreground sharp and clear. A perfectly captured London morning.

It took several minutes to clean up and remove her apron. Coming down the narrow attic stairs, she heard her parents arguing inside their bedchamber. She started to creep by, ensuring not to make a sound on the way to her room, when she heard her name.

". . . Violet's two suitors?" her mother shouted. "You are supposed to be hurrying them along."

Violet paused. Why were they discussing her marriage prospects?

"Only one now," her father said. "Wingfield's gone to Devonshire for the rest of the season."

Wingfield had left town?

"So marry her off to the other one. I need her settled, Charles. You promised me."

The other one? Violet had no idea who they were discussing.

"I don't know, Elsie. Sundridge seems a bit dim."

Violet put a hand over her mouth. Sundridge? He'd called her Victoria during their first two dances, even after she'd corrected him. He hadn't let her get a word in edgewise, either, talking about playing cricket each time she saw him. Her parents wished for her to *marry* him?

Her stomach turned over, her brain woozy. This could not be happening. And why was her mother so anxious to be rid of her?

Her father continued. "Perhaps we should let her finish this season and find her a husband next year."

"Absolutely not. I want her married as quickly as possible—and it hardly matters to whom. I will speak to Sundridge's father myself, if necessary."

"No, no," her father said. "I'll see it handled, though I cannot understand why you are in such a hurry."

"It's best for Violet. Prolonging a betrothal won't help her prospects. A second season will only make everyone wonder what's wrong with her."

"There's nothing wrong with her with the girl. A bit shy, is all."

"Because you've indulged her. Our duty is to see her married now that she is of age. You promised, Charles. Have a betrothal in place before the month is out."

Violet put a hand on the wall to steady herself. Before the month was out? That was little more than a week from now. Was her mother serious?

She hurried away, moving swiftly along the corridor, her ears ringing with impending disaster. She had no destination in mind, only the need to keep going, to put distance between herself and this information.

Her mother wanted Violet gone. Married off to whomever would have her.

What sort of mother had no regard for the match her daughter made? Charlotte's mother hovered at her daughter's side, ensuring Charlotte only spoke with bachelors from the very best families. Violet's mother, on the other hand, hadn't attended large social events in months and anticipated ridding herself of her only child.

Tears burned Violet's lids as she moved toward the front door, the desire to escape overwhelming her. Their butler appeared, and his brow lowered in concern when he saw her face. "Did you wish to go out, Lady Violet?"

"I'd like to take a walk and visit my friend Charlotte."

"Of course, my lady. Shall I send for your maid?"

"No need. I am not going anywhere but to Charlotte's and it's not far."

"Then allow me to fetch a groom—"

Instead of waiting, Violet opened the door and dashed down the front walk. When she was far enough from her house, she hailed a hansom to take her to the far side of Grosvenor Square.

To Ravensthorpe.

She needed him to comfort her, to tell her it would be all right.

Even if it was a lie.

Max's large home sat on the corner of the very public square. Considering it was the middle of the day, she could not pay a call on him. Instead, she instructed the driver to let her out a block over and she then snuck into the rear of Max's gardens.

Tears streamed down her face as she hurried along. Thankfully, the gardeners were on the far side of the property, their backs to the house. After slipping onto the terrace and through the French doors, Violet ran along the corridor, hoping to avoid detection by the staff on her way to Max's study, where she assumed he was working.

Not bothering to knock, she turned the knob on the study door and slid in. Max was seated behind his desk, a young man scribbling on paper in the chair across from him. The duke's head snapped up, dark blue eyes locking on her face—and his jaw dropped. She hadn't a clue as what to do now that she was here, so she waited, silent tears rolling down her cheeks.

Max recovered quickly, coming to his feet. "Webber, let's pick this up later. You have enough to get started."

The other man gathered his things and bowed. "Your Grace."

Violet moved aside to let the young man pass. When they were alone, she tried to catch her breath, but emotion clogged her throat. Max came toward her, concern etched on his handsome features. "Violet, what is it? What's happened?"

Without waiting another second, she threw herself at his solid chest. He caught her, his arms holding her tight to his frame, and she breathed in his now-familiar scent of orange and tobacco. He was strong and safe, a balm for her misery. After a few seconds, her tears dried on his necktie, her shudders ceasing. When he picked her up, she clutched at his shoulders and buried her face in his throat.

He lowered them into a chair near the empty grate. The moment stretched and he seemed in no hurry to make her talk. For some reason, his calm fortitude helped soothe her. Finally, she sighed. "I'm sorry. I shouldn't have burst into your home in the middle of the day."

"I don't mind, though I do hope you came in the back."

"I did. No one saw me except the man who was here a moment ago."

"Webber is discreet. His job depends on it. Now, are you ready to tell me what is wrong, or shall I give you a present?"

She leaned back to see his face. "You bought me a present?"

The duke appeared adorably embarrassed, with his cheeks turning pink. "Yes, I did," he said. "Shocking, but I am capable of simple kindness, Violet."

This was more than simple kindness. This was . . . monumental. He'd bought her a *gift*.

He cares for me.

Her spirits lifted immediately—a considerable feat, seeing as how she was to be betrothed by the end of the month.

Max slid out from underneath her and went to his desk. When he came back, he was holding a rectangle-shaped box wrapped in brown paper. "I hope you like it."

Was he serious? The box could contain rocks and she would treasure them always. She tore through the paper with all the restraint of a three-year-old on Boxing Day. She gasped. "You bought me a camera."

Max thrust his hands in his trouser pockets and gave her a half smile. "I did."

"I've wanted a box camera for months. How did you know?"

"I had no idea. The clerk at the store recommended it."

She stood and placed the camera on the chair, then wrapped her arms around his middle. "Thank you, Max. It's the perfect gift. I love it."

He squeezed her tighter. "You're welcome."

They stood there for a long moment, locked in an embrace, and Violet thought she'd died and gone to heaven. Her problems felt far away while in the warm security of Max's arms. "Why does my mother hate me?"

Max's lips touched the crown of her head. "Come sit." He led her to an empty chair and pulled her onto his lap once again. "Why do you believe your mother hates you?"

She relayed the conversation she'd overhead. "She wants me betrothed by the end of the month."

"Perhaps it is as she said, that she is worried a second season will harm your chances."

"Do you believe that to be the case?"

"No. However, I haven't any daughters and I only married to produce an heir, so I am hardly an expert."

He so rarely spoke of his late wife and his son. She was curious about them, about anything regarding his life. "Tell me about her."

"Who?"

"Your wife."

He started, his body jerking slightly. "Why?"

"Because I'd like to know her."

MAX DIDN'T KNOW what to say. Part of him wished to refuse. He hated talking about Rebecca, and Will had long stopped asking about his mother. Those were memories best not stirred.

But perhaps Violet needed to understand. Marriages in their world were not for love or happiness. They were for progeny and legacy, to transfer wealth and property. Moreover, she needed to know of his past and why he'd never marry again.

He cleared his throat. "I decided to marry when I was twenty-four. I'd wrangled the accounts into some semblance of order and made several wise investments on the Exchange. There was no reason to wait."

He'd been the last of his friends to marry. Charles had settled down two years prior and Violet had already turned one. There was no need to mention it, however. Doing so would only make him feel like an old lecher, and this moment was about comforting her.

"Rebecca was pretty, the daughter of an earl. Her father had a large farm in Scotland with some sheep that I envied. He offered it as part of her dowry and I accepted." He'd sold the farm ages ago, as it had only served as a bitter reminder of his failure.

He stroked Violet's leg through her skirts. Thankfully, she'd stopped crying—a sight that had shredded his heart—and seemed to be breathing easier. He liked having her here, even during the day. Returning to his tale, he said, "I had thought we were a good match, that we'd muddle through together, but Rebecca was scared most all the time. Scared of acting improperly, scared of the staff gossiping. Scared of me."

"Scared of you?" She leaned back to see his face. "That is ridiculous. I've always thought you quite kind and generous."

He shook his head. Sweet girl. "I mean in the bedroom. She could not stand for me to touch her."

"Oh." Violet's nose wrinkled in the most adorable way. "I see."

"She knew her duty, of course. She allowed me to visit to her room at night, take her only under the covers and in the dark. Never undressed. I suspect she gritted her teeth through the whole business, despite my concerted efforts to ensure she enjoyed it. But the harder I tried, the more miserable she became."

"Perhaps she found the pleasure shameful."

It had crossed his mind, but he'd never learn the truth, unfortunately. "Perhaps. She wouldn't discuss it, though, and when she began increasing, I assumed we were both relieved." He had been so happy, so eager to be a father. To nurture and love a child as he hadn't been by his own father.

"Assumed? You mean she wasn't happy about carrying your child?"

"No, about sleeping with her. I assumed she'd gladly see me go elsewhere for my physical needs. That I could fuck whoever I wanted, seeing as how she didn't want me."

She frowned, her nose wrinkling. "A mistress."

He sighed, wishing he didn't have to tell Violet of his sordid past. *She'll never look at me the same.*

Perhaps it was for the best.

He carried on. "There was a woman from before my marriage. She was the wife of a viscount and we got on well together. I thought . . . I thought I was doing the right thing."

"It was insensitive of you, but you would not be the first married man in the ton to take a mistress."

"I realize as much, but as time went on I didn't try to hide it, either. Call it hubris or the idiocy of a twenty-five-year-old duke. I started staying away for longer stretches of time. Then I took my mistress to Rome—despite her husband's objections." He'd felt invincible, a man who had everything that mattered: wealth, a child on the way, and a beautiful woman at his side. He was cocksure and fearless, certain he knew best. "Rebecca was eight months along when the viscount wrote to her, informing her of what I'd done."

Violet began rubbing his chest, as if to soothe him—him, the man responsible for it all—and something inside Max shifted, unlocked. No one had comforted him in quite a while. He hadn't wanted it, frankly. But it was different with Violet. She eased his troubled soul, smoothed some of the jagged edges that scraped and cut inside him.

Clutching her tighter, he finished it. "There was no denying the viscount's claims, as I'd just returned days earlier. The news sent Rebecca into hysterics. She was inconsolable, crying and refusing to eat. She resented that I'd taken a mistress while she was carrying our child and considered it a betrayal of our marriage vows. Because of the unrest, the baby came early. I had the very best doctors at her side, but they couldn't save her."

"They were able to save the baby."

"Yes. Will was small, but he lived." His son had been so tiny, so fragile. But Will had fought to survive and Max had done everything in his power to see that his baby thrived. He had wet nurses around the clock and an army of nannies to keep a vigilant eye over the future duke. Max hardly left his son's side during that time.

"Max, you don't know whether she would have survived or not. Many happily married women die in childbirth."

He pressed his lips to her hair. "There's no need to lie. I was responsible for her death." That shame would follow him to his grave. "Which is why I will never marry again. I have no intention of subjecting another woman to that life."

"What life?"

"With me, failing at faithfulness."

"Max, you were so young."

"Older than you. Old enough to know better."

"Perhaps you wouldn't be unfaithful next time."

The hopeful note in her voice caused his tone to harden. "There will be no next time, Violet. I have no need to tie myself down when I already have an heir." He was not interested in ruining another woman he'd promised to honor and cherish. Max wouldn't risk it. A second dose of guilt would bury him.

"What about love? What about companionship?"

He hated to shatter her illusions, but it had to be said. "My dear, I've no need of the first and can find the second anytime I wish."

She was quiet after that, but he didn't take it back. Someone must give her the unvarnished truth. Someone must lower her expectations, both with regards to him and her future marriage.

A marriage not so far in the future, it seemed. Max hadn't a clue as to why Lady Mayhew was in a rush to marry Violet off, especially to a twit like Sundridge. Lady Mayhew hadn't ever seemed cruel, but perhaps the resentment in the Mayhew marriage had bled into her relationship with her daughter.

Still, Sundridge and Violet, married? Max's gut cramped at the thought. That fool did not deserve someone with Violet's spark or adventurous spirit. To hear her moans or capture her sighs with his mouth. To suck on her gorgeous tits or tongue her luscious cunt. It was out of the question.

"I'll have a word with Sundridge," he said curtly.

"Why?"

"Because you don't want to marry him."

"You say that as if they won't merely find someone else, another hapless soul to take Sundridge's place."

He didn't care much for that, either. "I won't let you marry just anyone. I'll use my influence to help you make the best possible match."

"Such as?"

"There's . . ." Every name that went through his head was instantly discarded. No man he knew was good enough for her. "Hmm."

She studied his face, observing his indecision like a hawk searching for prey. "Well?"

"I shall need to think on it."

She snuggled into his side and buried her nose in his neck. "I cannot see why I must marry at all. I could move into a small apartment in Chelsea above a camera shop, then maybe open my own photography studio."

And leave herself open to all sorts of mashers, charlatans, and miscreants? He sat straighter. "Absolutely not. That would hardly be safe."

"Perhaps, but I would be independent. I'd be willing to trade some peace of mind for that."

"I wouldn't."

"And I could still see you."

Satisfaction raced through him as he considered it—and he was instantly ashamed. Violet could not become his mistress. To do so would ruin her social standing and likely get Max shot by her father. "You do not want that life, darling. You deserve the protection and security of a proper marriage. To be pampered and provided for until you die."

"By a man like Sundridge? No, thank you." Clever fingers played along Max's jaw, stroking the skin above his collar. "Will you grant me a favor, Maximilian Thomas William Bradley III?"

His lips twisted into an affectionate smile. "Indeed, someone has been studying Debrett's."

"I used to write it on paper when I was younger."

Surprised, he leaned back to lock eyes with her. "You did?"

"Yes, and I drew little hearts around it, too."

He dropped his head onto the chair back. "Violet, my God. I should toss you in a carriage and send you home." But he wouldn't. Good sense had departed ages ago when it came to this woman. He couldn't get enough of her.

He'd never felt this connection with a lover before, this consuming need to not only touch and kiss her, but to just be with her, to talk about everything and nothing. Maybe it was because he'd known her for so long. Or perhaps it was merely Violet, this daring and intelligent woman who challenged him at every turn.

She playfully pushed his chest. "Stop talking nonsense. Will you grant me a favor or not?"

He tapped his fingers on the armrest, thinking. He didn't like agreeing without all the terms. However, this was Violet. History had shown that he had a difficult time telling her no, unless the topic was marriage.

He kissed her temple. "It depends."

"On?"

"On whether this request involves a lack of clothing and a flat surface."

"As a matter of fact, it does. Would you like to hear what I want?"

Blood gathered in his groin as he considered all the ways he planned to defile her this afternoon. "Of course. Name it and it's yours."

"May I photograph you?"

He blinked. "But I thought you said . . .?"

"Oh, I did." She cocked her head, her eyes dancing. "I want to photograph you without your clothes."

CHAPTER EIGHT

WHEN MAX CHUCKLED, Violet did not join in. The request hadn't been a jest. Devastatingly handsome, the duke was a specimen of living, breathing art, and if he did not deserve to be photographed and preserved, then nothing did.

He angled to see her face, the light catching on the threads of silver in his ink-colored hair. Her lower half clenched at his beauty, so harsh and masculine it hurt to look at him. His dark gaze narrowed on her. "Why?"

"Why not?"

"That is hardly an answer."

She smoothed the fabric covering his chest, petting him. "Because you are so very pretty and I wish to try out my new camera."

"Violet . . ."

He sounded exasperated, so she explained. "It's not uncommon. Shops near the Strand sell all sorts of—"

"You should not know of those places," he said sharply.

"Everyone knows of those places, Max."

"Do not wander in there. If you wish to see those types of images, I'll purchase them for you."

"Why not pose for them instead?"

"Back to this, are we?" He shook his head. "Not the sort of portrait a duke poses for, darling."

The endearment warmed her insides, but she didn't stop pressing him. "Please? The light is gorgeous right now, with the perfect amount of afternoon sun. We'll lock the door and the photos will only be for me, I promise."

"Until you are angry with me and then copies are shipped off to my enemies."

That stung. "Do you honestly believe I would ever do such a thing?"

"No, but they could end up in the wrong hands. What if your mother or father discovered them?"

She sensed victory. "My darkroom is in the attic and they never go up there."

"And you'll lock them up?" He pinched the bridge of his nose with a thumb and forefinger. "I cannot believe I am contemplating this. My ducal ancestors are undoubtedly spinning in their collective graves."

"What if you turn your head, so the camera cannot clearly see your face?"

"That sounds better, but only if you allow me to take some of you as well."

"Nude photographs?"

"Yes."

She licked her lips and shifted on his lap. Did she dare? He would see all her imperfections and flaws, captured for eternity.

"Not so brave now, are you?"

The taunt hit home, making her feel foolish. "Fine. I will if you will."

He ran a hand along her side and cupped her breast. "As long as I am able to keep the photographs of you."

She arched her back, pushing into his palm. "What will you do with them?"

"Stare at them while I stroke my cock."

The place between her legs pulsed at the idea. "Perhaps I'll do the same with your photographs."

"You mean use them whilst you masturbate? Oh, my sweet girl, nothing would bring me more joy."

Before she melted into a pool of lust on his plush carpets, she got up and readied the box camera. Max locked the door and then disrobed garment by garment until he was naked, his long and powerful body making her mouth water. On display were wide shoulders and a strong chest dusted with dark hair that trailed south, toward his flat belly. His penis was half-erect, the crown peeking out from the foreskin, with dark veins running along the shaft. And his muscled thighs were—

"If you keep staring at me like that, we'll never get around to actually taking the photographs."

She shook herself and tried to adopt a more professional demeanor. "Let's move the divan to maximize the light."

He helped her arrange the furniture to her liking, and then she told him to lie down. "Stretch out so the camera sees all those glorious angles and ridges."

"I had no idea you were so enamored by my looks. You are embarrassingly good for my vanity."

Please. Every woman in London salivated over him, as he well knew. "Put your arm behind your head and lean back."

He did as she asked, taking direction as she arranged him the way she wished. Goodness, he was delicious, as perfect as any museum sculpture. The sun cast him in an otherworldly glow, though certainly not angelic. More like a sinful treat on a hot summer's day, wicked and irresistible. The path to ruin, one she would choose time and time again.

Crouching, she took the first photo from an upward angle, where she could see his body but not his face. "Good. Just breathe and hold still."

The box camera was easy to hold and manipulate, and she was able to get close on his bicep, his rib cage. The whiskers on his jaw. He was quiet, letting her work, the sound of the camera doing all her talking. She couldn't wait to develop the full-length photos, the ones with his face in shadow while the rest of him was on splendid display, including his rapidly hardening cock.

He was relaxed grace and banked power, and she struggled to breathe. Her skin was hot and itchy, the throb between her legs growing more insistent. A fine sheen of sweat broke out on her forehead, like a fever had taken up residence inside her veins and the only cure was to lick him from head to toe.

Ahem.

"Now roll the other way."

He cocked a brow. "You want a photograph of my bare arse, then?"

Her face flamed but she didn't shrink from the request. "Seems a shame to waste the opportunity."

Max presented her with his back, his muscles shifting as he settled. She quickly pressed the button to capture the shot and turned the key to advance the film, even before he finished moving. The impulse to save every bit of him, forever, burned through her. Who knew how long she'd have the privilege of seeing him unclothed? If her parents had their wish, she'd be betrothed to another man by the end of the month.

Ignoring the heaviness in her chest at the thought, she kept working to find the perfect image of him, her legs dipping and bending, stepping closer, then farther away, while the minutes advanced.

Finally, Max's hand drifted between his legs. "I cannot stand this any longer. The more you look at me the more I want you. Are you finished?"

She nodded, her mouth dry. He'd rendered her speechless.

"Violet?" He peeked over his shoulder. When she didn't speak, he offered up a smooth grin. "Oh, I see. Enjoying yourself, are you? Perhaps I might offer assistance."

The film had run out, so she carefully placed the camera on a side table. "Thank you for humoring me."

Now flat on his back, he continued to stroke his large erection. "Are you wet, my little mouse?"

She watched the slow movements of his hand, mesmerized as he pulled and dragged, the muscles in his forearms popping. "I wish I had more film," she murmured.

He chuckled. "Too bad you don't have a moving picture camera."

Oh, there was a fine idea. "Would you—?"

"Indeed, not. This is for your eyes only. Come here." She reached him in two steps, and he tilted his head to look at her, his stern expression full of lust. "Take off your clothes."

It took her longer to undress on her own than if she'd had his help, but soon she was down to her drawers, stockings, and shoes. Color stained Max's cheeks, his chest rising and falling rapidly with the force of his breaths as he stared. Deciding to tease him, she lifted her foot and placed it on his thigh, the heel of her boot digging into his flesh. He jerked, his pupils dilating until his irises were nearly black.

He grunted. "In the mood for a bit rough?"

She unbuckled her shoe and removed it. "Perhaps I wish to torture you."

"Then press harder," he said with a daring lift of his brow.

She brought her other foot up and leaned on him, slowly unfastening the buckle on her shoe. He sucked in a harsh breath, his body tensing. "Hurry with the rest of it and get up here."

She shed her stockings and drawers and started to stretch out next to him, but he grabbed her arm. "Sit on my thighs. Put your knees on either side of my legs."

Climbing up, she positioned herself, which left her sex completely exposed. It would have been mortifying if Max weren't focused on her like a starving man. "Like this?"

"Yes. Lean back and put your left hand on my shin, then use your right hand between your legs. Show me what you'll do when you develop the pictures you took this afternoon."

Oh.

He was ordering her to do . . . that. In front of him.

"Max . . ."

"You are gorgeous, Violet. Show me, please."

She bit her lip. He hadn't stopped pleasuring himself. Where was the harm if she did the same? No one would know except for him, and he wouldn't judge her. He never did.

"Go on," he urged, his voice a low rasp.

Arching, she steadied herself with a hand on his leg. The position thrust her breasts up, which Max must have enjoyed because his hand moved quicker. Emboldened, she slipped her fingers into her sex, dipping into the folds until she grazed her clitoris. Pleasure sizzled in her veins and she sucked in a sharp breath.

"Goddamn, that is beautiful. Keep going. Let me watch you."

Gathering her courage, she used the pads of her fingers to swirl and tease, the skin swollen and slippery, while the scent of arousal permeated the air. They observed one another, a shared and intimate experience with hardly any contact, and somehow that aroused her more. She tried to bedevil him, exaggerating her movements, thoroughly enjoying herself while her body climbed toward its peak. Max panted and cursed, his muscles straining as he pumped his fist, and his reaction spurred her on.

At some point, Max released his erection and placed his hands on her thighs, a light sheen of sweat coating his entire body. His penis was a dull red and fully engorged, resting on his stomach, waiting to be put to good use. And she wanted it. There was an emptiness inside her, an ache, and there would never be another man in her life like this one. Not like Max.

The time was right. She knew it in her bones.

"Max, I want another favor."

His gaze remained focused on the place between her legs. "Anything, darling."

"Will you be my first?"

He froze, his eyes locking with hers while his fingers dug into her thighs. "Your first time should be with your future husband. Not me. I cannot marry you."

Lord, she was tiring of hearing him say that.

She pressed harder on the taut bud and her eyes nearly rolled back in her head. "Why should I wait . . . to bestow this honor . . . on a nameless and faceless future husband?"

He licked his lips, his expression turning decidedly predatory. Like he was imagining all he wished to do to her. Streaks of white-hot pleasure rolled along her spine.

"You want me to ruin you." His voice was rough, with sharp edges and unyielding authority. He could command an army with that tone. God knew she'd do anything he asked when he spoke to her like that.

"Yes, I do." Then she landed a blow of her own. "Please, *Your Grace*."

As if on cue, his right eye twitched. "You'll regret it."

Impossible. She'd dreamed of this for so long, and he had exceeded her imaginings, the elaborate fantasies she'd concocted in her head over the years. The real man was infinitely more alluring, more caring, and there was no reason to hold back. She wanted to drown in him, to lose herself in his breath and surrender to his caresses. "No, I won't."

"Stand up."

She crawled off his lap and stood on the floor. Max rose and towered over her. "You still wish to do this? You want me to fuck you?"

"Yes."

"You are going to be the death of me. Let's go." Not bothering with clothes, he took a hold of her wrist and led her to the back corner of the study. Where were they going?

He pushed a section of the wainscoting, and the wall popped open.

"A secret passage?" How thrilling.

"Go." He ushered her into the darkness, then flicked a switch that illuminated a single bulb. A set of stairs waited to the left. "Climb."

She ascended the stairs, Max right behind her. She could sense him, large and looming, and her skin crackled with awareness, every cell vibrating with readiness. Was this truly happening?

At the top of the stairs, he reached to open a latch, then pushed on the wood. Beyond, a bedchamber was revealed. *His bedchamber.*

Her heart pounded, a steady thrumming of disbelief that she was finally here after so many years of dreaming about it. It was like she'd been invited into Heaven—or more like Hell. This was Ravensthorpe, after all.

She walked inside, her wide gaze taking it all in. A huge dark walnut bed dominated the space, while an armoire, side table, and single leather chair comprised the remaining furniture. Sparse artwork on the walls. As decadence went, the space left quite a lot to be desired. Standing by the bed, she dragged her fingertips over his simple bedclothes. "Hmm."

"You sound disappointed." He closed the panel in the wall. "What were you expecting?"

"Velvet and gilding, I think. A list of men you're exacting revenge upon. Perhaps a special coitus chair, like the one the Prince of Wales supposedly owns in France."

He made a choking sound, his eyes bulging. "How on earth do you know about that chair?"

"Have you seen it?" His lips flattened, and she had her answer. "Tell me. I overheard ladies discussing it in Paris at a ball."

"I will not. And I'd rather discuss you than Bertie. Are you certain about this? You may change your mind at any time, you know."

Even though she was feeling shy and longing for a dressing gown, Violet had never been more certain of anything in her life. "I want this. I want *you.*"

He pulled her close with one arm and used his free hand to roll her nipple between his thumb and forefinger. "Have I told you how much I adore your breasts?"

"You do?"

"Very much so. I would love to pierce these gorgeous nipples with jewelry. Did you hear of that when you were in Paris?"

That was something people did? "No." She watched his hand, her breath stuttering as his thick fingers pulled and massaged the tip of her breast. Each movement sent spikes of pleasure straight between her legs.

"It's in fashion these days. Rings that hang from the breast, sparkling with gems. I could tug on them gently, give you a tiny bite of pain. Would that be rough enough for you?"

"I think I might like that," she said, feeling dazed, drunk on his presence. Yet his talk of the future penetrated the fog in her brain. "So, does this mean we'll continue to see each other?"

CLEVER GIRL. Max should have known she'd pick up on that. "For now, let's focus on your request, shall we?"

She reached to stroke his shaft. "Just tell me what to do."

Max groaned and struggled for composure. He knew this was a mistake. He had no right to take her virginity, but he was past the point of talking her out of it. She was a grown woman and if this was what she wanted, then who was he to deny her?

His erection was so painful, he had to grit his teeth. Twice he'd nearly orgasmed while watching her pleasure herself and if he didn't spend soon, his balls might explode.

Still, he had to make this good for her.

He stilled her hand and gestured to the bed. "Lie back on the mattress."

The bed was the perfect height for him to feast on her cunt, and he wasted no time in doing so as soon as she was in position. He kissed and licked her, leaving no bit of skin untended between her legs. He even brushed his tongue over the puckered rose of her bottom, which caused her to gasp, and he made a mental note to return to that area someday soon. *Oh, the pleasures I will give you, my little mouse.*

"Max, please," she begged, her thighs trembling aside his head. "Your Grace. Oh, please."

He couldn't resist her when she begged in that tone, so he tongued her clitoris, suckling while sliding his index finger inside her. Her walls gripped his skin, reminding him of the narrow width of her opening. *You cannot hurt her.*

On his wedding night, he had tried to prepare Rebecca, but she'd wanted the whole business done quickly. Max had assumed his wife's reticence had been nerves during her first time, but it soon became clear Rebecca didn't enjoy their coupling. At all. No amount of preparation had pleased her.

He had to do better by Violet.

Her hips soon met the pumping of his hand, his finger slipping easily into her quim, so he added another. Violet's fingertips curled into the bedclothes, fabric bunching in her palms as she mewled in her throat, her body undulating toward its peak. "Oh, God."

By the time he used three fingers, she was drawn tight, shaking with need. Then the taut bud swelled and tightened in his mouth and she broke, her walls clenching around his fingers, milking them, and Max nearly came on the floor. Goddamn, he could not wait to be inside her.

Rising, he climbed onto the bed and slid between her thighs. "Lift your knees."

She obeyed without question, spreading herself open, her sex flushed from her orgasm, the skin glistening with her slickness. Had he ever seen anything more arousing in his life? Gripping the base of his cock, he lined up at her entrance then paused. His chest heaved as desire clawed inside him like a rabid beast, desperation a fever in his blood. "Are you certain?"

She widened her thighs even further and Max's brain turned to porridge. He pushed forward ever so slightly, working the head of his cock inside her tight sheath. The walls squeezed him like a fist, and he had to close his eyes, breathe deeply, to keep from rutting at her like an animal.

"Oh," Violet said.

He lifted his head and studied her. Violet's eyes were wide, as if she was surprised. "Are you in pain? Discomfort?" Rebecca had cried their first time, her tears soaking their bed. "Shall I stop?"

She shook her head. "Do not dare."

He exhaled, relief and affection settling in his chest, lightening his mood. Vowing to go slow, he moved carefully, steadily, watching her the entire time for signs of distress. She was breathing heavily, her skin flushed, as he slid into her body. It was bloody torture, with streaks of lust crackling along the backs of his thighs, his cock demanding friction.

When he bottomed out, he held there, motionless, sucking in air as he gave her time to adjust. Being inside her was heaven, a tight, wet paradise that he never wanted to leave. Violet was all he could see, all he could feel, and he wished he could stay right here, like this, for the rest of the day and into the night.

Soon he couldn't wait any longer. "All right?" he asked through clenched teeth.

"I expected to be torn in two. Instead I feel . . . full." She wriggled, causing him to shift inside her, and he screwed his eyes shut, struggling not to spend before they even got started. "I like it," she said.

Dear God.

Max gave a thrust of his hips, his shaft dragging along her sensitive tissues, and Violet purred. "Goodness, I like that even more."

He was done for.

Any civility he possessed disappeared and Max snapped, driving into her again and again. At some point she dropped her knees and clutched at him, pulling him closer as he fucked her like a man possessed. Her body slid higher on the mattress and he chased her, unwilling to let her get away even for a moment. A part of him knew he was being too rough, too barbaric for her first time. But she only moaned and scored his skin with her nails, telling him in breathy pants, "more" and "faster."

The woman would be his undoing.

He leaned over her, snarling in her ear as his hips worked, his cock plunging in and out of her channel. "You like this, my little mouse? You want more?"

"Oh, Max, yes. Please."

"You're going to let me fuck you whenever I want, aren't you?" He couldn't seem to stop talking, especially when her walls clenched every time he did. *She likes my dirty words.* "Your cunt was made for my cock. I've never had better."

It was the truth. But he knew it wasn't her body—it was *her*.

You're falling for her.

Unwilling to give credence to such ridiculousness, he shut off his brain and thrust hard. Then he used his thumb on her clitoris, stimulating the button until Violet's back began to bow, her breasts bouncing as continued to work himself in and out of her. Finally, she arched, crying out as her walls contracted around his cock. Flashes of heat streaked along Max's spine, through his bollocks, but he somehow held out while watching her orgasm, the sight more alluring than anything he'd ever witnessed.

As soon as she started to relax, it was tempting to let his body take over, surrender to the bliss that rocketed through his system. Yet he couldn't finish inside her. Quickly, he pulled out and crawled up her body, his knees astride her chest, and aimed the tip of his shaft at her mouth. "Open," he growled.

She parted her lips and he drove between them, groaning as her tongue swirled on the underside of his shaft as if coaxing his spend. Then it happened. The orgasm roared through him, sensation shooting along his thighs and out the tip of his cock. It went on and on, wave after glorious wave of euphoria, his muscles trembling as he gave her everything he had.

He slumped, nearly falling over, weak as a kitten in the aftermath. Violet continued to lick his shaft, her mouth gentle, and stared up at him with such adoration and satisfaction that his lips twisted into a half grin. He hadn't smiled this much in . . . ages. But Violet had that effect on him. In the short time they'd been lovers, he found himself thinking of her at the oddest moments, with small comments he wished to tell her, as if she'd invaded his brain with her sweet and earnest nature.

Running his hand through her disheveled hair, he almost blurted out a very stupid sentence.

You cannot ruin this girl's life. Begging her to be your mistress is selfish, Max.

God, but he wanted her. Day and night. Ready at his disposal, with her easy smile and keen observations, not to mention her delectable body.

He dropped onto his back and tried to catch his breath. Violet rolled closer, snuggling into his side, and he wrapped his arm around her.

"You are very good at that," she said, her head resting on his shoulder. "No wonder your mistresses fight to keep you."

It had never been like this, but he didn't tell her that. "I am pleased you enjoyed yourself. I haven't much experience with virginity." Only his late wife, and no one would deem that a success.

"Max, it was perfect." She pressed a kiss to his skin. "Just as I knew it would be with you."

He shifted to cradle her cheek in his palm. "I should be reassuring you. Did I hurt you?"

"No." She bit her lip and wiggled slightly. "I am a bit sore, but I cannot wait to do that again."

A chuckle escaped Max's throat. "What am I to do with you, my sweet girl?"

"I am certain you'll think of something, Your Grace."

CHAPTER NINE

VIOLET FORCED a smile at her dance partner. What on earth made her parents believe Lord Sundridge a good choice for a husband? While he wasn't particularly hard on the eyes, he talked nonstop. She'd stopped listening ages ago, instead memorizing three rote comments to interject whenever he paused for a reaction: "Indeed, I daresay you are right," "How clever of you," and "One can never know, I suppose."

Thus far, he hadn't seemed to notice that her mind was elsewhere. Or, rather on *someone*.

Max stood on the far side of the room, towering over the other men in his perfectly tailored evening clothes. His dark hair was expertly styled, his expression bored to the casual observer. Violet knew better, however.

The Duke of Ravensthorpe was watching her every move.

Oh, he might not have stared directly at her, but he observed carefully, keeping to her vicinity, and his keen gaze brushed over her person no matter where she was in the room.

She could swoon with the possessiveness of it. The duke, possessive of *her*. Her core squeezed in happiness, despite the soreness from yesterday. Though she and Max would never marry, she would never regret giving him her virginity. The experience had been utterly divine, satisfying in every way.

Which left her the problem of Sundridge. Her current dance partner was carrying on a one-sided conversation that seemed more like a lecture aimed at no one in particular. Above all else, she could not marry this man.

Had her father already spoken to Sundridge's father? Dread slithered over Violet's skin, turning her stomach. Why was her mother anxious to marry her off, even to a nincompoop? It made no sense.

Perhaps she should try and reason with Sundridge.

"My lord," she said, interrupting whatever he'd been saying.

Sundridge blinked at her. "Don't care for cricket, do you?"

Was that the topic on which he'd been rambling? "Our dance will end soon, and I wished to ask a question before we part."

"Oh. Has this to do with cricket?"

"No, actually." God help her. "It has to do with us. Are you . . . that is, our fathers . . ."

"Yes?" He had the nerve to sound impatient.

"Are you considering marriage? To me, I mean?" Two months ago, this conversation would have mortified her. Now, too much hung in the balance not to address it.

"I . . . yes. I thought my intent was quite clear."

"Why?"

"Why is it clear?"

"No, why me?"

He cleared his throat. "Well, why not?"

Hardly a statement of ever-loving devotion. "I cannot see that we have anything in common."

"You shall come to like cricket, Lady Violet, I swear."

"It's more than that. We hardly know one another." She lowered her voice. "Wouldn't you rather marry a girl with whom you are somewhat familiar?"

He gave her a look that suggested she belonged in an insane asylum. "You seem like a nice, quiet girl, docile. I think we'll get on just fine."

He made her sound like a cow. Her back straightened, anger burning her throat. "I am hardly quiet. I have opinions and thoughts of my own, which I cannot verbalize because you never cease talking!"

Heads around them swiveled. The other dancers looked shocked at the outburst, and she pressed her lips together, chagrined . . . but not apologetic.

Indeed, this was not the time or place for such a conversation, though she did intend to dissuade him from offering for her. Soon.

"Excuse me, my lord." Offering a quick curtsy, she dashed off the dance floor and headed toward the terrace doors. She kept her head down and hoped Max wouldn't see her. She needed solitude at the moment, not Max's insistence that all marriages were miserable or—God forbid—another offer to help find her a husband. How would she survive it if the only man she'd ever wanted arranged to wed her off to someone else?

Violet would rather die.

And what happened if she could not get out of a marriage to Sundridge?

A light mist fell onto the empty terrace, the dreary type of precipitation London served in a never-ending supply. Violet didn't mind the water. It felt cool on her overheated skin, a balm for the rawness in her chest. Was this her destiny? To marry a man she didn't want and relive memories of Max for the rest of her life?

She tilted her face to the sky and let the rain mix with the tears building on her lashes.

What am I to do with you, my sweet girl?

His words haunted her, even hours later. *Love me*, she'd wanted to tell him. *Never let me go.* But she knew what he would have said in response . . . and it would have broken her heart.

Can I do this?

Could she love a man who would never claim her publicly? Who would rather keep her hidden away in the darkness? Violet had once thought it wouldn't bother her, that she would do anything the Duke of Ravensthorpe asked.

But it *hurt*. Far more than she'd ever expected. She didn't want to hide or pretend. She longed to be at his side, in the daylight. Bear his children. *Be his wife.*

That would never happen. He'd made it painfully clear from the start.

A sound near the door had her wiping her face. Was it Max? She didn't wish for him to find her crying out here.

"Lady Violet?"

Sundridge. Her shoulders sank.

Turning, she folded her arms and inclined her head. "My lord."

After casting an unhappy glance at the sky, he drew closer, stopping just within reach. His dark blond hair immediately lost its artful tousling thanks to the water droplets. "I sensed you were upset on the dance floor and I wanted to check on your welfare. And apologize, of course, for whatever I might have said to aid in your distress."

Perhaps Sundridge wasn't so bad after all. "Thank you. I shouldn't have raised the topic of marriage in such a public place, I suppose."

"I had assumed . . . Well, I assumed when I kept asking you to dance that you realized I was serious about courting you."

"Why me?"

"As I said, I've found nothing objectionable about you. I think we shall get on quite well together."

"Is it the dowry?" Violet was aware that her status as an heiress would entice nearly any man. *Save Max, of course.*

"We do need it," he said. "I cannot pretend otherwise. That is not my only reason for choosing you, however."

Do I not get a choice, as well? She wished to shout the question into the cool night air, but what good would it serve? The answer was obvious, and everyone knew it. Still, she had to try. "What if I told you my heart was promised to another?"

Sundridge lifted a bony shoulder. "I think we should focus on friendship and compatibility. A marriage is a partnership, sort of like a cricket team. You see—"

"What about happiness?"

"If you are asking if I'll tolerate pursuits outside of our marriage, I won't object. We'll need children, of course, but that's no hardship."

Violet wilted, unable to countenance what was happening. Her life was spinning out of control, her future full of nothing but misery and compromise.

Sundridge gripped her arm and moved closer. "May I call you Violet?" Without awaiting an answer, he said, "Violet, I realize how young girls romanticize these things, but this is a time for strategy. Like in cricket, you might give up something now to gain a run or two later."

What in God's name was he talking about? She tried to pull free, to no avail. "You aren't listening to me—"

A voice cracked through the night like the lash from a whip. "*Release her.*"

The Duke of Ravensthorpe emerged from the gloom, looking like an avenging angel ready to lay waste to everything in his path. Violet's heart clenched as he stalked forward, his eyes burning into the younger man at her side. "I said to release her, Sundridge. *Now*."

Sundridge held up his hands. "I—I didn't hurt her, I swear."

Max glanced at Violet. "Are you hurt, Lady Violet?"

"No, Your Grace." She didn't know what do. Why was Max here? Had he been worried about her? She bit her lip and tried to contain the urge to throw herself into his arms.

You're a secret. You'll always be just a secret.

Max rounded on the younger man. "You are lucky no one else caught you out here. Were you trying to ruin her reputation? I hadn't thought you such a bounder, Sundridge."

"I came to converse with her. That's all." Sundridge sidled away from Max, his skin going pale. "I never meant any disrespect."

Max advanced, his hands curling into fists. "I saw her try to pull away when you grabbed her. Are you telling me I am wrong?"

Sundridge's back met the balustrade. He was trapped. Max didn't stop, snatching Sundridge's throat in a strong hand and leaning in. The younger man pleaded, "Your Grace, I swear. It was innocent. We were only talking. Tell him, Lady Violet!"

"I know what I saw," Max snarled and shook Sundridge once. "I ought to punch you in the mouth for lying."

Sundridge's face started to turn purple and Violet panicked. She'd never seen Max this enraged, this out of control. Would he honestly harm Sundridge in the midst of a ball?

Rushing forward, she put her hand on Max's arm. "Max, stop. Let him go!"

Max released Sundridge's throat and the younger man began to cough in an effort to breathe. Not quite finished, Max jerked Sundridge by a lapel and tossed him in the direction of the terrace steps. "Go home, Sundridge. And if I ever see you near her again I'll make certain you regret it."

Sundridge didn't look back. He hurried down the stone steps and disappeared into the gardens, likely headed to the mews. Max smoothed his jacket and pulled on his cuffs. She frowned at him, shocked by his display of irrational behavior. "Have you lost your—"

"What in the bloody hell, Ravensthorpe?"

Spinning, she saw her father near the French doors—and he appeared livid.

~

The rage-induced fog began to recede from Max's brain, only to be replaced by dread. Violet's father stood on the terrace, his mouth flattened into a furious line. Just how much had Charles seen and heard?

Max decided to go with the easiest reaction, which was righteous imperviousness. "I was returning from the gardens, Mayhew, when I happened along Sundridge manhandling your daughter. I assumed you'd appreciate my lending her my protection to avoid a nasty scene."

Charles stalked forward, his dress shoes slapping on the wet stone. "You were not in the gardens, Ravensthorpe, because I saw you slip out the terrace doors a few moments ago. I followed because I wished to talk to you—and then I catch you nearly strangling a man to death and my daughter calling you Max." He pointed in Max's face. "So I'll ask again, what in the bloody hell is going on?"

Shit. Charles had seen and heard most all of it, apparently. Though his chest burned with regret, Max forced out a lie. "I am saving your daughter's reputation, obviously."

"Violet, return inside," Charles barked, not taking his eyes off Max.

"But Papa—"

"Now, Violet."

Max raised a brow, using calm logic to diffuse this disastrous situation. "She's soaked to the bone, Mayhew. You cannot order her inside the ballroom in her current state."

Charles's gaze, full of fury and resentment, narrowed on Max before shifting to his daughter. "Go around the side of the house and find our carriage. *Now.*"

Max had to bite his tongue to keep from admonishing his friend for the way he spoke to Violet, who had done absolutely nothing wrong in this instance. Instead, he clasped his hands behind his back and tried to wipe any trace of emotion off his face.

"No, Papa. If you are going to discuss me, then I have a right to stay."

"Absolutely not. Get to the carriage this instant, daughter." Charles did not waver and Violet licked her lips, uncertainty creeping into in her expression.

Finally, she addressed Max. "Thank you for coming when you did, Your Grace." Her voice wavered slightly, making him long to pick her up and hold her, but he merely nodded instead. In a swirl of wet silk, she disappeared down the terrace steps.

"I want to know what is going on between you and Violet," Charles snarled. "You will tell me this instant."

"Don't be ridiculous," Max drawled. "There is nothing going on."

Charles's lips twisted. "She called you Max. She put her hand on your arm. I saw the way she looked at you, unafraid and adoring. There is a familiarity there, one that hasn't existed before, and I want to know why, goddamn it."

Max clenched his jaw, his mind spinning on a plausible response . . . but came up empty.

"My God." With both hands, Charles shoved Max into the stone balustrade. Anger hardened his features into a mask of rage. "You bastard. Have you compromised my daughter?"

There was no hope for it. Charles had seen too much and they knew each other too well. Max braced himself. "Yell a little louder, Mayhew. I don't think they heard you in Cheapside."

"How could you? My *daughter*."

Charles stripped off his right glove and pulled his arm back. Max knew it was coming, so he waited, holding perfectly still, aware that he deserved it. The fist connected with his jaw, driving him into the stone railing once more. *Bloody hell, that hurt.* Max bent over and dragged in a breath, struggling through the pain. "That's the only one you'll get, Mayhew."

"You goddamn arsehole. My only child and you had to defile her. What, are there not enough women in London already for you? No doubt you've given Violet the clap, you prick—"

Max grabbed Mayhew and reversed their positions, shoving the other man against the stone before leaning in. "I do not have the clap—and watch your mouth."

"She's not much older than your son. You've known her since she was a baby."

Stepping back, Max swept the water off his face. "She is not a child anymore. She is a grown woman. Nevertheless, I did not plan this. It just happened."

"I never thought . . ." Charles shook his head. "You've never gone for the young ones before. I thought she was safe with you around."

"She *is* safe with me around," Max growled. "I would never hurt her."

"She was an innocent, Ravensthorpe. By touching her, you've harmed her."

"I am discreet. No one knows of our association."

"Except for Sundridge. And now me." Charles raked Max with a look full of disgust. "All these years you've been coming to my home, eating dinner with my family, and you've been lusting after her. I ought to put a bullet in your rotten heart."

Anger swept through Max at the indecent implication. He pointed a finger in Charles's face. "I never lusted after her until recently. This all happened within the last month."

"Christ." For a moment, Charles appeared like he might cry. Then he drew himself up. "Is she carrying your child?"

"Absolutely not."

"Are you entirely certain?"

Max paused, because how could one ever be entirely certain? "I am fairly certain."

He'd taken precautions over the years never to subject another woman to childbirth. The possibility of death was too great a risk, and the idea of Violet writhing in agony, bleeding to death because of his lust, sent a bolt of cold fear through his veins.

Charles slapped the stone with his palm. "Goddamn you, Ravensthorpe."

"Even still, I won't marry her."

Charles's jaw fell. "You think I want my daughter married to *you*?" He gave a bitter laugh. "You killed your first wife. Do you actually believe I'd give my sweet and trusting daughter over to the likes of you?"

Max folded his arms across his chest and worked to remain calm. It wasn't anything he hadn't told himself, but it stung to hear it out of his friend's mouth. "No, I suppose not. Fortunately, no one knows of my association with her. Sundridge will assume my friendship with you to be the reason I intervened tonight. Her reputation remains pristine."

Charles acted as if he hadn't heard a word Max said. "Now the rumors about you and Wingfield make sense. I heard you accosted him at Brooks's, but I hadn't believed it. That was over Violet, wasn't it?"

"Do not make this into something it isn't, Mayhew."

Charles dragged a hand through his wet hair. "I cannot believe, after all our years of friendship, that you would do this. That you could care so little for my family. That you could be so callously cruel."

The moment stretched, the steady drizzle of rain continuing to soak them both, but neither moved. An awful sensation swept across Max's skin and burrowed into his chest like talons—a sensation he suspected was guilt. However, no promises had been hinted at between him and Violet. He hadn't lied—she'd known his intentions at every turn. He hadn't whispered pretty words merely to get under her skirt. He hadn't needed to.

Still, he didn't relish exposing the affair and hurting her. Damn Mayhew for forcing him to do it.

It's for the best. She was never meant for me, anyway.

The world believed him vicious and selfish. A monster who drove his first wife into the grave. It was past time to prove it.

Drawing himself up to his most menacing height, he drawled, "You are overreacting. I haven't hurt her or ruined her chances at marriage with Sundridge. 'Tis a lark between us. Nothing more."

"It had better be, because I'm betrothing her to Sundridge, if he'll still have her. As for you, I hope you rot in hell, Ravensthorpe."

Charles shoved Max out of the way and headed for the steps. "Oh, and Ravensthorpe?" He glared at Max. "If I ever see you in the vicinity of my daughter again, death sentence or not, I'll shoot you right between the eyes."

Then he disappeared and Max was alone, the sound of the raindrops his only company. He stared at his shoes and tried not to drown in his regrets.

I did the right thing.

There had been no choice but to tell Charles. Violet wouldn't agree, certainly, but she'd thank Max one day after she married some young lord and had a passel of children. A cantankerous, cynical duke such as himself had no right to a vivacious and optimistic young woman like Violet. She had years of joy and discovery ahead of her, while he had long crested that particular hill.

He rubbed the center of his chest, where a dull ache had set up residence. Yes, it was definitely for the best.

CHAPTER TEN

VIOLET COULDN'T MOVE, her back stuck to the stone as rain slithered into her bodice and behind her neck. Her stupid heart oozed misery, as if it had been sliced open to bleed out on the grass.

A lark. He'd called her a *lark*. Dismissed and diminished her.

That is what you get for eavesdropping.

Yet how was she expected to leave when her father and Max were discussing her? Of course, she had stayed—though a big part of her now wished she hadn't.

Chest tight, she lifted her face toward the sky, longing to start over again, back before she'd romanticized thoughts of a dark-headed duke with eyes like midnight.

It's better to know how little you mean to him.

She would never be more than a secret, a diversion he used to the pass the time. He would never love her, not as she loved him.

Indeed, she'd thought she could handle an affair, that having a piece of him was better than nothing at all. What foolishness. What hubris. Turned out it hurt to settle for scraps. She wanted every bit of Max, his body and his heart. His soul.

'Tis a lark between us. Nothing more.

Goodness, she couldn't breathe. She tapped her sternum with her fist, reminding her lungs to function. It must have worked because she was still standing when her father came storming down the stairs.

When he spotted her, he stopped. "I see you heard." Grimacing, he closed his eyes. "I would have spared you that, but I suppose it's best you learn what type of man he is."

Your cunt was made for my cock, Violet. I've never had better.

Even if he'd been telling the truth, their intimate moments had meant nothing to him. *She* had meant nothing to him.

Swallowing, she faced her father. "I'd like to go home."

"Come." He took her arm and towed her along in the rain. "God, Violet. I would have wished any other man in the entire world for you. He is the very last one—"

"Not now, Papa."

There must have been something in her voice, something desperate and broken, because he clamped his lips shut. They ended up in front of the house, and the Mayhew carriage was soon brought around. With the evening still in full swing, the streets remained quiet at this hour. Violet was grateful for the rain, as it washed away the tears leaking from her eyes.

When they were settled inside, her father handed her a dry cloth. Violet wiped her face slowly. "I am sorry, Papa."

"Sorry it happened—or sorry you were caught?"

She couldn't answer. The wound was too raw, her body still sore from Max's attentions yesterday.

Papa exhaled and pushed the wet hair off his forehead. "I am trying to remain calm, but it is a struggle. How on earth did this happen?"

She forced the admission past the lump holding court in her throat. "You mustn't blame Ravensthorpe. I threw myself at him—more than once, I might add—and he tried to warn me off many times. Also, he told me that he would never marry me."

"Then, why?"

"Because I've loved him ever since I was a girl."

And I thought I could make him love me, too.

"Your mother was right. I allowed you far too much independence with your camera and your classes. We should have kept you limited to traditional pursuits at home with a governess."

On the dark street were the familiar houses that lined their perfect little world, a society where young girls had no control over their future.

Where parents used their daughters like bargaining chips. There was a great fascinating city out there, one she'd never experience or explore because it had been deemed unsafe for girls like her.

"We'll marry you off to Sundridge and no one ever need know," her father was saying.

"Papa, he could barely bother to learn my name and all he talks of is cricket."

"You act as if you have options at the moment, Violet. Allow me to dissuade you of that notion. Sundridge is your only hope."

A sob worked its way out of her chest, but she pushed it down. There would be time enough for that later. "I do not want to marry him."

"You could be increasing," Papa hissed, his eyes full of disappointment and anger. "Have you thought of that?"

Max hadn't spent inside her, so she doubted a child would result. Those details were not something she wished to discuss with her father, however. "Nevertheless, that is no reason to rush into a miserable marriage."

Papa leaned in. "I will not have my daughter bear a child out of wedlock."

The absolute nerve . . . Her lips curved into a knowing sneer as she leaned in as well. "You mean like the child you fathered with a mistress two years ago?"

One could have heard a pin drop in the carriage. He stared at her as if she'd smacked him. "How . . . how do you know of that? Did he tell you?"

"Ravensthorpe and I never once discussed the particulars of your reprehensible behavior. I heard the maids talking about it. The woman came to the house when Mama and I were away, apparently."

He dragged a hand down his jaw. "You mustn't tell your mother. She'd . . . well, she has a weak heart and I'm afraid the news might kill her."

More like he feared Mama might kill *him* if she found out.

"Then you'll not marry me off to Sundridge."

"Are you—are you *blackmailing* me, Violet?"

She hadn't planned on it, but she wouldn't take the words back. Resolve hardened inside her, a small sense of satisfaction that eased her misery. "It appears I am."

"What happens if you find yourself with child?"

"Then I'll go away. No one will know."

"Absolutely not. It's too great a risk. You must marry quickly, Violet. For this . . . and other reasons."

Because her mother wanted her gone.

She turned toward the window. "I will choose my husband."

After a long silence, her father said, "He won't marry you, even if you're carrying his child."

As if she didn't know that already. Tonight, Max's position regarding her had been made abundantly clear. She fought to hold back the tears burning behind her lids. "I am aware. I want nothing more to do with the Duke of Ravensthorpe."

"Well, I'm relieved to hear it. He has promised discretion and I believe he means it. We'll find another suitor soon. Dowry's too large to ignore for most of these gents."

Violet didn't speak. She had no intention of entertaining another suitor, ever.

"Most importantly," Papa said, "I will ensure he keeps far away from you."

Max wouldn't chase her. Why would he? There were other larks, women who wouldn't hope for more. Women who wouldn't develop feelings for him. Sophisticated and smart women like Louisa, satisfied with stolen moments and the occasional tryst.

But that was not Violet, not any longer.

A LETTER. He'd sent her a letter.

A week had gone by—the most miserable seven days of Violet's life—and now Max had sent her a letter. She stared at the paper warily, as if it might burst into flames at any moment.

Why had he bothered?

"Lady Violet? Are you all right?"

Shaking herself, Violet looked at the housemaid who had presented Max's secret communiqué. "Forgive me, Katie. You said a boy delivered this?"

Katie nodded. "Yes, milady. He appeared while I was picking herbs in the back. Told me to give it directly to you and no one else."

"Thank you. I trust I can rely on your discretion."

"Of course, milady. I promise not to tell a soul." Katie curtsied and departed, leaving Violet alone in her bedchamber.

She placed the missive on her bed and studied it. The letter was thin, just a single sheet of paper, with no writing on the outside. Max's familiar ducal signet ring had been pressed into the sealing wax.

Part of her wished to tear it open and devour every word.

The more rational side, however, feared additional heartbreak. Hadn't she suffered enough? Unless his letter contained words of undying devotion and a marriage proposal . . .

A bitter sound escaped her throat. Max? A marriage proposal? Ludicrous. He would never marry her and she would forever be his secret.

Her door flew open and Charlotte appeared. "Violet, you missed our appointment."

Violet lunged for the letter and tried to shove it under the pillow. Unfortunately, her friend wasn't fooled.

"Is that a letter you're trying to hide?"

"No," Violet lied. "We had an appointment today?"

"Shopping and tea, remember? I cannot believe you forgot." She pointed at the pillow. "Was that a letter from one of your suitors?"

"No, definitely not." The idea of Max courting her was laughable.

Charlotte folded her arms, a determined set to her chin. "Out with it. You forgot our outing, there are dark circles under your eyes, and now you have this letter. What is going on?"

Violet waivered. The strain of keeping all this heartbreak to herself for so many days weighed on her chest. Ever since the night of the ball, she'd swallowed her grief, pushed her misery down to where no one would notice, and it made her brittle. A fragile creature who might break at any moment.

Perhaps sharing a slice of her anguish might help.

"It is from a man, but not a suitor."

"The plot thickens." When Violet remained silent, Charlotte removed her hat and tossed it on the bed. "Are you planning to tell me who?"

Before she could reconsider the wisdom of a confession, Violet let the words out. "The Duke of Ravensthorpe."

Charlotte gasped and clutched a bedpost. "Ravensthorpe? Have you lost your mind?"

"Yes, apparently."

"But he's . . . old. Handsome, but old. And Violet," she dropped her voice, "they say he killed his first wife."

Though he'd broken her heart, Violet still felt the need to defend him. "He didn't. She died in childbirth."

Charlotte studied Violet's face carefully. "I cannot believe this. You care for him."

Unshed tears scalded the backs of Violet's eyelids, and she struggled to retain the tenuous hold she had on her composure. "I love him. I have loved him for a long time."

"And you never told me?"

Charlotte's mouth flattened, hurt lingering in her gaze, and Violet added guilt to the mountain of emotion dragging her down. "Forgive me. Things with Ravensthorpe progressed quickly, and he made it perfectly clear that it was temporary. That I was temporary—"

"That bastard." Charlotte stiffened, her fingers turning white on the walnut bedpost. "He seduced you and then refused to marry you."

"More like I seduced him, but yes."

"Even if you threw yourself at him, he should have told you no. I cannot believe he ruined you and then tossed you away!"

"That's not exactly what happened. Sit down and I'll tell you everything."

Stiffly, Charlotte moved to the bed and sat. Violet took a deep breath and launched into the entire tale, starting with watching Max with Lady Underhill and ending with the letter.

"Wait, he called you a *lark?*" Charlotte's brows went up, outrage clear in her tone. "We should storm into his house and put a bullet in his black heart."

That sounded a tad extreme. "He never lied to me. He never led me to believe it was more."

"You should hate him for how he treated you."

"I don't hate him." She swallowed and tried to keep her voice from shaking. "But while I still love him, I cannot be a secret. I deserve better."

"Indeed, you do." Charlotte reached forward and grasped Violet's hand. "So what will you do about his letter?"

"I haven't decided." She lifted the note with her free hand and tapped it against her thigh. "At best, it's an apology for telling my father. At worst, it's a formal ending to our . . . friendship."

"Do you think there is a chance he's come around on marriage?"

I won't marry you.

"No. Absolutely not." Time and time again Max had made this clear.

"There's always Sundridge. He's not so terrible."

Violet gave her friend a disbelieving look. "He's awful, Charlotte. I won't marry him."

"Then what will you do? You must marry, especially now."

Because Max had ruined her.

Violet didn't feel ruined, however. She felt tired and deeply sad. Fed up with both her parents and society. Ready to make her own decisions and escape any reminders of Max.

This was not the future she wanted, years of circling ballrooms and watching as Max ignored her. How long before he followed another woman out to the gardens? Perhaps he already had.

She pressed a fist into her stomach. Everything hurt and staying here wouldn't solve any of her problems. Her parents would only marry her off to some fop and Max would carry on with his paramours.

She didn't want that life—one that would tear her down, bit by bit, day after day until she was absolutely nothing at all. No, she wanted love and a large family, a place where she fit in, but on her terms, with a man who cared only about her dowry.

It appeared she must find happiness all on her own.

"Violet, you're scaring me," Charlotte said when the silence stretched. "What can I do to help you?"

Plans began forming in Violet's mind, wisps of ideas that grew clearer, slowly revealing a path forward like an exposed image darkening in a developer bath. She could see it, a fate of her own choosing, even if the prospect seemed daunting at the moment.

Her heart pounded with renewed purpose and resolve. "Actually, there is something you may do. I need you to deliver a package for me."

MAX STUMBLED TOWARD THE CARRIAGE, his legs shaking like jelly. The dockside buildings dipped and swirled, the midmorning sun causing the world to look like a kaleidoscope. Somehow, he put one foot in front of the other and managed to reach his conveyance.

A groom rushed to assist him, but he held up a hand. He deserved the punishment. "No need," he mumbled. "Just allow me to get inside."

Once on the seat, he collapsed like a newborn foal and closed his eyes. He'd been rowing on the Thames for three hours, as he'd been doing every morning for the last fortnight. He hadn't rowed this much since Eton, and his body did not appreciate the punishment. There were blisters on his fingers and palms, his back screamed in pain, and he thought he might have cracked a rib.

But he would not stop. The torture was necessary.

Many times, he'd considered departing London. After all, he had three estates and several townhouses to choose from, including a beautiful apartment in Paris. Yet he couldn't bring himself to go. He couldn't bring himself to leave her behind.

You're a fool. She is better off without you.

He gasped when they bounced over a particularly nasty hole in the road, the agony in his side like being stabbed with a dull knife. Moaning, he clutched the leather seat and tried not to vomit on the carriage floor.

"Apologies, Your Grace!" the coachman called.

Several calming breaths later, the spots receded from his eyes. "Fuck," he whispered.

You cannot do this much longer.

There was no choice. He couldn't sleep at night and this was the only way to exhaust himself enough to rest. When he returned home, he'd fall into bed and finally find a few hours' sleep. It was a neat little system he'd worked out, one that was keeping him sane.

Last week, he'd broken down and written to her, stupidly confessing how much he missed her and apologizing for telling her father. He'd also asked to see her, certain that they could smooth over their troubles if given a chance.

She sent the unopened letter back.

And that wasn't all she returned. She also returned the photographs of him, the ones without his clothes. As if she couldn't stand to look at him. That had hurt worse than the unopened letter.

She must hate him—and he couldn't blame her.

So he rowed. When he wasn't on the river, he was brooding by the fire, draining every bottle of brandy in the cellar. He was pathetic, a miserable husk of a man, yet he couldn't seem to bring himself out of this funk. Nothing mattered. Work piled on his desk; food went uneaten.

He missed her desperately, like a piece of his soul had been removed. This was nothing like when he'd lost his first wife. Losing Violet was a howling despair haunting his every waking moment. He'd found happiness, had tasted salvation, and then let it slip away through his foolishness and vanity.

I hope you rot in hell, Ravensthorpe.

Indeed, he was already there.

Another carriage sat outside his home, but Max couldn't bother with callers at the moment. Or ever. "Send them away," he told his butler as he stumbled over the threshold.

"Your Grace," his butler said, following. "Lady Mayhew is here to see you and insisted on waiting."

Max froze. "Did you say . . . Lady Mayhew?"

"Indeed. She is in the front drawing room."

Why was Charles's wife here? They'd never liked one another. In the early days of her marriage, she had blamed Max for corrupting Charles. Out of loyalty to Charles, Max hadn't denied it, though Charles required no help whatsoever when it came to corruption.

Still, this visit might have something to do with Violet. "I'll see her now."

A horrified look crossed his butler's face—likely because Max wasn't bothering to change before receiving a caller—but Max didn't care. This might concern Violet, and that was far more important than the sorry state of his person offending Lady Mayhew.

He slowly made his way to the drawing room, doing his best not to crumple onto the Italian marble floor.

"Lady Mayhew. This is a surprise."

"Ravensthorpe. I have to say, you've looked better." She was perched on the edge of the sofa, appearing ready to bolt at a moment's notice. She and her daughter had the same hair, a similar chin and bone structure. It sent a fresh wave of agony through him just to look at her.

He cleared his throat. "What may I do for you this morning?"

"I've come to seek a favor."

"A favor from me?" This was unexpected.

She nodded once. "You see, when a wife is saddled with a lying, philandering husband, she must develop a trusted and reliable source of informants. These are often servants, which is certainly the case in my household. And I've recently been given an interesting piece of news."

"Oh?"

"According to Violet's maid, you wrote a letter to my daughter, which she returned along with some other papers. More letters, perhaps?"

Max braced himself, saying nothing and allowing her to come to the point.

"Regardless, my husband confirmed that you and Violet had been involved for some time."

"Our involvement has ended."

"I assumed as much, based on the returning of your note. Not to mention that she's disappeared."

He blinked. "What do you mean, disappeared?"

"She is missing. She left the morning after sending back your letter."

Max strangled the armrests in a death grip, his fingertips digging into the wood. That had been a week ago. Why hadn't he been—?

Fuck. Of course, he hadn't been informed. Charles didn't want him in the same room as his daughter.

Max had to find her. He would tear this city apart with his bare hands, if necessary. A hundred terrible things could befall a sweet young woman such as Violet in this god-awful city. "I assume the police have been summoned and are currently searching for her."

"No. My husband thought it best if we kept this quiet. Family only, that sort of thing." She studied his face. "But it's plain you still care for her."

"I do." He swallowed, his chest pulling tight. "I beg your pardon, but I didn't plan for it to happen."

"You needn't apologize to me. In fact, this makes things easier."

He bounced his leg, anxious for the woman to take her leave so that he could begin searching for Violet. He had to make sure she was safe. "Easier, how?"

"I need her married, Ravensthorpe. As quickly as possible."

His lips twisted derisively. "Yes, she was aware. Hardly matters to whom, does it?"

"You judge me, of course. As a man, you wouldn't understand that all women are pushed into marriage, whether we want it or not. We are traded like cattle, treated little better than dirt."

"Yet you treat your daughter the same."

"Violet is smart. Independent. A thoroughly likable girl. I love her, I do—but I have put up with Charles for long enough. It's time to be free."

Max sat up sharply, ignoring the pain in his side. "Free? Are you saying . . .?"

"I plan to divorce him as soon as Violet is married. The solicitor is ready with the paperwork."

"Divorce?"

She gave him a brittle smile. "I am tired of being disrespected and lied to. You, perhaps better than most, understand what I've endured for the last twenty years. He's fathered two bastards that I know of, probably more. I won't allow him in my bed any longer. Do you want to know why?"

Max remained silent, almost dreading the answer.

She continued, "My husband is riddled with disease. He's had mercury treatments to try and cure it. Lord knows it would be a miracle if I were not infected as well. I cannot stand to look at him any longer. If I must endure the scandal of a divorce to be free of that man, then so be it."

The explanation made sense. If Violet had known, it would have eased her mind regarding her mother's motives. His heart ached for his little mouse. "You should tell your daughter. She believes you want rid of her."

"And I am sorry for that. When I have the chance, I will explain it to her. I had thought to wait until she was married, when she would better understand what happens in the marital bed." She cocked a brow. "But I see you've taken care of that."

"I . . ." For once, Max was at a loss for words. He had taken Violet's innocence against his better judgment.

"Go and find her, Ravensthorpe. Use your considerable influence to locate my daughter and convince her to forgive you. Then marry her, quickly. You, more than most, are immune from any scandal. Your name will shelter her from any . . . unpleasantness during the divorce proceedings."

Marry?

He hadn't wished to marry again, yet he was miserable without her. He couldn't let her go—he needed Violet in his life, in his bed. In his home, making him smile and taking photographs. Being with her was easy, fulfilling in a way he hadn't experienced with any other woman before.

Could he try again? He'd failed with Rebecca, but Violet was nothing like his late wife. Violet was a spark of optimism and light, a beacon of joy and happiness. Intelligent and lusty, she would never bore him or let him run roughshod over her. Moreover, he was different than the selfish man of twenty-five, who'd believed himself invincible. He would treat Violet as a wife should be treated.

Violet . . . *his wife*. He liked the sound of that. Quite a lot, actually.

Suddenly, he didn't care whether Charles disapproved or whether people sneered at the age difference. He had to have her. To love and hold her until he took his last breath.

He tapped his fingertips against his thigh. She had disappeared, but Max would find her. In fact, he had an inkling of where she might have gone. "I cannot promise she'll forgive me, but I will try."

"Good," Lady Mayhew said, rising. "She is headstrong, but Violet's been in love with you for years."

Her mother had noticed when Max hadn't? Of course, he'd been busy avoiding Violet since her debut, terrified of his feelings for her. That ended now. He was ready to admit he loved her and that he couldn't live without her.

He stood. "I am not the only one who must seek Violet's forgiveness. You've hurt her, you know."

She winced, her brow furrowed. "That was not my intention, but I suppose I have been so focused on my own happiness that I forgot about Violet's. I haven't been the best mother."

"Help her understand. Be there for her."

Lady Mayhew cocked her head, her lips pursed in thoughtfulness. "You really care for her, don't you?"

"More than anything else in the world."

"Make her happy, Ravensthorpe."

Resolve settled in his chest like a rock, and he nodded. "You may count on it, my lady."

CHAPTER ELEVEN

Violet poured hot water into the teapot and returned the kettle to the tiny stove. Then she placed the lid on the pot to allow the leaves to steep. The stove had been a challenge, but she'd grown proficient with it in the past week.

Heartache turned a person productive, it seemed.

Since leaving home, she'd taken photos and explored the city. Walked the streets and observed the inhabitants. She'd also met her new neighbors, three other young women living in apartments above the camera shop in Chelsea. The girls worked in department stores and offices, each a new kind of independent woman, one in control of her own life. Just like Violet.

She hadn't told them of her aristocratic upbringing, but they knew. It was in the way she spoke, the way she dressed. Even in the tea she drank, apparently. But they didn't judge her. Instead, they fondly called her "countess," which Violet didn't mind. She'd never had a nickname before.

Actually, she'd never had this many friends before, either.

She still missed Max, though. He was in her head, her heart . . . in her bones. Part of her regretted not reading his letter, but it wouldn't have said what she wished to hear. Max would never tell her sweet words of undying devotion, the things a husband said to a wife. After all, she was a lark to him. A woman to pass the time.

Goodness, that still hurt.

Pouring her tea, she gave thanks that at least she hadn't conceived a baby. That was one worry she needn't add to the pile, which now included finding employment to cover her rent and living expenses. And those particular problems grew more pressing by the day as her funds dwindled.

Had he thought about her at all? Or had he picked up with one of his many mistresses?

A knock sounded on her door. She placed her cup in the saucer and stood, smoothing her dress. It was probably one of her friends stopping by to have a chat.

Opening the door, she jerked in surprise.

The Duke of Ravensthorpe stood there. Max. Here. In Chelsea. How . . .?

Oh, yes. She'd once told him about her camera shop idea. How had he remembered?

Dark blue eyes burned from under the rim of his hat, his mouth set in a firm, determined line. Though his face was gaunt, he was unmistakably a duke, with his frame draped in expensive fabrics and the gold of his watch fob glinting in the daylight. She could hardly breathe due to the need to throw herself at him.

No, no more playing the fool.

Her friend Irene stood next to him. "I hope it's all right that I let him in. He said he knew you." Irene leaned in. "Is he really a duke?"

"It's fine, Irene. Thank you." Drawing in a deep breath, she said, "Would Your Grace care to come in?"

Max removed his bowler and stepped into her tiny apartment. Irene's eyes were as big as saucers when Violet whispered, "I'll tell you later," and shut the door.

He dominated the small room, a force of nature in her private space. Violet wasn't certain where to go or what to do. Why was he here?

He held his hat and cane in gloved hands and inspected his surroundings. No doubt he found it lacking, but Violet certainly wouldn't apologize for where she lived. She loved this place.

Without prompting, she produced another cup and saucer, set it on the table, and poured tea for him. Then she retook her seat and calmly sipped her tea, waiting for him to break the silence.

After clearing his throat, he sat and removed his gloves. "Are you curious as to how I located you?" His voice was rough and cracked, like he hadn't used it in days.

"I once mentioned that I would rent a small apartment above a camera shop in Chelsea."

"Yes, and fortunate for me, there are just two camera shops in Chelsea, and this is the only one with apartments atop it."

She frowned, her brows lowering. "Why is that fortunate?"

"Because I needed to find you."

"Interested in a lark, were you?"

He winced. "I saw you leave with your father so it's obvious you overheard us, and I'm sorry I ever said anything as stupid as that. I didn't mean it."

"Why? It's true. That's all we were to one another."

"No, that wasn't all, not for me."

Bitterness welled up in her chest like a fog, its dismal fingers sinking into her heart to squeeze. "Forgive me if I have a hard time believing that, Max."

"Violet, I was trying to convince myself there was nothing between us. That I could go on living without you after you'd happily married your Sundridge or Wingfield. But I cannot do it. I am utterly miserable without you."

Hope fluttered in her stomach, but she beat it back with a ruthlessness that hadn't existed two weeks ago. "Because you need someone in your bed."

"Because I need *you* in my bed. In my life. With me, wherever I go. For however long I have left on this earth."

Her hands curled into fists, her skin burning with humiliation and anger. The gall of this man. "I see. You found me living here and assumed I would jump at the chance to become your mistress or whatever else you wanted. That I would be content to stay hidden and wait for your scraps. Well, you may return to Mayfair and shove that cane—"

"Wait." He reached into his coat pocket and produced a square box, which he sat on the tabletop. "I came here to ask you to be my wife."

The room spun, and Violet's mouth fell open. Was that . . .? No, it couldn't be. "But you said . . ."

"I know what I said, but that was before I tried to row myself to death in the Thames."

She shook her head, confused. "What?"

"Never mind. What's important is that I do not wish to exist in a world without you calling me 'Your Grace' in that breathy way of yours, or running your fingers through my hair. Or taking photographs of me, or talking of philosophy and history and all the other clever things in your head. I cannot do it. I need you."

"You want to marry me? Marry? Me?"

He sighed in that arrogant way of his, as if he hated repeating himself. The sound was so Ravensthorpe that she nearly grinned. "Yes, Violet. Please, marry me."

She bit her lip, not quite ready to give in, though her heart was nearly bursting with happiness. "I thought you were too old for me."

"I only care what you think. Do you think I am too old for you?"

"Of course not. What about my father?"

"I believe he'll soon be too busy with other matters to worry about us."

"Whatever does that mean?"

"Your mother came to see me. She plans to begin divorce proceedings. She was merely waiting until you were married off."

Divorce? Violet stared at the wall, her mind whirling. "Was that why she was so eager to see me settled?"

"Yes."

She paused, uncertain how to feel about this revelation. Looking back, the fights with Papa and the emotional distance from the family made a bit more sense. Mama clearly hadn't been happy, not for years, so if she needed to divorce Papa for her well-being then Violet would support the decision.

Yet why had Mama pushed for Violet to make an unhappy match, as well? If anyone knew the risks of marriage, it was her mother.

Mama should have tried to protect her, not sacrifice Violet for her own gain. Instead, her mother had washed her hands of Violet's future, practically pushing her out the door to any man who'd have her.

And why had Mama shared this information with Max, instead of her daughter?

Suspicion cast a shadow over the moment, and her stomach churned with emotion. "So this," she said, indicating the square box, "is your way of helping her?"

"No." Dipping elegantly onto one knee, he took out the ring and held it up in his fingers. "This is my way of keeping you all for myself. I'll never deserve you, not today. Not tomorrow. Never. You're beautiful and pure and I am the very Devil. But I love you, Violet Littleton, and I shall do absolutely everything in my power to ensure you never forget it, not for a moment."

She covered her mouth, her heart skipping in her chest. "You love me?"

"Indeed, in the very worst way."

She stared at his gold collar stud and voiced her deepest fear. "You won't hide me away? I'll be your wife in every sense of the word?"

With one finger, he lifted her chin to meet her gaze. A wrinkle had formed between his brows. "I'd be proud to have you by my side. I need you. Without you, I'm wrecked. You hold all my happiness in your dainty, camera-loving hands."

"I am not that powerful. After all, even you call me 'little mouse.'"

He stroked her jaw with the backs of his knuckles. "Violet, do you not remember the fable of the mouse and the lion? It is the mouse who shows great courage and bravery, saving the lion from a slow, painful death."

Oh, goodness. She hadn't considered that. Her belly dipped and swooped, as if she might actually swoon. "Are you saying I saved you?"

"Of course, you have, darling girl. You brought color and joy to a man who had lived in gray for so very long." He leaned in and pressed his forehead to hers. "You are the sunshine to my bleary dark soul."

"Max . . ."

"Is that a yes?"

Taking a deep breath, she steeled her voice into something more businesslike. "I have conditions."

The side of his mouth hitched, his expression soft as he rose to his full height. "Is that so?"

"I wish to keep this apartment. That way, I'll have a place just for me when I need to get away."

A muscle jumped his jaw, his dark gaze sparking as he studied her. "Is this about having a lover on the side? I won't share you, Violet. Not with anyone."

"I do not want another lover." She thought of his first wife. "And if we marry, I won't share you either."

"Agreed."

"That easily? Forgive my skepticism, considering your proclivity for lascivious behavior. Does the Duke of Ravensthorpe possess the ability for monogamy?"

"He does, if the woman in his life is you, with your clever brain and bold spirit. If you need to keep the apartment to retain a bit of your independence, then I'll not complain."

"Independence—and my photography. I'll use it as a portrait studio."

"As long as said portraits involve clothing."

She stood and closed the distance between them, using a fingertip to trace the edge of his collar. Goose bumps appeared on his skin and she smiled up at him. "You are the only one allowed to pose for my nude portraits, Your Grace."

A growl rumbled deep in his chest. "Yes to the apartment. What else?"

"I want to try for children."

His large body tensed. "No, Violet. I could not bear it if—"

"I am not your first wife." She stroked his lapel, soothing him. "I'll be fine. But I want a piece of you and a piece of me to live on, together, to make this world better a better place."

"Goddamn it," he said and shifted his gaze to the wall. "What if you die?"

"Death stalks us every day. I could choke on a fishbone at dinner and die. But I've spent my entire life watching, observing, never fitting in while waiting for something to happen, and I am tired of waiting. I want excitement and laughter, little feet running through the halls. Most of all, I want to see your face in our children."

"Christ, Violet." He bent to kiss her hard on the lips. "I suppose I'll need to find the best doctors in this bloody country to watch over you, then."

"Does that mean you agree to my conditions?"

"I don't have a choice, do I? I will give you anything you want to get my ring on your finger."

She nearly swayed, the exhilaration almost too much to bear. "Anything I want? Oh, the heady power of having the Duke of Ravensthorpe at my feet."

"As long as you never leave me, I'll lie at your feet anytime you like."

The afternoon light played across the angles of his face and throat.

Harsh and beautiful, he was hers, and she'd never tire of looking at him. "What about now? I like the idea of more nude portraits of you."

Taking her hand, he slipped his ring onto her finger. Then he reached into his coat pocket and withdrew a folded stack of photographs. She cocked her head. "Are those the pictures I took of you?"

"I thought I should return them to their rightful owner." When she moved to take them, he lifted the stack far above her head. "With one condition."

Crafty man. Of course he had his own condition. "Which is?"

"That you use them for their intended purpose while I watch."

He wanted her to do *that* in front of him? "Now?"

"Right now." His gaze burned with adoration and desire, but there was something else there, as well. Something new that was serious and far more meaningful.

He loves me.

Her skin could barely contain the joy coursing through her. Sliding her arms around his neck, she pulled him closer and put her lips near his ear. "Yes, Your Grace."

The End.

◞

Want more sinfully sexy heroes set in Gilded Age New York City?

Check out The Devil of Downtown!

ALSO BY JOANNA SHUPE

The Uptown Girls:

The Rogue of Fifth Avenue

The Prince of Broadway

The Devil of Downtown

The Four Hundred Series:

A Daring Arrangement

A Scandalous Deal

A Notorious Vow

The Knickerbocker Club:

Tycoon

Magnate

Baron

Mogul

Wicked Deceptions:

The Courtesan Duchess

The Harlot Countess

The Lady Hellion

Novellas:

How The Dukes Stole Christmas Anthology

Miracle on Ladies' Mile

ABOUT THE AUTHOR

Award-winning author **Joanna Shupe** has always loved history, ever since she saw her first Schoolhouse Rock cartoon. Since 2015, her books have appeared on numerous yearly "best of" lists, including Publishers Weekly, The Washington Post, Kirkus Reviews, Kobo, and BookPage.

Sign up for Joanna's Gilded Lilies Newsletter for book news, sneak peeks, reading recommendations, historical tidbits, and more!

www.joannashupe.com

CPSIA information can be obtained
at www.ICGtesting.com
Printed in the USA
LVHW111643021022
729794LV00001B/121

9 781949 364095